A TRAITOR TO HIS BLOOD

St Pauls, Bristol, 1980. Joseph Tremaine Ellington has long abandoned his former career as an enquiry agent for the safety of teaching. But his old life draws him back.

One of the very few lights from Ellington's dark and violent past has flickered out. His fiancée, Ruth Castle, is dead — leaving him heartbroken and alone, bringing up his fifteen-year-old niece Chloe. Ellington's days are long and lonely, his nights tormented by old ghosts.

When the wife of a respected Baptist minister vanishes into a seamy, dead-end world of users and abusers, leaving behind both her own family and a critically fragile premature infant daughter, Ellington is asked if he can help find the woman.

He was determined to keep his distance from the dangers of the Bristol night. But his inescapable obligation to an old friend keeps bringing him back like a moth to a flame . . .

M.P. WRIGHT

◆

A TRAITOR TO HIS BLOOD

Complete and Unabridged

LARGE
PRINT

ISIS
Leicester

First published in Great Britain in 2021 by
Black & White Publishing Ltd
Edinburgh

First Isis Edition
published 2022
by arrangement with
Black & White Publishing Ltd
Edinburgh

A catalogue record for this book is available
from the British Library.

ISBN 978–1–39912–520–8

Published by
Ulverscroft Limited
Anstey, Leicestershire

Printed and bound in Great Britain by
TJ Books Ltd., Padstow, Cornwall

This book is printed on acid-free paper

For Jen, Enya and Neve.

Prologue

Every night, as the curtain of dusk mantles the hours of light, I tell myself that I'll have a quiet evening at home. It's a tacit incantation, which is as much habit and superstition as it is a silent utterance of intention.

Home these days is 44 Banner Road in the heart of St Pauls, Bristol, an inner suburb of the city that I've been part of, on and off, for the better part of fifteen years. A red-brick, two-up, two-down Victorian-built tenement is where the peace is. The house, once the rented abode of my late aunt Pearl and uncle Gabe, offers the kind of tranquillity and peace of mind that in the past has long eluded me.

Most evenings, after I've fixed supper, I draw the curtains, kick off my shoes, perhaps pour myself a couple of fingers of rum and allow Otis Redding's sweet crooning to mask the brawl and chatter of the outside world. But the sanctuary found behind four walls, with its joyous music and the intoxicating properties of strong spirits, can only slake the troubles of the outside world and a man's inner demons for so long. Sooner or later bad news or some kind of vexation breaches the strongest, most impenetrable of citadels, no matter how high or formidable you build your fortifications; and deep down, I've always known my home to be no different.

I have spent most of my life in rooms like the one I sit in now; modest and unassuming. In my youth I'd moved around like a hermit crab, only settling down after I found the love of a fine woman back on

1

the island of my birth. My first wife, Ellie, created an idyllic home, a beachfront chattel dwelling where we lived with our beautiful daughter, Amelia. But personal tragedy had forced me to leave Barbados long ago.

I'd made the miserable ten-day journey across the Atlantic Ocean to Southampton in the winter of 1964. I'd set foot on English soil, a disgraced former police officer and widower; my beloved kin murdered; the men responsible for their horrific demise unpunished; my own future far from certain. For years afterwards, other people's misdeeds and adversities mapped out my own pending fate. I became an unwilling survivor, desolate in a hostile new realm, dealing in the detritus of my fellow man while still burdened with my own sorrow.

Lost in those dark days, I mourned behind closed doors and worked for every wretch or miscreant that crossed my path.

In the passing of time, my own grief slowly abated its grip and I found myself lucky enough to be blessed again with the gift of love and the comfort of a warm home. For eight years, my partner Ruth Castle and I shared our lives happily together along with my adoptive niece, Chloe. I gave up the shady world of private investigation and held down a job with the Bristol Bus Company while Ruth continued teaching at the city polytechnic. We lived a quiet and contented life, tucked away in the Gloucestershire countryside. Those halcyon days seem almost ethereal and illusive to me now. As if I had cruelly dreamed them.

Ruth was taken from me almost eighteen months ago, pancreatic cancer doing its very worst in the blink of an eye. Our previously serene moment in time quickly replaced with sackcloth and ashes. The familiar, unwelcome lament I had carried in my mind for so long after Ellie's death returned on the day we buried Ruth, a funeral song that still dwells in both daydream and nightmare. Mine to know and grieve upon.

All the people I met, helped or hurt, all those faces and voices, real or imagined, had remained cloaked and unspeaking while Ruth was alive. When Chloe slept, and I felt alone in the house, the whispers of my past, the beat of sorrow and regret in my blood, the haphazard apprehensions that made me the man I once was, slowly returned. The 'Duppies' were out there in the darkness once again, all of them standing at the barricades in my mind waiting for me to join them in their foul perdition. My strong resolve held such miserable entities at bay for most of the time, but on occasion, when I was at my lowest ebb, I believed I may have succumbed to their inhuman desires.

For the sakes of Chloe's future happiness and my own sanity we packed our bags, hitched up the wagon and returned to where I knew deep down my niece wanted to be. St Pauls is where she belongs. Where she feels safe. Where she is not ridiculed or mocked because of the colour of her skin or how she speaks, or the way she dresses and braids her hair. It is the place her family have lived, where their memory remains and where her friends still reside.

It is home.

It's also my old haunt.

I still own the small cottage in Hambrook and I rent it out to a family, whose happiness and well-being appears to mirror our own when we inhabited the place. Some of my new neighbours in St Pauls still have their misgivings about the kind of man I once was. Folk with long, unforgiving memories who still like to keep me at arm's length, the shadow of the Heartman, an unwelcome presence.

Those I care about believe that I am no longer cheek-by-jowl with the dark side. Trouble is not my business and as the passing years attest, it's been a long time since I last undertook the kind of favour that would bring me to the attention of the local law or into the clutches of the criminal underworld.

Occasionally, I ponder on the fact that I have come a long way from my journeyman days operating in a corner of society where life was fought for as much as it was lived. Such fleeting reveries feel hubristic and mythical. High-hat reminiscences that are undeserving of my previously questionable deeds and actions.

As twilight slips ever closer, here in this familiar room, in this brooding moment before a crueller world returns in a rush and bears me back into it, I will tell you what I know to be true:

It is still not yet dark.

At night I sleep with my old service revolver tucked underneath my pillow.

And old ghosts return to haunt my sleep and torment my waking days.

1

Friday, 14 March 1980

I was sprawled out on a deep curve of the corner couch, reading my battered copy of *King Lear* and trying to work up enough enthusiasm and energy to get up off my ass and go make myself something to eat. It was a little after ten and I'd been wrestling with the bard's blank verse since getting in from work. My day job nowadays finds me sat behind a desk, plying my trade part-time for the Bristol West Indian Friends Association. We're a kind of Caribbean Citizens Advice Bureau, a free, confidential information group that helps out local folk in dealing with their troubles. Four days a week, you'll find me sweating blood at the bureau's office on Wilder Street, up to my neck dealing with the rest of mankind's woes. Right now, my own personal headache was whether or not I could be bothered to pad into the kitchen to heat up some of yesterday's brown down chicken stew I'd made the night before. While I'd been lost in Lear's treacherous world, I'd managed to down a quart bottle of hooch without breaking a sweat and by Act IV my barren insides were starting to rumble for something other than seventy-five per cent proof Barbadian gut rot.

Chloe had gone out for the evening, sleeping over at my old friend Loretta Harris's house. It was Mother's Day weekend, and in many ways, Loretta had become the maternal rock that Chloe needed to cling to after

5

Ruth's death. My niece had barely known her own mother. My sister, Bernice, had been murdered when Chloe was only six. In the winter of '67 I'd returned home to Bim to settle an old score as well as conclude my sister's affairs. In doing so, her orphaned infant daughter became my ward. Over time, as Chloe grew and learned, I became 'Uncle Joseph'; by the time she was ten or so, she was calling me 'JT' like everyone else did; now a few months shy of her sixteenth birthday, she simply refers to me as 'Pa'.

The ticking of the wind-up clock and the crackle of the fire's dying embers were the only sounds in the room. The clock, a much-treasured possession of my aunt Pearl's, had been sat on the chimneypiece for as long as I could remember. Encased in fine dark wood, its numerals wrought in pale pink metal — copper and tin most probably.

As I stared at the black hands on the dial, I heard the sound of a car slow down and pull up outside, its tyres squealing against the kerb at the front of the house. The vehicle's engine died, quickly followed by a car door opening and slamming shut. None of that meant anything to me, but the unmistakable din of heel and toe caps tapping up the path towards my front door quickly got my attention. The brass horse-tail knocker had already cracked three times by the time I'd got to my feet, the metallic kickback reverberating into the hall and through the closed door of the living room. By the time I had my hand on the front door handle whoever was on the other side had hammered at it again twice more for good measure.

One of the things the street teaches you is that if you bend over, you're bound to get kicked. Whoever was outside wasn't just passing by. This was no courtesy call. There was serious intent in their hammering, and I muttered something under my breath about an ill wind and immediately regretted doing so. Nothing seems to tempt fate more than mentioning the possibility of something bad happening. I heard myself curse as I put on my meanest expression and yanked open the door.

A face out of the past, from a long-forgotten era, stared back at me from the porch step. Evison Foster smiled nervously, his arm dropping like a stone at his side. Foster was a tubby, serious-looking guy with deep eyes set under shaggy brows. His broken nose and heavy jaw gave off a vibe of an old-time prize-fighter, but in truth, Evison, who was originally from Antigua, was considered in the community at large to be one of the most devout and gentle souls around.

He was a slow, lazy-moving fella, whose age I guessed to be around sixty. He had a reputation for being a good, uncomplicated and kind man. But I wouldn't have called Evison a friend, so his unexpected appearance at such a late hour immediately set me on edge.

'How you doin', T?' Evison spoke the 'J' in an unvoiced breath. I could never tell if he had an impediment or if the 'J' was just too much effort for him.

'Good, Evison. Been a while.' I stepped onto my front porch, stuck my head five inches or so out into the street and saw he was alone. I edged back inside and set my gaze back on Foster. 'What can I do for you?'

'Hoping I could get a moment of your time?' Evison stood awkwardly, his smile revealed crooked, gappy teeth. But they looked strong, like brown and white tree stumps that you'd need dynamite to remove.

'That's if it wouldn't be too much trouble?'

I held out my hand. 'You'd better come on in.'

Evison wiped his feet on the hessian mat and stepped over the threshold into my domain, his eyes adjusting to the hall light as he eyed me up apprehensively. He wore a thick woollen black overcoat, grey slacks and a green cotton shirt with blue flowers on it that was open at the neck. His polished loafers were buffed military style, his polyester strides hitched up high on his portly waist to reveal bright white socks. This impressive, if odd-ball look was topped off with a battered gold Timex watch with a cracked face and a row of clip-on ballpoint pens sticking out of the top pocket of his coat. I noticed he was wearing his shirt outside his trousers to hide his massive paunch and love handles.

We shook hands. His rough and scarred skin bleached in patches to a whitish, putty-like grey, elsewhere stained darker, by the cleansers and chemicals he used in his work. Evison restored old buildings and, occasionally, churches. One of the few times I'd had a proper conversation with him was around a year or so past when we'd sat in the bar of the Inkerman pub on Grosvenor Road sharing a pint and he began talking about the chapel he was working on: 'You wouldn't believe what-all these ole roosts have wrong with 'em. Every'ting on God's earth looks to be out to destroy 'em. Death watch beetle, the size you've never seen. Mould and rot everywhere. Ground settles, trying to crack the walls open, an' when that don't work, it moves off someplace else and tries to tear 'em down anyway it can. Amazes me how these old piles manage to stay upright as long as they do. Only the good Lord keeping 'em up, I expect.'

I knew that whatever Foster wanted with me, it sure as hell had nothing to do with old crypts or crumbling stonework. I gestured with my head towards the living room. 'You wanna take a seat by the fire?'

Evison shook his head politely. 'No, I'll be just fine here, thanks.'

I rested against the passage wall and waited for my visitor to start up the conversation. After a few moments of awkward silence, I decided to shift matters on. 'So, what is it I can do for you, Evison?'

Evison's rotund face suddenly tightened. 'Somebody in need of your professional services, 'T.'

'Then tell 'em to come down and see me at the bureau.'

'Oh, they ain't looking for that kinda advice.' Evison hunched his shoulders then pulled out a white handkerchief and dabbed at his brow and lips. 'This a matter that's best not discussed in public, if you get my meaning. It's a thing that's gonna need some discretion.'

'Been a long time since anyone came knockin' at my gate door after dark talkin' 'bout discretion, Evison.'

Foster gave me a nervous grin, his gaze reluctant to meet my own. 'Yeah, well like I said, this a kid gloves kinda thing. Needs a sensitive touch. Your name came to mind when I taking contemplation at my church.'

'Huh-huh, is that right. Where you praising the Lord these days then, Evison?'

'Old King Street Baptist Chapel.'

I nodded my head. 'Pastor Walker's joint, right?' Evison winced when I referred to his place of worship as a 'joint'.

'Yeah, me an' my wife, Carmen, are members o' Pastor Walker's flock.' Foster hesitated for a

9

moment, clearing his throat before continuing. 'It's the minister that's in need of your assistance, if truth be told. Folk say you and him go back a way.' Evison dithered again, stared down at my linoleum before focusing back in on me 'And he got the kinda problem only a brother could handle.'

The 'brother' remark was enough to raise my hackles; I should have ushered Evison Foster back out into the street there and then. I knew nothing good was going to come from our conversation or his plea, and yet for some foolish damn reason that I can't explain, I let the big man keep on standing in my hallway.

'I've known Mervyn Walker 'bout as long a time as I've known anybody since I've been over here. Don't recall him ever needing my guidance or, for that matter, me asking him for it.'

Evison straightened, forcing his round shoulders back and his big belly out. He looked up towards the ceiling, his eyes closed. ''Do not withhold good from those to whom it is due, when it is in your power to act.'' Then his pious bearing quickly evaporated and he opened his eyes and mumbled in hushed tones the words, 'Proverbs, chapter three, verse twenty-seven.' He flashed me a righteous beam.

I pulled myself off the wall, the heat rising across the nape of my neck, my heart going like a bird in flight. 'I know the scriptures, Evison. I don't need it reciting to me in my own home if it's all the same with you.'

Foster bowed his head in embarrassment, a gesture that immediately made me regret voicing my snappy remark. He shuffled his size elevens from side to side like a scolded schoolboy. Rather than watch him squirm any longer I fired off another question.

10

'If the pastor's in need of my help, why ain't he here asking for it himself?'

Evison shook his head slowly, not meeting my eye again. 'It ain't as easy as that, 'T I'm the only person in the congregation knows 'bout his plight. Ain't many souls a man of God can turn to when he finds himself in trouble. The pastor would rather his parishioners were not aware of his burdens, if you know what I mean. That's why I'm here on his behalf seeking your good grace now.'

'My grace?' I replied. 'That's pretty rich, Evison. I thought one of the reasons people pray was so they could get the good Lord's guidance and protection?'

Evison clasped his hands together and swallowed hard. For a change, he looked straight into my face. 'Pastor Walker, he's boxed in wid a problem that even prayer can't fix.' He reached into his coat pocket and took out a piece of folded notepaper then inched his way over and handed it to me. I noticed his fingers were trembling as he stepped back towards the door. 'Please, go see the man yourself, make your own mind up whether you can offer him a helping hand after he's told you 'bout his predicament.'

I curled the paper up in the palm of my hand then looked up into the man's now placid face. 'I'll see what I can do.'

After Evison had gone, I went to my bed and drank four glasses of rum way too fast. I passed out thinking that I should never have opened my damn door.

11

2

You could tell by some folks' houses that they'd left St Pauls and moved the half mile up the road to live out their dreams. When I was a kid, your home was not a place to dream. At home you had to do like your father and mother did and that was to live with your lot and never complain, no matter how bad things got. Home meant that everybody inside the place already knew what you were like and what you'd turn out to become, and if you did the slightest thing different, they'd laugh you right down into a damn big hole. You lived in that hole. Festered in it. After a while you either accepted your hole or you got out of it.

There were all kinds of ways to get out. You could get married, get drunk, get next to somebody's wife. You could take a shotgun and eat it for a midnight meal.

Or you could move the hell out of town and never come back.

Pastor Mervyn Walker had done just that. He'd moved ten minutes up the road to Montpelier and was never looking back. The piece of paper that Evison Foster had handed me last night had the pastor's new address written on it. I'd woken late and had a leisurely breakfast, so by the time I was sat behind the wheel of my car to drive over to Mervyn's place it was a little after midday. I pulled my rusting Ford Escort up outside the plush, detached Georgian pile that was the Walker residence, an etched brass plate proclaiming the high-end bricks and mortar behind the neatly

12

clipped hedge to be The Rectory.

I entered sacred ground via a scrolled metal gate and wandered up the garden path towards Eden. The minister's house sat behind an expansive and well-maintained lawn, the elderly black man on his knees working the border with a hand trowel clocking me before I had chance to press the doorbell.

'If you lookin' fo' the pastor, you ain't gonna find 'im home.'

'Any idea where he is?'

The gardener kept eyeballing the soil, finally pointing a finger back towards the path. 'He'll be doin' the Lord's work over at the chapel, I sus'pec.'

I thanked him and headed down towards the street. As I closed the gate, I looked back up to the house and saw that the old fella was stood on the edge of the lawn watching me like a messenger of doom, claws forward, resembling one of the biblical prophet Daniel's four beasts, an archaic creature ready to devour my soul.

As I turned away, in the distance, I heard a baby cry.

* * *

Old King Street Baptist chapel in Montpelier was a small, pretty, salmon-coloured building, built on the model of an old American-style Antebellum church. There was a large crucifix stood high on the outside wall; Jesus already suffering for the congregation before they set foot through the door. On Sundays, the devout were unlikely to notice though. It was a time to feel and look good not to be staring up into space. Pastor Walker's flock would be dressed in their best, waiting for the word of the Lord without letting it cramp their style. All the men and women, and children too, would be decked out in their finest. Fancy dresses and pressed suits, patent-leather shoes and the occasional pair of white gloves. The smiles and bows that passed between the sexes on Sundays before the morning service would have been scandalous any other day of the week.

I stood outside the church for a few moments, weighing up in my head what kinda mess I might well be getting myself into. In two minds whether or not to get back in my car and drive away. I caught sight of the bloodstained Christ figure out of the corner of my eye, and although I'm no true believer, some kind of hunch in the pit of my belly told me that the Good Shepherd was giving me the once over. Still wavering, I headed up the narrow path and reluctantly headed on inside the chapel.

'Old King', as the faithful referred to it, was beautiful on the inside too. A cosy rectangular room with a wood frame ceiling and space for a hundred chairs.

The podium that stood upfront was adorned with fresh yellow lilies and draped in deep purple banners. Behind the minister's place slightly off to the left, rose thirty velvet chairs, in three rows, for the choir.

There were six stained-glass windows on either side of the room. Jesus on the mount, John the Baptist baptising Jesus, and Mary Magdalene prostrate before the cross. Bright cellophane colours: reds, blues, yellows, browns and greens. Giants of the Bible shining down on us mortals. We might have been poor folk but we sure as hell knew how to build a house of prayer, and how to bury our dead.

I found the pastor at the side of the altar with his

back to me, standing over the communion table sifting through a pile of books. I came to a halt underneath the leaded light depiction of the Baptist, the prophet's gaze scrutinising me from above.

'Mervyn.' The pastor gave a startled jump, spinning around on his heels to face me. His expression a confused blend of sudden bewilderment and awakening insight. We nodded a silent greeting at each other.

'Joseph, well, this is a pleasant surprise.' Walker peered over my shoulder then gave an equally fleeting glance around the chapel before drawing his attention back to me. 'I didn't expect to see you setting foot inside God's house.'

'Well, you know me, Mervyn. Full of surprises.' I folded my arms across my chest, hoping that Walker would perhaps make the first move. I knew Mervyn was a cautious and prudent man. Not the kind of fella to spill the beans on a personal matter or problem to a stranger. The two of us went back a while, but we weren't close. It was becoming clear that the pastor was going to need a kindly nudge to help him unburden himself. So, I started prodding. 'A little bird told me I should stop by, pay you a visit.'

Mervyn Walker smiled nervously, slowly edging away from the table. I watched him take a couple of paces backwards, as if he suddenly felt an urgent desire to get a little more distance between the two of us.

Like me, Walker was in his late fifties, but he held himself like a mature statesman in his seventies. An act that he carried off with great aplomb.

His hair was cut short on the scalp and into his neck, and unusually for a black fella, straight. He was tall, at least six-four with a pencil-thin moustache the only

15

decoration on an otherwise serious face. The man was handsome in a mean sort of way — I'd heard that the women of the congregation all coveted his attention, but once they got it, the pastor left 'em high and dry at home crying with the good book.

'What is it that I can do for you?'

'I think it maybe the other way round, pastor.'

Walker clasped his hands and looked at the ground for a moment. 'I beg your pardon?'

'Evison Foster.'

The preacher's brow furrowed. His eyes glassing over a little, the tell-tale sign of a man caught between feeling flustered and cagey. He added a little catch in his throat, sort of like a nervous chuckle as he spoke. 'Yes, what about him?'

'Well, he paid me a visit last night. Said I may be of service to you. That right?'

The pastor didn't answer straight away. If he was already looking uncomfortable with me mentioning Evison's name, announcing that I may be of help to him clearly put him on the back foot.

'Did he now?'

The pastor wiped his palms against his trousers and gave me a sly once over before he beckoned me with a tip of his head to follow him. We headed across to the other side of the chapel towards a small green door. Before opening it, he asked: 'I take it you've come here alone?'

I nodded.

'And Evison offered you no prior knowledge of why he asked you to seek me out?'

'Other than to say you had a problem that I may be able to assist you with, I'm in the dark.'

The pastor smiled. 'As our good Lord said: 'What's

done in the dark will come to light." Mervyn swung open the door and flicked on a switch to reveal a steep staircase. 'This way.' He led me downstairs and into a small annexe room where he and his deacons probably suited up before each service. Mervyn Walker still didn't strike me as being desperate. Cagey yes, but not despairing. But I knew whenever a fella wanted to speak to his fellow man out of earshot of anyone else, there was trouble in the air. I didn't know how this latest hazard was about to show itself but I was hell-bent on avoiding it. I slumped back against the wall and waited for the pastor to turn and face me. When he did, I could see the sleepless nights in the dark circles under his eyes.

'So, you gonna tell me what's going on, Mervyn?'

The pastor raised his head, fixing me with an anxious stare. 'It's my wife, Trista. She's gone missing.'

At that moment I felt, keenly, a sense of desperation instantly fill the cramped vault. 'Missing. How long she been gone?'

Mervyn looked down at his hands for maybe two or three seconds; long enough for the average person to formulate a lie. 'Two days. I came home on Thursday afternoon around four-thirty. Found Noah, our six-month old, in the nursery swaddled up in his cot crying and the house empty.'

'Your wife ever walked out on you and not come back like this before?'

'No. Never,' he said shaking his head like an old Roman general after his last defeat. 'This is totally out of character.'

'You think her disappearance has anything to do with any other troubles you could have? Maybe a fight beforehand over something?'

17

The pastor looked at me warily. 'There was no fight. We have no troubles.' Walker's eyes were piercing and intelligent, generous rather than cruel, despite his austere demeanour.

'Come on, Mervyn. Everybody has something to get vexed about. You tellin' me there was nothing your wife might take up and leave over. Nothing she may have been upset about?'

The pastor hunched his thick shoulders. 'She'd been suffering a mild malady this past week or so, but nothing of great concern.'

'What kind of malady we talkin' 'bout, Mervyn?'

'It was nothing serious.' I could see something else in his eyes. A deep pain. It made me feel strangely sad. I watched him fumble to find the right words, the uncertainty all too evident in the fluttering pitch of his voice. 'Trista became low in mood very soon after the birth of our son, Noah.'

'Low mood. You talkin' 'bout her being depressed?'

'Nothing as severe. More like bouts of anxiety followed by a little malaise.'

'A malaise? Mervyn, mothers — they don't walk out on their new-born child for no reason. It goes against the grain. To do a thing like your wife gone an' done, it implies she's a lot more desperate and unwell than you perhaps realise. She taking any kinda medication for this low mood you're talking about?'

'Not that I'm aware, no.'

'She perhaps not take too well to being a mom?'

The pastor gave another curt shake of his head. 'No. Trista is a devoted mother. She showed no signs of being unhappy around Noah, the opposite in fact.'

I knew I was pushing Walker and was wishing I wasn't having to. But something bothered me about

18

the pastor's story and it got me wondering about the kind of woman who'd take off, leaving her young son alone in his crib. 'You think your wife's recent low mood could be the reason why she abandoned your son and left without telling anyone?'

'It's possible. But I can't be sure.' The pastor stiffened, his jaw tightening defensively. 'Listen, I don't like you using words like, *abandon*. Trista has neither abandoned me or our son.'

'Then what would you call it?'

Walker was silent for a few heartbeats. 'I really don't know how to describe it.' He waited for his heart to beat some more and then said: 'I don't understand any of it. That's why I confided in the Fosters.' I could now tell by the pastor's lost gaze that he was suffering. I hoped Mervyn could see in my eyes that I sympathised, even if I didn't understand. I decided to take a less confrontational approach, going left field with my next question.

'Does your wife work?'

Mervyn Walker shook his head. 'No.' A puzzled look appeared on his face. 'What does her working have to do with anything?'

'Nothing really. Just trying to get some idea if she had colleagues she may have gone and bunked down with.'

'There are no work colleagues. Just friends of the church. Trista is the chair of the St Benedict Trust. That was a role which kept her busy before our boy came along.'

'The Benedict Trust?'

'Yes, it's our church charity. You've not heard of it?'

I shook my head. ''Fraid not.'

'Trista was particularly involved with the Five

Loaves and Two Fishes Project.'

'And what's that?'

'You, of all people know how folk in this area find it a daily struggle to make ends meet? Loaves and Fishes hands out food packages to those in need. They also give out hot drinks and sandwiches to people at the door of the charity's mission house on St Andrews Road. It's the Lord's work for the people.'

'Okay, so how come you got Evison Foster tangled up in all this?'

'That would be due to his wife, Carmen. They are both long-serving members of our church. Carmen was gracious enough to come over and me help out with Noah this past forty-eight hours. Neither my wife nor I have family here in Britain. No one I could call on to assist at home. I confided my concern about Trista's sudden disappearance to Carmen. She in turn suggested I reach out to you.' The pastor hung his head for a moment, staring at the ground before fixing his focus back on to me. 'I was reluctant to approach you personally.'

'If you're so worried, why not go to the police? They have the manpower. The right kinda resources.'

The pastor gave me a withering look, then did something that took me by surprise. He stuck his hand in his jacket pocket and pulled out a packet of cigarettes. He flipped open the box lid and offered me a smoke. After I'd politely declined, I watch him light up with trembling hands. When he finally spoke again, wisps of smoke escaped his nostrils making his previously clean-cut face resemble that of a dragon. 'The police bring a great deal of unwanted attention, especially to a man such as myself, living in the close-knit community in which we do. I have no doubt that they

20

have their place in such matters, and do a fine job for the city, but you know as well as I do, they don't look kindly on the lives of black folk, nor do they treat our trials and misfortunes in the same conscientious and diligent manner as they would our white neighbours.'

Walker pulled on the filter of his cigarette, blowing a thick plume of grey smoke towards me. 'Black folk around here, they have all kinds of difficulties, you know that. A kid gets mixed up in the wrong crowd, a car goes missing. Fingers get pointed. People round here calling the police can sometimes just makes something bad that much worse. This situation with Trista could easily spiral out of control in the wrong hands. What's needed is tact, a lightness of touch. Do you think the Bristol constabulary could bring those qualities to the fore in aiding people of colour like ourselves?'

I gave a sigh, a sudden awkward boxed-in feeling dropping around me, my chest feeling as if it were being squeezed hard from the inside. 'So, if you're not prepared to go to the law, what is it you actually want from me?'

Walker smiled and screwed up his face at the same time then inclined towards me in a confidential manner, his voice little more than a murmur. 'This is a domestic problem, not a crime. I am all too aware of your past, Joseph. I know what you used to do for a living. Your specialist skills have not gone unnoticed to me in the past. I was hoping that I could persuade you to use your expert knowledge to perhaps do a little sensitive digging around, to try and uncover where Trista may be at?'

I found myself shaking my head again. 'No way, Mervyn. I ain't done that kinda work for a very long time.'

Mervyn smoothed one side of his moustache with a long, slender finger while he peered into my eyes. 'But you could, if someone were to ask you to, yes?'

'Ain't nobody bin fool enough to ask. And I ain't bin stupid enough to let 'em either.'

'A man works for money or family or,' the pastor shrugged, 'some men work for God.'

I pointed at my chest. 'The kinda way I earn a crust these days ain't complicated and I don't do it fo' the Lord either. How I earn my cash is legal, Mervyn. More importantly, I don't come up against the kinda nasty individuals I'd rather be leaving alone.'

The pastor threw his cigarette to the floor, stubbing it out with the toe of his shoe before holding up his palms, pleading fashion. 'I'm not asking you to break laws or put yourself in any danger, Joseph. I merely wish you to discreetly enquire locally if anyone has seen Trista or has knowledge of her possible whereabouts.'

There was that damn word 'discreet' coming back at me again. I felt the blood rush into my cheeks. My tone was light, which probably made my words sound more threatening than I wanted them to be. 'Mervyn, back in the day when I did the kinda question axin' you're talkin' 'bout, I was appealing to people on the wrong side of the tracks. I was peeping on flea-bag hotel rooms, untying marital knots, blackmailing blackmailers outta business, and in general peering through dirty glass at the dirty lives of people in a very dirty world. You tellin' me that you think your wife has gone an' crossed over into that kinda place?'

Mervyn showed me a mouth of gritted teeth before answering, his fingers curling up into knotted fists. 'I do not.'

'Then go get the police an' let them help you any way they can.' I turned to leave, but the pastor snatched at my elbow pulling me back.

'Please, Joseph, I can pay you! Name your price.'

I turned to face Walker, yanking my arm out of his grasp. 'I don't want your damn money, Mervyn.' I tried to leave again, but he reached out and took hold of my upper arms, pushing me back against the wall, his body shaking uncontrollably. I could smell the heat and funk and rage trapped in his clothes, saw the tiny scar on his face, the grease in his pores and the moisture lining his brow. Red and blue veins surfaced on his cheeks, his hot, stale breath fanning against my face.

'Listen to me, man, I'm begging you. Just give me a couple of days of your time. Forty-eight hours, that's all I'm asking. Not a moment more.'

Walker released one of my arms and hurriedly reached his hand into the inside pocket of his jacket. He pulled out a brown-leather wallet and began to tear a handful of ten- and twenty-pound notes from the bill fold, forcing the cash between my fingers. 'Please, if anyone can find her, you can.' Mervyn's voice was childlike in its pleading, his body quaking like a scared dog. He grabbed my hand in a vicelike grip, the tears welling up in his eyes. We stood there holding hands and looking at each other until the pastor realised that I was more than a little uncomfortable. As he reluctantly let go, he whispered: 'Please, in the name of Christ, please, just do whatever you can to find her. Find her quickly, Joseph. I just want her home, safe.'

Without thinking, I heard myself mumble the words, 'Okay, I'll do it.'

23

I stumbled towards the door and stared back into the clergyman's tortured, sobbing face, and at that very moment realised, that if anyone was in need of God's all-encompassing grace, his truly loving favour and comfort, it was surely his faithful servant, Pastor Mervyn Walker.

Me, I could have killed for a stiff drink.

Right now, hard liquor was about the only thing capable of calming me down. Three shots of neat rum would do the trick. Enough booze to settle my nerves. Give me time to ruminate. To ask myself that all-important question:

How could I have been fool enough to be drawn into another man's misery?

3

I got home a little after three. My tongue felt like a cactus pad, the blood pounding in my temples and Pastor Mervyn's pitiful pleading still rattling around inside my head like it was on a tape loop. I could hear the phone ringing inside the house as I got to the door. I tried to get the key into the lock, but I was in too much of a damn hurry and dropped it into a pile of fallen dried-up leaves and twigs that had blown on to the front step. The phone kept on ringing, though, and it rang until I'd rummaged around, found the key, and made it inside the door. Once in the hall, I tripped on the doormat and by the time I'd got up off the floor and limped to the coffee table the ringing had ceased.

I sat on the edge of the sofa, massaged my bruised knee then emptied Mervyn Walker's blood money out onto the seat next to me. There was at least two hundred quid crumpled up on the cushion of my battered Chesterfield. I stared at the cash for a couple of minutes, thinking how bloody stupid I'd been to have accepted both the dough and another man's troubles. It wasn't the first time I'd brought home that kind of blood money. Another thirty pieces of silver that was most probably going to land me in deep water again.

I heaved myself off the couch and hobbled down to the bathroom. Just as I began to take a pee the phone started ringing again. But I had learned my lesson. The phone rang while I rinsed my hands and dried them. It rang until I made it back to the living room

25

and then it stopped again.

I was in the kitchen with a quart of rum in one hand and a tray of ice in the other when the phone rang again. I considered ripping the line out of the wall, thought better of it, walked back into the living room and finally answered the call.

The first thing I heard was Loretta swearing at her teenage son, Carnell Jnr. When she realised I was on the other end of the line she switched her bile towards me.

'Where the fuckin' hell you bin?'

I tried to shake the gloom out of my voice. The nightmare of the pastor's earlier incessant begging still hanging heavy in my thoughts. 'Church.'

'Bullshit. I know you bin crashed out in that scabby ole pit o' yours. Man, I bin callin' you fo' the best part of an hour. You remember tellin' me how you'd come ovah an' mow my lawn today?'

'I recall saying something of the kind.'

'Recall, my ass! You said you'd be here by two. Clock on my wall just struck t'ree!'

'Look, I'm sorry. I had a few errands to do, I guess the time kinda ran away with me,' I lied. There was an unhealthy silence on the line for a moment.

'Time ran away, he says. Why don't you try runnin' your butt over 'ere. Keep me waitin' much longer, the fuckin' grass'll be growin' up underneath my back do'!'

'I hear you, okay. I'm on my way.' I was anticipating the phone being slammed down on me when I heard Chloe's voice talking to Loretta.

'Pickney 'ere says you need to stop by at Brittan's butcher's an' pick up some blood sausage if you all want feedin' later!'

26

Loretta had hung up on me before I had a chance to say another word. The disconnect tone ringing in my ear like an angry wasp trapped in a sealed jar. I dropped the receiver into its cradle, limped back to the kitchen, put the ice into the top box of the fridge and looked at the rum bottle in my hand. Ten years ago, after the kind of morning I'd just had, I'd have come home and downed half the bottle by now. But the passing of the years has mellowed me a little, and thankfully sated my overeager thirst.

There are few things as beautiful as a glass bottle filled with rum. Liquor shines when the light hits it, reminiscent of precious things like jewels and gold. But rum is better than some lifeless bracelet or coronet. Rum is a living thing capable of any emotion that you are. It's love and deep laughter and brotherhood of the type that bonds nations together. Rum is your friend when nobody else comes round. And rum is the solace that holds you tighter than most lovers can.

I thought all that while looking at my sealed bottle. And I knew for a fact that it was all true. True the way lovers' pillow talk is true. True the way a mother's dreams for her napping infant are true. The kind of parent's fancies that meant they'd never turn their back on the thing they loved the most.

A rum mind and my feverish musings couldn't think its way out of the many questions I still had in regards to the unusual predicament of Pastor Mervyn and his missing wife, Trista. To work out those kinds of convoluted problems required a steady hand and a sober head.

So, I took that fine bottle of Mount Gay rum, put it back in its box and placed it on the shelf where it belonged.

Loretta Harris lived in a white terraced house on Brunswick Street. It was a tall, two-storey building with a latticed skirt of criss-crossed green slats under the eaves. The front was walled in red brick and behind it an unkempt flagstone base with a cracked concrete path that travelled up to the front door. Out back, the yard, the place I'd come to work on, was big and unruly. Long shaggy grass grew around a rusty old slide left out there to remind Loretta of when her son, Carnell Jnr, was still a small child.

In the centre of the lawn stood a half-dead crabapple tree that had been covered in some kind of blotchy, white fungus for years. Around the dying tree, during the summer grew a garden full of eggplants, snap beans and rows of tomatoes. Loretta liked to be surrounded by things that were bountiful, and enjoyed having familiar fruit and vegetables that she'd seen grown in the old country now growing in her own garden.

Although she rarely spoke of them, Loretta had endured hard times in her past. Food had been hard to come by, and there were many days when she'd go hungry. Her father had disintegrated into a helpless drunk. Back home she worked and farmed and smiled for white store owners. I didn't know the half of it, but I knew that her life had been tough. As a child, barely fifteen, she'd nursed her bedridden mother until the suffering woman began to hate her.

All that bile and bitterness never stopped Loretta from caring for her ma. Bleak experiences like that toughen up a person's soul, and Loretta could be as hard as granite if you got on the wrong side of her.

She was a foul-mouthed, no-messing, fiery piece of work and I rarely ever found the courage to cross her. But she was also loyal and kind to those she cared about.

Loretta would have been Rodin's model if he were a black woman. She was big and strong like a man but still womanly — very womanly. Her face wasn't beautiful so much as it was handsome and proud. 'Noble' was too weak a word to describe her looks and bearing. She owned the Déjà Vu barbershop and hair salon on Moon Street. Loretta still worked a few hours each week, alongside the half-dozen other hairstylists she employed, but the high-end St Pauls crimping parlour was a lot more than a local place to get your hair jazzed up and jaw to the staff and fellow customers. Behind the gleaming glass mirrors, the white porcelain backwashes and dryer hoods stood an off-shoot of the vast criminal empire that she ran for my cousin, Vic. Loretta never spoke of her 'other' business, and I knew better than to ever ask about it.

I found Chloe sitting at Loretta's kitchen table doing her homework. She was concentrating so hard that I had to stand real close to her and cast a shadow over the book she was reading to get her attention.

'What you got there?'

Chloe looked up at me blankly. 'A book.'

'I can see that. What's it 'bout?'

Chloe flipped the pages to show me the cover. I read the title out loud. '*Saturday Night and Sunday Morning.*' Chloe immediately went straight back to reading. 'It any good?'

'Um, uh-huh.'

'So good that you can't take your nose out of it for one minute to say 'Hi' to your old man?'

After a moment's hesitation she said, 'Hi, Pa.'

'So, come on, what's the book about?'

'It's about a guy called Arthur Seaton. He's a hard-drinking, hard-working, working-class, womanising, glib liar from Nottingham who gets his comeuppance for behaving like a damn fool, but bounces back pretty much undented.' Chloe grinned. 'Remind you of anybody?'

I dropped the wrapped blood sausage I'd just picked up from the butcher's on the table, bent down and whispered into her ear. 'Lady, I ain't no Casanova and I never lie to you.' I took off my jacket and hung it on the back of one of the kitchen chairs. As I was heading out towards the garden, Chloe called after me.

'No, maybe not, but you are a damn fool sometimes.'

It was a low blow.

Low, but true.

* * *

Loretta was standing in the yard hanging washing on the line and waiting on me to start sweating cutting her lawn. She was wearing a yellow wraparound dress with a red and blue silk cloth coiled in her hair. Her feet were bare. I never minded seeing Loretta nor helping her out whenever I could. We'd been good friends for a long time. Over the years she'd helped me out of more serious scrapes than I cared to remember.

Her late husband, Carnell Snr, had been one of the few friends I had when I first came to England in the sixties. His tragic murder and the unwitting part I'd played in his death continued to haunt me.

'So, you finally got round to grace us wid your

presence.' Loretta glanced at her wristwatch and made a tutting sound. ''Bout time too.'

I decided not to bite and headed for the garden shed to fish out Carnell's old petrol mower. Before I'd the chance to get my hand on the starter grip and fire her up, Loretta was back at me fishing for trouble.

'Chloe bin waitin' on you. You know how the child likes you around fo' Mother's Day weekend. Ain't much that pickney ask you fo'. Least you could do is be 'ere fo' her when she needs you to be. She ain't no baby no mo'. She got feelin's. All her friends, they got mommas. All of 'em buying flowers, an' chocolates, an' that kinda shit. You'd need to remind yourself o' that fact. Kids be cruel, Joseph, 'specially when they knowin' one of 'em ain't got no mom at home.'

'Has somebody at school said something unkind to her?'

Loretta waved a hand dismissively. 'Ain't no body bawled her out. But tha' ain't tha' point. The pickney, she at a funny age. Needs you to be solid.'

'You're right. I'm sorry. I just gotta lot on my mind today, that's all.' Loretta turned on me some more. I could see the pointed questions tallying up in her eyes.

'You gonna tell me where you bin all mornin'?'

'Like I'd said earlier, I had some errands to run.'

'What errands?'

'Stuff fo' work, that's all.'

'You expectin' me to believe that shit?'

'Believe what you want.' I ambled back to the shed. Fetched out a rusting spade and a fork and rested both against the garden fence. Loretta flashed an angry glance at me.

'Sum'ting you ain't tellin' me. Sum'ting that stinks.

31

I know you. What gin on?'

I blew my breath out hard. Loretta knew I was caught, and that I wouldn't find a way out of her constant quizzing. Best that I come clean now, rather than face her full wrath.

'Evison Foster, he paid me a call last night, that's all.'

'Yeah.' I watched the radiance drain out of Loretta's face. It was like a façade, a mask. Suddenly she was hard and angry — close to downright ugly. 'Well, whadda tha' ole prick want wid you?'

'To ask a favour of me.'

Loretta shook her head at me solemnly. 'What kinda favour?'

I reached down for the starter grip and yanked it back, the motor whirring but not kicking in.

'Kind I don't do no more.'

Loretta came in close and put her hand on my arm, squeezed and said in a conspiratorial tone, 'I told you 'bout you an' trouble, ain't I, Joseph?'

'Yeah, yeah you have.' I suddenly felt a little dizzy. 'You think I'd go lookin' fo' trouble at my age.'

Loretta shrugged and stared deep into my eyes. 'Trouble it don't set up like rain, Joseph. You best remember that.'

★　★　★

At around five o'clock, Loretta called me in for supper. I washed up at the kitchen sink and joined Chloe and Carnell Jnr at the dining table. Loretta had fried the blood sausages with onions and a tomato sauce and heated up a saucepan of red beans and rice. Her cooking was always a treat. The tomato sauce was dark

32

red and spicy, the salad dressing full of parmesan and garlic. It tasted wonderful, but I wasn't enjoying my meal as I should have, my mind on other things. I kept taking deep breaths through my nose, but still had a strange feeling of slow suffocation.

Loretta gently laid a couple of fingers on the back of my hand. 'Sum'ting you wanna git off your chest, man?

'No,' I said sharply. 'Why you axin' me that?'

''Cause you keep fuckin' sighing, that's why!'

'Listen, there ain't nuthin' wrong. Nuthin' I need to spill. You been pesterin' me since I come in the door. Give it a rest, why don't ya.'

That silenced the table for more than a minute. It would have been longer but I spoke again. 'I'm going out for a while,' I said, standing up from the table. I felt my bruised knee spasm, a feeling of anger wrapping tight under the skin in my hands as I fought to keep my balance.

'Don't go, Pa,' Chloe pleaded. Carnell Jnr gave me a hard stare, his mouth loaded up with sausage and rice.

'Where the hell you goin', Joseph?' Loretta asked in an unusually reasonable tone.

I took another deep breath that came out in a sigh. 'Into the yard. Finish off the job I came here to do in the first place.'

I sidled back out and ran the mower one more time over the lawn. It didn't need it, but I wanted to brood over the things Mervyn Walker had told me, and working in the garden almost calmed my nerves.

Half an hour later, as I was stowing the mower back into the garden shed, I felt a strange sensation creep through me. When I turned to admire the freshly cut lawn and survey all my hard work, I saw Chloe was stood at the kitchen door. She looked at me with clear serious eyes. I waited for her to say something, but the words never came. I put my fingers in front of my lips and blew her a kiss then waved. She just stared at me.

God knows what she was thinking.

4

I woke from a dark dream feeling completely calm. But when I opened my eyes, terror crept over my heart. It's funny, the things you see in your sleep. My nightmare had me chasing a faceless black woman through the alleys and side streets of St Pauls with what felt like death's hand clutching at my back. I was bleeding from a gash in my forehead, the blood dripping down my cheeks and nose and into my mouth. I couldn't see the face of the woman I was running after, but I had a feeling in my bones that it was the missing parson's wife, Trista Walker. I closed my eyes again and tried to shake the gory image out of my mind, finally opening them again when I heard footsteps on the bare floorboards in my room. Chloe was stood at the bottom of the bed, dressed in her school uniform, smiling at me. 'Pa, I'm making breakfast. You need to get up now if you don't wanna be late into work.'

I peered across at the brass alarm clock on the bedside table: it was a little after seven. I rubbed at my face with my palms and sat up gasping, my mouth dry, a bitter taste on my tongue. I struggled to raise myself off the mattress. The room began to shake slightly — an almost negligible shiver that came from my tentative hold on consciousness.

'Are you okay?' Chloe was already heading for the door when she asked.

'Yeah. Just a nightmare, that's all.'

My girl turned and raised an eyebrow at me. 'I thought only pickneys had those kinda bad dreams?'

35

I smiled at her, mute. The sound of my long dead father's gravelly voice suddenly echoing in my head:

'Boy, it hard to tell da trute when it' a lie folk need to be hearin'.'

I finally made the effort to climb out of bed, rolling to the edge and swinging my legs over the side one at a time before getting to my feet. I felt dozy and listless as I made my way down the landing, lumbering but silent, like a bear, into the bathroom. I shaved and showered, standing under the hot water for the next ten minutes hoping it would bring me around a little. As I towelled myself dry, every muscle in my body ached, as if I'd just ran a marathon. My hands shook, the vision of the anonymous fleeing woman still kicking around inside my head. I lingered in the doorway a moment before girding myself to step out on to the landing, taking my morose thoughts with me.

It was the warm aroma of coffee brewing in the kitchen which finally brought me closer to feeling alive and attempting to shake off the stupor I was lost in. The weekend had flown by in an unpleasant blur. Mervyn Walker coming back into my life with his missing wife problem left a dark cloud over what should have been a fairly relaxed couple of days. I'd taken Loretta's advice and spent most of Sunday doing stuff with Chloe and trying to make amends for my sniffy behaviour the day before. We baked bread while listening to the Jamaican DJ, Leroy Anderson, on the Dread Broadcasting Corporation, prepared jerk chicken and rice and peas for lunch and later in the afternoon we took a drive over to Arnos Vale cemetery to place flowers on my old friend Mrs Pearce and Ruth's graves. Then, before dusk hit, we headed out to Clevedon beach and sat quietly together and

36

ate ice cream on the sea front, our mismatched shadows fused into a single contented shape under a slowly rising moon.

Back in my bedroom, early sunlight danced through the window and made interesting patterns on the white walls. I pulled on a dark brown linen suit, a milk-chocolate turtleneck pullover and my best brown leather brogues.

As I looked back into my closet, I caught sight of my old Aquascutum trench coat hanging in the far corner. I'd ignored the coat's existence for longer than I cared to remember. Now, I found myself reaching for it, holding the waterproof fabric against my chest, like a tearful child clinging onto their favourite comfort blanket.

As I was heading downstairs, I spotted a large brown envelope lying on the rug in the hall. I hung the overcoat over the wooden newel cap at the foot of the banister, made my way across to the hessian mat and picked it up. The flap was sealed, an adhesive label bearing Mervyn Walker's full name and his upmarket rectory address. I felt my stomach sink as I tore open the top and pulled out a letter written on Basildon Bond blue stationery along with a Kodak snapshot of the pastor's wife, Trista. It was a flattering image, one which had the reverend's wife smiling at the camera in a way that would have worked its magic on child or fella alike.

Dear Joseph,

I've heard no word from Trista overnight. I thought this recent photograph may aid you in your search for her. You can reach me on 0272 741686,

37

please do not hesitate to call, day or night.

I am grateful to you for extending to me this kindness.

In my despair, I am reminded of the scriptures and Jehovah's blessed message: 'For the Lord is the God of recompense, He will surely repay.'

Sincerely, your friend,
Rev Mervyn Walker

Reading Mervyn Walker refer to himself as my 'friend' made me feel uneasy. It was an odd thing to write: we'd hardly been bosom-buddies in the past. I put the photograph and note back and walked down the hall into the kitchen where I found Chloe making scrambled eggs and toast. I smiled at her and sniffed the coffee bubbling away in the percolator on the stove top.

'Smells real good.' I inhaled deeply again and took a seat at the dining table, still hanging on to the manila envelope.

'Are you in some kinda trouble, Pa?' Chloe asked, putting a plate of eggs and a coffee down in front of me.

I remained silent. Chloe's question told me two things. First and foremost, she was all too aware that my snappy mood at Loretta's on Saturday night had been out of character and had set alarm bells ringing in her head. And the second, although she was not aware of the fact, my agreeing to help out the pastor had brought out the worst in me. A crankiness which was at odds with my usually mild manner.

Chloe could see that the job I'd secretly taken had gotten under my skin and into my unconscious mind.

I looked like I was in trouble because trouble had coloured my mood.

'No,' I said. 'Why?'

'You always get a serious look on your face and stare into space when you are in trouble.'

'How'd you come up with that theory?'

'I remember that look from when I was a kid.'

'You're still a kid.'

'Are you okay?'

I nodded. 'You remember Pastor Walker?'

'Yeah. Everyone knows Elder Slick.'

'Elder who?'

'Elder Slick, that's what all the kids round here call him.'

I shrugged. 'I don't get it. What's with the slick claptrap?'

Chloe shook her head and laughed. 'For such a smart guy, you sure can be thick sometimes, you know that?'

'Well, how 'bout you enlighten me, smarty pants.'

'Well, flash car, big house, pretty young wife. That's pretty slick for a man of God, don't you think?'

I fought back the urge to laugh. Chloe had made a good point, but I bit my lip rather than agree with her. The pretty young wife observation for some strange reason rang an alarm bell inside of me, but I wasn't sure why. I wagged a scolding finger, the tone of my voice pitched between rebuke and praise. 'That ain't no way to speak 'bout the minister.'

Chloe gave me an icy look. 'I'm just repeating what other people say 'bout him, that's all.' Her grimace quickly turned to a girlish grin, a swift indicator that she was taking charge of the conversation. 'So, what's this you were gonna tell me 'bout *Mr Slick*?'

39

I felt myself cringe at the word 'slick'. 'Ain't nothing important. The man just asked me to pay him a visit yesterday. Turns out he wants me to do a little work for him.'

'Work? But you already gotta job.'

'Yeah, I know I have. This is more a kinda favour to the man, than a career move.'

'What kinda favour's he axin'?'

'The pastor needs me to try and help him find something he's lost, that's all.' I took a mouthful of egg.

'This thing Slick's lost, make a man antsy and bad-tempered?' she said with almost no hesitation.

I choked back my food and swallowed, then began to cough; my eyes watering. 'Why you cheeky little . . .'

Chloe's beautiful face broke out in a resplendent grin. She burst out laughing as I was trying to compose myself. Looking at her was like staring into the once pretty face of my deceased sister, Bernice. She shared her momma's hazel eyes, which had a little green in them as well as a heap of sassiness. When I finally got my breath back, I pointed at the food on my plate. 'Aren't you eating?' I asked.

'I already did.' Chloe winked at me and reached for the blue school blazer that was hung over the back of the chair opposite me. I watch her put it on, then pick up her heavy leather satchel from the kitchen floor and sling it across her shoulder.

'Have a nice day, honey,' I said as she began to walk away.

Chloe stopped, sidling back towards me. She bent down and kissed me on the temple then stroked the top of my head with her slender fingers. 'Love you, Pa.'

I turned and watched her walk down the hallway and head out the door. A feeling of coming awake hit me for the first time since opening my eyes in the upstairs bedroom.

I still felt dead on my feet . . .

But now I had a jig in my heart.

5

One thing I learned in almost twenty-five years as both a policeman and private operator, never trust your first impressions about anything.

Mervyn Walker was a man of the cloth. Pious. Devout. Any true believer worth their salt is gonna tell you that a servant of the Lord don't lie, right?

The pastor's early morning mailshot had done little to ease my inner disquiet about taking on his missing person's crusade nor did it settle my growing inner misgivings about his honesty. I was slowly starting to firm up the notion that Trista Walker's disappearance was going to cause me grief in the coming days. I've always believed that those kinds of sneaking suspicions are worth paying heed to, and yet here I was considering the notion of entering the lion's den again. I'd been handed plenty of sob stories in my time. Some of 'em bona fide; most, little more than grift and hustle. Was the minister's tale of woe just another way for somebody to put the squeeze on me?

There was nothing worse than being played for a sucker. I'd found that out the hard way. Walker's honey-tongued note smacked both of desperation as well as a suggestion of sainted arrogance. In between all his flowery words and excessive gratitude was the lousy feeling that I was being bought to stick my head above the parapet and do another guy's dirty work.

Or, maybe, just maybe I'd got the padre all wrong. Perhaps he'd turned to me, as he'd inferred down in that dingy chapel catacomb, *because he had no one else to turn to.*

I considered myself a man of fair intelligence. I know what secrets I should keep. Know when a man needs a helping hand. Know when not to take unnecessary risks; just like a married man knows that he shouldn't bed Pam Grier with his wife in the next room. But, sometimes, when the real world comes knocking, as Mervyn Walker had, all we can do is hold on tight and hope the roof doesn't fly off.

In for a penny, in for a pound.

Now, I'd convinced myself to bite the bullet and give Walker the benefit of the doubt. All I needed to do now was let the office know I'd be absent from duty for a few days. I dialled the bureau's number and let the phone ring for the better part of a minute, still thinking about the pastor's predicament and my next move. These thoughts reverberated in my head, like loose change rattling round the inside of a washing machine drum, until somebody picked up the receiver.

'Friends Association,' an elderly woman said brightly.

'Hey, Harriet.'

'Who's this callin'?'

'Joseph Ellington.'

'The Prodigal Son,' she declared. 'Ain't like you to be makin' no call 'ere. S'up?'

'Everything's fine. I just wanted to let you know I ain't gonna be in till later in the week, I'm afraid.'

'Oh, I'm sorry to hear tha', Joseph. You sickly?'

I cleared my throat and said, 'No. No, I'm fine. I've just had some unexpected personal stuff drop in my lap. Something I gotta deal with sooner, rather than

43

later. I should have it wrapped up by Wednesday, latest.'

A moment passed before Harriet spoke again. 'Any'ting I can duh to help?'

'I wish there were. I hadn't bargained on making this call. I'm sorry it's at such short notice.'

I heard the old woman sigh. 'Ain't a problem, bossman. Bothcration cithcr nipped in the bud or it nip you in dey arse. Don't you be a stranger fo' too long, now. This place always feel empty without you 'bout.'

'Be back before you know it. Take care of yourself, Harriet.'

'You too, son,' she replied, and we both hung up.

My mouth was dry after that brief conversation. I'd not told Harriet Tyler the full story for my sudden absence, but neither had I imparted to her a lie. Call it a well-intentioned untruth. A red herring rather than flight of fancy. Either way I cut it, I still felt like I'd just hoodwinked a kind soul; a decent human being who didn't deserve to play a part in the shifty dealings I was about to take part in.

I could have sunk a nip of rum before heading out but knew better. Drinking and dealing with broken hearts are okay as long as there were no car keys or a loaded .45 in your hip pocket.

I intended on driving my old heap across town today. As for my handgun, that was safely entombed in a place only I was privy to.

Concealed in darkness where it could harm neither man nor beast.

6

Once I was in my car, I felt a moment of exhilaration. Strange, because I'd spent the better part of the week-end feeling gloomy about my decision to go looking for Trista Walker and what little joy that search would no doubt bring me. Turning the key in the ignition and hearing the engine fire up seemed to shock me out of the melancholy that had settled in on me. The kinds of investigation work I'd undertaken in the past, while being far from a perfect way to make a living, had on the whole given me a sense of purpose, and a decent living.

I remembered what it was to be a man living in the cracks back in Barbados. My enquiry agency had elevated my position within the community. I was self-employed, made my own money and answered to no one. And yet, at the same time, there was both dis-trust and hostility from many in my own community for the kind of work I did and my past history working as a serving police officer.

Away from St Pauls, walking down the Bristol streets of white gentility, I was always a target. A target who couldn't fire back on the men who used words like spear-chucker, jigaboo and darky-boy for sport. Back in the mid-sixties all a man like me could do was wait for the sun to go down and move through the darkness hoping I could play private detective with-out getting my head kicked in or worse. Fifteen years later and the racism and bigotry of the past was fad-ing a little, but it had far from gone away. The start of a new decade and I was again stepping back into a role I swore I'd never toil in again. It was dangerous work to undertake any way you cut it, and no matter how many years had passed since I'd last taken on a case the risks to both my life and limb were still very real. The times may have changed for many since 1965, but not for me. I was a British citizen, but a citizen who still had to watch his step, a citizen who still had to distrust the police and the government, public opinion and even the history taught in schools.

It was odd that such negative thoughts would somehow now invigorate me. But knowing the truth, no matter how bad it was, in my experience gave you some chance, a little bit of an edge. As much as I may have wanted to deny it, pulling on my old overcoat this morning, knowing I was walking out of my front door to return to a job I'd once been good at, gave me a thrill. I put my foot on the gas, telling myself such a spirited feeling would soon wear off once the first fling of shit hit the fan.

★ ★ ★

It took me less than ten minutes to drive across town and over to my first destination, the Young Women's Christian Association on Wells Road in Totterdown. I'd decided to check out all the usual haunts a woman may decide to take up refuge if she found herself either on the streets or trying to keep her head down and out of the hands of some fella who was making her life a misery.

At the reception desk I was greeted by a portly, stony-faced woman with a brusque Somerset accent who regarded me with the kind of chary disdain normally

46

offered to death row prisoners. My polite enquiry was treated with mistrust and barely hidden scorn, and I walked out of the building and back towards my car having learned nothing other than the fact that, 'Men aren't welcome at the YWCA.'

I soon got the feeling that I was on a fool's errand after I drew a blank over at the Spring of Hope Women's Shelter in the Old Market area of town, and likewise was shown the door at the Salvation Army hostels in both Knowle West and Two-Mile Hill Road in Kingswood. Two and a half hours of leg work and polite questioning had produced nothing more than the reality that I was probably on a hiding to nothing. A needle in a haystack search, looking for a woman who likely didn't want to be found, and who, if she still had her wits about her, was probably miles away from Bristol by now. But I had to consider other options. If she was unwell, physically or as Pastor Walker had suggested, mentally, there was a remote chance she may have checked into one of the local hospitals.

I pulled over at a phone box on my drive back into the city, and with the help of the Yellow Pages called the Bristol Royal Infirmary, the Frenchy Hospital on the north-east outskirts of town, Brookland Hall psychiatric unit in St Werburghs, and lastly St Michael's maternity hospital; the receptionists at each establishment informing me in no uncertain terms that nobody with the name of Trista Walker had been admitted for treatment or placed onto a ward in the last four days. Before I'd left the Old King chapel on Saturday afternoon, Mervyn Walker had told me that, apart from her purse and a black, hooded winter coat, his wife had taken no overnight bag or, to his knowledge,

47

any spare clothes, cosmetics or toiletries. Why, if the woman was so desperate to get away from her home and, perhaps, the pastor, had she not packed a suitcase with the most basic of personal belongings before taking off? It made no sense whatsoever.

Clutching at straws, I headed over to the city's coach station on Marlborough Street and checked out the ticket office.

'May I help you?' a white-haired woman, who had no such intention, asked me. Her nameplate read, Monica Shaw. She was very pale and on the bulky side. There was a ring with a large garnet stone on her right hand. The gem looked like a knot of blood that had congealed on her finger. A cup of tea steamed next to her telephone and a curtain of cigarette smoke rose from an ashtray next to her. I smiled politely, flashed Trista Walker's mugshot at the woman and asked if she'd seen her come in and buy a ticket to any place special? The combination of my vocabulary, grammar and the politeness with which I spoke meant nothing. I got the same monosyllabic replies to my prying. Another blank runaround, just as I'd been given at the YWCA and the half dozen other places I'd already set foot through.

The woman and I didn't speak another word to each other. There was no need to. I walked out of her ticket office feeling like I was being turfed out rather than leaving of my own accord. As I was about to close the door, I turned to say, thank you. The woman was staring back at me in a way that made me avert my gaze and look out across the terminus. There was hatred in her eyes. Real hate. It should not have shocked me, but it did. For a man like me, the only thing you can expect from your own courtesy and decency is hatred in the eyes of another.

I continued to wander round the bus station for the next half hour, showing off Trista Walker's photograph to anyone who cared to look at it. Asking those folk waiting for or about to ride a bus if they may have seen the parson's wife hanging around. Afterwards, I trawled the city streets, going into various cafés, pawn shops, pubs, hotels and then the harbourside doss houses; every joint sending me away with my tail between my legs and clueless. By three-thirty I was ready to throw in the towel.

On the drive back home, I had time to ponder my situation. I'd spent the better part of the day looking for someone who most probably didn't want to be found. A desperate soul, probably mentally ill and in need of professional care and medical attention. Trista Walker was clearly more than a little unhappy with her lot. A woman didn't just up sticks and walk out on her marriage and leave her young child without damn good reason. Mervyn Walker had offered up plenty of fire and brimstone, but he couldn't adequately offer up any reasonable grounds for his wife's disappearance other than she was suffering some kind of malaise. And why the hell didn't he want the police to be involved?

It was true that the law would stop a black person in the street just for walking, but to not involve them when the person you loved had gone missing without word or reason seemed more than a little suspicious. I was slowly coming to the conclusion I'd perhaps been a chump to say yes to the pastor's request to help him out. Nevertheless, such a prudent verdict still didn't stop the nagging feeling inside me that gave voice to push on with my search.

I was a fool, I knew I was a fool, and still, perhaps stupidly, I didn't care. Trista Walker was missing. I now had the bit between my teeth and wanted to find her.

The Five Loaves and Two Fishes Project on St Andrews Road in Montpelier sat on an ugly spread of nothing that led to no place worth talking about. A pot-holed tarmac artery set either side by dilapidated pre-war, red-brick houses that cut along the outer boundaries of both the suburbs of Stokes Croft and St Pauls. An eyesore in the cold light of day and equally miserable after night had descended, the rundown ward was very much the poor cousin to the otherwise up and coming bohemian residential neighbourhood it partially shouldered. Even in the relatively cool March air the Andrews Road residents sat out front of their rented tenement homes staring at me as I pulled up in the street.

I wasn't what you'd call a stranger to the area, but neither was I homegrown and held without suspicion. The locals would have stared at each other if I wasn't there, but me parking up outside their pads offered a titbit of interest to their otherwise uneventful day. Kids screamed and ran in and out of the road and along the pavement. Boys played war while little girls watched, half in envy, half bewildered.

I crossed the road and walked along the slender passageway to the rear of the Five Loaves and Two Fishes Project building. It was a large single-storey wood and brick pile occupying what had once been a mortuary. In the old days, before I moved to Bristol, I heard that the undertakers had a bar fitted behind the coffin repository. Mourners would come in grieving and leave with new hope.

The back door was open and an old woman sat in front of it in a deck chair. Behind her, stood at a workbench, I could see a man I recognised to be Floyd Council eyeballing me suspiciously. Council was known to most people in St Pauls and the surrounding area as 'Dipper'. A former habitual criminal, Council had been a notorious house burglar, thief and pickpocket who had spent as much time confined as he had living in the free world. Word on the street was that after breaking into the home of the much-respected Bristol clergyman, Canon Malcolm Widdecombe, he'd being caught red-handed by the kindly reverend. Dipper, after being shown his unchristian ways, had, if it was to be believed, seen the light, given up his felonious ways and turned to God. I wasn't convinced. I'd known men like Dipper my whole life. His type was crooked to the bone and his supposed religious conversion didn't fool me one bit. I was, however, a little flummoxed to see him stood inside the premises of a charity. A place recognised for its goodwill and giving to others. Dipper's reputation was for taking without asking or the kind of jobs where there were no questions asked, and not doing a kindness for his fellow man or woman. I ignored his questionable presence and focused on the formidable gatekeeper sat in the deck chair.

'Hello. My name is Joseph Ellington.' I held out my hand. The brief smile that came across the old woman's stern face didn't reach her eyes. She reached up, took my palm in hers and we shook.

'How can I help you?'

'I'm looking for Mrs Walker.'

Even sitting down, I could see the elderly custodian had been a formidable soul in her time. She was short, with a slender frame. Her eyes were a piercing dark brown, and though her face was not particularly attractive, there was something otherworldly about it. She was dressed in a cranberry one-piece that hung around her ankles. Grey hairs battled with the dark ones across the woman's head. There was a bald patch towards the top of her pate.

'Trista?' the woman said without hesitation. 'The minister's wife?'

'That's the very lady. She about?'

She shook her head. 'Ah-ah . . . I can't help you, sorry.'

'I was told she sometimes works here.'

'She sometimes comes and helps out, but she ain't here now.'

The old woman gave me a bitter glance then turned in her seat and stared at Floyd Council, mouthing something to him that I could not make out. Then, without saying another word to me or before I had chance to question her further, she got up and went inside, taking her chair with her, closing the door in my face. I heard the lock turn and voices talking on the other side. As I turned to leave, I heard the bolt rattle and the door open up again.

Floyd Council came blustering out. He wasn't over five feet tall. In fact, he probably might not have made the full sixty inches. He wore navy blue overalls and a tired black Crombie overcoat, his curly hair cut short, with wispy sideburns. His large brown eyes offered up very little wisdom. It was obvious that Council had been monitoring every word of the brief conversation I'd just had, but the little fella wasn't embarrassed by this exposure.

'Hey, Mistah Ellington.' Dipper hesitated a

moment, wiping the back of his hand across his nose and sniffing loudly. 'I tou't dat were you talkin' to Miss Grace. How you doin'?'

'Good, Floyd. You?'

Dipper shot me a grin. 'Can't complain, man. Can't complain.'

I pointed back at the project. 'What you doing at the Loaves and Fishes, brother?'

'Me?' Council held up a hand. 'Shit, I'm straight these days, Mr Ellington. The Lord got me doin' his work!'

'That so.' I directed my eyes from Council's feet up to his face. 'Well, that's real Christian of you, Dipper.' Council dropped his arm to his side and shuffled on the balls of his feet, nervously. He clearly didn't like me using his street name, or the up and down look I'd just given him.

'I heard you's lookin' fo' Pastor Walker's woman?'

'Yeah. She been around here, lately?'

'Not that I've seen.' Dipper shot me a snide glance and moved in closer. His voice hushed. 'Though, if she ain't hanging out at that fancy vicarage pad o' hers, you could seek her out at a couple o' other places.'

'You know where I can find her?'

Dipper shrugged. 'Not exactly.' He broke off and turned, glancing back at the closed door before quickly training his piggy eyes back on me. 'But I've bin tol' the kinda places she likes to hang out.' There was suddenly a deep certainty in his voice. He began to rub his thumb across the tips of a couple of his sticky fingers. I reached into my jacket pocket, took out my wallet and wafted a five-pound note under his nose. Dipper snatched the cash out of my hand faster

53

than a cat on a mouse. 'You try Dingy's on Nicholas Road.'

I went to grab the money back, but the sneaky little shit was already stuffing the note out of sight. I took Council by the arm, pulling him towards me.

'You are kidding me, right. What the hell would a minister's wife be doing in a dive like Dingy's?'

Council sighed and shook off my grip. 'I 'ear tings 'bout duh woman, dat's all am sayin'.'

'What kinda things?'

'Jus' dat the pastor's wife, she like to live danger-ously.' Council flashed me a dirty grin then turned on his heels and bolted for the project door. I yelled after him.

'I find out you've pulled a fast one on me, I'm coming over to your place to get that cash back. You hearin' me, Dipper?'

Dipper took hold of the door handle before turning back to face me. He pressed his lips outward and then pulled them back in before giving a little nod. 'I 'ear you, brother. Look, all I can say is, you get no joy with Dingy's, you come knock ma' gate door. I'll see if I cain't put you right someplace else. I do a little axin' round in the meantime. P'haps cook up sum'ting tasty an' help you out some more, yeah?'

There was something ugly in Dipper's choice of words and the way he said them.

Walking back to my car, I was watched by more than a dozen pairs of eyes. Most of that part of the street seemed to have stayed out to view me leave. I couldn't blame them for their curiosity or their idle chatter. Most had little else going on in their lives. I knew their interest in me would be as fleeting as Dipper's pledge to help me out in the future. It didn't matter that neither would last.

In my experience, an inquisitive mind is often squandered on the misfortunes of others and promises rarely kept.

7

I cooked dinner that night. Fried chicken, macaroni cheese and greens, served with the homemade lemonade Chloe liked me to make for her. We sat at the kitchen table and Chloe served. My little girl had matured early. She could easily take care of herself when I was at work, could hold down a grown-up conversation with folk much older than herself and she was as sharp as a pin. A real smart cookie. These traits may have had something to do with my child-rearing, but I couldn't be sure. I was a single parent who was often out in the world rather than home. I had moved Chloe from one place to another when she was young; we'd both lost the woman who had been our saviour and who in my niece's eyes was the mother she both craved and deserved. She'd also been, these past eighteen months, subject to my often-sour moods. That was something I wasn't proud of.

'You mind going over to Loretta's tonight?' I asked when we were both seated.

Chloe nodded while she chewed on a piece of chicken. 'To sleep over you mean?'

'Yeah. I already checked in with Lol. She's looking forward to you keeping her company for the night. You'll need to take your uniform and pack for school in the morning. I want you to call me when you get there, let me know you're safe. Okay?'

'Okay.' Chloe's voice contained the lilt of the English Caribbean. The tone was both soft and strong. She swallowed another mouthful of food and gave me a quizzical look. 'Where you going?'

'I'm just finishing up on that favour for Pastor Walker. But I might be out late.'

'Who you going with?'

'No one. I'll be on my own.'

Chloe stared down at her plate, swallowed another mouthful of food and then reached out to rest her palm on the back of my hand. 'Be careful, yeah?'

'Always,' I said in a joking voice. The two of us carried on eating, an awkward silence filling the room. The only noise the sound of the metal cutlery tapping against our plates.

'Pa?'

I knew from Chloe's tone that something serious was about to hit me. Something that had nothing to do with my being out for the evening or her sleeping over at Loretta's for the night.

'Yeah?'

Chloe looked from side to side as if there might be spies in the kitchen. 'You ever meet my father?'

I swallowed hard, clearing my throat before speaking. 'I did.' I shifted in my seat, unsure where to look. I decided it best to keep my head down. My nose stuck in my chicken dinner. 'It was a long time ago.'

'What was he like?'

I stared at my adopted child, a helpless feeling creeping over me. 'He was a businessman. Wealthy. Quite powerful. Our paths never crossed that much,' I lied.

The story of Chloe's parents' lives, and deaths, had always been a subject that I'd been reluctant to discuss with her, and in fairness Chloe had surprisingly never asked me to tell her what I knew. She shouldn't have had to hear the truth until she'd at least reached

57

her twenty-first year, not her fifteenth, but I knew I couldn't avoid it for another six years.

'How'd he die, Pa?' Chloe said, raising her voice ever so slightly.

'It's a sad story,' I said. My little girl shifted herself closer to me.

'But you'll tell me 'bout it sometime, right?'

I leaned over and kissed her on the cheek. 'Sometime.'

We ate the rest of our meal in silence. When Chloe had finished, she asked to be excused and told me that she was going to her room to pack. I watched her walk down the hall and climb the stairs. Heard her bedroom door click shut.

I sat at the kitchen table a while longer, in that little pocket of uneasy peace. A minute or two of silence before I stood myself up and returned to the war.

★ ★ ★

Chloe called me from Loretta's as soon as she'd set foot through the door, just like she'd promised. I left the house a little after nine and headed for Dingy's Blues Bar. The streets were empty and dark. As I walked, I got to remembering the times I'd spent traipsing the same part of St Pauls with my old friend Carnell Harris. I was back in 1965. Carnell plodded alongside of me in the snow, chattering away about a card game or some horse he'd just backed.

My reverie saw him come to a halt. He smiled, mouthed words I could not recognise, his hand dropping at his side, blood slowly seeping through the gaps in his fingers. A fog rolled in around our feet and he slowly left my side, stumbled, picked up pace and broke into a sprint. A half-dozen faceless, silent, cloaked demons began to pursue him. There were no cries, no pleas for help. I watched both the fog and my friend disappear. I was certain the spirits chasing my long-dead comrade would never catch him. His soul was still alive and breathing — somewhere.

★ ★ ★

Dingy's Blues sat on the junction of St Nicholas Road and Grosvenor Road. The main joint comprised of a room built around the remnants of a large brick oven that had once been used to make bread for the parson's bakery empire in the twenties. The oven had been twelve feet in diameter. Theo Sweet, the bar owner, had long ago installed a circular mahogany bar around the old oven and, on busy nights, he had as many as four barmaids working back to back, serving a mainly black clientele.

Outback there was a dozen tiny rooms, where for a set fee a fella could lay low or get laid. There were no windows in the walls of Dingy's main bar, but the roof was one big skylight, and so it was exceptionally sunny during the day, but at night as dusk fell, the place gave many of its more enigmatic drinkers a subdued, cossetted atmosphere to relax in. Theo used the old exhaust fans left over from the bakery to keep the place at a reasonable temperature during the summer, while in winter two roaring wood fires kept the joint cosy.

In the far corner of the bar sat an old upright piano on a wide dais for a jobbing musician or diva to keep the mood cool. Tonight, there were no sounds playing. Dingy's was practically empty and Sweet was the only person working.

'Theo,' I said as I approached.

The barman winced, straining to find my name. The rundown bar was the place that local folk who liked to keep a low profile patronised. It wasn't a joint I frequented often on account it was one of the few drinking dens in St Pauls that wasn't owned by my cousin Vic and it was renowned for selling more skin than it did booze. 'Joseph, right?'

'Yeah.'

'What you drinkin'?'

'Bottle o' Dragon stout.'

Sweet was in his early sixties but was still a nearly perfect specimen of manhood. He was five eleven with maple-brown skin, wide in the shoulder, with only around ten pounds more than he needed on his frame. He had a small scar under his left eye and eyebrows that even a vain woman wouldn't have touched up. His lips were generous and sculpted, his oiled hair was combed back in perfect waves. He carefully poured my stout into a half-pint glass.

'You still hitting a bag over at Vic's place?' Mentioning my cousin's name got the big man's attention.

The barman handed me my beer. 'Nah, I ain't boxed fo' years, man. Most o' the fightin' I do these days is with the drunks I sling out inta the street.'

'I saw you get into a fight there one night, must be ten years ago or more.'

'Yeah, did I win?'

'Oh, yeah. You sure did. It was a big dude, name of Fairfax, you put him down and they had to carry him outta the ring.'

'I don't remember any fights but the ones I lost,' Theo said in a rare show of pride.

'How many you remember?'

'None that come to mind.' Sweet had a sharp laugh, like the chatter of a dozen angry hens. I laid down a pound note He pocketed the cash, keeping the change for his tip.

Sweet picked up a wet cloth but then became serious, eyeing me suspiciously as I sipped at my drink. 'We might as well cut the shit.'

I felt a sudden tightness grip at my insides. 'What's that you say?'

Sweet straightened his shoulders and began wiping at the polished bar with the rag. 'You want sumpin', son?'

I let the question hang for a bit. 'What makes you think I want anything other than this glass o' Dragon?'

The barman stopped wiping, raised an eyebrow and laughed. He paused a full fifteen seconds longer. Long enough for me to know that he was already on to me. 'You ain't no regular. Nevah seen comin' in 'ere to kick back.' Sweet buffed his bar top a while longer before giving me a mean look. 'Gotta be more than that pound's wort' o' piss water you got in your hand to bring you breezin' ta my place. Just can't tink why.'

'No good me telling you I fancied a change of scenery, I suppose?'

Sweet shook his head. 'Any fool round 'ere knows 'bout my door. Knows what goes on inside o' 'ere. We got t'ree tings goin' down. Ganga, fuckin' an' domino.' Sweet looked me up and down. 'Don't look like you after any blow, a bitch or to slam duh bones. So, I gonna axe you again. Whadda you want?'

I took Trista Walker's photograph out of my pocket and placed it on the bar. 'I got it on good authority

61

that the woman in this picture sometimes takes a drink in here, that right?'

The barman peered at the photo, took his time looking at it, then pushed it back towards me. Sweet's only imperfect features were his eyes. They weren't set deep in his head like most folks. They were right out there competing with his nose for facial real estate. As a result, even I could easily read the hesitation when it entered his gaze.

'You the Jah's kin, right?'

I nodded my head. 'Vic's my cousin.'

The barman's dull gaze came to life, he leaned across to me, his dry breath kissing my cheek. 'I maybe seen her come in a couple o' time, but that's all.'

'On her own?'

Sweet shook his head, not meeting my eye. 'Couldn't say.'

'You know who she is, right?'

'Naw, man. I got no idea who tha' floozy is, jus' that her face looks familiar.'

'Familiar enough to perhaps know her name and who she hangs out with?'

'I bin runnin' this place too long to remember every bitch walks thru' my door.' He said it as if he were proud of the fact. 'What you want wid the woman?'

'It's a family matter.' The family remark finally got the barman's full attention.

Sweet stared at me for a moment then scratched his high cheekbone. He gave a sideways glance towards the back room where the scabby bunks were located. 'There's a young fella name o' Loudon doin' a bit o' bid'ness out back. Might be able to point you in the right direction. Boy ain't evah long. Be out just in a minute.'

62

I slipped the photograph back into my pocket. 'That the same Troy Loudon who put Chris Sanigar down in the fourth?'

'The very same.' Sweet gave a low cough, his eyes shifting towards the rear of the bar. When he spoke again it was almost a whisper. 'Go easy on how you go 'bout axin' him questions. The boy gotta temper on him.'

When I looked away from Theo, I saw Troy Loudon coming from out back and heading towards the door at real speed. He was short and stocky, welterweight size. I had seen him fight a few early bouts, but I'd heard he was fond of the bottle as well as the bookies and was always looking to make a fast buck any way he could. Troy's fists were like hammers: insistent and right on the head. But he ignored the body, and that's something Vic had told me a boxer should never do. I thanked Sweet and followed Loudon out into the street.

'Troy!' I called after him. He looked back in my direction and waved even though in the dark he didn't recognise me. 'Hold up, man.' Loudon came to a halt on the pavement and waited for me to catch him up, a puzzled look on his face. Boxers know so many people, and they have to give the time of day to most fellas because it's the man on the street who mostly pays their salary. Loudon was no different.

Troy and I had been in various places in the past, parties at shebeens, I'd seen him at the gym years back, but we'd never actually met. I knew who he was by reputation and I was aware that his standing in the community these days was fairly down at heel.

'Joseph Ellington,' I said to help him remember what he didn't know. 'What's happenin'?'

63

'Not much. Goin' fo' a workout.' He cocked his head across the street in the general direction of the gym and flexed his muscles almost unconsciously. Like most boxers I knew, he kept his head down. I glanced down at my wristwatch.

'Kinda late to be working out, ain't it?'

'I ain't evah off the clock when it come to punchin' a speedball.' Loudon rolled his shoulders at me, the bewildered expression on his face becoming increasingly more evident.

He was a sand-coloured man, but there was something else about Troy that I couldn't put my finger on.

Maybe it was his buck teeth or the way he walked. It was as if he had the rhythm of a white man. A stride instead of a walk in his gait.

'You wanna make an easy twenty quid?' I asked the young prize-fighter.

His smile showed me three teeth capped in silver and two that were missing.

'I'm looking for a woman by the name of Trista Walker.'

Troy swallowed the grin and turned away from me. 'I ain't seen her.'

'Hey, hold up will ya, man.' I ran up beside Loudon and stopped.

'What?'

'Word is you know her. I was hoping you could put me in touch?'

'That's some real shit you bin hearin'. I hardly even know the bitch.'

Loudon made to walk off, but I stood in front of him. I was close to a foot taller.

'I could go to, say, thirty if you'd consider helping me out?'

64

'Get the fuck outta my way, man.'

It was putting my hand on his shoulder, that was my mistake. Terry brought up his left arm to block me and then he threw a quick jab to my head. That was okay, even at my age, I could still take a welterweight jab. I reached my arms out around to catch him in a bear hug, but Loudon was too fast. He unloaded a half-dozen uppercuts to my middle, two of them landing real hard. I was on the ground as fast as I could get there and Troy Loudon was running down the street.

He disappeared into the night while I held on to my ribs.

'You okay, Mistah Ellington?'

Theo Sweet peered down at me. A worried look on his face. He held out an open palm by way of solidarity. I didn't take the barman's hand because I didn't want to owe the man anything. After about a minute or two I pulled myself up in a stooping stance.

'You okay?' Sweet asked again.

'Yeah, yeah, I'm fine.'

'Man, what'd I tell you 'bout axin' that big fool questions. He could 'ave put you in your grave.'

I don't think I answered Sweet. Maybe I gave him a nod.

But I knew he was right.

8

I stood in the street outside of Dingy's, gasping for air, holding onto my ribs and sweating like a pig. My knees buckled when I tried to move, so I gave up on the idea real quick. Theo Sweet was at my side giving me the kind of withering look a man would normally get from a scornful wife whose anniversary he'd forgotten. I watched him take a cigar from the top pocket of his shirt, unfurl the cellophane wrapping and light it with a match. The big barman chugged on the end of his stogie, screwed up the cigar's wrapper and spent match in his palm and dropped both at his feet. He took a lungful of smoke then hit me full in the face with a plume of grey fumes.

'You must have really given tha' boy sum backchat fo' him to take you down like he did.'

When I tried to answer I made a noise like I was gargling. I clung to the wall, a life raft in a stormy sea. After a moment or two, I slowly started to get my breath back, the red mists starting to part, my head less woozy. 'You know where Loudon lives?'

Sweet froze like a wary fly when a man's shadow passes by. 'Why?' he said through nearly closed lips.

'Why? Because Loudon knows something about the woman in that photograph I showed you. I wanna find out what, that's why.'

Sweet rubbed his hand over his face and turned to me. 'You gotta be fuckin' crazy, man! Troy, he'll tear you a new arse'ole you go near him again.'

A sharp twinge brought tears to my eyes as I drew

in another breath. 'Didn't say I was gonna go bother the fool tonight, did I?'

'If I was you I wouldn't be tinkin' 'bout botherin' the big bastard again, inny time soon.'

'Man didn't knock me to the ground and run for nothing. He had a scared look in his eyes before he took off.' I flinched as I straightened my back and turned to face the barman. 'You know where I can find him, or not?'

Sweet twisted his face and spat a wad of brown spittle at his feet, the tone of his voice becoming conspiratorial. 'You didn't hear this from me, right?'

I nodded my head. 'Right.'

'Loudon got a pad on Albany Road. The house is abandoned. He tol' me he moved in a couple of weeks ago. Had me take him a couple o' old wooden chairs I had no use fo', no mo'. Place's a white joint. Got a fucked-up fence, ain't got no paint on it. That's 'bout as much as I know.'

'It's enough.' I forced a smile by way of gratitude.

Sweet took another deep pull on his cigar, then spoke through the fog he exhaled. 'Okay, but it's your funeral. I tell you, best you let him cool off 'fore you go talkin' to him. Whoever you helpin', you gotta still be breathin' to do it.'

'Thanks for the good advice.'

Sweet turned and nodded. He rubbed his face again. 'Ain't no such thing as good advice, brother. I'm jus' givin' one man's bullshit to anutha.'

He shambled back towards the bar. I'd never really liked Theo Sweet. I'd always considered him 'the opposition' on account that he wasn't part of Vic's employment stable. I'd seen the barman as the enemy, someone to distrust or steer well clear of — now all I

67

saw was a kindred spirit; a man trod on by his history and dismissed because of the colour of his skin. A man who knew that the majority of people in this land would never notice his hardships or sorrows, and if they did, they would blame him for his own misery.

I hobbled after Sweet, tapping him on the shoulder as he was about to enter the bar. I put out my hand and said: 'Thanks, man.'

★ ★ ★

The walk back to my house was a painful one. Taking a beating was nothing new to me. In the past, as stupid as it might seem to those unaccustomed to it, even fear had become an old friend. These days, things are different. For years I'd been far removed from the kind of life that involved other people's misfortunes and me being on the receiving end of a hefty punch, and by the time I'd walked back through my front door, my aching body was telling me so. For almost a decade, I'd been getting up and going to work, receiving my salary into my bank. Paying bills by cheque instead of cash. I was a member of Chloe's school parents' teachers' association.

I slept in my own bed every single night from Christmas to Christmas. I'd followed the same routes every day and toed the line, but all of a sudden I seemed to be lost, and all because of a missing preacher's wife. It was like I was a young man again, back on the beat, every morning leading me someplace I never would have suspected I'd end up at. The main difference now was that I wasn't enjoying myself. I didn't want to lose my way. But something inside of me, something I couldn't explain, was telling me I had to keep looking for Trista Walker.

I had to be sure that her disappearance had been of her own choosing.

* * *

I'd gotten myself around five hours sleep. I was woken by my alarm at six, bleary-eyed and aching. I rose from my bed, groaning to myself after catching sight of the bruising down one side of my ribcage. I limped down to the bathroom, my knee still smarting from my fall, feeling like I'd just gone twelve rounds with Marvin Hagler. I took a shower, turning the water as hot as I could stand it, pointed my face with my mouth open into the shower head, washed the cigarette smoke from the bar out of my hair and scrubbed my skin till it was raw. Then I turned on the cold water full blast, propped my arm against the tiled wall and counted slowly to sixty. Afterwards, I sat on the edge of the bath, my nerve endings feeling like they'd been touched with lit matches. Once I got my strength back, I dried myself, returned to my bedroom and dressed.

In the kitchen, I made a pot of coffee. I rested my back against the draining board, thinking to myself, my body throbbing. I drank two cups of the black liquid along with a couple of aspirin in quick succession in the hope that the caffeine and painkillers would knock a little life into me.

By seven I was sitting in my car across the road and down the street from Terry Loudon's squat on Albany Road. I was expecting trouble. Hell, I was looking for it, I just wasn't that eager to go face it. As a police officer back on Bim, I'd learned a valuable lesson when it came to arresting crooks. Whether they were on the run and in hiding or they were unaware that you were on to them, it was always best to get 'em early; preferably while they were still slumbering in their bunks. A man fast asleep, tucked up underneath a warm blanket or eiderdown is a damn sight easier to handle than one facing you off with a knife in his hand and a bellyful of hooch inside of him. I wanted to catch Troy Loudon while he was sleepy-eyed. Dozy. On his back and hopefully a lot easier to communicate with. Better to introduce myself while he was still unsteady on his feet than upright and ready to swing at me again.

Outside the street was as quiet as the grave. Not even an early riser walking the dog. Curtains were drawn upstairs and down across most of the few houses that were still occupied. From their dilapidated state, there couldn't have been many folks who were still calling the rundown dwellings home. I gave it another couple of minutes longer, partly because I didn't like the idea of taking another pasting from the quick-tempered boxer and partly because I wanted to make doubly sure I could get inside Loudon's doss-house without being spied on by a passer-by or one of the up-with-the-lark nosy neighbours. I got out of the car and headed across the street with my coat collar turned up and my chin dipped low to the ground. I didn't look up until I was stepping out of the gutter and facing the fleapit I was going to try and get inside of.

★ ★ ★

Troy Loudon's squat was just as Theo Sweet had told me. The derelict alabaster-coloured tenement was

70

surrounded by a fallen down fence that was covered with a weedy vine of hardy blue flowers. The grass was overgrowing and there were no cultivated plants in the yard at the side of the building. The wind had brought rubbish from the street to litter the little front porch. Gum wrappers, soft-drink cans, leaves and newspaper sheets were scattered across the path. The mouldy wooden steps that led up to the door felt soggy under my weight.

The door still had two glass panels framed either side of a central wooden panel. I had no intention of knocking, expecting my nearly sixty-year-old shoulder to be doing the work of gaining me access. But there'd be no need for that. The door had been left slightly ajar, which I thought was more than a little unusual. I took the easy access as being a 'gift horse' and walked on in. Inside, the hallway was misshapen, lit only by the daylight coming through the glass in the door behind me. The stink of damp seeped out of the walls. The floor was warped and sagging, the ceiling slumped.

The hallway started out wide, but it narrowed as I neared what I thought would be the living room. Now I was inside, I felt the courage drain out of me. The place had taken on a sinister air. I don't know why, but something inside told me it would perhaps be in my best interests to let Loudon know that I was prowling round his lair.

'You here, Troy?' I called out nervously. I got no reply and slowly continued to head towards the living-room door. 'Troy, it's Joseph Ellington. I ain't looking for no trouble, man. I just want to talk to you, that's all.' I left the passageway and stepped cautiously into the room. The lounge, if you could have called it

71

that, was as barren as the yard and porch. There was no sign of Loudon. The room could have been a flop house in a frontier town in the Old West. The walls hadn't had a lick of paint in years and a splinter from the rough floor would have sent you to the hospital with lockjaw. A mismatch assortment of furniture was dotted around the room.

There were no mementos from Loudon's boxing career. No trophies, jewel-crusted belts or gold-braid sashes, just a few tatty fight posters sellotaped to the walls. Ashtrays were filled to the brim with cigarette butts and reefer roaches. A torn couch faced the wall and two wooden chairs lay on their sides on the floor. The thin, moth-bitten shades were pulled, the room bathed in semi-darkness.

I stepped back out into the hallway and called out again, louder this time. 'You here, Troy?' Still no comeback. It was then that I was hit with an unwelcome but all too familiar whiff. A smell like that of rusting metal lying in stagnant water. The unmistakable odour of blood, coming from the closed kitchen door behind me. I suddenly felt light-headed, my ears ringing with white noise. Every fibre in my body was telling me to walk on out of the place, get back in my car and drive away. But the familiar stink and my own foolish curiosity drew me closer.

I reached out and slowly pushed open the door. Though I'd seen violence and death many times before, the sight still made me stagger backwards. Troy lay sprawled on the kitchen floor, the whole back of his head shot off, his brain fanned out like a halo on the tiles beneath him His eyes were wide open and his mouth too — as if he'd been trying to suck down one last breath before it was all over. The scene reminded

72

me oddly of a beached sea lion, washed up and left by the tide.

A piece of notepaper was pinned through his T-shirt and most probably into his flesh. Written in what looked like red lipstick was the word TRAITOR.

I held my breath and made my way around Loudon's body carefully, keeping my feet away from any of the wet stuff. Next to Troy's body was a black gym bag, the contents of which had been turned out all over the floor. I squatted down on my haunches and took a biro out of the inside pocket of my jacket to open up the lip of the bag so I could get a better look inside.

The stink of drying blood was starting to get to me and my gag reflex was weakening by the second but still I was curious. Troy's killers had obviously been looking for something — had they found it? The bag stank of old sweat and seemed completely empty. I was about to withdraw my arm when I noticed something tucked into the lining. I reached back in and pulled at the edge of what turned out to be a small colour photograph.

The photo looked like it had been taken fairly recently. Two men were sat on a large bed. A naked woman lay between them, the crook of her left arm hung across her face making her unidentifiable. I immediately identified Troy as one of the men.

He was beaming a smile that could have made a new sire out of an eighty-year-old man. The other fella was black. A short afro, cropped tight on his scalp. He was dressed in a pair of leather trousers and a white shirt that was unbuttoned down to his waist. A thick gold metal chain and medallion hung around his neck. The lower part of his face, from what I could

73

see of it, looked to be handsome, the jaw chiselled and smooth. The rest of his face was hidden behind a colourful masquerade mask, the type I'd seen many years before, hanging in the windows of countless New Orleans gift shops.

I pocketed the photograph and looked back down at Troy Loudon's body. Suddenly I was sorry about the fight we'd had. Had I had something to do with his death? I got the awful feeling that maybe if I hadn't tried to strong-arm him last night, he'd have talked to me and lived.

I used my sleeve as a glove to wipe the kitchen door-knob and did the same again at the front door, before leaving through the back door. I ducked low in the bare back yard and headed for the fence. Over that hurdle, I made it to the next street and the short walk back to my car.

Most people in the neighbourhood were either getting ready for work or still in bed, so I wasn't too worried about being seen. I turned the key in the ignition and drove away slow and easy. I had no desire to draw attention to myself. No wish to be fingered for a murder I'd not committed. I was back inside my own home a little after seven forty-five; the ripe hum of death caked all over me.

I slung my coat on the hall floor and ran up to the bathroom. I filled a glass with tap water, drank it down, then threw up in the toilet. My hands shook, the backs of my legs quivered, flashes of colour popped like lesions behind my eyes. I tore off my clothes and stood in my underwear in front of the washbasin, cupped water onto my face, brushed my teeth then threw up again. My stomach went into spasm, my eyes stinging, my face cold and twitching; there was a pressure

74

band across one side of my head as though I'd been slapped with a thick book, my breath sour and trembling in my throat each time I tried to breathe.

Weak, I wiped the sweat and water off my face with a towel, my stomach still doing vicious somersaults. I stared into the bathroom mirror through watering eyes.

For a moment, I did not recognise the man staring back at me.

9

I'd managed to get to my bed without vomiting or falling over again and I was asleep before my head hit the pillow. It wasn't what you'd call a good rest. Less than three hours later, I was sat bolt upright in bed with violent tremors after waking from a nightmare where I'd been buried alive, in a wooden casket alongside Troy Loudon's rotting corpse. For some time, I'd perched on the edge of the bed trying to glean meaning from the bad dream. After failing at that I lugged myself to my feet to shower for the second time that day. I was dressed and stood in the kitchen watching the washer spinning the clothes I'd been wearing earlier before the downstairs clock struck midday.

I put a pot of coffee on and made myself porridge with hot milk, then sat at the table trying to figure out what the hell to do next. I rested the photograph I'd found at the bottom of Troy Loudon's gym bag against the sugar bowl on the worktop and tried my best to ignore its presence while I ate, but no matter how hard I endeavoured to snub the three-by-five print, my eyes kept being drawn back to the image of the three people framed in the colour shot.

I'd had a chequered history when it came to photographs. I always felt uncomfortable viewing them, as if I was trespassing into memories or special moments which I had no right intruding upon. I owned very few photos of my late wife, Ellie, and our daughter and none of my life back on Barbados. The family albums were all destroyed in the house fire that had killed them. Gabe and Pearl had left me a few old sepias of my parents, pictures they'd stashed away over the years and, of course, there were the yearly school snapshots of Chloe that I'd proudly displayed around the house after she'd brought them home from class.

There was, however, one photograph I'd kept for some time, one that I rarely viewed and which depicted two deceased souls who were neither relatives nor friends. The greyscale monochrome image was that of a middle-aged black man and a little black girl, who I later found out to be a Jamaican alderman called Earl Linney and his adopted six-year-old niece, Stella Hopkins. The girl was sat on Linney's knee. She was smiling, both dressed in their Sunday best. The photo appeared to be a vision of a happy family life, one that I later found out to be anything other than joyful.

Like the print I'd just retrieved from the dead man's gym bag, I'd found the earlier photograph while searching the rented home of the then grown-up Stella. She had concealed the snapshot in a brown manila envelope which she'd then taped to the back of an old scrapbook and hidden underneath her bed.

Both Stella and Earl had died in tragic circumstances. Both taking their own lives.

I'd kept the photograph as a reminder to never again involve myself in the plight of strangers.

Fifteen years on, and I was failing to heed my own council.

★ ★ ★

I've never really been what you would call a friend to the Bristol police. In the past we'd been on very awkward speaking terms only because they needed my help from time to time. And also because I used to be fool enough to put myself in the way of them when somebody in the community was getting the short end of the stick from one copper or another.

Finding Troy Loudon's body was enough reason to be making a call, anonymous or otherwise, to the local constabulary. A dead body in St Pauls, whether the corpse was black or white, would make the news in the local rag. The *Evening Post* liked to print bad news, especially when it was coming out of St Pauls.

Loudon's bloody remains eventually turning up would bring both the press and, worse still, the police on to the streets. Having those guys sniffing around would make any underhand errand for Mervyn Walker all the harder to undertake.

I didn't have a lot of concrete information to go back to the pastor with. Nothing to confirm his wife's whereabouts. No sighting of her by anyone. She'd not bunked down in any of the local hotels or hostels and, from what I could make out, hadn't sought sanctuary at the women's refuge. I had nothing to ease the man's mind, other than my suspicion that his old lady may have been connected to a dead boxer. Although I couldn't put my finger on it, my head was telling me that Loudon and Trista Walker had history; I just didn't know what kind. I was basing such an off-kilter feeling on nothing more than pure instinct. The years of being lied to for a living.

Rather than make the unsung call to the police I'd been considering, I picked up the telephone and dialled the pastor's number. When the reverend eventually answered he sounded aloof and preoccupied. I went straight for the jugular and told him that I needed to speak to him urgently. I listened to Walker sigh, then ten seconds of uneasy static on the other end of the line before the cleric offered his cold reply.

'You better come on over, then.'

The line cut; the metallic sound of the dialling tone left ringing in my ear. There were no virtuous thanks. Not even a goodbye.

The receiver in my hand felt as heavy as lead.

10

I was thinking about what I was going to say to the padre when a woman answered the door. She was tall and imposing, with a round face unadorned by make-up and piercing brown eyes that immediately began inspecting who was stood on the front step. She seemed all the more noble because her salt-and-pepper hair was wrapped high on her head with a dazzling orange and purple scarf. Her flower-pattern dress was long and flowing, the wide hem almost touching her ankles. It set off her dark skin in a way that spoke of the islands.

'Yes?' Her voice was musical and deep; pure Antiguan burr.

'My name is Ellington. I'm here to see Mervyn Walker.'

'He expectin' you?'

I nodded. 'Called him a half-hour ago. He told me I should come straight on over.'

The woman continued to stare at me for a moment longer before opening up the door. 'You better come on in, then.' I felt her gaze on me, watching me wipe my feet on the mat before I dared to step across the threshold. The air was heavy with the smell of cooking mixed with incense. On the wall to the left of me hung a spooky-looking Veronica Veil portrait of Christ. The woman circled around to face me. She was older than me, maybe sixty, sixty-five at a push, and commanding in the way she held herself. I guessed that the pastor's formidable sentry could well be Carmen,

80

Evison Foster's wife. I saw her lips go in and out a little and her neck quiver ever so slightly before she spoke again. 'You wait 'ere. I'll git the pastor.'

She disappeared up the wide staircase and the house suddenly felt empty, silent and sad. A few moments later came the sound of hushed voices speaking on the landing, then the shuffling of feet followed by the sight of Reverend Walker trudging down the flight of stairs to greet me. He was dressed in a white shirt, open at the neck, black trousers and polished blunt-toe black brogues. He cleared his throat when his foot hit the bottom step and broke the briefest smile at me by way of greeting.

'It's been a rather daunting kind of morning, Joseph. I'm sorry if I sounded off-hand with you earlier.' Walker showed me a perfect set of front teeth. A skull's grin. He looked right at me, but I could see that the effort to hold his head up was born out of fatigue and worry. He reached out his hand to shake mine. We shook; his cold grasp felt as if it were siphoning off my living heat.

'It's no bother, man. We all get mornings like those every now and then.' I smiled and we stopped shaking. I glanced quickly around the hall and back at the pastor. 'You have anywhere we could speak a little more privately?'

'Of course.' Walker's voice sounded muffled, like there was wet cotton stuck down his throat. He held out a limp hand. 'This way.'

The living room the pastor led me into was large, but there was very little floor space because of a crowd of furniture. Bookshelves covered with wooden and silver crucifixes, religious ornaments and theological books lined every wall. Two cracked red-leather couches, three stuffed armchairs, a walnut coffee table, a cherry dining table, and an upright piano were stabled there. The deep green carpet was thick. It swallowed up the sounds walking might have made. The walls were papered green too.

'Have a seat.'

'Thank you.' I sank into one of the big armchairs and looked around. 'You have a nice house.'

Walker frowned, ignoring the compliment. 'You said you needed to speak to me, urgently?'

'That's right, I . . .'

Walker held up his hand to stop my words. 'If . . .' He stammered a moment and then halted. 'If . . . I could just stop you there . . .' The pastor wouldn't meet my gaze, stared down at his polished shoes before continuing. 'You . . . you are not the only person who has been insistent on talking to me today.'

'Say what?'

The pastor raised his head. When I saw his face, I knew there was trouble coming; some kinda crap that was about to rub off on me. 'The police . . . the police, they were here earlier.'

A spasm went up my spine. 'They were? Whadda they want?'

'To ask me a heap of questions, that's what.' Walker cringed at the crackling sound of his own voice. 'There was two of them. White, plain-clothes detectives. They knew about Trista, about her going missing.'

'How'd they know? You speak to anyone else about what's gone on?'

Walker shook his head. 'I did not. Just Evison and his wife. The two detectives didn't divulge where they got their information from either.'

'What about Evison's wife, upstairs? You think she

maybe let the cat outta the bag?'

He shook his head again. 'Mrs Foster? No, absolutely not. I can assure you that it was neither her nor her husband.'

'Well, somebody went an' tipped 'em off.' My heart started pumping blood at a fast pace. 'What kind of questions these two coppers ask you?'

The pastor rubbed his hand across his mouth. 'They wanted to know how long she'd been gone. If I knew of any reason why she would leave without saying. If she'd been unwell, that kind of thing?'

'And what did you tell them?'

'The very same thing I told you.' Walker let his eyes get heavy, so they almost closed. 'I gave them the information they asked for. They wrote it all down in their notebooks. You could tell from their demeanours, by the way they spoke to me, that they didn't believe a word I was telling them.'

The pastor squinted at me, scratched at the top of his head. 'They also wanted to know why I hadn't contacted the police and reported her missing.'

'And how'd you get out of that one?'

Walker ran the four tips of the fingers of his left hand around his cheek; an insincere smile suddenly creeping across his lips. 'By telling them that I had consulted you on the matter, and that you had agreed to investigate the matter on my behalf.'

I shot up from out of Walker's comfy armchair. 'You did what, dammit?'

'What else could I do?' The pastor was becoming sweaty. His eyes were shiny like he was starting to come down with a fever. I watched while he fumbled to think of what to say to me next. 'I explained to them . . . explained that I didn't want my congregation to find out. That I needed such a delicate matter handling with some sensitivity.' Walker sounded like he was starting to wheeze. He took in a depth breath and gave me a hard stare. 'It was the truth, after all.'

'Yeah, the kinda truth that could easily put me behind bars.'

'Don't be a fool. What you have been doing is completely legal. I explained that you were a trusted friend, that you had previous experience in such matters, and that I expected you to continue with your enquiries.'

'Hold up, man,' I said, intent on stopping Walker's soft soap. 'The police are involved now. Just let 'em do their damn jobs.'

Walker reared up like a king cobra. 'No!'

'You've gotta be mad if you think I'm gonna start poking my nose into police business.' I went to walk away. The pastor grabbed my upper arm, squeezing it so hard that I could feel my fingers filling with blood.

'Will you just hold on a minute!' I came to a halt, the muscles in my jaw and upper body tensing. The minister loosened his grip on me, taking heed of the rigidity now coursing through my limbs. He let go of my arm and I felt him back away.

'Joseph, we're the same. Blood and bone. History and heart. It's just like I told you only a few days ago. The police cannot assist me with this problem. Any efforts they may make will be half-hearted. I could tell that from how they were speaking to me earlier. They see the colour of my skin before they see anything else. They were more interested in knowing whether I'd harmed my wife, whether there were darker forces at work, rather than offering support and guidance. If you were in my shoes, it would be exactly the same.

The law couldn't help you or anyone in our community if you were looking for their help. You have a crime committed against you; the law isn't interested, and you know that. They only come knocking on a black man's door when they want to throw the cuffs on him.'

'Yeah, well, that's just what I'm worried about. I've been arrested. Felt those cold handcuffs on my wrists. I've seen the inside of a British police cell. I ain't in any rush to be put inside one again any time soon.'

'If you don't help me, then no one can.'

'Why the hell the law knocking on your gate door if it ain't to help you out, Mervyn?'

'They were here because of who I am. What I represent. The church. The good standing they hear I have in the community.' Walker stabbed a finger at his chest. 'I don't trust the law in this country, just the same as you don't. I know that the Bristol constabulary came to the aid of the dog collar, not the man.'

'I ain't buying it, Mervyn.'

'You don't have to buy it. It's the truth. The police won't . . . can't help. They'll just muddy the waters, like they always do. Every time a policeman enters our world, he just brings more trouble. Brings unrest to our streets and misery to our neighbours. You know that.'

I tried to interrupt, but the pastor was having none of it. I got the feeling that people didn't get to speak once Walker mounted his soap box.

'If Trista isn't found soon, the police are going to start looking at finding a way of pinning her disappearance on me. You can be sure of it.'

I went to turn away. The brief silence that followed was the pastor's declaration. He could have been on a stage or in a courtroom. Something told me Walker's performance was far from over.

'Joseph, God has provided me with you to offer up the answers I seek, I'm sure of it. Please, I beg you, please keep searching.' Walker shifted his watery eyes directly towards me. 'If it's more money you want, I can . . .'

I shook my head. 'It ain't a question of the money, Mervyn. I told you that.' My head was telling me to hurry up and get the hell out of the cleric's front room, but something was holding me there. Some unseeable force keeping my feet pinned to the deep pile of that green Axminster. I wasn't afraid, exactly. I rarely got frightened unless I was faced with immediate danger. But standing in front of the pastor there was anxiety rooting around in my gut and I didn't like it one bit. Walker backed up a couple of paces and sat down heavily on one of couches, like a man at the end of an especially hard day's work. He gazed up at me, his face taking on a grave expression, the water clearly welling up in his eyes. 'Please, Joseph. Please keep on looking.' The pastor's voice was so light that it could have been a child asking.

I took a deep breath, then another. I should have turned the reverend's pleading down out of hand. But again, I just couldn't.

In truth, I had sympathy for his plight and an undeniable understanding of our mutual brotherhood. The look I gave Mervyn Walker told him that I would continue to do his bidding. I knew it wasn't a wise move. In life, I've learned that all good things come hard, but wisdom is the hardest to come by.

At that moment in time, I knew I was pretty much going to have to forget all about such valuable human qualities as foresight and common sense. Ignoring both at my own peril, I found myself reaching into my inside jacket pocket and handing the pastor the snapshot I'd found in Troy Loudon's squat. He focused in on the image and began to scrutinise the faceless naked woman, the mystery masked man and the dead boxer.

Mervyn Walker looked at that picture for a long while. He didn't move or speak. When he finally lifted up his head to look at me, the tears flowing down both cheeks, I was left in no doubt that the pastor had identified at least one of the individuals in that miserable photograph.

I felt a sudden wave of embarrassment hit me. This was the second time the cleric had turned on the waterworks, and hearing his blubbering was unsettling. Rather than have to watch the man shedding so many tears, I slowly walked back across the room, stopping to look out of the window and tried to admire the well-manicured lawn while the reverend carried on weeping. After a while he began to quieten, and I could hear the sound of bird call in the distance. The harsh *caw-caw* became louder; an eerie chorus made up of a murder of crows and a conspiracy of ravens. I could see the birds starting to gather in the trees outside. As their cries became louder, it felt as if the flock were waiting noisily for the pastor to finish his sobbing.

It was as if the full-throated, ravenous carrion were hungry to swoop on down, to descend into the man's desolate home and pluck the flesh from his pitiful bones.

87

11

'I don't normally take hard liquor,' Mervyn Walker informed me as he shakily poured three fingers of Macallan malt whisky into two heavy crystal tumblers. He wiped at both cheeks with the back of one hand before setting the bottle on top of a tall mahogany drinks' cabinet. He took a sip of booze before turning and handing me a dram. When Walker finally turned to face me, the expression on his mouth bitter, his eyes seemed to have changed colour, as though a terrible sadness or great darkness was having its way with his soul. He gestured to the photograph.

'The woman with those men.' There was a pause, a silence in which I could only guess at his thoughts.

'Yeah?'

'It's Trista.'

A mule's kick would have seemed like a kiss from an angel alongside that bombshell. It took me a moment to get my tongue back into gear. 'You sure?'

'I'm a preacher, Joseph. Not a monk.' He slugged back the rest of his booze. Stared at the floor, unable to look me in the face. 'I think I know what my wife's body looks like.'

'That woman, she's got her face covered. That could be any black woman lying on that bed.'

Walker nodded his head solemnly. 'Vitiligo, Joseph.'

'Beg your pardon?'

'Vitiligo . . . It's a rare condition where pale white patches develop on the skin. Trista had it. If you look very carefully, you'll just about be able to make out

88

such a blemish on her body.'

I held up the photo to my face, my eyes zeroing in on the woman's body.

'Top of the right hip. It's not difficult to make out, if you know what you're looking for.'

Walker was right. There it was, a small white oval shape on the skin, below and to the side of the ribs, just where the man said.

'Where did you get that photograph?'

'It belonged to one of the men posing in it. A fella called Troy Loudon. I found him dead last night in a squat he'd been dossing down in.'

The pastor appeared to be frozen for a moment, his face sick. 'Dead . . . dear Lord.' Walker took a solid hit of his whisky. 'How . . . how did he die?'

'He'd been shot in the head.' I heard the reverend mutter something under his breath, words that I couldn't make out. He looked deathly ill. 'The photo was at the bottom of Loudon's gym bag. I found it while I was rifling through what few belongings he had.' I took a moment to let what I was telling the reverend sink in. 'You know this guy Loudon?'

Walker looked me square in the face, his eyes holding mine. 'I do not.'

'You've never heard of him?'

The pastor huffed something out of his throat, his gaze holding onto me. 'Should I have?'

'Not especially. He was a boxer. Not top class, but he'd made a bit of a name for himself in the ring. He was fairly well known round these parts. It looks like he'd fallen on hard times. A bit of a booze problem from what I can gather. No fixed abode. Spent most of his time either drunk, drugged or swinging his fists at a punch bag. The night before he died, I got a tip off from a guy I know over at Dingy's Blues Bar. This fella said Loudon was worth speaking to.'

'And did you?'

'I tried. I followed him out of the bar later that evening. I stopped him in the street and mentioned your wife's name, said I was looking to catch up with her. Loudon said he hadn't seen her. When I pushed him for more, he put me on my back.'

Walker's eyes popped, his face darkening, as though someone had lowered a shade on it. 'The man hit you?'

'Well, he sure as hell didn't give me a kiss, Mervyn.' I stared at the pastor, more than a little dumfounded by his naivety. I decided not to labour the point with him, and stuck to the matter in hand. 'One thing for sure, Loudon knew Trista.'

'And what makes you think that?'

'Because, before he laid into me, he told me as much.' I let my eyes slip off the pastor's for a second or two. 'I hardly even know the bitch,' were his exact words.'

Walker got to his feet and walked back to the drinks' cabinet, swaying slightly, as though his gyroscope had stopped working. He poured himself another two fingers and immediately sank half of the spirit in a single gulp.

'You need to start giving it to me straight, Mervyn.'

The pastor eyed me suspiciously. He attempted to sneer then faltered in his resolve. 'What are you talking about?'

'I'm talking about the fact that for a man who wants to keep his private life private, a helluva lotta folk seem to know stuff about your wife.'

Walker shook his head, his lips crimped. 'That's

90

not true.'

'No? I paid a visit to the Loaves and Fishes yesterday.'

I heard the pastor breathe loudly through his mouth, as if his tongue had been scalded. 'And?'

'And . . . there was this old woman sat outside at the rear of the place. When I asked her about your wife, she gave me the cold shoulder. Had a face on her like thunder. As soon as I mentioned your lady's name she headed back on inside and left me standing on the back doorstep.'

'That would be Viola Saunders. She's one of our church's longest-serving sisters.'

'You any idea why she would have been so offhand with me?'

'I have no idea. Viola's a gentle, kind soul. It doesn't sound like her at all.'

'Perhaps your wife may have confided in this Saunders woman?'

'I think that's highly unlikely.'

'Where's this Viola live?'

'Why?'

'Why? Because you're asking me to find out where or what the hell has happened to your wife, Mervyn. If you want me to do that and get you some results, quick, I need to start talking to anybody who knew her. And that includes the kind of folk who'd rather not speak to me. If you've got it, write her address down on a piece of paper for me.'

The pastor put his whisky glass on the coffee table and walked out of the room; when he returned a few minutes later he was holding a piece of blue notepaper. 'You'll find Mrs Saunders here.'

I took the slip of paper, glanced at the address

written on it then held the photograph out at arm's length in front of me. 'Are you sure you didn't know Troy Loudon?'

Walker winced then pressed his fingers against both temples as though they were drilling into the sides of his head. 'I'm certain.'

'Then, how'd you think your wife knew him?'

'I'm not sure. Before our son was born, Trista would have the occasional evening out. A night at the theatre, sometimes the cinema. Perhaps she met him at one of those places?'

'Who'd your wife have these nights out with? You told me she had no work colleagues, just friends of the church.'

The pastor looked at me from under his brow. 'She'd often go out alone. I have no fondness for either the stage or film.'

'You think many of your congregation would know a man like Troy Loudon?'

'Perhaps, I can't be sure.'

'Loudon ever attend Old King Street?'

Walker stiffened, insulted by the thought. 'No, never.'

I kept pushing. Waiting to catch another possible lie. 'How about the other guy in the picture. The one in the strange mask. You any idea who he could be?'

Walker's eyes lifted to the ceiling. 'Of course not.'

I placed the photograph back inside my jacket pocket. 'You gotta fella called Council helping out at the Loaves and Fishes, don't you?'

The pastor looked at me and nodded. 'Floyd, yes. Why? What does he have to do with all this?'

'Council was sniffing around me at the mission house. He was the one put me on to Dingy's Bar.'

92

'You think that Floyd perhaps knows more than he's letting on?' The tremolo in Walker's voice was of the subdued kind that I always associated with people whose sleepless nights of worry and uncertainty had left them in a desolate place. The pastor sounded to me like he was in just such a forsaken frame of mind. Getting the reverend to come clean was like pulling hen's teeth.

The same old story. Secrets and lies.

'That's what I need to find out.'

Just as Mervyn Walker had done to me earlier in the day when I'd called him up on the telephone, I didn't offer my gratitude to him nor bid him farewell. I just spun on my damn heels and got the hell out of his home.

My life had once again started to feel like a glass-bottomed boat ride through the city's sewer system.

12

When I pulled up outside of Floyd Council's ground-floor flat the front door was wide open. I almost drove away. Another dead body was the last thing I needed. Council's weathered apartment building on Albany Road was a two-storey, stucco-covered tenement surrounded by a fallen down fence. Grass was overgrowing in the yard at the side of the building. Rubbish littered the front porch.

I knew that Council had the thieving inclinations of a magpie but even I wasn't fully prepared for what greeted me when I walked into his living room. The soot-stained gas fire and threadbare nets covering the window were obvious, if unpleasant fixtures and fittings, standard to most of the other apartments in the block I suspected, but the rest of the stuff that was piled up around the lounge was reflective of Council's unique thieving personality. Eight televisions, stacked one on top of the other, a half dozen Betamax video recorders, boxed, all with a label stuck on one side of the carton, stating in black lettering, WATER DAMAGED. There was a large box of plastic toilet seats stood next to an old broken Welsh dresser. A complete set of Encyclopaedia Britannica, brand new, upside down on a shelf on the back wall and a rusting, fold-out camp bed with a base that looked like a platoon of British infantry had slept on it in full kit and battle dress. The room stank of stale ganja and mouldering paper.

No wonder folk called him 'Dipper'.

Photos from old pornographic magazines were pasted to the walls, but over the mantlepiece, clearly in a place of honour, was a portrait of the Emperor of Ethiopia, Haile Selassie. On the fireplace itself were countless dusty books; novels, cookery journals and works in Latin.

A collection of 'increase your word power' handbooks and countless self-improvement manuals. There wasn't a copy of the Bible in sight. Everything else stacked up around the place was cheap and nasty and most of it pilfered from someone else's house. It was all very Floyd 'Dipper' Council. Frightened of his own shadow and defects, always meaning to do something about them, never getting around to it — and never bloody well around when you needed to speak to the man.

I sat down on the only chair in the room, a high-backed, winged affair with a massive tear in the seat, and prepared to wait.

★ ★ ★

Even from outside in the hallway I could pick up the smell of curry. I sat in silence and waited for Dipper to walk through the door.

'I hope you brought enough for two?'

Dipper Council jumped like someone had just stuck a knife in his back.

'Raaaahhhs-sole! Man.' Council came across as tough but immediately started to back pedal when he caught sight of me. He quickly gave up the gruff voice and went back to being his cowardly self. I knew if the aggressive tone he'd come in with had been in his hands, they'd have been up over his head if I'd have

95

snapped back at him. Dipper's bloodshot eyes went to the floor before cagily looking back at me. 'You scared da livin' shit outta me.'

I got to my feet. 'Shall I get the plates?'

Council snatched the bag tight to his chest. 'It's ma dinner, Mistah Ellington.'

I shook my head. 'Our dinner.'

Dipper sighed and slowly let the carrier bag drop at his feet. He threw off his coat and then began to struggle to open up one of the dresser doors. Inside, when he'd finally prised his way in, was a stack of enough stolen dinnerware to stock a restaurant.

'How'd the hell you git in, Mistah Ellington?'

'How'd you think?'

Council stopped rubbing and shrugged.

'Your damn door was open you goat head. You're getting careless, Dipper. One of these days you might have burglars.'

'Nuthin' much 'ere wort' thieving.' Dipper smiled to himself. 'It's what you call sentimental value mostly.'

I looked around Dipper's dive. 'What if the police paid you a visit?'

'Bagged it all at a jumble sale. Babylon can't prove a ting.'

'That?' I pointed at the rotting camp bed. 'At a jumble sale?'

'Nah, man. Tha' legit, tha' bed is. Bought an' paid fo', years ago.'

Dipper set out the two plates and a couple of dessert spoons on top of the dresser. I didn't know anything about antiques, but the type of glazed crockery he was showing off looked like it was top quality stuff. I winked at the little thief. 'You have been busy.'

'Lord says it don't pay to be idle.'

'God say anything in the good book about members of his flock nicking other people's stuff?'

Council ignored my sarcasm and began to tip the first of three cartons of Indian takeaway onto one of the two plates. As he moved to drench the second in some kind of orange-coloured sauce, I held up my hand.

'Not for me, thanks, Dipper.'

Dipper gave me a puzzled look. 'But you say you wanted to eat!'

I sniffed the air. Grimaced. 'I just lost my appetite.'

Council shrugged again. 'If you 'ere 'bout dat five pound, I al'ready spent it.' Dipper was in his forties but had the body of a boy. When he smiled, you could have been forgiven for thinking he was the model for the original Cheshire Cat.

'I ain't here about the cash,' I said in a commanding voice that somehow felt like it was not my own.

'Naw?' Dipper's body relaxed a little. He rubbed at the tip of his nose with the back of his wrist and gave me a curious look.

I shook my head. 'No. It's a little more information I'm looking for.'

Dipper became wide-eyed, rubbing his fingers against his thumb. 'Am always happy to help a man out if you kna' what a mean?' Council winked at me then began to shovel a spoonful of curry into his mouth.

'You can start with this.' I took the photograph I'd found at Troy Loudon's flat out of my pocket and laid it next to Dipper's plate. Council, expecting to see hard cash, craned his neck to get a better look at the print, then started to choke on his food.

'Kawblema! What you showin' me tha' kinda shit fo'?'

97

'You recognise any of these people?'

Dipper kept chewing and peered down at the photo then swallowed and sucked air through his front teeth. 'To nuff a do. Big fella one side o' the trio is tha' nasty piece o' wuk, Troy Loudon.'

'And the other two?'

Dipper chuckled to himself. 'Don't be dumpsy, man.' Council shoved another spoonful of food inside him before continuing to speak with a mouthful of unchewed rice. 'The nuk-nuk showin' her belly gotta face covered wid her skinny arm an' the utha nigger wearin' a damn mask. How you expectin' me to recognise 'em?'

I knew better than to spill my guts to someone like Floyd Council that the boxer was dead. Parting with that kind of grim news could easily put a noose around my neck if Dipper became privy to it. I tapped the photo with my finger. 'You hear anything useful about Loudon?'

Dipper's face lit up. 'He gotta spooky tart lives above the Miner's Arms on Mina Road.'

'What's so special about her?'

Dipper spooned more rice into his mouth then spat most of it out at me when he replied. 'Loudon an' his woman, dey sum' time run parties.'

'What kinda parties?'

Council coughed and stabbed a finger at the photograph. 'Dem kinda parties.' The thief gave me a wide smirk. 'Skin n' devil stuff.'

'What the hell you talking about?'

'Am talkin' 'bout tha' hard mout' cow o' Loudon's bein' an Obeah. She a dark bitch inta sum crazy stuff. I 'ear dem shebangs her an' Loudon got goin' git real messy.'

'How messy?'

'I 'ear talk o' voodoo. Chantin' shit. Blood bein' sprayed up the walls, cuttin' chicken's heads off an' throwin' 'em 'bout the place. The ole nine yards o' foolish craziness.'

I tried to read Council's eyes, to see if he was being sincere, lying to me or was just plain crazy. Dipper was a real pro. A born street hustler and all-round con and I knew it would be near to impossible to truly pick the truth out of his words if the slimy little git chose to give me the runaround. There was, however, one way to ensure that he was being on the level with me.

'You know who I'm related to?' It was a pleasure to see Floyd Council's eyes widen in fear at the unspoken mention of my cousin Vic's name. We had a moment of silence. Dipper looking over his shoulder for my vengeful relation before training his gaze back on me.

'Fah real, man. E'rybody 'naw you the Jah's kin.'

'Then don't fuck with me, Dipper. You need to be righteous, brother.'

Dipper held up both hands, his palms facing me. 'Mistah Ellington, ah wouldn't lie to you.'

'You do and I swear the Jah, he'll burn you, man.'

Dipper dropped his spoon into his food and pushed the plate away from him.

'Man, you ain't gotta vex 'bout me tellin' you the trute.'

'Good.' I waved the photo in Dipper's face. 'You think this photograph could have been taken at one of those parties?'

'It could 'ave bin. Hard to say. I ain't nevah had an invite. Jus' 'naw what I 'ear.'

'You gotta name for this girlfriend of Loudon's?'

99

'Yeah, it's Queenie . . . Queenie Blue.'

'What's this Queenie Blue look like?' I asked.

Council twisted his face, trying to remember. 'She a proper dirty sket. Jamaican. Skinny arse. Thirty-five, mebbe even forty. Hands an' fingers covered in nasty tattoos. She bin on de game fo' years. Her an' Troy always bin tight. Always hangin' out together.'

'Okay . . . what else can you tell me about Reverend Walker's wife?'

'I 'naw she like to kick off her 'eels. Likes to live on the wild side, but likes to keep it hush-hush, if you git me drift?'

'You know anywhere else she's hung out at in the past? You're saying that she likes to live dangerously?'

'Tha' right. I see the woman all ovah the place. Always at night. The Black and White Café, Inkerman pub, the Shady Grove.' Dipper glanced back towards the door as if he was afraid someone was about to burst in and tear out his tongue. I saw the fear knit across his brow. When he spoke again, it was in a whisper. 'I even seen her in the Gambling House.'

The Gambling House was a renowned shebeen at the end of Campbell Street. Local folk, mainly men, would gather there to drink knock-off rum and smoke dope. The place was teaming with bookies' runners, dealers, and a lot worse. The police gave it a wide berth. Never bracing or raiding the place. Folk went there to bet, play dominoes, cards and to seriously kick back. Unless you were really from St Pauls, you wouldn't go nowhere near the joint. It was only for proper hustlers. It was Vic's premier spot.

'You remember seeing her in the House with anyone local? One of the regulars maybe?'

A shadow moved over Dipper's already dark visage.

I got the feeling he was about to say something and then decided against it. 'Nah, not dat I evah saw. She was real cool. Nevah seen her tek a jump-up on the dancefloor. Always kept hersel' outta the way. Always stood in the shadows. Strange woman.'

'What can you tell me about Viola Saunders?'

'You gawh be kiddin' me.' Council pursed his lips and spat on the floor. 'Tha' ole hag. She anutha witch.'

'Did Viola and Trista Walker get on?'

'How'd the hell wud I 'naw.' Dipper kicked at the foot of the Welsh dresser with the toe of his shoe. Cursed under his breath. 'If the damn pastor's woman like trow'in' 'bout hexes, an' sorcery shit dey gonna git along like a house on fire. I keep outta ole girl Saunders' way. Woman gives me the fuckin' creeps!'

I stuffed the photo back in my pocket. Headed towards the door and stopped as I drew next to Dipper's side. 'One more thing.'

Dipper let out a heavy sigh and looked up at me. 'Yeah, wus dat?'

'Give me the name of the top man you ratting for, Dipper?' I watch Council squint back at me. He licked at his lips, but there was no saliva on his tongue, his agitation plain to see. 'Come on, which copper you grassing to?'

'Ahh, shit, man. Don't be axin' me dat.'

'I want a name.' I watched Dipper making a mental calculation. Who was he more afraid of, the Bristol constabulary or the Jah? I didn't have to wait long to find out.

'It . . . it . . . dat rassclaat Detective Superintendent Eve.'

'Don't know him.'

'You don't want to. Round 'ere we call 'im 'Eve tha

Squeeze' on account o' how tha' bastard pinches you fo' any'ting he feel like.'

'You wouldn't happen to have mentioned anything to him about the pastor's wife?'

Dipper shook his head and scowled. 'Naw, why wud I do dat?'

'Didn't say anything to him about me asking you questions about Trista Walker?'

The little thief remained silent, his Adam's apple swelling in his throat, the words he was trying to mouth stuck in his gullet. Real terror had suddenly taken hold of Dipper. He began to tremble, the beads of sweat bubbling up on his forehead and brow. I smelt the faint, unpleasant hum of the man's body odour starting to waft up from underneath his armpits and the perspiration slowly starting to trickle down his scared face. He inched his way along the dresser, creating welcome space between the two of us and trying desperately to keep on looking me straight in the eye, and I in turn was determined to hold his gaze.

I knew that whatever devious and pathetic notions were going on behind Floyd Council's treacherous, frozen stare they were simply too vast for me to comprehend.

13

On the ride home I pondered on the complex weave of Pastor Walker's problem. I was still no wiser as to what was really going on between the cleric and his missing wife. Whatever it was, it was more than a simple husband and wife tiff. There were clearly problems in the relationship, something that the minister was unwilling to divulge or discuss with me. Trista Walker had, for whatever reason, abandoned her new-born son, and quit her marriage. She'd left home without taking any clothes or other belongings. There had not been, to my knowledge, any letter of explanation left on the day she'd walked out, or any contact made to anyone the couple knew. It was as if the woman had woken up that morning and decided to just disappear clean off the face of the earth. The whole thing stank to high heaven.

Gut instinct told me that Mervyn Walker clearly had something to hide, but for the life of me I didn't know what the hell that was. One thing I did know was that the cops were now breathing down the reverend's neck and that could easily open up a serious can of worms for me. I had no urgent desire to find myself being reacquainted with the local law. I'd been a chump to the police on more than one occasion in the past and I had no intention of finding myself in that unenviable position again.

I also had to ask myself what I'd actually achieved by questioning Floyd Council. He'd coughed up word that Trista Walker enjoyed mixing it up with more than just the genteel company of local fellow churchgoers. Council had mentioned a number of St Pauls dives that seemed unlikely places for a clergyman's wife to be hanging around in; how much of what he'd told me was actually true?

Dipper may have been the font of all knowledge when it came to the word on the street, but I wasn't so sure how reliable his information was when it came to dishing the dirt on folk far removed from his usual food chain. He may have been on the level with me and, in truth, the only way I'd find out if his information was legitimate or not was to dig a little deeper, and start sticking my snout into some of the unpleasant dives he'd told me about.

One thing I was sure of, was that Dipper was in the pocket of the police and that could only spell trouble for me. I was pretty certain that Floyd had tipped off the Old Bill after I'd been nosing about after Trista Walker at the Loaves and Fishes mission house. Did Council know more about the pastor's wife's disappearance than he was letting on? Had he perhaps encouraged them to pay Mervyn a visit? Someone had put the law on to the minister? I just wasn't sure who.

Even though Dipper was still unaware that Troy Loudon was dead, showing him the photograph had been a risk. I was putting myself in the firing line if and when Troy Loudon's body was finally discovered. Council may not have been the sharpest knife in the drawer, but even that dummy would put two and two together fairly quickly and then go blabbing to his overseer at the Bristol constabulary, Detective Superintendent Eve.

I needed that kind of grief in my life like a dog

needs fleas.

As I drove into Banner Road, I caught sight of Chloe sitting on the wall outside our home, still wearing her school uniform, her satchel hung on the gate post, a teenage black boy, maybe a couple of years older keeping her company. I gripped the wheel tightly as I pulled up to the kerb. My chest rising and falling, crazy paternal thoughts suddenly flitting through my head of their own accord, like flying leaves in the wind.

I sat for a moment, the engine still running, looking daggers at Chloe's new admirer, who in turn clearly wasn't taking a blind bit of notice of me eyeballing him. He was kitted out in a wide-collared psychedelic print shirt, washed denim jeans and a pair of expensive white Adidas tennis shoes. His eyes were screened by a pair of dark aviator shades. As I got out of the car, Chloe put on a big grin, saw the agitated look on my face and dropped her smile.

She hesitated before bouncing off the brickwork and heading towards me to kiss my cheek. The fact her lips didn't quite touch my skin told me more about how she was feeling than if they had. She smiled at the boy stood in front of me and I felt my stomach turn. 'Joseph, this is Dimitri.'

The kid stood erect, rolling his shoulders at me. He took a cocky peek at Chloe from over the top of his oversized sunglasses. That bold gesture really set my hackles up. Chloe sensing bad blood shot in between the boy and myself and continued her introduction. 'But everybody calls him D.'

'Call you D, young brother. Not a chance in hell.'

I shifted around Chloe and reluctantly held out my hand. 'How you doin', Dimitri?' The kid looked at my mitt for a moment before clicking on to the fact that

105

I was expecting him to take up my palm and shake it. By the time he'd actually reached out to take it, my arm was already back at my side.

'Yo,' he said to me, half smiling. When I didn't beam back at him, the kid's face blanched. I savoured a moment or two of awkward silence while he tried to figure out what to do or say to me next. He looked down at the ground for a second or so then raised his head to regard Chloe. I saw her sway back an inch. Not wanting to lose face in front of her, Dimitri decided to open his mouth.

'Chloe's told me a lot 'bout you.'

I raised an eyebrow. 'About me. You're kidding, right?'

The boy called D shrugged. 'Nope.'

I pointed at Chloe without looking at her. 'You talking 'bout this pickney here?'

'Yeah. She bin biggin' you up, Mistah Ellington.'

I looked at Chloe, feigning a smile and set a hard gaze back on Dimitri. 'Man, this girl, she never says more than t'ree words to me most days. How come she's singing my praises to you all of a sudden?'

The look on the kid's face was one of wide-eyed bewilderment. He had no pre-packaged answer. No other bullshit to offer. That told me something.

'I . . . uh . . .' he said.

'Joseph,' Chloe said in her best maternal voice. 'That's not very polite.'

'So, come on, what did Chloe here tell you about me?'

'She . . . sssaid that you used to be some kinda policeman.'

'Did she now.'

'An' that . . . that . . . that, you all related to the Jah.'

106

Dimitri's stare shifted off mine, as though they were trying to wish himself away from my presence. I took hold of Chloe's wrist in one hand and snatched her school bag off the gate post with the other and padded both up the path. 'My daughter tell you what I think of kids who don't know how to shake a fella's hand properly, too?'

I didn't wait for Dimitri to reply. Couldn't have cared less if he spoke or not. My only concern was getting my child inside the house and my front door closed to the world outside.

'Why were you so rude?' Chloe snatched her arm out of my grasp, backing away from me with pain in her eyes. 'There was no need for you to be so damn nasty.'

'Hey, I'm just looking out for you, that's all.' I didn't want the conflict that was coming. I wanted to find the child in her, to tell her a joke or tickle her and make her laugh. I wanted to dismiss her serious stare, but I could not. Chloe balled her hands into fists. This gesture made me feel very uncomfortable. It wasn't the father and daughter relationship I'd grown used to. Chloe was almost a woman, and I was being a fool not accepting that fact. 'There's nothing to look out for. D's my friend!'

'That all the boy is?' I snapped.

The little girl's eyes no longer glittered. What replaced the innocent gaze I long cherished was now something altogether more adult. 'D's as much a friend to me as anyone I know. He'd do anything for me.'

I dropped Chloe's school bag on the hall floor but stayed put by the door. 'Would he now?'

Would this kid worry about you, like I do? Lose as many

107

sleepless nights as I do? Would he love and care about you like I do? I thought all these things, but I didn't say them.

'You're just jealous!' Chloe stretched out her fingers in agitation before knotting them back into fists again.

'No, I'm just concerned that you don't get hurt, that's all.'

'Why should I get hurt?'

I let out a deep sigh. 'Because that's what happens, child. Boys can be cruel. They can be devious. You need to be more careful who you get close to, that's all I'm saying.'

'Not every boy is like that. D's different.'

'Is that what he told you?'

Chloe's face pinched. 'It's what I know.'

'And I know, in life you've gotta choose your friends carefully.' I saw the tears welling up in her eyes,

'Who the hell do you think you are, telling me what I should do and who my friends should be?'

'I'm your father.'

'No, you're not!'

I'd been called names many times in my life. It was always a painful, enraging experience. But it was nothing compared to the simple truth that had just been spoken.

Chloe stormed down the hall and pushed past me. As she ran up the stairs, I wanted to call her back, to tell her that I was sorry and that I understood what she was saying and that it was true. I opened my mouth and a sound came out, but it was not words. It was a small croaking utterance, something that had never before come from me. A mixture of pain and regret. When Chloe heard this muted cry, she stopped

108

and turned, hurt and anger etched across her face. I dropped my head and found a spot on the hall carpet to stare at, trying to find the right words to convey to the child.

'What?' she shouted.

I didn't answer.

The two of us stood in silence for a second or two. By the time I looked up, ready to speak again, Chloe was already gone. The sonic boom of her bedroom door slamming rang across the landing, down the stairs and hit me square in the face.

My little girl was nearly sixteen.

I remembered the degree of judgement I had at that age and shuddered.

14

I cooked and ate supper alone. Chloe had collected her fish and rice and gone back to her room to eat, not something I'd normally ever allow her to do. I had no heart for another quarrel with her and, in truth, I was ashamed of how I had reacted, embarrassed to face her after behaving so badly. Maybe, I thought to myself, there was a God. He wasn't some gigantic and powerful deity but just the vessel of all knowledge and therefore a judge of candour and honesty. Now and then he inhabited some person and made them say the words that had gone unsaid. Chloe had been the expression of that God. He was using her to condemn me for my ignorance and rash temper. What Chloe had said wasn't pleasant to hear, but it was, for the most part, the truth.

I'd lost my appetite as soon as I'd sat down at the table. I stared at my plate while the food slowly got cold, my head continuing to fill with muddied abstractions. Rather than reflect on my earlier misconduct, I chose to mull over the pastor's predicament and the things Floyd Council had said to me — his strange notions about Trista Walker and his offbeat opinion of his fellow Loaves and Fishes volunteer, the witch, Viola Saunders.

I looked at my watch; it was a little before six. I didn't feel like hanging around the house to find myself either picking another fight with my daughter or to sit in silence, alone, mulling things over and licking my wounds like some beaten up alley cat. It was still early, still just about the right time of the day to be making polite house calls. I decided to get the hell out and go pay Mrs Saunders a visit. See if I could glean anything from the old woman which could perhaps throw further light on Trista's strange disappearance. Resolute, I washed and dried the pots then headed upstairs, stopping outside of Chloe's room. I put my cheek to the door, hesitant to speak at first. When the words finally came out, they were sapless and low.

'I have to go over to St Werburghs. See somebody who may be able to help Pastor Walker out. I'll be back in an hour.' I stepped away from the door hoping for a reply, but didn't get one. 'You want me to stop off at the shop on my way home, bring you anything back?' No answer.

I walked away, feeling foolish and inadequate, as though I were starting to lose part of myself. I closed my bedroom door and sat on the edge of the bed, trying to will myself into some kind of normality. Chloe's words had cut so deeply that I couldn't see past the pain. After what seemed like an age, I changed into my old brown two-piece suit, knotted a tie and splashed on a little aftershave. Deciding on a pair of socks took me five minutes; putting them on took ten. I took a small notebook and pencil from my bedside cabinet and picked up the slip of paper that the pastor had written Viola Saunders's address on and the colour photograph of Troy Loudon and Trista Walker. I slipped them into the inside pocket of my jacket then reached up to the top of the wardrobe and took down my old brown felt fedora. I dusted it off and stuck it on my head, pulling the brim down low across my brow.

As I came out of my bedroom, Chloe was waiting

111

for me on the landing. She walked over, and without saying anything put her arms around me. I held her against my chest, the heat of her body radiating through her clothes. I dipped my head, my chin grazing the top of her scalp. I could smell her hair and the sweet deodorant on her skin and felt her heart beating when I pressed my hand against her back. She buried her face in my chest for a long time before finally releasing her hold on me. 'I'm sorry, Papa.'

I smiled down at her. 'It's okay, honey,' I whispered in constricted little words. 'It's me who should be apologising, not you.' I felt Chloe's body jerk as she took in my contrite words. 'I'm sorry. I was talking gibberish earlier. It's like you said, I have no right to judge your friends or who you choose to spend time with.' Chloe took my hand and squeezed it. She didn't say another word. Didn't need to.

She was still the same little girl I'd brought home with me from Barbados when she was just an infant.

The years between then and now meant absolutely nothing, and I knew that she was my daughter and I was her father and that I always would be, and that Bernice, her mother, would remain our guardian angel forever.

I knew such sentiment wasn't the kind of thing that would change the world, but by the same token the world would never change us.

★ ★ ★

It was just shy of seven by the time I pulled up into Conduit Road on the furthest fringes of St Werburghs. Viola Saunders lived in a flat-topped, large bungalow, dirty white in hue. It looked more like a council worker's outhouse than it did a residence. This industrial cottage consisted of two apartments; Viola's was the door on the left.

I knocked and waited, knocked again.

'Yes?' came a voice from inside the house.

'Mrs Saunders?'

'Yes?'

My name's Joseph Ellington. We met recently at the Loaves and Fishes mission house. I wanted to know if I could ask you a few questions?'

'I don't know any'ting,' she bellowed at me from behind the door. Her bitter words could have been the first sentence out of a Jean-Paul Sartre monograph. That brought a smile to my face.

'Please, Mrs Saunders, it's just a few questions.'

'Who the hell are you?'

'Joseph Ellington. I'm undertaking some enquiry work for Pastor Mervyn Walker.'

'So, whadda you want?'

'You attend the Old King Street Baptist Chapel?'

'Yes.' There was reluctance in her tone because with those words I was insinuating myself into her life.

'Is Carmen Foster still with the congregation?'

'You know Carmen?'

'I know her husband, Evison.' I watched as she pressed her face against the frosted glass panel in the centre of the door. 'Do you have a telephone Mrs Saunders?'

I could see the outline of the old woman as she struggled to eye me up. 'I do.'

'Why don't you give either the Fosters or Pastor Walker a call, ask them about Joseph Ellington.'

'You wait here.'

'Yes, ma'am.'

★ ★ ★

'Pastor Walker say he sent you to ma' gate door,' Viola Saunders said through the glass a few minutes later. A few more moments passed and then the chain rattled and more than one latch clicked. The brown door in the dirty white wall pulled inward. Mrs Saunders stood back in the shadowy room. She wore a full-length pale blue cotton dress with tiny yellow flowers printed on it and was barefoot. Perched on the bridge of her nose was a pair of brass-rimmed, half-moon spectacles. She peered over them at me suspiciously.

'You go to church, Mistah Ellington?'

I shook my head. 'Not since I was a small boy.' I inched forward to the threshold. 'You let heathens into your home?'

Viola couldn't help but smile. 'Come on in, son.'

The small sitting room was candlelit, with one small and heavily curtained window. Three padded chairs were set in a semicircle around a walnut coffee table. A coal fire burned in the grate, surrounded a ceramic tiled mantle and two large ivory church candlesticks flickered at each end of the inglenook. There was a partially completed two-thousand-piece jigsaw puzzle of a Caribbean beach scene, complete with coral blue sea, white-tipped waves and golden sand. The place wasn't much, but people like Viola Saunders and I had learned long ago to live with not quite enough and then make do with somewhat less than that.

The old woman pointed at one of the chairs. 'Sid down.' It was more order than invite. 'I don't 'ave nuthin' to offer,' she said after we were seated.

'That's okay. I'm only here to ask about you about Mrs Walker.'

114

'I didn't tink you was 'ere to do de Lord's work. Whadda 'bout de pastor's wife?'

'When was the last time you saw her?'

''Bout a week ago, mebbe a little longer,' the old woman said with almost no hesitation.

'Was that at the mission house?'

'It was.' She scratched her forearm, her face empty. 'Why you axin'?'

'Did you know that she was missing?'

'Ah didn't, but I do now.'

'Pastor Walker has asked me to see if I can find out where she may have gone to.'

'Dat poor man be betta off not 'nawin' where she slinked off to.'

'What makes you say that?'

'Duh is more in the mortar dan the pestle wid the pastor's wife, Mistah Ellington. You 'naw whadda mean.'

I took the photograph out of my pocket and covered the part showing Trista's naked body and the masked man with my fingers then reached over and held it close to Viola Saunders' face.

'You recognise this fella on the left?' Viola Saunders inched herself forward in her seat and squinted at the print, a grimace quickly arcing across her face.

'You showin' me pictures o' a punch-drunk fool, so wha'?'

'You know him?'

'Course I 'naw him! Dat's de Loudon boy. 'Bout as much use to his fella man as a cat flap in an elephant house.'

'Did you ever see Troy Loudon with Trista Walker?'

Saunders shrugged. 'He come by de mission house a few times. Used to deliver notes to her.'

115

'Notes, what kinda notes?'

'How de hell do I 'naw! Most probably be the kind o' post a pastor's wife wouldn't want no ole woman like me to see, I sus'pec.' Saunders' phlegm-thickened laughter rose to the ceiling like the barking of a trained seal. 'Mistah,' she continued to chortle, 'you ain't gonna get very far axin' me dese kinda questions.'

'Why not?'

'Why not? I'll tell you why not. You need ta start openin' your eyes, son. You wanna see the trute? Well, you only gonna do dat if you start axin' me questions 'bout the real Trista Walker, not dis minister's wife you searchin' fo'.'

'What kind of questions should I be asking, Mrs Saunders?'

'Kind dat Pastor Walker should 'ave bin axin' years ago, dat's what kind.' Saunders cackled to herself. 'Look, son, first off, dat woman probably the most unchristian pastor's wife you ever likely to meet.'

'What makes you say that?'

'You the one bringin' pictures o' fellas like Troy Loudon into mah house. Naw God-fearin' woman on earth wud wanna 'ave any'ting to do wid scum like dat if dey had de Lord wid dem. Trista bad to de bone same as dat hard mout' boxer.'

'You're not painting a very pretty picture of her, Mrs Saunders.'

'Am jus' tellin' you what you came 'ere lookin' fo'. Tellin' you de trute. You don't like what you 'earin', you can git de hell outta ma home. Makes no difference to me.'

'Can you tell me anything else that might help?'

'I knew her momma.'

116

'Her mother? Mervyn Walker said that Trista had no family.'

The old woman made a tutting sound and shook her head. 'Is dat what she tell de pastor? Dear God.' She shifted in her seat before continuing. 'Trista's momma nevah had no husband, that's fo' sure. She musta bin in her late forties when she had de child. Wus a miracle de infant lived. De woman brought de pickney up on her own most o' de time.'

'What, here in Bristol?'

'Yes, man, 'ere in Bristol.' Viola Saunders sat forward, her milky eyes centring in on me. 'Her momma she flitted from one place to a'nudda. Most a de time dey lived in a big ole place on Melita Road up de way in St Andrews. De woman had a way o' keepin' de child outta sight most o' de time. Sum time, when her momma was tryin' to keep outta de way o' de police, de girl wud be shipped off to sum place or 'udda, den sum floozy wud bring her back when all de trouble had died down.'

'Trouble . . . what kind of trouble?'

'De kind no chil' has a right to be around.' She hesitated for a moment. 'Her name not Trista you 'naw.'

'What?'

'Trista not a real name.'

'Then what is it?

'It's Celestine.' Viola Saunders put her palms on the arms of her chair and raised herself up on to her feet. 'You best come on this way.' She picked up one of the candles and gestured her head towards the rear of the cramped chalet. I followed and stood in the hallway while she kneeled down over a drab-green army surplus trunk in her tiny bedroom. There were box springs under a single mattress for a bed, which was

117

made, and the oak floor was swept. The metal caddy looked like it worked as both a night table as well as a closet. The window above her head shone enough light to help her see. I looked out onto the tiny back-yard, the hole in the wall not wide enough for a man to squeeze through, giving the old woman's bedroom the feel of a jail cell. Nailed to the wall were a series of framed Bible pictures each depicting various scenes from the Old Testament.

Mrs Saunders gazed up at me, studying my features for a moment or two.

'You 'naw when Celestine was a child, her momma used to tell folk all kinda crazy tings 'bout dat pickney o' hers.'

'What kind of things?'

'Said de pickney saw de duppy, dat kinda ting.' She shifted her weight and looked up at the picture of the Virgin Mary on the wall. 'Naw surprise when you 'naw what kinda woman Celestine momma really was.' She said this to the wall rather than directing the words at me. She stayed staring at the picture for a second or two then shook her head as if to drag herself away from unpleasant reminiscences she'd rather not be having. She lifted the lid of the trunk and began fishing around inside, finally retrieving a large square tin box from underneath a pile of old newspapers and other belongings.

The metal box, which had once been painted red, was flecked with rust, the word OXO barely distinguishable on the top. Viola Saunders pulled herself upright. It seemed to take all she had in her to get the job done. She opened up the tin, mumbling under her breath and began to thumb through a pile of old letters and photographs before finally lifting out what

118

looked like a folded sheet of old newspaper. Viola's spectacles slipped down her nose and, as she lifted the paper up to me, her hands began to shake as though she had suddenly been struck down with some kind of palsy.

''Ere, this . . . this Celestine's momma.'

I slowly unfolded the paper and held it up against the light of the candle. It was a partial page cut out from an old copy of the *Bristol Evening Post*. The date at the top said, Friday 16 October 1964. The headline in large, black print read:

BRISTOL WOMAN ACCUSED OF
KEEPING A DISORDERLY HOUSE.

Below the headline and to the right of the article was a faded image of the woman in question. It was a standard mugshot, the type of which would have been taken after being charged with an offence by the police. I felt my stomach sink as I concentrated on the black and white portrait. The familiar countenance that starred back at me was that of a black woman from my past. Distinctive features of a cruel and dangerous individual who I had long since chosen to wipe from my memory.

It was the face of Clementine 'Hoo Shoo' Dupree.

15

I couldn't sleep that evening. There was a breeze wafting through the bedroom: a chilly night-time draught that made me shiver even underneath the bedclothes. The discoloured newspaper cutting Viola Saunders had given me lay on my bedside like an unwelcome portent. I stared at it until my eyes stung, thinking about the revelation the old woman had dropped on me and how my unwelcome past was once again tipping into the present. Trista was Celestine, the daughter of a powerful voodoo *mambo*, Hoo Shoo Dupree, a woman I'd had the misfortune to cross back in the winter of 1965.

I finally dropped off a little after two-thirty. I was walking through the empty streets of St Pauls, stalked by some unseen predator, with the echo of voodoo drums in the distance. In the darkness, I heard a woman scream then call my name over and over again. I bolted from one narrow passage to another, searching. Finally, I broke out into a desolate, mist-filled street. Lying in the middle was a woman's body.

A man stood over her, his face obscured by a dark, hooded cowl. He held a knife, the blade smeared with blood. I heard the woman's voice call out my name again. The man dropped the dagger and ran. I gave chase. An enormous church, as tall as a skyscraper, loomed ahead. I followed the man inside. He made the sign of the cross with a bloodied hand before disappearing behind a curtain. He reappeared behind the altar. I lunged and seized him by his arm, spinning him around, pushing him back against the wall. The cloak hood fell away. Staring back at me was my twin. It was like looking in a mirror.

I heard him whisper the words, 'This is from Celestine,' then I felt his teeth. His kiss grew savage. Blind panic filled every fibre of my being. I struggled, and we thrashed on the hard, nacreous floor. His face was suddenly a shapeless pulp, lacking bone or cartilage and when I pulled away my hands, gone was my own grisly image; instead, staring up at me, was the disfigured and crimson-soaked face of my cousin, Vic.

I woke up screaming.

★ ★ ★

A hot shower slowly settled my nerves. I was shaved, dressed and at the breakfast table with Chloe just before seven-thirty. She'd poured my coffee and sat down opposite me. I didn't feel much like eating. I stared at the plate of scrambled eggs and toast Chloe had made and felt my insides roll. My stomach felt like it had shrunk overnight to the size of a walnut, and it ached after the first mouthful of toast went down.

'Something wrong with the food?' Chloe asked.

'No . . . not at all.' I pushed a small piece of egg around the plate with my fork. 'My mouth thinks it's great, but my gut is telling me that it's on strike.'

Chloe frowned. 'So, what was all the noise about this morning?'

'What noise?'

'The noise coming outta your room? You were yelling at the top of your voice like a madman.' Chloe bit into a piece of toast before continuing to speak through a mouthful of unchewed food. 'Your screeching woke

121

me up before the alarm had chance to.'

Ignoring Chloe's question and desperate to change the subject, I pointed my fork in her direction. 'Hey, quit speaking with your mouth full.' I watched her eyes dip to the table and saw her swallow. When she looked back up at me, I held my breath, unsure what she was going to come back at me with.

'Loretta called while you were out last night.'

'Yeah, what'd she want?'

'To ask if I wanted to go to the cinema with her and Carnell Jnr tonight.'

I sipped at a cup of black coffee. 'To see what?'

'*The Wiz.*' Chloe heaped up another forkful of food. 'It's on at the Gaiety.'

'You've already that seen that film, twice.'

'So, that was last year. I wanna go see it again. That alright with you?' Chloe shovelled in her breakfast and eyeballed me, waiting for my reply while she munched away.

'Yeah, that's fine by me. I'll leave some money down here for you for drinks and sweets, or whatever.' Chloe beamed. I pushed my plate away from me and took a swig of coffee. 'You think Loretta would mind you staying over with her for the night?'

My daughter's happy face suddenly became sombre. 'You know Loretta never says no to me stopping with her. Where you gonna be?'

I felt a shudder run through me. An almost negligible tremor that came from my child's pointed questioning. 'I wanted to follow up a few things from last night.'

Chloe stroked the back of my hand with her fingertips. 'You sure you're, okay, Papa?'

I took her fingers and squeezed them lightly. 'I'm

fine. I just need to work through this problem of Pastor Walker's, that's all.'

'You need to be careful, Joseph.' Hearing Chloe use my Christian name unsettled me. I preferred being called 'Papa' a whole lot better.

'I can take care of myself. You know I come from a hard place,' I said.

'I know,' she replied in an exasperated tone. 'St Philip parish, Barbados. Tough policeman chasing down the bad guys. Knocking down doors and fighting the good fight for queen and country since you was nineteen.'

I laughed. 'Am I that predictable?'

'I've been listening to you tell me those stories my whole life.' Chloe pushed what was left of her breakfast to one side, quietly placed her knife and fork in the centre of her plate and got to her feet. She walked around to where I was sat and kissed me on the temple. 'Sometimes you should listen to me too.'

I looked up into my child's face, feeling all the fierce love that only a father can know, neither of us saying another word. Chloe cleared the plates and cutlery from the table and took them over to the sink then made her way down the hall. I sat there, staring at my child until she was out of sight and climbing the stairs; her sage-like counsel still replaying inside my head.

* * *

'Bye, Papa,' Chloe said before crossing the street to leave for school.

'Look both ways.'

She laughed at my feeble attempt to make her stay

123

a child.

Walking back to my front door, I glanced to the right and saw two white men in suits and ties coming towards the house. They were both the same height and had virtually identical haircuts, and probably tipped the scales within a few pounds of each other. I considered the trouble heading towards me and thought about backing into the house, slamming the door and legging it out back and over the yard wall. I turned my head to catch a glimpse of Chloe, but she was gone.

'Mr Ellington?' one of the men, who wore a dark grey suit, said.

'Yes?' I answered, addressing both the fraternal twins.

'I'm Detective Sergeant Locke and this is my colleague, Detective Constable Mapp. We'd like to have a word.'

'Is that right?'

As they stepped off the pavement and through my gate, I took a step backward so that I was standing in the front doorway.

'We've been informed that you are looking for a Mrs Trista Walker.'

'Yeah, by whom?'

'That's not important,' Detective Constable Mapp, who wore a suit of dark blue, said.

'It is to me.'

'May we come in?' Locke asked.

Neither man, at any point in our conversation, smiled nor was anyone flashing Bristol constabulary warrant cards.

'No, you may not.'

'We have to talk to you about the disappearance of

Mrs Walker.'

'That's your problem. I ain't got nothing to say to you.'

'We believe that you are getting involved in an ongoing investigation,' Locke replied. 'If you don't cooperate and tell us what you are doing, we can have you arrested for interfering in police business.'

'Okay.' I shrugged. 'If you got a warrant or you are thinking I committed some kinda crime, you got your duty to do. But I'm telling you that I ain't done nothing to concern you or anybody else over at Bridewell police station. I'm a law-abiding citizen and I won't be bullied by loose talk from strangers.'

The copper called Locke looked over my shoulder and down my hallway then zoned his attention back in on me. 'This case, as I believe you well know, involves a missing person. We have concerns that kidnapping may be a serious consideration in regards to our enquiries.'

Officer Mapp felt now was the perfect time to chip in his two cents' worth. 'It's your duty to cooperate, Mr Ellington.'

I disregarded the constable and focused in on the higher-ranking Locke. 'How'd you find me?'

The detective sergeant sighed. 'Pastor Mervyn Walker told us about you. He kindly gave us your address.'

'Is that so?'

'May we come in?' Locke asked again.

'No.'

'Have you been in contact with Pastor Walker in the last twenty-four hours?'

'Yep, saw him yesterday morning.'

'He hired you to look for Mrs Walker, yes?'

'I didn't say that I'm looking for her, and even if I was I ain't got anything of use to tell you fellas.' I took another step back. 'I don't even know if you two are really police officers.'

Locke grinned at me. 'You're a relation of Victor Ellington, yes?'

I nodded. 'I was wondering how long it would take for you to bring his name up.'

'What do they say . . . no smoke without fire?' Locke winked at me.

'Yeah, well, any family flame my cousin and I once burned was put out a long time ago, I can assure you of that.'

'Do you really want to run foul of the police, Mr Ellington?' Mapp warned.

'There anything else?' I asked.

Locke's face flushed. 'Are you going to answer my questions?'

'I am not.'

The two police officers turned their heads to regard each other. Should they arrest me? Should they push me into the house and force me to answer their questions? I had no doubt that they might utilise such tactics. And if I was another kind of man, say an obedient, compliant white fella, I might have tried to placate them.

Maybe if they had shown me their identification, asked for my help or at least smiled, I might have been persuaded to accommodate them. But the freedom I had to refuse had its own story. There were black men and woman still dying for my freedom and my right to say no.

Maybe one day officers Locke and Mapp would understand that simple fact.

126

'This isn't some kind of game, Mr Ellington,' Locke barked at me. 'I'm telling you to stop any activity you may be involved in that has anything to do with Trista Walker. Understand?'

I gave the detective a weak smile and a crooked nod, then closed the door in his face.

16

There was half a cup of cold coffee left in the white and blue mug sitting on the kitchen table. I sat and took my time drinking the bitter dregs, trying to make plans for the day as well as I could. Despite covering a lot of ground in the past few days, I was still completely in the dark about the case I'd agreed to undertake. The pastor had paid me pretty well for my trouble, but not enough for this kind of confusion.

In the past, when I'd been dealing with a case where a person of colour was in the hot seat or needed my assistance, I usually spent most of the investigation giving them a helping hand in the black part of town. I'd talk to family and friends, loved ones and those who hated them across a very defined local area. The crime they were suspected of or problem they had generally took shape in some place around or in St Pauls.

But Mervyn Walker's wife didn't exactly fit into any of the above. Yes, she was black, and would not escape the harsh truths of prejudice and racism, but her apparently comfortable way of living, tucked away in a swish vicarage in a cosseted area of Montpelier, was a world away from the boarding houses and hand-to-mouth existence that was a reality for most of our community.

Such hardships, the effects of poverty and crime, were practically on her doorstep and yet, Trista, or Celestine or whatever the hell name she was using, had been privileged enough to distance herself from such bleakness thanks to being married to the pastor and, just as importantly, the degree of comfort, security and elevated social status that the church afforded her. The fact that the police were making such a big noise about her vanishing off the face of the earth told me that either influential outside forces were at work, and that could perhaps mean some exalted clergyman from the diocese using their influence on Mervyn's behalf or, more likely, the Old Bill had been tipped the wink by someone looking after their own interests.

On the face of it, Walker's disappearance appeared to be totally out of character; the reason for her unexpectedly walking out of her home, as the pastor had claimed, more to do with her perhaps unsound mental state or some kind of dissatisfaction with her life than it was foul play or, as the police had just informed me, a possible kidnapping.

Finding Troy Loudon with the back of his head blown off, as well as the photo of Celestine naked with the dead boxer and some masked stranger, and the shock of discovering that Hoo Shoo Dupree was possibly her mother, had put a very different spin on things. I didn't know if Dupree was alive or dead. I did know that the woman was poison. She'd spelled trouble for me back when I was searching for Stella Hopkins in '65. I had the awful feeling that the old witch's bad blood was somehow connected to Trista Walker's disappearance; the Voodoo religion the *mambo* priestess had so vehemently practised making itself felt from afar or from beyond the grave.

I may have been in the dark over Walker fleeing her home and still being on the lam, I did however have a few leads that could perhaps enlighten me as to the possible reasons why. Floyd Council had coughed up a few local joints that he assured me he'd seen Trista Walker hanging out at in the past: Shady Grove shebeen and the Gambling House, the Black and White Café, the Inkerman pub. The Shady Grove and the Gambling House were after-dark haunts and I'd only be able to sniff around those places at a time when most sensible folk were tucked up in bed. I'd head out to both those places later tonight and concentrate my efforts on the other two dives during the day.

I knew that once I walked out of my home and headed into any of the four establishments that 'Dipper' Council had told me to sniff about in, as soon as I started to ask questions in those places about Trista Walker, I would most likely arouse the attention of the kinds of flinty, ruthless types I would be wise to stay clear of.

I knew those types of shady individuals all too well.

Crooks. Thieves. Dealers. Whores and their miserable pimps. Desperate or violent types who'd prefer to beat you to a pulp first and ask questions later.

Dangerous men. Men like my cousin, Vic.

The thought of re-entering that tenebrous world suddenly filled me with dread.

A dear old friend, and former neighbour of mine, Mrs Pearce, an elderly and kind woman, had once told me that the lives we lead, the things we do, good and bad, the kindnesses offered, the misdeeds undertook, the art we create or artifacts we produce, are all but scrims, one layer over countless others; some that reveal, some that conceal. I'd learned to hide much over time. And while I can never bring myself to accept Christian notions of sin and atonement, there's definitely something to karma. The things we store up, locked away inside, do pile up on us, weigh us down.

Ten years ago, I saw a man called William Ryder killed. He was shot in the head in front of my very eyes. His execution was ordered by my own kin, Victor Ellington. Ryder was a local Bristol mobster; a cruel deviant who, in all honesty, deserved his grisly end. Looking back, all these years later, I know that I have played my part, one way or another, in the killings of a number of men, including Ryder's, albeit none by my own hand. Nevertheless, although I may have not pulled the trigger or taken a life personally, being part of or around such savagery taints the soul. It contaminates the heart and mind in the same way ink stains the skin.

I try not to think about those dark days. Though from time to time, such as after being questioned by those two police officers just now, I see something in their inquiring, bitter eyes that drags me back to the person I once was, and what I feared I was quickly becoming again.

17

Hidden behind deeply tinted windows, the Shady Grove café on Ashley Road was the kind of joint that didn't begin to liven up until well after dark. So, it was no surprise that when I walked in just before noon there was no one there eating or drinking, and not a domino or card player in sight, and that's just how I wanted it. The Shady's owner, Gilbert 'Ajax' Watson was a king of kings, a legend, and known right across St Pauls as 'Mistah Community Man'.

'You 'avin' the red beans an' rice, bossman?' Ajax asked in a voice so deep that it was disturbing; like the rumble of a wild animal that was considering a roar.

'Tell me they're not left over from Monday?' Monday was traditionally wash day right across the West Indies. Fix-head pots of red beans and rice would be left simmering on the stove while the women grafted. Most cafés and homes carry on this practice. St Pauls is a place that likes to embrace tradition.

'Joseph, you 'naw I mek a fresh dutchie o' 'em every damn day.' Watson was somewhere between fifty-five and sixty, not heavy or thin, and a little over six feet tall. He was standing at his waist-high counter at the back of the café. Behind him was a kitchen full of his family members, their spouses and friends. None of them looking like they were doing a lot of work, just smoking and chatting to each other.

Shady's served as a place for the community to socialise, drink and dance together. I'd always known it as the place to go if you wanted to fill your belly with 'homecooked food' or when the outside 'white' world felt like it was against you. The bar-cum-diner always reminded me of the kind of place I sometimes ate in back home. The inside was like a time capsule dedicated to all things Caribbean. Neon clocks and bright Red Stripe and Dragon stout beer signs hung on the walls. Formica, fake-wood panelling and cheap plastic was everywhere and Lord Kitchener, Desmond Dekker and Bob Marley always playing on the jukebox. There were eleven square tables for customers and a long counter behind which Ajax ruled.

At the far end of the bar there was a payphone on the wall. I took a seat next to it and ordered some jerk chicken, a bowl of rice and beans and a cup of black coffee. Ajax turned around and shouted, 'Esther! Bring Joseph some a dat chicken an' rice!

'Okay,' bawled a young woman's voice from the kitchen.

Ajax didn't let anyone eat at his counter. You went over there to order for sit-down or take-out. But he didn't want you loitering around and obstructing his view. Most men who tried to start up a conversation with Ajax were told, 'Sit your arse down, man. I ain't got time to fool wid you. This 'ere's a bid'ness.' The fact that he could stare or shout down most of his clientele said quite a lot, because the men and women that patronised Shady's were not to be pushed.

'So, Joseph,' Ajax said. 'What you doin' 'ere?'

'Thought I'd get myself an early lunch.'

'Uh-uh. You gotta do betta 'n dat. I ain't seen you in 'ere in, must be t'ree year. Last time I saw Loretta she tole me you left the bus depo an' dat ole place you had out in da sticks and was back livin' n' workin' in St Pauls.'

133

'That's right.'

Ajax shook his head, eyeballing me for a moment. He strolled round the counter, pulled up a chair and plonked himself down on the opposite side of the table from me. 'Well, all dis time not showin' you' face, gotta mean you want sum'ting comin' 'ere to me, right?'

'Here you go,' said a young woman, placing a heaped plate of chicken and rice and my coffee down in front of me. She smiled at me. She was wearing a bright pink top and leggings and had a large white ribbon holding back her long braids.

'Was' wrong wid you, Esther?' Ajax asked angrily.

'What?' Esther complained.

'Go git him some greens n' corn. He ain't no animal jus' gonna tear at meat. Man needs a balanced meal.' Ajax shook his head and his waitress pouted.

'You want collard or callaloo greens, Joseph?'

'Collard.'

'Yeah, man. Dat's what I always go for. Dem callaloo greens is bitter.' He sang the last word to accent his distaste.

'Ajax, you mind if I quiz you a minute?' I asked when Esther had slouched away.

The café owner laughed. 'Now we gittin' down to it. You started nosin' 'bout in other folks bid'ness agin, yeah?

'Let's just saying I'm helping an old friend out.'

'Is dat right?'

I nodded. 'Yeah, that's right.' Ajax chuckled to himself. I blew at my coffee before taking a sip. It was a strong, bitter brew, made just the way I like it. 'You know Troy Loudon?'

'Troy Loudon.' Ajax sighed. 'Mm, mm, mm. Now

134

dat boy is trouble an' he don't even 'naw it.'

'You know him well?'

'Well enuff. Troy gotta chip on his shoulder, a temper dat nevah tires, eyes fo' de wimin an' a heart drippin' right off his sleeve. If a man could be too much fo' life, it's Troy Loudon.'

Esther brought up a big plate full of greens. The collards gave off a sharp aroma laced with a hint of vinegar.

'I hear he'd fallen on hard times?'

'Hard time. Bad time. Troy nevah de same from one day to de nex'. One day he come in 'ere sayin' he gonna be de nex' champion o' de world. Nex' week he wanders de wrong way down de street an' now he's tellin' folk he gonna be sum kinda night club big wig. He bin in 'ere befo' now tellin' me am jus' a slave wukin' fo' de white master. Can you imagine such claptrap?'

'Brother got it wrong there, Ajax.' I spooned a heap of rice and peas into my mouth and savoured the earthy flavour. 'Man, this is the best damn food I've eaten in many a day. Many a day.' I wasn't lying either. When you get soul food right, it feeds the spirit, and my spirit was flying with those rice and peas.

'Okay, Joseph. You done et fo' free and I answered you question. You got any'ting else you wanna axe befo' I git back to wuk?'

I took the photograph of Trista Walker out of my inside pocket and slid it across the table. 'You ever see Troy in here with this woman?' Ajax gave the snapshot a long hard look.

'I 'naw who she is.' Ajax shook his head, a bitter look sweeping across his eyes. 'An' I ain't evah seen her in 'ere wid Loudon. If you friend is involved with

135

either Troy or dat woman, he messin' wid a world o' trouble.'

I nodded because my mouth was busy chewing. Ajax handed back the photograph. 'I ain't got nuthin' else to say 'bout either of 'em.' He was about to rise from his seat, but I held him back with another question.

'You remember Clementine Dupree?'

Ajax's keen and amiable eyes studied me for a moment. 'Everybody round 'ere remember Hoo Shoo.'

'You know what happened to her?'

'I 'ear all kinda ting 'bout what 'appen to dat ole girl. Most o' it jus' nincompoops talkin' dottish.'

'You think she's dead by now?'

'Dead . . . Where you bin, man?'

'You know something I don't?'

'Looks like it . . . She up at Long Fox.'

'Long Fox . . . you talking about the mental hospital?'

'Course I am . . . Place called Brislington House, dese days.'

'When did she end up there?'

'I heard dem honky doctors carry 'way her crazy arse off 'bout t'ree year ago. Bes' place fo' her, if you axe me.' Ajax tilted forward on the finished wood table, lacing his fingers and planting his elbows so as to form a perfect equilateral triangle. 'Joseph, when it come to people an' problems, folk round 'ere have al'ways said that you de smartest man dey evah 'naw.'

I laid my spoon down at the side of my plate and straightened my back. 'Thank you, man. That's kind of you to say so.'

Ajax Watson slowly rose to his feet, his eyes widening. 'If you still so smart, tek my advice, man. Stay

136

the hell away from all t'ree o' dese raasclaats. Poking round in dese people's bid'ness likely to git you killed.' I stared at him until he looked away. A vein was pulsing in his temple, his eyes were suddenly cups of sorrow.

'Staying away might be easier said than done.'

Ajax shook his head and scowled. 'Okay, it's your funeral.'

18

I'd almost reached the top of Ashley Road, my head still taking in Ajax Watson's words and his stark warning. For some reason, maybe because of Watson's shot across the bows at me, I suddenly felt tired. An odd twitching sensation underneath the skin around the nape of my neck and my jaw. I felt a bead of sweat roll down the side of my head, and I was happy that the traffic lights in front of me had just turned red. I propped myself against a lamppost and sighed.

Then I heard a car pull up behind me and its doors swing open.

'Hey, you!' somebody said.

The voice came from behind me, but I didn't need to turn around to know who it was. Two boys in blue were coming at me like twin hyenas on a wounded antelope.

'Officers.'

In the blink of an eye, the luxury of being a free man was abruptly snatched away from me. Now I was a soldier and the enemy was standing right in front of me. When the enemy pulls up a black man in the street, they don't ask you how you are, or if you're too tired to stand your ground or stick up for your rights. The enemy has many wounds of his own and he hates a black fella for every one of them.

'Let's see some ID,' the cop on the right said.

They were both young and white and had been after me as long as all three of us had set foot on the earth.

I reached inside my jacket pocket and handed over

my driving licence. 'Name's Joseph Tremaine Ellington. Live on Banner Road.' I pointed my finger towards the end of the street. ''Bout five minutes' walk away.'

'You been drinking, Joseph?' the copper on the left asked. I could distinguish him by the tiny scar above his lip and the ivory hue of his teeth, which he showed in a false smile.

'I have not.'

'We're going to have to search you,' the other cop said. 'Put your arms out to your side.'

'I thought you were asking me if I was drunk?'

'You might have an open half-pint bottle of grog in one of your pockets.'

I did as they told me. I didn't like it, but I had more pressing things on my mind and I wanted to get on my way as quickly as possible. They went through my pockets and patted me down to the ankles. One of them, the one without the scar, had breath that stank like a fetid drain. It took me all my inner reserve not to retch in front of him.

'Okay,' the scarred copper said when all they found on me was my wallet, two pound thirty in change and some lint. 'Now we're going to have you walk in a straight line for us.'

'Hey,' a stranger's voice proclaimed. 'What you botherin' that man fo'?'

It was a man whose face I recognised, but whose name I didn't know. He worked in the Langford abattoir across the road from where I was stood. He'd been watching what had been going on, I supposed.

'This is none of your business,' the unscarred cop informed the newcomer.

The abattoir worker was wearing white, bloodied overalls, the skin on his face crinkled up like old parchment.

'Man wasn't doin' nuthin',' my new-found defender said. 'Man's jus' walkin' up to the corner and restin' himself against dat pole. He ain't drivin' no car, so who cares if he had a drink?'

'I won't be warning you again,' Scarface said. I saw him lift the front of his tunic and reach for his truncheon.

'Yeah, coon,' the partner agreed.

I was starting to become worried about the well-being of my good-intentioned advocate when yet another voice joined our impromptu chorus.

'What did you say?' This from a tall white fella, also in blood-smeared overalls stretched tight over his big belly. 'What did you call my man?'

'Hey, Gordon, wus goin' on out there?' another deep voice chimed in.

The abattoir was a low, whitewashed wood and brick building that encompassed an open space like a hanger for a small aircraft. Instead of a front wall, the property had a huge metal gate that rolled up when the place was open. Behind the men, I could just make out decapitated animal carcasses hanging from the ceiling on metal chains and hooks.

'Some young copper out here called Roy a coon,' the foreman shouted back.

More men came rolling out of the slaughterhouse into the street. Now there were nine of them stood outside, more than one of them holding razor-sharp butchering knives in their hands.

'That fella ovah there wus jus' walkin',' the man I now knew as Roy said to his gaffer. He pointed across the road towards the offending police officer. 'An' den dis one 'ere, plain as day, up an' call me a coon.'

140

Fear was starting to register in the white policemen's eyes: the fear of a complaint lodged against them; the fear of a roust escalating into a minor riot; the fear of them losing control in a situation they were not prepared for. But most of all they were afraid of their fellow white man. The foreman who was stood with his work colleagues. I didn't matter. Roy didn't matter. But if a white boss stood up against the cops, then they transformed from law enforcement into what they really were — hired help.

'Why'd you call him a coon?' the head man, Gordon, asked the clear-skinned copper.

'I didn't,' he replied, gesturing vaguely at me.

'Not him,' Gordon snapped. 'Roy.'

Cars were now slowing down in the street, all of them driven by black folk. A couple of vehicles had pulled to the kerb. Gordon was angry and so was Roy. The rest of the slaughtermen, who were all black, were now stood around their colleague and boss, all of them looking mightily aggrieved.

I suppressed a snicker. It was as much a nervous laugh as an evil one: a chuckle spawned in the hell of my early life. Even though I couldn't have thrown a punch at that moment, I wanted to cut loose and fight.

Luckily for all of us, the policeman's radio started making noise. Scar man went to the car and grabbed the microphone. He said something, and I heard a tinny response.

'Hey, Trevor,' he said. 'Emergency on the Portway, underneath the suspension bridge. Sounds like a bad one. We gotta go.'

They both jumped into the car and took off.

I waved my thanks to the men across the road as

they began heading back into the abattoir. Roy shot me a smile and followed on after his work mates. I'd just been accused by the police of being drunk and disorderly even though not a drop of booze had touched my lips. I decided I'd head over to the Beaufort Inn on York Road. Get me a nip of rum, and a pint of stout chaser to wash it down with.

I stood on the street a moment longer, weighing up my bad luck in life. Those two cops would have liked to have either thrown my arse in a cell for nothing or perhaps at a push even have left me for dead in a ditch someplace. Apart from this latest madness I'd just gotten myself mixed up in, I had, in the past been shot and sapped and kicked by the police. I'd been on a few of their hit lists over the years, and as of this afternoon, had for the first time fallen foul of their godforsaken SUS law; that was section 4 of the 1824 Vagrancy Act, a parliamentary decree created by our Whitehall betters which gave police officers the discretionary power to arrest anyone they suspected of loitering with intent to commit an arrestable offence.

In reality that meant no bookings, no charges, just a heap full of bruises.

A feeling of anger wrapping tight underneath my skin, my hands balled into fists. Fear on one side of me, defeat on the other.

19

The Beaufort Inn was more than just a pub. It was a bar and restaurant, club and private meeting room, and was one of the first public houses in St Pauls that my cousin, Vic, purchased outright for cash, no questions asked. The old Victorian building was home to much of his St Pauls 'business' operations, the imposing building taking up a huge chunk of York Road. It had a kitchen out back and round folding tables in the hall, which came out once a year to fill the street outside for the Caribbean carnival. On any given evening the Beaumont could be hosting a gospel recital by some local church diva and later that night there'd be a high-stakes poker game for local high-rollers. There'd be birthday and retirement parties taking place at the weekends at the same time as bookies' runners were heading in and out of the place.

Most people never just walked into the Beaufort for a pint; punters always had another reason for visiting the pub than to simply slake their thirst. A lot of folk didn't enter the place unless they were invited. For a few people the door was always open. I wasn't always one of them, but my earlier run-in with the police had spooked me, so much so that I was prepared to frequent a pub I normally stayed well away from to try and reach out for my reclusive and mercurially feral relation, Victor.

Horace Rayford stood at the alley door that led up to the rear of the Beaufort. Horace was a big man, with a heavyweight's physique and an old man's face.

His hair was a tangle of thickly knotted locks that hung down almost to the base of his spine. Horace had a countenance of sad kindliness, but I knew that the man was capable of great violence if provoked, and word was that he'd killed at least three men back in Jamaica before moving to Britain and coming to work for Vic. He wore a dark wool suit and a purple silk shirt, opened at the neck with a gold chain in evidence. A white rose drooped in his lapel.

'Horace,' I said in greeting.

He raised his head in a half salutation, watching me with watery, elder-statesman-like eyes. 'JT.'

I leaned against the frame of the gate, the huge doorman still blocking my entry. 'I just got pulled over by the police. Stopped me for no damn reason other than to see the look on my face.'

Horace nodded. 'First time it 'appen to you?'

'Yeah.'

'Shit, you should tink yourself lucky. Last month, an' dis all in a fortnight, me stood outside de Mina Road post office. Babylon pull up an' git out, say I was loitering to dip an ole lady's handbag. I look at dese two spotty young coppers thinking dey gotta be joking wid me. Weren't no joke. Bastards charged me wid intent to commit an offence. Week later charge gits chucked outta court.' Horace spat at his feet before continuing his tale of woe:

'De very next day am walking down Grosvenor Road. Babylon in a squad car a'gin. Blue lights, siren blaring away. Dem pigs say dey wants me fo' possession o' drugs. Den dey find out I ain't got none so dem say I've flogged 'em. Fat copper runs me down to Bridewell, stick t'ree fingers up me arse. Said he's doin' it in case I'd hid 'em up there. What de raaangate!

144

I was stuck in a cell fo' six hours. Six fuckin' hours! Two day later, dey pick me up on Portland Square. Police bundle me into de back dis crappy blue and white panda, said dey wus lookin' fo' a house te'ef'. I said, I ain't no fingasmit an' I ain't nicked nuthin' from nobody. Pig backhands me cross de face an' says, 'Den we'll do you fo' motors or possession, you choose.' I said, I ain't particular on either, man, an' de fucker kicked me outta dey car an' drive off.' Horace grunted, shifting from one huge foot to another. He heaved his chest out from under his jacket. I knew that close to those expanding sinews there'd be a gun. 'Whaddya want, JT?'

'Looking for Dutty,' I said.

'Not 'ere.'

'Then, if it's okay with you, I'll just go get myself a drink.'

Horace's nostrils flared. He took a deep breath then nodded and stood to one side. As I neared the bar an ebony wood door on the other side swung open and Wallace 'Half Pint' Holt came out to meet me. Half Pint's skin was toasted gold. His features neither Caucasian nor black. Wallace was always grinning. And I knew that if I hadn't gotten the signal from Horace, he would have been ready to slit my throat or put a hole in my forehead.

'JT,' Wallace said. 'What's you' bid'ness, man?'

'I'm looking for Dutty.'

'Not 'ere.'

'That's what Horace just told me.'

'Then Horace tole you right.'

'Well, my relation's skivvy needs finding, and sharpish,' I said, knowing that even the self-important dogsbodies at the Beaumont wouldn't want to cross

145

the 'Jah Rhygin'.

The man I was looking for was a creature of habit, rarely venturing outside until after dark. Gut instinct told me the Beaumont's off-the-books landlord, Dutty Ken, was holed up inside. I wanted to see the man and wasn't about to take no for an answer. Half Pint knew he had to let me in to see his boss or meet my cousin's wrath. He wouldn't like the fact, but at the same time he'd not want to be put in the position of explaining himself to either Dutty or worse still, Vic, if either should find out that Wallace had refused me entry. The little minder sniffed, considering if he had anything else to say to me before deciding he was best keeping his trap shut and waving me on in. I strode across the lounge and through a door with a central frosted glass panel. A brass plate above it read snug in bold, black-etched lettering.

Dutty Ken was sitting at a small round table against the far wall. There was a crystal tumbler half-filled with white over-proof rum in front of him, also a copy of the early edition of the *Bristol Evening Post* opened to the racecard's page. A half-smoked cigar burned in a yellow glass ashtray next to him.

At over two hundred and fifty pounds in weight, Dutty still managed to look dapper. He wore a dark blue suit, an ivory satin shirt and a navy-blue tie held down by a gold lion's head pin. His hair was close cropped in thick curls and his skin as black as his polished brogues. He peered up at me and then stuck his nose back into the list of riders and nags. 'I gotta sweet accumulator runnin' at Bath dis afternoon,' he said, not offering me a seat. I made my way over to the bar and perched myself down on one of the high, full-back stools then rapped the bar with my knuckles.

'You still serving stout in this place?'

Dutty made a slow hissing sound before reluctantly lifting his fat carcass out of his chair and lumbering around the bar to pull me a pint. I could feel those cold, pale eyes of his on me as he yanked the hand-pull back and forth, filling a thin glass with black ale. 'Dat's on de house.' Dutty slid my beer across the bar then walked back to his seat and began reading the sports page again.

'Will Vic be in later tonight?'

Dutty shook his head. 'The Jah is away on bid'ness an' he didn't leave any messages when he comin' back or for me to give you either.'

'I gotta get hold of him,' I said.

'Uh-huh.' Dutty's eyes had no sparkle in them whatsoever, giving the impression that he'd seen such bad times that all of his hopes had died. 'What you want?'

'That's between me and my blood,' I said.

Dutty stared at me for a few seconds then called out: 'Delyse!'

'Yeah?' a high-toned woman's voice called back. She came into a doorway at the back of the bar.

'Bring me de phone, woman.'

'Yes, Dutty.'

Delyse belonged to Vic's mob. She had a wild look about her and from what I'd heard, a wilder temper. She wore no bra, and didn't seem to be missing it. Her skin was reddish brown, her lips poised in the permanent expectation of a kiss. She balanced precariously on high heels that were on their way to becoming stilts. The black dress she wore was mid-thigh and she walked in a circular movement that made her seem like she was dancing. She brought out a black phone

147

on an extremely long cord and placed it on the table in front of Dutty and offered him the handset. He declined, saying, 'Dial de Jah.'

Delyse did so, though she seemed to have some difficulty maintaining her balance and dialling at the same time.

The moments idled by.

'Jah?' she asked in a quiet voice. 'Hold on I got Dutty on the line.' She handed the receiver to Dutty. He took it while staring at my forehead.

'Jah? . . . I got JT 'ere sayin' he got a message fo' you.' Dutty listened for a moment then went to hand me the phone.

'Just tell Vic, I said, 'manchineel',' I said, not taking the handset.

Dutty gave me a confused look before speaking into the phone again. 'JT, he says to tell you manchineel. Uh-huh . . . Uh-huh . . . okay, I'll tell him.' He handed the receiver back to Delyse and she sashayed away.

'The Jah travellin' back from London tomorrow afternoon, says you should go ovah to Cuckoo Lane after seven.'

I took a swig of my pint. 'Thanks, Dutty.' I sat quietly for a moment before sinking the rest of the pint, then stepped down from the bar stool. Dutty held up his big paw to get my attention.

'Jah said you should bring de pickney wid you, too.' I thought I saw a flicker of goodwill in Dutty's expression, but I suspected I was foolishly erring on the side of charity. I nodded my head. 'Okay, whatever Vic says.'

As I was walking away, a thought suddenly came into my head. I turned and headed back to Dutty clicking my thumb and middle finger at him.

'What you know 'bout a boxer name of Troy Loudon?'

The landlord moved his head in a circle. His neck bones cracking loudly. 'Same as everybody else round 'ere 'naw . . .' Silence trailed in Dutty's wake while he flipped over the pages of the local rag he'd been reading. He held it up at arm's length to reveal the *Post*'s headline.

MAN DISCOVERED DEAD IN MONTPELIER SQUAT.

Dutty dropped the newspaper down in front of him, pushed back in his seat, a big smile on his lips, the unexpected mirth not quite reaching his eyes.

'Dat wufless raaaahhhs-sole stiffer than a wedding day dick.'

149

20

The manchineel tree graces Barbados's beaches providing shade from the blazing sun for locals and holidaymakers alike as they enjoy themselves on the beach. But the island's citizens know something that most tourists don't. Those magnificent shade trees with their little apples hanging from the branches are probably the most dangerous thing folk will encounter on their vacation to Barbados. The tree with its dark grey bark, shiny green leaves and small white-green flowers is a beautiful thing. The apples are a greenish-yellow with a pleasant, sweet-smelling fragrance when they ripen. The leaves, bark, sap and apple-like fruit of the manchineel are all poisonous. Contact with any of these will cause severe blistering, burning of the skin and, for some poor souls, even death.

Manchineel was what Vic and I had agreed as a code word if I ever needed him and I didn't want anyone else to know the reason why.

Manchineel meant that I was in trouble. And as I turned the corner into Banner Road. I was about to find out just how deep in the shit I really was.

The police were waiting for me outside my home. The same two plain-clothes fellas, Locke and Mapp, who'd come knocking my door earlier were standing round my car. I thought about turning around and making a run for it, but one of the coppers saw me, pointed and shouted out: 'Finally, the wanderer returns.'

Apart from not informing the police that I'd found

Troy Loudon's body earlier in the week I had, to my knowledge, broken no law. Rather than make life any harder for myself, I decided to go and meet my fate.

'Hello, officers.' I smiled as I approached them.

'Mr Ellington.' Detective Sergeant Locke grinned back at me. 'A few questions down at the station if you don't mind.'

'What about?' I asked as I drew closer.

Locke winked at me. 'You're under arrest, old son.'

Detective Constable Mapp was a pro at slapping on the cuffs before I could think let alone speak.

'Get in the car,' Locke whispered in my ear.

I let my body go loose to oblige him but DC Mapp pushed me when I was off balance stepping into the backseat. I'd barely got my foot in before he slammed the door.

''Scuse me,' I said as we cruised away down the road. 'What's the charge here?' I was feeling playful. Perhaps it was the pint of stout on an empty stomach. Maybe it was lack of sleep or the fact I was tired of being rough-housed by white policemen. Maybe it was just that I'd given up like so many black men in my position, tired of putting up their fists against batons, rubber bullets and hatred.

Locked turned and said, 'Murder,' in a bland tone. 'And conspiracy.'

I was quiet for the rest of the ride.

* * *

I hadn't been to Bridewell Police Station for questioning in many years. It looked older for sure but it still smelled the same. A sour odour that wasn't anything exactly. It wasn't living and it wasn't dead, it wasn't

151

food and it wasn't excrement. The stink wasn't anything I could put my finger on, but it was wrong, as wrong as the stench that came out of Dipper Council's front room.

The last time I was at the nick I was taken there under arrest and the police put me in a cell before shifting me to a raw-walled room that was made for questioning prisoners. The kind of cross examinations that were punctuated by fists and boots. This time, though, they sat me at a desk with Detective Constable Mapp on one side and the higher-ranking Locke with his back against the wall on the other side of the room. I'd not been searched nor asked to empty my pockets. Mapp had a blue-white form and police notebook in front of him. He was clearly going to be asking the questions, while his comrade in arms looked on.

'Name?'

'Joseph Tremaine Ellington,' I answered.

'Date of birth?'

'That would be twenty-first June 1923.'

'Height?'

'Close to six foot two.'

'Weight?'

'Thirteen stone, three, except at Christmas and Easter. Then I'm about fourteen.'

He asked more questions like that and I answered freely. I knew I had to. Back on Bim and here in England, I'd been beaten, robbed, shot at and generally mistreated by more white men than I had black brothers. That's just the way it was. I trusted a black man before I'd even think about a white one and the idea of trusting a white copper simply went against the grain.

152

Mapp looked at his pocketbook. 'I see you were stopped and searched by two of our officers earlier today.'

I nodded my head. 'I was being rousted for no reason.'

Mapp shook his head and sighed. 'Rousted? How very unfortunate.'

Locke decided to put his two cents' worth in. 'Look on the bright side you weren't nicked then.'

'There was no reason for them to stop me, let alone nick me. No evidence I'd broke a law. No witnesses. No crime.'

Mapp made a tutting sound. 'Temper, temper.'

'I don't lose my temper.'

'Wise. Especially with policeman,' heckled Locke.

I smiled at him. 'Lose your temper with a copper, well that'd be assault. They lose their temper with you, it's called resisting arrest.'

'Sounds like semantics to me,' said Mapp.

'It can sound like whatever you want it to. I got witnesses back where those two officers stopped and rough-housed me.'

'Witnesses?'

'Yeah, folk that can confirm I've done nothing wrong.'

Mapp sniggered. 'How's that? I mean, how does anyone witness nothing?'

I was about to answer the snotty detective constable when Locke placed his hand on his colleague's shoulder to interrupt proceedings.

'Okay, Joseph, we've got the basics here. Now, if you'll come this way, please. My gaffer, Detective Superintendent Eve, would like a word with you.'

The superintendent was waiting for me in his office,

a familiar room that once belonged to Detective Superintendent William Fletcher — a policeman I'd known who I'd had a long-standing love–hate relationship with and whom I'd been with on the night he was killed by a sniper's bullet the better part of ten years ago. Outside, on the door, I'd just managed to make out the outline of Fletcher's name under black letters that now spelled out the office's new occupier, Detective Inspector Robert Eve.

Eve took my cuffs off when we were secure behind closed doors.

'Why am I under arrest?' I asked as soon as I heard Eve turn the key in the lock.

The inspector was a tall, lean man. He had tight black eyes and black hair. His box-shaped head and squared off jaw gave him a military appearance; his gruff, dismissive voice was the kind I'd heard barking at me when I'd been on the force. The inspector took off his thick, black-rimmed glasses and pressed down on the bridge of his nose and then across both eyes.

'Because, from what I understand, you're in it up to your neck, Joseph.'

Suddenly there was an animal trying to claw his way out of my chest. I had to catch half a breath to sound normal.

'Up to my neck. What you talking about? What's the problem, man?'

The copper pointed at a chair. 'Sit down, Joseph.'

Hearing my Christian name being used by a stranger, and a white man at that, threw me off kilter a little. 'I don't wanna sit down. I want you to tell me what the hell is happening here.'

Eve walked behind his desk and sat. He clearly didn't mind if I stood over him in such a small room.

It was his office, plenty of other men and women had to remain upright at his behest. Eve didn't look like the kind of man who could be intimidated and, clearly, he didn't really care if I stood, sat or was kicked into a corner.

'I've been reading all about you, Joseph.' Eve tapped at a manila folder with his exceptionally long and bony finger. 'Very impressive. Barbadian police force. Joined at eighteen, rising to the rank of sergeant. Awarded the Barbados Star of Gallantry for an act of conspicuous courage in circumstances of extreme peril. A few years working as a private detective when you first came to Britain.'

'Enquiry agent,' I interrupted.

'I beg your pardon?'

'I wasn't a private detective. I made enquiries for folk when they had a problem. Calling me a detective makes me out be some kinda Sam Spade.' I took a breath, my pulse throbbing at my temple. 'But that was all a long time ago.'

Eve smiled. 'It would appear that it's a former calling which you have recently decided to renew.'

'Sorry, you've lost me.'

'Really? Why don't you let me try and help you find your way, then?' Eve opened up the file in front of him. 'Pastor Mervyn Walker.'

'Yeah, what about him?'

'I'd be right in saying that you have been undertaking some . . . enquiry work on his behalf, yes?'

I nodded. 'His wife, she's gone missing. Mervyn asked me to sniff about, as a favour to him.'

'A favour?'

'Yeah. Mervyn knew I'd gone looking for missing folk in the past. Wanted me to do the same, see if I

155

could turn up his wife, Trista.'

'Any success with that?'

I shook my head. 'No.'

'Shame.'

'Look, all I've been trying to do is find the rever-end's wife, that's it. What the hell's that gotta do with me being arrested fo' murder?'

Eve consulted the document on his desk. 'In the early hours of yesterday morning, a man was found dead in Montpelier.'

'Yeah, so I see from today's *Bristol Evening Post*.'

'The dead man's name was Troy Loudon. He was found slowly becoming maggot food with the top of his head blown off. The word 'traitor' had been writ-ten on a piece of paper in lipstick and pinned to his chest.'

I shrugged. 'And?'

'And, I have it on very good authority that you've been bandying Loudon's name about St Pauls while you've been searching for Mervyn Walker's missing wife.'

'So, that don't mean I killed the fella.'

'No, but I think it means that you know more than you are letting on. Correct?'

'I know I should keep my mout' shut until I gotta solicitor sitting next to me. That's what I know, Inspector.'

Eve smiled again, looked at the chair on the other side of his desk, then at me. 'Sit down, Joseph.' The inspector's beam widened, but only a fraction. 'Please.'

I stood for a moment, looked at the padded swivel chair next to me then back at the waiting policeman before deciding to park myself down. Eve smiled again. I liked him. I liked him in the same way a prisoner

156

develops an affinity with his warden. Robert Eve was the white man in charge. He was another well-fed, pompous official who was, in my opinion, the source of our problems. I wondered in that very moment if I shot up out of the chair and killed the man, would the problems of my people become that much lighter? Of course, the idea was ridiculous. Realising the impotence of my fantasy, I laughed.

'Something funny, Joseph?'

'Not you, sir.'

'Then let's get down to business, shall we?'

'It's your show.'

'It is, and that's why I'm hoping that you'll have no need for legal representation.'

'Is that right?'

'Yes.' Eve nodded to himself before continuing. 'I don't believe that you are involved in Loudon's death. I do however think that you have certain valuable skills and are appropriately placed within your community to assist the police in finding out who did. That's why I'm hoping we can come to a very specific mutual agreement, an accord without the need for further legal intervention, shall we say.'

'What kinda agreement you talking about, Inspector?'

The blood rose in the inspector's face. 'The kind that prevents you rotting in a cell for the next twenty-five years for a crime you didn't commit, and that helps this city find a killer and a missing woman.'

'Go on.'

'Tell me everything you know about Trista Walker's disappearance and Troy Loudon's death.'

What else could I do? I was being interviewed by a white police officer in a black man's hell. I did as the

157

man asked, and I started talking. I gave that copper everything I had; everything except me finding Troy Loudon's dead body in a rundown tenement building nor the colour photograph I'd discovered of the boxer and the mystery masked black man sat next to a naked woman; a woman I believed to be Trista.

After I'd finished Eve looked at the wall to the left of him, not addressing me directly when he spoke. 'And you've found all this information out in how long?'

''Bout forty-eight hours, or so.'

The inspector focused back in on me. 'That quickly? That really is excellent investigative work.'

'I suppose I got lucky,' I lied.

'Do you know what my men meet as soon as they set foot inside of St Pauls, Joseph?'

I shrugged again. 'No. Whadda they meet?'

'A great big wall of silence, that's what.' Eve looked at his watch. 'The kind of hush that dramatically slows down a police investigation, if you get my drift?'

'I get the picture.'

'Good.' The inspector stroked the lower half of his face and regarded me. I noticed a small dark blemish on the back of his left hand, immediately reminding me of Trista Walker's skin condition, vitiligo. 'It wouldn't be the first time you've assisted the Bristol constabulary, would it?'

'Me and the late Superintendent Fletcher . . . I suppose you could say that we had an understanding.'

Eve cleared his throat. 'I'd like you to extend that *understanding* to me, Joseph.'

'Would you?' My heart was going like a bird in flight.

'Yes.' The inspector's smug, superior attitude didn't waver. He was clearly enjoying having the upper hand. 'It is our belief that a member of the pastor's congregation alerted someone at a higher level within his church in regards to his wife's disappearance. We know that Mervyn Walker is a well-respected member of the Montpelier and St Pauls community. He's been a tireless campaigner for social welfare and reform in the region for many years and is very highly connected with both the Church of England and Catholic diocese here in Bristol.

'The man is also, much to my surprise, highly respected with the powers that be over at City Hall. Such top-level regard, and being a man so well respected in his local area is, I believe, the reason that the reverend was initially reluctant to approach the police in regards to his wife going missing and for employing your services.'

'In my experience,' I replied, 'ain't nothing knocks a man of God from his high station than the whiff of scandal or some kinda personal misfortune.'

'Exactly, and why I want you to hone all that 'experience' of yours to assist my men on your home turf.'

'You've gotta be kidding me?'

'I am not.' Eve turned his eyes directly on me. He started from my waist and worked his way up to my face. I knew what he saw; he was eyeballing a scared brother with no choice but to do what he asked me to.

'I want Mrs Walker found, alive and well, and I don't want to see a murderer go free either,' Eve said. 'No matter his colour. In this case, if it came out that a white man killed Troy Loudon or has anything to do with the Walker woman's disappearance, then I want the right person going on trial and I think you can help me achieve that. The people of Bristol should see that its police force means to maintain the balance

159

of justice, no matter the colour of a person's skin. Understand?'

Eve pulled out a white handkerchief and dabbed at his brow. 'Now, if you agree to this request and I let you go and then, say, come morning, I find out you have not been straight with me; that I find out you know more than you've already told me and that you decide to leave town and make a run for it, where does that leave me?' Eve pointed at his office door. 'What happens when Detective Sergeant Locke and young Mapp out there say, 'Well, sir, we brought the coon in for you. We had him bang to rights.' Whose arse would be in a sling then? You do see my point, Joseph. You do see that a man who either lied to me or went on the run would risk having the full might of the British law thrown at him once I'd caught up with him, yes?'

'Oh, yeah. I see your point.'

'Good. So, if you leave here now, I want to know that I have you firmly in my pocket, Joseph. That our mutual 'understanding' means you are all too aware that from now on, you'll be doing any further snooping for me. For Queen and Country. Got it?'

Logic is perhaps the most frightening talent that a man has. A man with logic can see death coming where a fly only sees a shadow. I saw death in Eve's reasoning.

'Yeah, I got it.'

Eve might have been smiling at me again, but I couldn't quite tell. His lips moved about an eighth of an inch and the flesh around those dark eyes seemed to ease up a bit. 'The city appreciates your goodwill, Joseph. It's too bad that your community doesn't have more citizens with such a sense of civic responsibility.'

160

Before I could come up with a fitting reply Eve was lifting the receiver of his phone and dialling a number.

'So, can I go?' I asked.

Detective Superintendent Eve didn't look up. He just waved the handkerchief out in front of him as if he was bidding farewell to a loved one from Temple Meads station.

I was up and out the door before either of us could take another breath.

21

There was a phone booth right there in the station, but I went six streets away from Bridewell to make my call.

'Loretta?'

'Yeah, Joseph. What's the matter?'

'I need you to go over to my place, check on Chloe, then take her back to yours.'

'Okay. Where de hell are you?'

'I'm in a call box on Wine Street.'

'Wine Street . . . You broke down o' sum'ting?'

'No. My motor's parked up right outside of home.'

'How so?'

'Let's just say I had myself a one-way lift into town earlier, care of the Avon and Somerset Constabulary.'

There was a long silence on the line. The only sounds, our breath and the occasional car passing by.

'Muthafuckas!'

★   ★   ★

I took a bus back to St Pauls.

It was a little after five, and the streets were filled with people: workers leaving the office for the day and shoppers wandering from one store to another. On the bus there was a mixture of young and old, young mothers and teenagers coming in late from school. Most of them were black folk.

There were women with eyes so deep that most men can never know them or the trouble or pain they held inside them. Women like Trista Walker. And there were children, like so many in St Pauls, with futures so bleak that it could make you cry just to hear them laugh. Because behind the music of their laughing you knew there was the rattle of chains. Shackles we wore for no crime; manacles that had been fitted on to us for so long that they melded to our bones. We all carry those cold bonds, but nobody can see them these days — not even us.

All the way home I thought about freedom coming for us at last. Emancipation escaping the West Indies, rolling across the waves of the Atlantic, our liberty swelling up along the Severn estuary and washing onto the streets of Bristol.

But, I asked myself, what about all those centuries in chains? Where do our fetters and cuffs go when you think that you're finally free?

I picked up my car and drove the short distance to Loretta's. Before I'd left Banner Road, I'd checked for any obvious police presence. My home and the street I lived on had been free from the prying eyes of the law, but I doubted it would be that way for long. From now on I'd be assuming that I'd have officers Locke and Mapp clinging on to my every move, like lions chewing on a gazelle's arse.

Aretha Franklin was belting out Otis Redding's song 'Respect' on the radio when I walked into Loretta's place. I found her pushing a mop in the kitchen. She was looking almost mean enough to dissuade me from approaching her. You learned where we were reared to avoid tough-looking women with sticks in their hands.

'Hey, Loretta.'

She kept pushing the mop. A couple of days ago

163

she was mad at me for looking for trouble, now she was furious 'cause she knew I'd found it.

'Don't go droppin' your jaw on de floor expectin' sympathy outta me.'

'Say what?'

Loretta rested her mop against the kitchen table. 'De Babylon, what want wid you?'

'Me at their beck and call, that's what.'

'An' you went and tole 'em to tek a runnin' jump, right.'

I shook my head. 'Nah. There's some inspector sitting in his office wants me wrapped round his little white finger doing his bidding or he's threatening to put me inside.'

It took her a moment to let her anger go. 'Why, man?' Loretta had a hatred for the police that stirred in her heart. And, you know, hatred has deep roots in a black woman's heart.

I told my friend everything, from getting myself mixed up in Pastor Mervyn Walker's plight to finding Troy Loudon dead and everything else in-between and after. When I'd finished Loretta said nothing. Instead, she took me in her arms. Our embrace would have hurt most people. It was strong and straining. She smelled of cleaning wax and freshly baked bread, of the sweat from hard work. 'You a damn fool, you 'naw dat, don't you, Joseph Ellington?' she said in a voice with no sympathy.

I nodded. 'I know.'

We looked at each other, our smiles little more than sorry grins.

'I'm gonna be out tonight and busy for a few more days; are you okay to keep an eye on Chloe for me for a while and for her to stay here with you?'

Loretta stood away from me, a glassy look creeping across her eyes. 'Ain't no need fo' you to ever be axin' me that kinda question. That chil' knows she always gotta place 'ere.'

I nodded my gratitude and looked round me. 'Where is she, anyhow?'

'Chirren sat glued to de TV in de front room.'

'Children? How many kids you got in there?'

I went to make my way back down the hall. Loretta yelled after me. 'T'ree. She in there wid Carnell Jnr an' some real good-lookin' young fella.' I felt my stomach take a sudden tumble. I opened the lounge door and was greeted with the howl of juvenile laughter and the blaring sound of music coming from the television. Chloe was sat on the sofa, Carnell Jnr one side of her and the boy I knew as 'D' on the other. An earthenware mixing bowl, filled to the brim with popcorn was sat on Chloe's lap, the two boys both had their mouths full of the stuff. My child gave me a hesitant, almost fearful look. I winked at her and received a relieved grin for my trouble.

'Hey, honey.'

Chloe looked at me with a hard gaze and then she mouthed, 'Are you okay, Papa?'

I winked at my girl, jawing the words, 'I sure am.'

'Good,' she grunted back at me. Chloe took a handful of popcorn out of the bowl, threw it into her mouth and began to chomp. I gestured my head at the two other teenagers cosied up next to my daughter.

'How's everybody doing?' I had to shout to be heard over the din.

'All cool, Joseph,' Carnell Jnr pitched in without taking his eyes off the TV screen.

I smiled at Dimitri.

165

'Good to see you, D,' I bellowed. Dimitri, a surprised look on his face, nodded his head in greeting at me then smiled. I made a mental note to myself that I owed the kid an apology and would give it to him as soon as I was living some kind of normal life again. I waved my hand at Chloe to get her full attention.

'I'm taking a trip over to see Vic tomorrow night.' Chloe's eyes lit up. 'And your uncle's asked you to tag along with me, that okay?'

Chloe's eyes widened further, a bright look of excitement breaking across her face. She wagged her head at me. 'Okay,' she said, then she blew me a kiss.

I closed the door, my ears grateful for the respite, my heart swelling with pride and love. When I turned to head into the kitchen, Loretta was stood blocking my way.

'I 'ear right, you goin' to see Vic?'

'Yeah, why?'

Loretta shook her head, a huffing sound catching deep at the back of her throat, and gave me one of her best dagger stares.

'Brother, you must really be in fuckin' trouble.'

166

22

Cheltenham Road was real red-light Bristol history. A crooked spine of three-storey sandstone buildings that ran for almost a mile into town. The road was broken and desolate during the day with its tired-looking laundrettes, kebab houses and mangy hotels. But at night the 'Chelt', as it was called, was a centre for late-night reggae houses and white rum so strong it could grow hairs on the glass it was served in. When a fella said he was heading for the Chelt he meant he was going to lose himself in a dark world of dub sounds, booze and women.

Dipper Council had told me that Troy Loudon had a regular floozy hanging off his arm most of the time, a woman called Queenie Blue. I took a guess that Loudon would have spent some of his nights hanging out at either a cat house, shebeen or a bar on the Chelt, and if he hung out down there, chances were Queenie did too.

The Locarno was in an alley halfway down the Chelt. Over the years, it had gone by many names — the Grog Shop, Barber's Ballroom and Tavern, the Rapture and Ada's — but these days the Locarno was known by its regulars as 'The King Dick'. The Dick was a legal bar, more or less, run by Mitzi Jerman. The bar staff were mainly scantily clad girls and the police found it proper to shut it down every once in a while.

The Locarno was long, narrow with a low ceiling and a stage dressed in fairy lights at the far end.

167

Down the left side of the room ran an oak bar tended by Dickie.

Dickie and Mitzi were a husband and wife team who had somehow drifted into the low-rent bar scene. The whites of Dickie's eyes were yellow and he stooped over his workstation like an old timer, but his arms were as strong as iron cables. He looked at me when I walked in and nodded at an empty table, but I walked up to the bar.

'Hey, Dickie.'

'JT.'

'Mount Gay,' I said.

The landlord turned away to grant my request.

The room was dark. The jukebox was playing the Paragons' 'The Tide Is High'. With no introduction, a buxom woman well into her sixties jiggled onstage. She wasn't wearing much and what she did have on was a shiny turquoise colour against high-brown skin. She carried a long white feather, which she waved along her breasts and thighs.

The patrons were sitting around half a dozen tables opposite the bar and close to the stage area. Fragile ribbons of smoke rose from dented aluminium ashtrays. A waitress moved petulantly from table to table in the hope of keeping Dickie busy at the bar, but from where I was standing it looked like few folks were interested in ordering more than the one shot or half-pint that they already had sat in front of them.

This had to be the early crowd. Not huge tippers or drinkers, the kind of pre-midnight revellers who were a warm-up act for the customers, mostly men, who rolled in later.

Mitzi sat right up close to the stage, sipping at a tall glass filled with bright red liquor. Mitzi always claimed that none of the girls working here ever did anything that they didn't want to, but both Loretta and I had known girls who'd been given the push because a punter had complained to Dickie that they'd been 'unwelcoming'.

I took my rum and moved to where the action was happening over at the stage.

'Joseph Ellington!' Mitzi roared.

I took her hand and pecked at her clammy cheek. 'Mitzi.'

In a fit of improvisation, the woman with the feather moved downstage and brushed the back of my neck with her tatty plume.

'Sid 'own, baby.' Mitzi pulled an empty chair away from a table where an old man had been resting his head in his hands. I looked around.

'Still kinda slow, huh?' I asked.

Mitzi pawed at me with a thick, red-nailed hand. 'Still early, JT. Old Pauline just do her lil' ting out there to git the stage ready for the real action later.'

I smiled and finished my drink. Mitzi lit up a Park Drive, inhaled deeply then waved over to Dickie to bring me another.

Sat there, I didn't have a plan. I wasn't a cop, even though I was now doing their dirty work for them. Maybe I'd ask about Queenie Blue. Maybe not; it was all down to how much Mitzi felt like talking. Dickie rolled up behind me and dropped my tot of rum down on the table, collected up the empty glass and headed back for his bar without uttering a word. Mitzi looked at me, a hint of suspicion in her eyes.

'So, what you doin' in 'ere, Joseph? Been a long time since you set foot inta de King Dick.'

169

'Needed to get myself a drink,' I said non-committedly, casting my eyes at the stage then back at Mitzi.

'Perhaps you wanna play 'round too? I got girls 'ere would love to take a bite outta you.' Mitzi's business wasn't a subtle one.

'Nah.' I shook my head and smiled. 'But while I got you with me, I just wanted to ask you a question.'

'Okay, baby.' The landlady pulled on her smoke and blew grey fumes into the air. 'But you need anything, you 'naw where to come. Gettin' people together is my bid'ness.'

'Business good?'

Mitzi nodded. She watched two men walk through the door. Dickie was looking too. He may not have said much but he could pour liquor and look at the same time.

I snapped my fingers trying to remember something I was struggling to recall. 'You ever see Queenie Blue in here?'

'That fuckin' tramp!' she said in machine-gun chatter.

'Sounds like she's not welcome.'

'Listen, Queen Blue is a frowsy skank. She come in 'ere tryin' fo' a job. I tole her to git her scrawny arse the hell outta my place. I 'naw she be out in half a dozen joints along this damn road any night an' then out on de corner if that don't work.'

I nodded. Sipped. 'You hear about her boyfriend, Troy Loudon.'

Mitzi jutted her chin out. 'I 'eard, alright. Everybody talkin' 'bout it. He may have been Queenie's squeeze fo' a time, but he was her damn pimp fo' most of it. Word is another John wanted her too, an' that

170

fella had more muscle than Loudon. Whatever 'appen to that boy, most folk round 'ere will be sayin' he had it comin' to 'im. If you got any sense, fella, you'll stay well clear o' the likes o' Queenie Blue.'

I let her wisdom settle for a moment, then said, 'I better get going.'

When I stood up, I felt the room sway a little as if I were on board a ship in rough seas.

'See ya.'

'Bye, Joseph.' Mitzi smiled. 'You take care, sweetheart.'

I paid Dickie on the way out and didn't look back at the misery that was slowly unfolding at the tables and on stage.

In the alley outside I leaned against the wall of the bar, breathing in a lungful of the cold night air. I stayed pitched on the Locarno's brickwork until my insides began to feel cleansed of the muck I'd just been inhaling. Dante's Inferno had nine circles of hell. Mitzi's place could have easily competed for tenth place.

Something told me I'd be sucking in a lot more filth before the night was over.

23

There were many bars and clubs on and around the Chelt. I wouldn't have been able to walk into all of them in one night, but I didn't have to because I was looking for a special type of joint. A place like the Locarno that catered to love- and sex-starved men, and sometimes women. A place that offered more than whisky and reggae. There were just a half dozen places on Cheltenham Road that fitted those kinda needs.

There was Vicki's, a strip house run by Bennie 'Red Line' Anderson, a former Trinidadian wrestler whose motto pinned on a plastic plate over the front door of the bar proudly announced, 'My Girls Are Cleaner Than Lux!' Then there was Martell's, a pick-up bar where the 'staff' had a couple of drinks lined up for their 'customers' before heading out to a flat, an alley or a no-questions-asked hotel.

The Hi-Ho Lounge and the Black Penny were one step down on the evolutionary ladder. These were pubs-cum-knocking shops where the criminal fraternity liked to hang out. Gamblers and thugs. Men who had done long stretches inside. Both these pubs had upstairs rooms where some off-the-book quack would turn up to patch a gunshot or knife wound. Where ambulance-chasing solicitors met clients, who preferred not to be seen out in daylight. And where girls got on their knees for five minutes and five quid, for a man who may well have been kept at Her Majesty's Pleasure and not seen a woman in five years.

I'd been away from the Bristol bar scene for years, so most people were still happy to see me stick my head through a door. They were happy to talk. I picked up a gem in the Hi-Ho from Kermit Sullivan, a low-life pimp and high-grade drunk who spent more time wasted than he did cashing in on the local red-light scene. Kermit had the biggest neck I have ever seen on a man. It was as wide as his jowls, his tie and collar pin looked like formal dress on a pig. He chewed gum and drank beer at the same time when he spoke to me.

'Yeah, I 'eard 'bout poor ole Troy. Damn shame, man.' Kermit was sat at a table outside of the pub. He wore a white polyester suit and cream loafers, his hair a knotted tangle of grey curls, his shoulders stooped with bone loss, his face netted with the lines of a chain smoker. 'You 'naw, his woman, Queenie? She done found him dead.'

I finally found the full two-pound nugget when I ran into an old acquaintance at the Black Penny. Ezzard was a good friend of Vic's when they were younger. He was only perhaps five foot five, but he had the shoulders of a heavyweight. He'd been pie-eyed pissed in a pub in the centre of Bristol years back and, as the story goes, Ezzard wanted 'one for the road'. The landlord had told Ezzard to sling his hook, and Ezzard said: 'One more drink, mistah.'

That's when the six-foot-six landlord made a grave mistake. He put his hands on Ezzard, and Ezzard put him down with a single blow. The landlord was dead before he hit the floor. Ezzard had done thirteen years straight for manslaughter. If the landlord had been black, Ezzard would have done half that time.

'JT,' Ezzard said. He was hunched over a table at

the back of the bar, his big hands wrapped around a pint glass, half-filled with stout.

'Ezzard, so, you're out at last, man.'

'Not fo' long,' he said, nodding in a way that made him seem like some kind of wise old owl.

'You paid your dues, Ezzard. Police can't take you back inside unless you give 'em cause to.' I pulled a chair up to his lonely table.

'Fuckin' Babylon.'

Ezzard was drunk and was known to be loose in the tongue. I knew that if I let him rattle on a while, I might strike it lucky. I also knew that if I stuck around, I'd probably hear things that I didn't want to hear. Ugly stuff that would set my teeth on edge. I was half-drunk myself and rather than wanting more booze I was craving my bed and the warmth of a blanket over my shoulders.

'Fuckin' police al'ways on my back. Knockin' me gate door all times o' de day an' night. Harrassin' me. Jus' a bunch o' bastards.'

The glass cracked in Ezzard's mighty grip. Beer mixed with the man's blood ran over the table and on to the floor. I handed Ezzard my handkerchief and collected a towel from the bar to soak up the mess, then ordered him another drink. I returned with Ezzard's stout and placed the glass in front of him. The man looked up at me with a depth of gratitude.

'T'anks, JT. You a friend, man. A true friend.'

Vic always used to say to me, 'Jus' remember when you lookin' to find sum'ting out . . . you can buy a drunk's friendship wid a handful o' feathers an' a sprinkle o' salt.'

He was damn right.

I leaned across and patted Ezzard's rocky shoulder

across the table. 'I'm tryin' to find something out.'

'Yeah . . . wha's dat?'

'You knew Troy Loudon, right?'

'De dead boy, I jus' 'ear 'bout?'

'Yeah, that's right. Loudon, the boxer.'

'Uh-huh, yeah I knew dat young fool.' I watched the blood soaking into my handkerchief.

'Hold that rag tight, Ezzard. You bleeding a lot, there.'

Ezzard gazed down at his hand and seemed surprised to see the bloody cloth. He clenched his hand into a fist and the handkerchief disappeared into his palm.

'Whaddya wanna 'naw 'bout Loudon?'

'It ain't Troy I'm interested in, it's the girl he hung around with, Queenie Blue.'

Ezzard nodded his head slowly, his eyes rolling in his head as he did. 'Queenie sum bad bitch,' he whispered. His breath was so rank that I had to swallow twice before speaking.

'You know where she hangs out?'

Ezzard peered into my face. He took a deep breath and leaned back. 'I don't wanna cause you no pain, JT. Dat woman tear your heart out, man.'

'No pain to me, Ezzard. You know where this Blue woman is, then you'd be doing me a big favour in telling me.'

Ezzard's face broke into an unfriendly grimace. 'I tink she down on Smokey Row.'

I tried to look like I was bothered by what he was telling me. When somebody said 'Smokey Row' they meant a whorehouse run by Eddie 'Happy' Riddle and his wife, Connie.

'Thank you, Ezzard,' I said as solemnly as I could. I

175

took a note out of my wallet, folded it in half and slid it across to the old man. 'Get yourself a pint for your trouble.' I got up and backed away from the table.

Ezzard snatched the note up inside his crimson hand. 'You don't need to do dat, JT.' He followed me with his eyes. I smiled and decided to let him keep the handkerchief, too. Maybe in the morning when he looked at the bloodstained rag, he'd remember who had given it to him but little else about our meeting.

As I left, I half expected someone to grab me, to interrogate me, to threaten my life, but no one even noticed. I slipped through the throng, no more remarkable than a shadow.

24

It's not a long way from Cheltenham Road to the Bishopston suburbs.

It's the same city, but a darkness descends as you progress northwards. You pass from black and brown realities to the beginning of white dreams. A mile and a half to cover from one part of town to the next. But distance was the least of it. It was another world where I was going. I felt drunk and shouldn't have been behind the wheel of a car. The only reason I didn't have an accident going the short distance I travelled was because I didn't think about driving and somehow steered from instinct.

The Smokey Row was a three-storey featureless pile that sat on the corner of Kings Drive and Bath Road. There was no sign or promise on the tar-coloured door that got you inside the brothel, and if you didn't know what lay on the other side, you'd just walk on by. I knocked and a slit in the door slid open above my head. Yellowy eyes anchored in dark flesh glared at me, and then the black door opened.

Seated on a tall stool was Abe Bolden — twenty-two stone and then some extra pounds of muscle, hard fat and nasty intentions. His skin was only a little lighter than mine and the baseball bat in his hand was in lieu of the .38 tucked in the waistband of his trousers hidden underneath his jacket. Abe's shiny, silver Moss Brothers suit had been stolen to order straight off the peg. The red tie around his neck was dragged so far down his chest that the knot was almost in line with his belly button.

'If it ain't Joseph Ellington. The Jah's kin,' he said aloud, as a servant to royalty might announce an arrival at a monarch's ball.

There were maybe a dozen patrons in the illegal bar that separated the incoming customers downstairs from the brothel business above. Thomas 'Tommy-A' Charles Anderson was standing behind the bar. His darkness, strength and proportions were mythic. He was both ugly and handsome. Tight-lipped with heavy-lidded eyes that told you all you needed to know. I walked up to where he was drying a glass and took a seat.

'What's wrong wid you?' he chided.

'I'm sitting in this place, ain't I?'

There was both evil and forgiveness in the man's grin. He took a bottle with no label from under the mahogany bar and poured a long drink in a slender glass that he then set before me. I looked at the high-proof white rum a moment; a spirit I was sure had been illegally supplied by Vic's organisation, and swivelled around to take in the view. The Smokey Row's clients were mostly around my age. Black and white, and mainly all men. All of them hardened by lives of crime, drink, gambling or drugs. I truly felt out of my depth, and yet strangely at home.

'You gonna take a drink o' that liquor?' Tommy-A asked me.

'Don't know yet. I've just about had my fill of booze tonight. Was hoping for something that would ease my weary bones rather than dull my mind any more than it already is.'

Tommy-A laughed and pointed at a metal door on the other side of the room. 'You want easing, you best go axe Lulu.' I nodded my gratitude and got to my feet. 'Jus' press the lion's mout',' said the barman.

I made my way across to the other side of the room. There was a small man, the colour of buffed bronze, sitting at a table about two feet from the door. He was maybe in his sixties and nursing a beer the same way that Ezzard Randolph had been. The old fella looked at me as I approached, quickly shifting his gaze towards the spirit I'd just left. 'You gonna drink that hooch?' he asked.

I shook my head. 'No, man. Help yourself.'

The man got up out of his seat and headed for the bar. I watched him hop up on the stool I'd been sat at and knock back the special bootlegged brew that John kept for his supposedly 'special customers'. I returned my attention to the iron entry and pushed the bell button in the centre of the roaring lion's mouth.

A mule-faced woman answered. She was aged any-where between forty and sixty-five and didn't look pleased to see me. Her fake platinum-blonde hair cas-caded onto her black shoulders. Her face looked tired, a bruise above her left eye was barely masked behind cheap foundation and her eyes were the colour and sheen of wet sludge. I caught sight of her small hands, which she held before her gold satin bathrobe, tiny fingers that still looked as if they could crush stones.

'Lulu?' I said. I had a stupid grin on my face. I could see it in the bronze-framed mirror that dom-inated the wall at the woman's back. Lulu peered at me blankly. I grinned on.

'What you want?' she asked without a hint of warmth or charm.

'Was looking for some company an' perhaps another drink.'

179

'You smell like you already had enuff drink. Doubt you could tek on a real woman.'

'Business so good you turning it away for Eddie Riddle?'

Lulu pushed at a loose lock of her wig and the thing fell to one side of her head. 'Ain't nuthin' dat good. I jus' don't trust you, man. I know who you are. Heard all kindsa tings 'bout you.'

'You know me so well, you'll know you I'm related to the Jah, right?'

Lulu's hard face softened, but her attitude didn't. 'What you want? I ain't axin' no more.'

I tried to make my smile a little more sincere by looking at my own eyes in the mirror. 'Like I said, I want a drink and some companionship, and in the same room.'

'Why come 'ere?'

'I've been told this is the place to meet up with Queenie Blue.'

Lulu's eyes turned to stone. 'Yeah? Well, Queenie ain't gonna wanna fuck some half-cut ole peeper like you.'

I stuck my hand in my hip pocket and produced a folded wad of bank notes. Twenties and tens. I rubbed the cash between my fingers. 'Why don't you go ask Eddie?' Lulu's mug could have deterred a rhino from charging, but she knew better than to turn away hard cash. She scowled at me for another thirty seconds or so, but I could tell that her eyes were never far from the money in my hand.

'You betta come on t'ru.'

We went down a hall that was papered with purple and grey velvet flock. There were a series of dark-stained, waist-high coffee tables every few feet with clean metal ashtrays and glass dishes with gold foil-wrapped chocolates in them. It led to a largish room with deep-red sofas along each cream wall. There were lamps here and there, all of them turned on, the 25-watt bulbs casting very little light across the already dingy foyer.

'Wait 'ere,' Lulu snapped, tapping her wig. She exited from a door on the opposite side of the room.

I wasn't kept waiting long.

Eddie 'Happy' Riddle came through the same door Lulu had. He got his unusual moniker on account of the fact that he rarely, if ever, broke out a smile. He had a full head of long black hair, braided close to his scalp, and wore an old-fashioned, three-button black suit with a starched white shirt and a silken navy-blue tie. His black leather shoes shone in the same way that his raven-like eyes did; the look they gave me bordered on hatred.

'Happy,' I said.

Riddle curled a lip and flared one nostril. 'This a rare surprise, Mistah Ellington.'

I didn't hold out my hand and he kept his claws in his pockets.

'Have a seat.' Happy pointed at one of the sofas. 'How's the Jah doin'?'

'Vic's real good, thanks.'

I sat and Happy stood before me. His skin was crinkled and as dark as bitumen. He blinked and I crossed my legs. Somewhere outside I heard a police siren.

'What you want 'ere, Mistah Ellington?' He made the question bluntly straightforward.

'A woman,' I said in kind.

Happy's smiling lips quivered. 'I don't tink so.'

181

He blinked again. I uncrossed my legs and I reached for the wad of bank notes in my back pocket. I thumbed five crisp notes out of the bundle and held them out in front of me. 'Queenie Blue.'

I saw Happy wince, his misgivings clearly etched across his lined face, an off-white incisor biting at the corner of his bottom lip. After what seemed like an eternity of internal deliberation the pimp snatched the cash from my fingers. He brought one bill right up to his face and squinted.

'That dough resting in your hip pocket, better than a visit from the Jah, right?' I said.

Happy thought of such a terrible prospect for all of a second and nodded. He pocketed the cash then went back the way he'd come.

A few minutes later Lulu returned. 'Com' on,' she barked.

I followed her through the doors and up a single flight of stairs, her gold gown barely hiding her ample modesty. We went down a hallway that looked like it belonged inside the cheapest of motels. There were doors on each side with brass numbers on them and Lulu opened door 9 and ushered me inside, then closed it behind me.

A small black woman walked out of the shadows and stood close to the dull glare of a lamp on a small table next to a single bed.

'How you wan' it?' she asked.

'I want to talk.' I don't think I stuttered, but the woman smiled as if I had.

'What you wanna talk 'bout?' One of her front teeth was solid gold. Her chest, and both arms and hands, were decorated in an ornate series of tattoos.

'You Queenie Blue?'

182

'Come on.' She pointed at the bed. 'Sit 'own.'

We sat side by side with her thigh against my trouser leg.

'You Queenie?' I asked again.

'Uh-huh.'

'I wanna know about Troy Loudon.'

I saw Queenie's eyes harden. 'He's dead.'

'I know that. I heard you found his body?'

'Yeah. Whadda 'bout it?'

'Who'd you think would want Troy dead?'

Queenie laughed. ''Bout half o' Bristol.'

'Anybody specifically?'

Queenie sat back with her hands propping up her body from behind. 'You workin' fo' de Babylon? 'Cause de pigs already came to me place an' I tole 'em I didn't 'naw nuthin'.'

'I just wanna find out what happened to him, that's all.'

'Why you axin' 'bout Troy? I don't evah remember seein' you round when he was livin'.'

'I'm looking for a woman that I think Troy knew.'

Queenie's eyes glassed over and her shoulders rose. 'What woman?'

I took out Pastor Walker's photograph of his wife and showed it to Queenie. 'You know her?'

'Mebbe.'

'What can you tell me about her?'

'Bitch likes to fool 'bout. Likes to git her claws inta a brother an' mess wid 'is head.'

'She ever try diggin' her talons into Troy in the past?'

Queenie laughed, shaking her head. 'Celestine knew betta than to be touchin' ma man.'

'You have any idea where I can find her?'

183

'Naw.' Queenie smiled. 'Mebbe de cemetery. Celestine crazy 'bout dead tings. She a high-type *mambo*, like to be close to dem dat 'ave passed on. Dat woman only deal in de blackest o' magic.'

'The woman you call Celestine has gone missing. I've been asked by her husband to try and find her. You know any place that she might be?'

Queenie stroked at her mat of tangled hair. 'Husband betta off not 'nawin' where his woman gone. Like I say, Celestine fah real Obeah, like me. She says, jus' like a mama was. You ain't gonna find Celestine she don't wan' findin'. You might as well be searchin' fo' a duppy in dey night. I don't 'naw where de bitch is. Don't wanna 'naw either. Witch like Celestine need leavin' alone, if you 'naw what good fo' you.'

'How about this fella in the mask?' I reached into my jacket pocket again and took out the Kodak snapshot I'd found in Loudon's gym bag. 'You ever see this guy hanging around with Troy?'

Queenie peered at the photograph. She bit at her lip, tilted forward to shake her head, and I realised that, like Lulu's, Queenie Blue's hair was a wig. 'Uh-huh, that's Zorro.'

'Very funny.'

'Oh, brother, you de comedian, axin' all dese questions. Happy says I betta watch out 'bout you. Says you bad news an' I jus' betta fuck you an' keep my mout' shut.'

Three raps rattled the door. 'Five minutes!' a man's voice said. It wasn't Happy's.

'You gotta give 'im anutha twenty-five if you wanna stay in 'ere wid me.'

'How come? I just paid Happy a hundred for the pleasure of your company.'

'The boys runnin' the landing only give you ten minutes an' they knock after five to, you know, hurry you up. But you pay anutha twenty-five to 'em they leave you alone fo' ten minutes extra.'

I gave Queenie the money.

She ran out into the hall without putting on a stich.

Alone in the room I considered going out the window. Something didn't feel right. I knew I'd boxed myself in. There was no place to run if things turned tricky. Maybe Queenie Blue was out there right now telling Happy or 'the boys' what I'd just asked her and they'd come gunning for me. The booze inside of me was wearing off and I wasn't feeling much like getting into a scrap with Eddie Riddle's hired help.

The door opened and Queenie came back with a bottle of rum, two glasses and enough charm to fill the rooms either side of us. She was grinning. 'One o' de girls said we could 'ave a slug.' She poured the two glasses full and settled on the bed beside me, her legs open wide. I was eager to find out what Blue knew and make tracks as fast as I could. I took a swig of the rum she'd given me and held up the photograph of Loudon, Trista and the masked man.

'The man wearing the Mardi Gras get-up. You have any idea who he might be?'

Queenie opened her legs wider. 'You wanna fuck me or not?'

I inched back across the mattress and stabbed a finger at the photograph in my hand. 'I wanna know who the fella in this picture is.'

Queenie Blue sank the contents of her glass. She made a face like she'd just tasted something sour and began to pour a refill.

'You axin' de wrong girl.'

The door got hit with another trio of heavy thuds. 'Move your arse, man,' said the same voice, this time more impatient. More aggressive. I got off the bed, put my glass on the bedside table and the photographs into my jacket pocket and backed away across the room. Queenie Blue's eyes widened. She bit at her knuckle and frowned, inching herself back against the headboard of the bed.

I held my finger to my lips. 'Then who should I be asking?'

Queenie's amused look contained more than a trace of scorn. 'Try quizzin' de husband who sent you on dis fool's errand. Man o' God like 'im, he bound to 'ave all de right answers fo' you,' she whispered.

I turned, walked across the room, my hand at the brass door handle. Blue murmured at me in a hushed tone.

'When you see de pastor, tell 'im dey Heartman waitin' fo' him. He'll 'naw what you mean.'

When I walked out into the hallway, a man was standing at the foot of the stairs. He wore a pin-striped suit, the jacket open to reveal an off-white shirt that was unbuttoned to almost the waist. I saw his eyes turn into me, focusing in the dim light, his hardened stare tightening. He brushed his hands together and slowly began to walk towards me.

'You finished grilling Queenie?' he hissed. I saw the expression change in his eyes; the way green water can suddenly cloud with a groundswell. 'Fun's over, mistah.'

I was drunk, but not so drunk I didn't know that my reflexes were shot. I loosened my shoulders, remained quiet, gathering all of my strength for one move.

'Happy wants to know why you givin' one o' his

186

best girls the third degree?' He began to pace towards me, raising his eyes a little to glance over my shoulder as he was gaining speed.

I heard the floorboard behind me give, the creak it made barely audible. That was enough warning for me to avoid the leather cosh aimed at my head. I moved to the right long enough to see a squat black man stumble behind the force of his thrust. I let him fall and threw a punch that landed on the side of the running man's jaw. He fell hard against the wall then dropped in a heap.

Little men, on the whole, are more agile than larger ones. The smaller guy with the blackjack was already on his feet and swinging his sap. I shifted to my left enough not to take the full brunt of the blow, but I felt it graze my head above my right ear. The impact felt much like I'd been hit by a lorry. I reeled towards one of the room doors, my eyes watering, bright colours erupting across my vision; red dots cut through by yellow shards and peppered with black holes.

I aimed my fist for the place I'd last seen the little man's face. Felt my fist impact against flesh and bone. I kept punching until there was no more skin or cartilage to beat. Snatching up the cosh at my feet, I stumbled along the hall and down the stairs. I didn't look back nor did I say a word. When I walked out into the foyer, the Smokey's doorman, Abe Bolden, was stood at the entrance to the bar blocking my way. He beamed at me then smoothed the top of his lip with his fingers. Those two fleeting movements gave me just enough time to hide my hand with the sap in it behind the back of my thigh.

'We really gotta do this, Abe?' I asked.

Bolden shrugged his huge shoulders. 'Boss, he

don't like nosy niggahs, Joseph.'

Adrenalin electrified my senses. I saw everything around me with an exaggerated clarity known only to madmen and fanatics. I took a step forward and watched Bolden run at me like a charging bull. I darted to my right as he was about to career into me, springing up and around on the balls of my feet and raising the cosh as I lifted myself into the air. The bouncer by that time knew it was too late, his left arm already rising to shield his head. I slammed the blackjack down across the big man's face as he was about to try and take a solid swing at me. The cosh made contact with the top of his skull, raked down across his left eye and then the bridge of his nose. Bolden's legs gave way and he clattered against the empty table and chair by the stair door, one hand cupped to his face, the blood roaring between his fingers. I knew if he managed to get to his feet, I'd be heading for my grave. I darted forward and kicked the doorman once in the ribs then, as he sank forward again, stamped my foot down on his right hand. I felt his fingers snapping through the heel of my shoe. The big man screamed, rolling over onto his back, his body trembling.

The room was silent. Tommy-A the barman, the hookers, the Johns, the handful of waitresses in their pink shorts and cut-off black blouses all stood like statues in the floating layers of cigarette and ganja smoke.

I heard someone dial a telephone. I went out the door into the night air counting heartbeats and breathing as slowly as I could.

25

I was startled awake by a raspy chatter in the early dawn. Two magpies were scrabbling in a thin film of dew that had formed on the boot of my car. I'd been sleeping, sitting behind the steering wheel. My shoulders and back were stiff, my hands bruised and swollen and my head throbbed from the crack it had received from one of Happy Riddle's cosh-wielding goons.

The magpies were stood so close to each other that their tails were touching. They were staring off in different directions, watching each other's back. I was starting to wish that I had some kind of brother-in-arms to rely on. All I'd ever had was Vic, and standing side by side with him was like pressing up against the devil himself. I knew now that in taking on Mervyn Walker's shifty errand I'd opened up a real can of worms. I was in way over my head, and with little to show for all my efforts. In less than a week, I'd trawled across half of Bristol, been in two fist fights, wandered the city's red-light district, spoken to drunks, pugilists, grasses and whores, and made an enemy of a local pimp and, worse still, the city police. Now, I was about to once again pal up with Satan himself. Seeking out my cousin's help was a last resort. Vic would know that I'd have had to have hit rock bottom to seek out either his favour or protection.

Vic was the ghoulish tricker of West Indian folklore. He was the Jah. God-raging. The bane of fellow gangsters and police officers alike. He was the nemesis of authority figures and a hostile opponent to anyone who sought power over others; a one-man demolition derby who had murdered both criminals and those who upheld the forces of law and order. Many likened him to a mythical creature. A revenant of revenge and retribution. His enemies were many: fellow gangland heads, vindictive bent coppers and judges who wanted him taken off the board. Over the years he'd been shanked, shot and part blinded. But all the aforementioned were amateurs when it came to hurting Victor Ellington. Vic's most dangerous adversary lived in his own breast.

When I finally threw off my idle musings about my wayward cousin and roused from my seat, one of the magpies took off immediately. But the other one cocked his eye at me, looking me up and down. His hard dull eye sizing me up and classifying me a fool.

Even getting out of the car and slamming the door didn't rid me of my black and white angel. He just hopped to the side to keep his eye on my disgusting display of human sloth and called out to his cowardly partner as I relieved myself against the trunk of a tree. He opened his beak and screeched when I rested against the wing of my car and looked out across the North Somerset countryside and the city of Bristol.

I hadn't driven up to Dundry Hill for many years and I was damned if I knew why, in the small hours of the morning, half-cut, I'd decided to head out of town and pull up in a layby, next to a field in the middle of nowhere and bed down in my car for the night. The hill visually dominates the surrounding areas and from its highest point, on a clear day, you can see Clifton Suspension Bridge, the housing estates of south Bristol to the north and the farmland and villages of the Chew Valley to the south.

Dundry was a special place. My very first experience of being in the English countryside, away from the bustle and noise of the city, was coming up to the hill. The alderman, Earl Linney, had arranged for me to meet him at its peak one cold afternoon in the winter of 1965, where he'd spoken of the bombing of Bristol by the German Luftwaffe during the Second World War, and gone on to charm me with his wisdom while embroiling me in a very different type of destruction and downfall, partially of his own making. Years later, Ruth and I would drive up to Dundry with Chloe to walk and picnic. Ruth loved the serene escape that the rolling hills offered. Most summers we'd come up to lose ourselves down winding country lanes or wander for miles across lush fields. Those idyllic, sun- and laughter-filled days now seemed distant and cold.

I lowered myself behind the steering wheel again and gawked at myself in the rear-view mirror. Staring back at me was a man I barely recognised. Tired and beaten up. I could see what I thought to be a haunted look in my eyes, not unlike the thousand-yard stare that soldiers bring back from places no one should ever have to revisit. As I turned my face from the mirror, I could have sworn I heard Ruth's voice in my ear whispering the words: 'Take that sour look off your face and give me a smile.'

Behind me, the magpie cackled. I turned and the bird remained stock still. 'What you lookin' at?' He answered by jumping off the hood and pecking at a stone on the ground.

As I sat looking at my new-found feathered friend, I smelled what those two birds must have smelled: it was the cloying odour of Queenie Blue's strong perfume mixing with the lingering foul scent of other men's sex, both of which had permeated my clothes as well as the iodine twang of the dried blood that was caked to my fingers and the backs of my hands. The magpie stared up at me from the dirt as if to say: 'Brother, you stink like you bin in a whorehouse.'

When I started the engine, the bird finally took off. I saw him and his buddy gliding over the woody escarpment behind me as I drove away towards the spiralling chaos that was swiftly taking over my once harmonious life.

26

Most people think of violence as an abstraction. It never is. It's always ugly, it always demeans and dehumanises, it always shocks and reels, and leaves its witnesses sick and shaken. It's meant to do all these things.

My fight with Abe Bolden and Eddie Riddle's men had left me feeling empty, washed-out inside, my skin tight and clammy, my eyes jittering with refracted light that seemed to have no source. Rather than just the rum I downed last night, I felt like I had been drinking neat moonshine for three days straight. Locking horns with Riddle's cronies had disconnected me from the peace and tranquillity that I depended upon with the religious love of an acolyte. Apart from some bruising on my hands, shoulder and scalp, there was no real physical pain to speak of. All the bad stuff I was feeling inside me was due to my recent violent behaviour. My skin felt like ants were crawling across it. Broken razor blades were twisting inside my conscience; an emotional numbness was washing over me; a kind of visceral paralysis that only occurs when decent folk resort to the lowest form of human communication.

It was a little after nine by the time I got home, and I felt exhausted. The air was heavy and cool and I smelled the sulphurous twang in the light breeze that blew over from the docks. Once inside, I filled a glass with warm water and salt and drank it to make myself throw up. Afterwards, I ate a handful of aspirin and multivitamins, then stripped out of my clothes and threw them in the laundry basket. I took a shave and showered in hot water until there was none left in the tank, then I kept my head under the cold water for another five minutes.

Dried and smelling sweeter, I put on a fresh pair of trousers and a clean blue shirt. I then went downstairs to the kitchen and downed two glasses of orange juice before making myself a bowl of All-Bran with banana and sitting at the table alone with my thoughts.

For years, when I was working as a not-so-private investigator, I'd met more than my fair share of people struggling to cope with the hardships life had thrown at them. I'd heard the well-worn phrases, the 'need for discretion', and 'no wish to involve the authorities in my affairs' and 'complete respect for confidentiality', et cetera. That was the thing about my old job, people were always telling you how to conduct their case, almost as if they didn't quite trust you, almost as if you were going to have to improve your standards in order to work for them. Mervyn Walker had behaved in the same crabby manner when he'd asked me to help him. I'd been stupid enough to lend him a hand and now I was paying for my foolish lack of judgement.

As a kid, reading my battered copies of the American comic strip Dick Tracy, I used to think that a detective was the daring hero, solving crimes in an hour, putting the bad guys behind bars and having an attractive blonde sweetheart like Tess Trueheart hanging off your coat sleeve for company.

That was never going to be me.

No, I was the man who helped put a blood-stained white shirt on a naked man and drive him to the infirmary after his wife has stabbed him in the back after a bust-up over an infidelity. I was the fella who stood between the loan shark sniffing for his hiked-up weekly payment and the poor fool he was happily swindling. I was the guy with the sack of corn, the goose and the fox trying to get across the river in the boat that could only take two passengers.

Today, I'm back juggling another man's mess, trying to stay afloat doing the kind of questionable work I'd sworn never to undertake again.

Now the police had their hooks into me, I couldn't quit the job, but I could pretend that I wasn't on it, at least for a few hours. I made a call to my work colleague, Harriet Tyler, over at the Friends Association, made my apologies and informed her that the unexpected personal stuff that had kept me away from my work at the advice centre was going to be a little more protracted than I'd expected and that I would not be in for the remainder of the week. Harriet was, as ever, kindly and sympathetic.

'You sure there's nuthin' I can duh to help, son?'

'I'm fine, Miss Harriet.' I heard the old woman sigh on the other end of the line. 'But thanks for thinking of me,' I added.

'Sum'time, Joseph, dealin' wid other folk's problems, well dey ain't an easy burden to bear. You remember dat.'

Hearing the front door knocking was a relief, a lifeline thrown out to me from an unknowing stranger. Rather than have to expand on my own woes I made the excuse to Harriet that someone was at my door and I had to go. I was about to say goodbye but the line had already cut before I'd had chance to utter my farewell.

The man standing on my front porch was a bright

195

young thing for sure, and with some heft about him. While he had the poise of a toff, his stony eyes and hard jawline spoke of the streets, replete with hand-cuffs, riot canes and water cannons.

'Mr Ellington?'

'Uh-huh.'

He produced a ratty, worn-out leather wallet dis-playing a police identity card complete with fetching mugshot.

'Richard Peace.' I was happy that he didn't offer to shake hands. 'Detective Superintendent Eve asked me to drop by.'

'Well,' I said reluctantly, 'come on in, I guess.'

I led the big man into the living room and offered him a seat on the sofa. I took the armchair. My own simple throne in this tiny kingdom of mine.

'What can I do for you, Mr Peace?'

'I thought I'd introduce myself.'

'Yeah, what for?'

'Superintendent Eve thought it advisable that there was an official representative to liaise between your-self and his squad.'

'You a copper, right?' Richard Peace's suit was pure Savile Row. Stiff lapels and only two buttons. Dark grey in colour, crease in the trousers, almost a uni-form.

'Let's just say I work across a number of important legal areas for both Bristol City Council and the Avon and Somerset constabulary.'

'What does that mean exactly, Mr Peace?'

'It means from now on I'm your official police con-tact with Superintendent Eve.' Peace reached into his breast pocket and came out with a thin brown enve-lope. He handed the packet over to me. 'You'll find

196

details of all the phone numbers you can get me on. Office, home and answering service. Call me if you have anything to report or update.'

'Eve said I was to report to him.'

Swaying back again, Peace said: 'The Superintendent is running the investigation officially, and will, of course, be kept fully appraised. We'd just like to be kept in the loop as well.'

'Whose we?'

'Interested parties, Mr Ellington.' He crossed his legs.

'You perhaps wanna expand on who these specific parties might be?'

Peace looked surprised for a moment, then smiled. 'People who have the best interests of our city at heart. People concerned about its citizens' welfare.'

'All of its citizens?' I asked.

Peace tapped his left hand on the arm of my sofa. He was staring hard at me, wondering if I was trouble.

'All, Mr Ellington. It's clear that the work that you agreed to undertake for Pastor Mervyn Walker, your ongoing attempts to locate his missing wife, has become a criminal case. This chap in Montpelier found dead, who it's now believed had some kind of association with Mrs Walker.' Peace stopped in mid-sentence, clearly trying to recall the dead man's name.

'Troy Loudon,' I volunteered.

'Loudon, that's the fella.' Peace sat up straighter. 'Well, this Loudon was clearly close to the line. His police record showed numerous arrests: encouraging soliciting in a public place, kerb crawling, owning or managing a brothel, pimping and pandering, and I believe a conviction for grievous bodily harm. All unsavoury stuff at the best of times, and even more troubling when the dead man is perhaps connected to a prominent member of both the church and the St Pauls local community. This kind of situation can turn from bad to worse very quickly. That's why I have been brought in. The last thing this city needs is the wagging black finger of suspicion being pointed at either the police or the church.'

Peace clearly saw me grimace at his insensitive remark. He uncrossed his legs and sat forward. 'You know as well as I do.' He turned to briefly look out of the window, his glare cutting through the net curtains, his true focus out into the street and then back on me. 'St Pauls is like a powder keg of trouble just waiting to be ignited and explode. No one wants dead bodies turning up, minister's wives disappearing, or God forbid, the kind of ludicrous civil unrest that was seen in London last year erupting here in Bristol. The Southall situation was abhorrent, the death of that poor teacher, Blair Peach, was tragic. Rioting and looting are not something we'd like to see repeated here in the city. We want the lid firmly fitted on our keg of gunpowder.'

I liked the 'we' bit. Oddly Peace's circuitous threats soothed my nerves a little. I was used to white men in authority trying to either intimidate or fool me. It almost always meant they had something to protect or hide. I made a mental note that Peace could easily recall the name of a murdered white man, but not that of a black fella whose life was taken in the same violent manner. Peace shifted in his seat, the ruddy expression on his face making me all too aware that his stony-hearted words had offended me.

He offered a placating grin which did nothing to

soften my dislike of the man.

'Whether the shadow falls across the pastor at this juncture or not is unclear. What we do know, thanks in no small part to your investigative work, is that his wife's disappearance appears to be connected to a dead man who one wouldn't have expected to have been seen sitting in the first three rows of pews at the Old King Street Baptist Chapel.' Peace cocked his head, adjusting to his new view of me. 'All you have to remember is my phone number. No matter what you come across, legal or illegal, you are to call me first. I don't care if you sniff blood in the air, you call me and leave the regular cops out of it.'

'What if someone else turns up dead?'

Peace's face turned to stone. 'I'm the contact.'

'And will Detectives Locke and Mapp be hanging on my tail?'

That got my new police liaison man to laugh out loud.

'No, no, no, Mr Ellington. You're safe. That's why Superintendent Eve had you brought in. Find out from the horse's mouth whether you could be trusted or not to help out. To see if you . . .' Peace rubbed at his chin with the tips of two of his well-scrubbed fingers, giving me the once over, getting his smooth patter straight before speaking again.

'To see if you were the kind of chap who flew straight. The inspector thinks you're a straight flier, Mr Ellington. He believes most of the residents of St Pauls and Montpelier aren't going to look twice at a black man asking the kind of questions you'll continue to be asking. I agree with him. The officers you mention will be undertaking their own enquiries of course, but it's my understanding that they'll be

199

leaving you alone, for now.'

It was the 'for now' bit of the man's soft-soap spiel that had me most worried. Peace got to his feet. 'If you come up with anything at all just call me. If you can't get me directly, I check into the answering service every hour or so; if you tell the operator, it's an emergency, they'll make sure they find me.'

He walked to the door.

'Many thanks, Mr Ellington. Don't forget — call me and only me if you find anything. Anything at all, remember.'

He walked down to the kerb and climbed into a red Mini Cooper. As he drove off, I thought that I would never have imagined a big, dangerous fella like Richard Peace squashing himself inside a tiny tin box.

27

Richard Peace's visit earlier in the day had made me sit up and think. Having the police muscling in on the matter of the pastor's lost wife was one thing, but some cloak and dagger civil servant knocking my door unannounced told me that I was well and truly in over my head in regard to Trista Walker's disappearance. A black woman vanishing in St Pauls was nothing out of the ordinary, so the fact that the police spotlight was shining so brightly on Trista going missing told me that I needed to tread carefully. In the past, if it had been any other job, I could, and would, have dropped it. But Peace knew he had me over a barrel. Knew that I couldn't say no to him, not with the police already on my back, making all kinds of threats. Peace was clearly pulling Superintendent Eve's strings, and Eve in turn barked out orders at his foot soldiers, Detective Sergeant Locke and Detective Constable Mapp. All three coppers were like hunting hounds, and I was either going to point out the prey or fall victim to their snapping jaws.

I also took Peace's promise that Locke and Mapp would not be sniffing around me with a big pinch of salt. I was fairly sure I'd find myself being followed at some point or return home to find an unmarked police car sat outside my home, a polite reminder from the boys in blue that they had their eyes on me.

I thought of old Marley in *A Christmas Carol*. He dragged the chains of mortal life behind him like some slave that had escaped with the manacles still attached to his wrists and ankles. I was free, but every step was a challenge.

Richard Peace had insinuated that I was still my own man; but that man still owed his soul to the company store.

I'd agreed to pick Chloe up from Loretta's place at six. I knew she'd be excited to see her uncle and likewise Vic would, as he always did when Chloe came over, want to huddle up with her on the quiet, charm her with his many tall tales then, again as he always did, go on to increase the balance of his niece's 'rainy day' savings account by slipping her a roll of cash.

To my reckoning Chloe never left her uncle's place without being in receipt of at least fifty quid. I was expected to turn a blind eye, which I reluctantly did. Chloe idolised Vic, and Vic in turn was a devoted and loving uncle. Over the years, Vic had stuck his hand in his pocket for everything from money for a new bike to paying each year for his niece's school uniform. Vic had 'people' to handle every part of his life if he needed them. Gofers for this, a flunky for that; Vic couldn't tell you, or care, what time of day it was most of the time, but he never forgot Chloe's birthday, or to send cards and gifts at both Easter and Christmas. After the death of his parents, my Uncle Gabe and Aunt Pearl, Vic had channelled much of his unspoken grief into building up a close relationship with Chloe. To say that the two of them were as *thick as thieves* would have been an understatement.

While that pair would be in cahoots, I needed to corner Vic to discuss my own problems and to reluctantly seek his counsel. I knew Vic already had his people with their ears to the ground for the slightest titbit of information from which he could perhaps benefit. Very little 'street news' escaped Vic's attention thanks to countless local informers and stooges that he had in his pocket.

During the afternoon, I nervously paced every room in my house waiting for the police to perhaps come knocking again. I sat and made a few calls to people I knew and trusted, folk who worked in the pubs and bars around the area, asking them to keep an ear out and an eye open. Any news on Trista Walker would be gratefully received. I swallowed more aspirin to help fend off my continuing aches and pains and to reduce the swelling in my hands. Late in the afternoon, hit by fatigue, I fell asleep in the armchair. I woke an hour or so later, confused, my body hot and trembling from a bad dream, my clothes damp with perspiration. I sat on the edge of the seat, my head bent down, my jaws clenched tight to keep them from shaking. I stayed like that, staring at the patterns on the rug at my feet for some time, my fuddled head someplace between the real world and the fool's paradise I'd just stirred from.

I took my time to come out of my stupor. Rough sleeping in my car the night before had knocked me for six. My body felt as heavy as lead as I climbed the stairs to the bathroom. Every joint smarted. My bones felt liked they'd been disassembled and dropped back inside my skin. I threw cold water over my face and soaked my swollen knuckles in the sink. Back in my bedroom, I'd decided to dress casual for my evening audience with my cousin. I changed into a pair of khaki chinos, a soft blue flannel shirt and put on my comfortable brown loafers. I headed back down to the kitchen and made a pot of strong black coffee. Sinking two cups helped to liven me a little, but only just.

203

Just before six, I grabbed my jacket and coat from the stair banister and climbed into my car; my emotional gauge set somewhere between elation and panic. My breathing heavy and uneven.

For maybe five minutes I sat outside my home, thinking.

I thought again of Richard Peace stood in my living room, assuring me that I was safe because I would be a black man among black men doing his and the police's dirty work. The fact that I took Peace's words as truth made me laugh; a white man telling a black one he was safe because of his skin colour. For a minute or so I luxuriated in the solace that I knew the man was a fool. Then I thought of Vic. Suddenly any fears I may have had about how the police or the law could coerce or hurt me paled into insignificance when I considered my cousin's spine-chilling reputation for putting the fear of God into someone.

Strangely, this terrible thought made me laugh very hard. Anyone passing in the street would have thought that I'd gone insane behind the wheel.

* * *

Chloe was already waiting for me outside of Loretta's when I pulled up. She was wearing an off-the-shoulder blue Lacoste sweatshirt which hung down over jeans, her hair pinned high on her head. She beamed at me as I opened the passenger door for her to climb in and angled her body over to kiss me on the cheek. Pointing a finger at the windscreen, she said: 'Come on. What you waitin' fo'?'

For the first fifteen minutes of our journey from St Pauls into rural Somerset, Chloe was quiet, her face turned towards the window, looking out at the countryside. I took a deep breath; my adopted child was in many ways more intelligent, more mature, than me. I knew if I was going to break the silence anything I said needed to be something that either piqued her intellect or made her laugh. I needed to keep Chloe on my side because I knew I'd be asking her to stay with Loretta for a few more nights until things had calmed down. One thing I knew I had to steer clear of was fishing for personal stuff: if I tried to dig into her closed adolescent life, I'd come across like an overprotective parent.

I opened my mouth without thinking and went straight with goat head.

'So, how's things with Dimitri?' No sooner had the words had come out of my mouth, I felt myself grimace.

Chloe turned to give me a vexed look.

'What's with the eyeballing? I was just asking how things are going, that's all.'

Chole rolled her eyes. 'We're just friends, okay?'

'Okay.' I heard Chloe tut to herself, either out of anger or embarrassment. 'Any chance you thinking you might become good friends?'

'Papa!' she said in faux exasperation.

I took a deep breath, kept my eyes on the road, tried my best to button my lip and still failed. 'Look, all I'm saying is . . . is that, you two . . . you looked kinda happy together when I saw you last night.'

Chloe turned fully round, taking in my words seriously.

'You really think so?'

I nodded, keeping my expression blank. 'Yeah, course I do. Did an old fool like me good, seeing you

205

smiling and happy.'

Chloe sat still. I could sense her staring at the side of my face as I took a sharp bend in the road. A few moments later she shifted closer to me; the tone of her voice was softer when she spoke.

'You know, you really don't need to worry all the time.'

I kept watching the road. 'Uh-huh. Is that right?'

'Yeah. I know right from wrong. I'm not seven years old anymore, you know.'

'You don't have to tell me that.'

'You always told me to be careful how I chose my friends, right?'

'Right.'

'Well, D was chosen carefully, okay?'

I felt my throat tighten, a tingling flickered inside it, like a heated wire touching a nerve. 'Okay.' I turned my head to briefly look at her.

'And,' she said before I could speak again. 'D would never intentionally hurt me.'

I looked back at the road, biting the corner of my bottom lip before speaking again. 'Worth remembering, we get hurt worse by the people who we care about the most. And they seldom mean to do it.' I glanced back at her face. Her eyes met mine, then they looked away. 'That's what's makes it so painful, kiddo.'

Chloe was quiet for a moment. The earlier downpour had begun to slacken. The inside of the car felt humid, the air oppressive. I cracked open my window. The wind pouring in smelled of the rain and the nearby sea. Out of the corner of my eye I saw Chloe puff out her cheeks.

'You know what Loretta says about me and you?'

206

'No, what's she say?'

Chloe started to laugh. 'Chip nuh fly fur fram de blak.'

I felt a blooming sensation in my chest and nodded my head.

The car fell silent again for a while. It took a minute or so for my fears for my child to settle, then another to appreciate that Chloe saw it as her duty to calm me when I worried about her. When I was a young man back home, girls could wrap me around their little fingers. All they had to do was whisper my name and I'd be all looks and smiles. Chloe had that impact on me, and I was sure she would rather remain mute than lie to me when it came to matters of the heart. All this instilled an uneasy feeling that I couldn't quite describe. I was trying to put that feeling into words when she interrupted me, and, to my surprise, for the next ten minutes of the journey Chloe's palaver was all about D and how wonderful he was, and smart, and how cool his damn ma was.

'She's a healer, you know.'

'She's a what?'

'D's mama. She heals sick folk. She has this paste that she can put on a wound or a cut and it heals in less than a day and a half.'

'I know that paste.'

'You do?'

'Yeah. It's called Anamu.' I glance back over again. 'Your gran'ma and her folk were using the very same homemade ointment to rub on her and your grandpa before you or I were even breathing.'

Chloe raised her eyebrows, her gaze shifting across my face. She smiled at me and moved across her seat, resting her head against the top of my arm. I felt a

207

gentle shudder go through me like tension leaving a metal spring. She remained motionless next to me as I drove; the trees along the roadside beating in the wind, the last of the rain falling against the windscreen.

It had stopped raining completely by the time we reached Clevedon. The character of the coast changed around the mouth of the River Parrett, the rocky cliffs and shingle giving way to sand flats that run all the way to the promontory which was home to the tiny fishing village of Brean Down.

I parked opposite the lane that headed out to Vic's place, and Chloe and I walked down to the beach and along the water's edge. The tide was on its way out, the long strip of sandy beach slick with water and tiny crustaceans in the sunset, the bay shimmering like a bronze shield. The waves broke into a thin froth on the shore which blew into the air. High up against the darkening dome of the sky, cormorants drifted in formation on the wind stream.

We walked out to the end of the point, neither of us feeling the need to engage the other in unnecessary chit-chat. The clouds in the west looked like strips of flame above the green horizon. We stopped at the shore's edge to spend a while skimming stones out into the ocean, then Chloe linked her arm in mine and we slowly made our way the half mile or so back up to the road.

Fifty yards from the slipway down to the beach was the turn off into Cuckoo Lane. A two-mile channel which had been cut through dense woodland on one side of the road and acres of grazing fields on the other. The untarmacked road, a narrow single lane, grew thinner as it wound inland. The Flint, as it was called, was hidden away at the end of the road. It was former watermill, which had grown in scale and splendour in direct proportion to the previous owner's fears of either marauding tenants or local common thievery. The Flint's current owner had, over the years, done more than his fair share of stealing. Vic had his own nefarious reasons for creating a remote fortress for himself. A hideaway in which to maintain his privacy, a secure home that provided him with high-level security and kept his enemies at bay.

The main house was situated at the edge of a huge artificial lake. The old watermill stood next to the water; the two buildings connected by a short, thatch-covered bridge. A miniature jetty invited what few visitors were allowed to ignore the road if they wished, to arrive at the Flint by boat. It was impressive and absurd at the same time; my cousin's vain re-creation of something that had already been vain and extravagant to begin with.

The light had all but faded from the sky and rain had started to slowly fall, the drizzle slanting across the flood lamps anchored high in the trees as we pulled through the iron gates into Vic's drive. Gator Hebert, the Flint's rugged custodian, appeared from out of the side door of the tiny lodge house. Gator was well named. He had the same evil grin as an alligator and seemed to come up from nowhere each time I met him.

Tonight, he cruised silently towards us like a huge predator dressed in white slacks and a blue striped sports coat, a gap-toothed smile breaking across his scarred face as he approached the car. I wound down the window, held out my arm and Gator took my hand and shook it warmly.

'How you doin', Gator?' I asked.

'Good, JT, real good.' Gator turned and pointed a finger someplace between the watermill and the lake. 'You 'naw where to go, reet?'

I said that I did, gave my thanks and pulled the car into a parking area hidden among the trees. Chloe and I walked the last hundred yards over the footbridge, leaving the world as we knew it behind.

We headed across a gravel frontage and mounted the double flight of stone steps to the front door. I had not seen Vic in over eight months and was still wondering if it was wise to invite the past back into my life or into his. I rang the chimes. In retrospect, I wished that I hadn't.

Bitter Lemon, Vic's right-hand man, swung open the door. He was the colour of a well-used penny. Stubby in his build, with large strong hands. He wore black work pants and a brown short-sleeve shirt and perched on the back of his head was a black felt porkpie hat. We shook hands, his grip relaxed and cool, with no sign of the power it actually contained.

'Joseph, it' bin a while. How you doin?' Bitter didn't wait for a reply, focusing his attention towards Chloe.

'Chil', you have grown. Tell me you 'ungry?'

Chloe nodded excitedly.

Bitter closed the door behind us and curled a huge arm around Chloe and guided her towards the kitchen. 'Good, 'cause I got jerk chicken rollin' on de rotisserie.'

Chloe could not have looked happier as Bitter began to guide her towards the kitchen. He called back to me, his muscular arm raised, a single thick digit pointing in the direction of the large patio doors at the rear of the house. 'Go on up, JT. He's expectin' you.'

210

The foyer at the front of the house was softly lit, the windows hung with red velvet curtains and that subdued lighting carried on throughout the entire house. The place felt calm, serene almost. I made my way through the dining room, past Vic's study and library and into a long hallway, both lined with bookshelves, into a thickly carpeted living room with high French doors and a cathedral ceiling. Beyond that was a door that led out to a covered, windowless atrium which took you out to the garden. More sober illumination shimmered outside. Dimmed floodlights picked out the path that snaked along the edge of a well-maintained lawn. Vic's private apartment was partially hidden behind a large oak. A two-storey barn, a once humble building, now palatially converted, where my cousin held court and kicked back in.

The door to the apartment was ajar and those stairs were daring me to set foot inside. It was twilight and the world around me was slowly blending into grey. Going to Vic over my problem would, I knew, create problems of its own. With no exaggeration. Vic was by far the most dangerous man I have ever known, getting him on board was like unleashing the Kraken. Once he was free any kind of carnage could ensue.

And so, I stopped to consider.

But I knew that I didn't have a choice.

I took the stairs one at a time.

Somebody in Vic's apartment had a very bad cough. I'd heard it from the bottom step. It was one of those deep, wet rolling coughs that, in my childhood days, almost always preceded a funeral. Vic's apartment door was slightly open. I heard women's voices inside. They were laughing and cooing, not coughing.

'Vic?'

'Com' on in, cuz.'

The lounge I walked into was what I imagined a first-class room at the London Savoy would look like, if styled by a wealthy Barbadian. There were tall marijuana plants growing in large decorative terracotta pots by the sliding doors at the rear of the place. The white carpet was two inches thick, the red leather chairs and couches fitted with large silk cushions. All the furniture was bespoke, mostly imported from the West Indies or the US.

Vic was sat in the middle cushion of one of the sofas, and flanked by two large, shapely women.

'Shit, look who it ain't.' My cousin sank back into his seat, one arm stretching out across the top of the couch. 'Where de fuck you bin, man?'

'Getting into trouble,' I said.

Vic grinned, and hacked into his closed hand.

'Sounds nasty. You okay?'

Vic waved off my concern. 'It ain't nuthin'.' He turned to one of his companions. 'Dis is Crystal,' he said waving a hand at the woman on his right. 'Crystal, this my blood, JT.'

She stood up and stuck out her hand. 'Hi, JT. Pleased to meet you.'

She was tall, perhaps five-foot-nine or so, the colour of tree bark. She couldn't have been older than twenty-five, which is why the weight she carried seemed to defy the pull of gravity. For all her size her waist was slender, but that wasn't her most arresting feature. Crystal gave off the most amazing scent. It was like the smell of pineapple and all-spice, earthy, sweet and pungent all rolled into one. I took her hand and raised it to my lips so I could get my nose up to her skin.

She giggled and I remembered that I was still a

212

grieving widower.

'An' dis 'ere is Roxy,' Vic said, suppressing another cough.

Roxy's body was similar to her friend's. She didn't stand up, instead only waved her hand and gave me a half smile.

I hunkered down in one of the huge seats that sat behind an onyx-topped coffee table.

'How you all doing?'

Vic chuckled and coughed at the same time. 'Shit, man, we all ready to party — ain't dat reet, girls?'

They both laughed. Crystal leaned over and gave Vic a deep soul kiss. Roxy smiled at me and shifted her butt around on the cushion.

'You gonna spit out what you doin 'ere, den?'

'Perhaps best if we speak alone, Vic.' Seeing the two girls snuggling up to my cousin I was expecting him to tell me I had to wait till tomorrow so I was surprised when he sat up straight, peeling the women off him.

'Okay,' he said. 'Ladies, why don't you go wait fo' me in de bedroom.' He reached into his pocket and came out with a handful of crisp notes. Crystal snatched at the cash.

'Com' on, Roxy.' The other girl got to her feet. 'These men got some bid'ness to discuss befo' we party.'

When Crystal walked past me, she held out her hand again. I kissed that sweet-smelling skin as if it were my own mother's hand reaching out for me from long ago. I felt her shudder. I did, too.

Vic would have killed men for lesser offences, but I was in the frame of mind where danger and the risk to my own life was a forgone conclusion. After the women were gone, I turned to Vic. He was smiling

213

at me.

'I see dem eyes, man.' Vic began to laugh. 'Cuz, I gonna mek a dirty dog outta you yet.'

214

28

'What do you think?' I asked Vic after I'd finished telling him my woes.

'All sounds fucked up,' Vic replied, his brassy remark, I sensed, part of a greater response. He took a joint from a silver cigarette box on the table next to him and lit it with a match. He sucked on the end of the reefer, inhaled deeply, then began to hack like an old man, something I'd never heard him do before. He hammered at his chest with his fist and wafted a grey cloud of smog away from his face. 'Man, I t'out you'd thrown de towel in wid all dis detective shit?'

'You know damn well I had.' I pinched at my temples with my fingers and sighed. 'I thought I was doing Mervyn Walker a favour.'

'A favour, shit!' Vic slumped back and blew a fresh cloud of smoke at the ceiling. 'Fuckin' trouble got you name tattooed on the inside o' his eyelids. Trouble be studyin' you in his sleep. Trouble bin after you' hide long as I can remember. You the only niggah I 'naw can git himsel' stitched up by a vicar.'

'Why'd you think I've driven all the way out here?'

Vic hunched his shoulders. 'To bring de pickney to see a favourite uncle.'

'Very funny.'

Vic peered over my shoulder. 'Where'd the hell is de chil'?'

'In the kitchen with Bitter, stuffing her face with jerk chicken.'

I saw Vic break out into smile. 'Damn, that big ole

215

bastard, he cooks up a mean pot a suppa.' My cousin sniffed the air. 'You 'ungry?'

I held up my hand. 'No, I'm not hungry. But I could use your help.'

'Brother, it looks like you could use t'ree days in bed.'

'I could do with that too.'

Vic shook his head and laughed. He slapped a hand on the seat next to him. 'Shift you' arse ovah 'ere.' I moved over to the couch. Vic slid to the side to give me room. He was wearing what he liked to call his work clothes. Black Levi's and matching poloneck pullover, and black leather ankle boots. His long dreadlocks were scraped back tight against his scalp and tied with black cord. On the little finger of his left hand, he wore his cherished gold and diamond encrusted Lion of Judah signet ring.

My cousin, two years my junior, still looked remarkably young for his age. Time had been kind to his natural good looks, and even the salt and pepper grey curls embedded in his well-maintained goatee did little to age him. Where he had once worn a leather patch, his right eye socket now sported a prosthetic glass eye, the white around the iris crafted meticulously to match the shade of his left, the pupil never flickering.

Vic's hard stare out of that fake eye may have been crafted in an ocularist's workshop, but that didn't stop him from ever missing a trick. He was the perfect criminal. A killer without a conscience, a warrior without fear, his IQ was most probably off the charts for all I knew, and even if it wasn't, his whole mind paid such close attention to his profession that there were few who could out-think him when it came to

216

breaking the law.

I fished the colour photograph of Loudon and Trista Walker out of my jacket pocket and handed it to him. He whistled to himself when he saw Trista Walker's naked body stretched on the bed, and sucked air through the gap in his front teeth as he scrutinised the other two characters in the picture.

Vic stabbed his finger into the centre of the photo. 'Dat's Elder Slick's woman?' Hearing Vic refer to Mervyn Walker as Elder Slick immediately made me think of Chloe using the same nickname for the pastor a few days earlier.

'Yeah.'

'Shit. I need to git me next to Jah, iffa man o' de cloth can bag himself a piece o' fine skin like dat.'

'What if I told you that piece of skin was the daughter of Clementine Dupre?'

Vic's eyebrow rose a quarter of an inch before looking at me. 'Dat . . .' He stared back down at the photograph, frowning, then after a moment fixed his eye back on me. 'You tellin' me dat's Hoo Shoo's pickney?'

'Yeah. Hoo Shoo gave her the name Celestine when she was born. Lords knows why the hell she started calling herself Trista.'

I heard my cousin mutter something under his breath but couldn't make out what he'd said. Vic continued to scrutinise the print, his dark skin and lone grey eye made him appear wraithlike in the low light. 'Obeah's gone an' hexed you a'gin, bwoy.'

'What you talking about?'

'Any'ting dat come outta dat ole witch Hoo Shoo gonna let a man 'naw what he made of.'

'Yeah, flesh and blood. I thought you didn't believe

in curses and spells?'

'I don't.' Vic forced a grin. 'Dis Celestine any'ting like her slippery ole lady, you gonna need iron an' gunpowder an' mebbe a little luck to find her.' Vic gave the photo a final once-over before handing it back to me. 'Loudon's al'ready bin clipped. De vicar's put de finger on his ole lady, so you 'naw it's her laying on dat crib in de nuck-nuck.' Vic pulled on the end of the joint, inhaling the vapours deep into his chest. 'So, who de fuck is de fool wearin' de mask?'

'That's what I'm trying to find out?'

'You say you axe dat skank Queenie Blue 'bout this fella?'

'Not a lot. I paid Eddie Riddle a hundred quid to speak to her alone. She gave me a load of voodoo mumbo jumbo, tried to fill me with cheap rum then charged me another twenty-five quid and told me to go ask the pastor what was really going on.' I rubbed at the back of one of my hands and winced. 'Eddie clearly didn't like me sniffing around Blue, so he sent in his boys to have a word with me.'

''Ow many of dem?'

'Two.'

Vic grinned. 'Pickney in ma kitchen could floor two o' Riddle's bwoys.'

I chuckled. 'And Abe Bolden.'

Vic began to laugh, almost hysterically, the laughter turned to a bout of serious coughing. When he finally managed to contain the barking and rasping, my cousin looked at me, his right eye fixing in on me. 'You put Ade down?'

I nodded my head. 'Uh-huh . . . Used a sap.'

'Muthafucka! I'd 'ave paid good money to have seen dat shit.' Vic took a deep draw on his reefer to stem the urge to laugh further and immediately began to hack again.

'What's going on, Vic?'

'Wid what?'

I pointed at his chest. 'With that cough?'

Vic took another draw on his joint. 'I tole you, it ain't nuthin'.'

I was about quiz him a little more, but my cousin beat me to it with a question of his own.

'You still have yourself those creepy dreams?'

I laughed: partly because of the dream I had had earlier in the day and partly to put my cousin at ease.

'Sure, I do. Matter a fact, dreams been kicking my arse this past week or so.'

'Yeah? Me too, man.' He shook his head and reached for a crystal tumbler filled to the brim with rum that sat on a table at the side of the sofa. He pointed at the bottle next to him. 'Get yourself a drink, JT.'

I shook my head. 'In a minute . . . what you dreaming about?'

'Home,' he said, after taking a long swig.

He looked across at me. I would have seen his wide-eyed vulnerability as fear in another man's face.

'Home?'

'Yeah. I'm back on Bim an' I'm seein' folk we used to 'naw as kids. All dem ole niggahs down by the port. Your mama, an' mine too. Dey all walkin' past me on de beach back in St Philip parish. One ole fella he walkin' reet into me and me shoulder, it starts to crumble.'

'Crumble?' I said, as a parishioner might repeat a minister's phrase for emphasis.

'Yeah. Fuckin' arm turns to sand. Tings start comin' offa me an' dey fallin' to de ground. I try an' catch stuff wid my utha hand, but dat's turnin' to sand too. Me legs start doin' de same. An' folk was jus' walkin' by not tekin' any notice.'

'Damn,' I said. I was amazed not by the content but by the sophistication of Vic's dream. I had always thought my cousin to be, for most of the time, something of a brute who was free from complex thought or imagination. I'd known him since we were kids and I was just now seeing a whole different side of him.

'An' dat ain't all. Dem niggahs dey jus' start walkin' ovah me. Den, when am crushed into dust de wind come an' all I am is dust blowin' in de air.' Vic knocked back a mouthful of rum. 'What de hell all dat 'bout, hey?' he asked me with all the innocence of the child he never was.

'I ain't gotta clue. It's just a dream, man. Nothing else.'

'Funniest fuckin' dream I evah had.' Vic coughed into his hand again, his chest rising and falling. His gaze went away from me a moment then came back, as though he had gotten control of his emotions and refocused his thoughts.

I shook the photo in front of me. 'Where'd you think I should start looking for this mask-wearing guy?' Vic's jaw tightened, a malign look on his face. He cleared his throat.

'Let's start by payin' dat toe rag Queenie Blue anutha visit.'

29

Vic had spent most of the rest of the evening sat with Chloe in the library, leaving Bitter Lemon and me to chat among ourselves in the kitchen. When I asked Vic about his two companions, Crystal and Roxy, still waiting for him in his bedroom, he gave me a heavy frown, rolling his head in a circular motion, his neck bones cracking loudly.

'Fuck 'em. All dey wanna do is laugh an' drink ma liquor cabinet dry.' He winked at me. 'Dem bitches can wait. I got more important bid'ness to be attendin' to.'

Vic was happy again. The challenge of helping me locate the masked man in the photograph, which in turn I hoped would lead me to Trista Walker's whereabouts, had clearly brought him alive. Over the years I'd come to realise that everybody has different jobs to do. There's your wage job, your responsibility to your kin, and then there are some special duties that every man and woman takes on. Some people are artists or have political interests, some are obsessed with collecting stamps or movie stars' autographs. One of my special duties had always been to keep Victor Ellington from falling into a dark place. Because whenever Vic stopped having a good time someone, someplace was likely to die. And even though I had pressing business of my own, troubles that I needed him on board to sort out with me, I knew that he valued his time with Chloe above all else.

It was midnight by the time Vic walked the two

of us to my car, the floodlights in the trees casting shadows on the gravel drive. Chloe give her uncle a big hug, and Vic in turn pushed a wad of banknotes into Chloe's hand and planted a kiss on her forehead. He opened up the passenger door, watched his niece climb inside then closed it behind her. He rested his arm on the car roof. I gave him a knowing look, which he ignored.

'I'll see you tomorrow.' Vic backed away from the car. 'De Alexander club, midday.' He pointed at my chest. 'An' bring dat picture o' de floozy an' de utha two fools wid you, okay?'

'Okay.' Vic bent down, smiled and waved through the passenger window at Chloe then turned without saying goodbye to me. I watched as he took a joint from his back pocket and lit it as he slowly started to walk back towards the house.

A reefer burning in one hand, a half-filled crystal tumbler of rum in the other.

Chloe fell asleep in the passenger seat. I drove and she snored. That's a song I'd never tire of. Before she dozed off, we'd agreed that she would go and stop at Loretta's after school tomorrow for a couple more days, or better still, until I had sorted out Mervyn Walker's missing wife problem. Chloe wasn't happy about it, but at the same time she didn't kick up the stink I was expecting. I got the impression that her uncle had cajoled her earlier on with the promise of more cash as long as she didn't give me any grief about being sent to stay with her Aunt Lol.

We got back into St Pauls just after one. The coast road and those going back into Bristol were all but deserted. It had turned much colder, a wolf's howl of wind whipped at my face as I got out of the car.

The street was quiet and thankfully looked free of unmarked police vehicles staking out my home. I carried Chloe, who was still sound asleep into the house and put her, still partially clothed, into bed.

As I was about to walk away, something inside told me to leave the bedside light on and her door open. Chloe wasn't normally afraid of the dark, and she was too dead to the world to notice that it was on. Perhaps I was hoping that the soft glow of the lamp would cast its dull beam along the landing, into my own chamber and offer me a little comfort and security as I turned in for the night.

★ ★ ★

In my dream I was walking, wearing only a T-shirt and shorts. It was freezing. The carcasses of black men and women hung from hooks. I recognised all of them but couldn't put a name to anyone. It occurred to me that I might be in hell.

Then I came across Queenie Blue. Her throat had been slit; her hair plastered down over her eyes. I stared and almost brushed the hair from her face. I turned and saw Chloe and Vic hanging side by side on dreadful hooks. I reached out . . .

The moment I touched Chloe's face a hand fell on my shoulder and span me round. It was Trista Walker, Obeah Queen of her own underworld.

'Come and join them, Joseph,' she proclaimed.

I screamed and sprang up in my bed. A numb chill gripped me. My heart felt as if it had grown two sizes too large for my chest.

30

Chloe's room was the colour of a half-rainy day, dominated by mild blues and gentle greys. School books were stacked neatly in one corner of the room, and soft toys were strewn at the foot her bed. I peeked around the curtains, the glass fogging before my face. I wiped at the pane with my fingers. What looked like snow clouds, silver and black, hung in the air in a multitude of precious-metal hues, adorning the early morning sky as if they longed to kiss the pavement. I checked the street for any unwelcome signs of police presence, but thankfully there were none.

Chloe's head was sunk into a plump, sea green pillow, and her bare leg stuck out from under the matching duvet cover. When I pulled the duvet over her leg she stirred and looked up at me.

'Hey, Papa.'

'Hi there,' I hailed, sitting down at her side.

Chloe looked at the bruising that ran across the knuckles on my left hand. She frowned. 'How are you?'

'Better now I've seen your sleepy head.'

She grinned and sat up, holding the duvet up to her neck. 'I've missed you being around these past few days.'

'Well, I'm right here.'

'When will you be finished with Elder Slick?'

'Hopefully I'll have everything sorted for him by the end of the weekend. You head over to Loretta's later. Okay?'

Chloe's grin shifted to a desolate stare. 'Whatever you say.'

'Well, I say that you get your butt over to Loretta's after school.'

Chloe drew the duvet closer to her face, her mouth partially obscured by the thick quilt. 'Loretta's okay with D coming over to see me. That alright with you too?'

I shrugged. 'Loretta's joint, Loretta's rules.' Chloe grinned again, happy with her little victory. I sat looking at my girl for a moment.

'What?' she asked.

'You,' I said.

Her fingers tightened around her quilt. 'What about me?'

'You look just like Bernice did. Like your mama did when we were kids.'

Chloe's fading grin suddenly broke out into a larger smile. I started to rise from the bed, but Chloe grabbed my arm anchoring me back down on the edge of the mattress.

'Uncle Vic's gonna be helping you out, yes?'

I nodded my head. 'Yeah, that's right.'

'Please, just be careful.'

I nodded my head and glanced down at my wristwatch. 'You need to get moving if you don't want to be late for school.' I creaked back up on to my feet. 'I just came in to kiss you good morning because you were asleep when I kissed you goodnight.'

Chloe proffered her cheek and I kissed it.

'Jeez, Papa! And you need to get yourself a shave.'

* * *

Changed, showered and shaved as instructed, I headed to the kitchen to make breakfast for Chloe and then helped her pack a small canvas bag for her stay with Loretta. After she'd left for school, I sat down on the sofa and pulled the telephone directory from the newspaper rack.

'Brislington House,' a woman's friendly voice said.

'Resident services please.'

'We don't have such a department, sir.'

'I need to talk to someone about a resident staying with you.'

'The administration office is what you want, sir,' the officious switchboard operator informed me.

The next thing I heard was another ringing telephone.

'Admin,' a mature woman's voice said.

'Who am I speaking to?'

'Miss Leslie.'

'Good morning, Miss Leslie, my name is George Pagett. I'm calling from the Social Security Invalidity Benefit Department.'

'How can I help?'

'I have a giro payment for one of your residents, £527. This amount is part of an Invalid Care Allowance and the payee is . . . er, one moment, please.' I flicked over pages of the phonebook on my lap, hoping to give Miss Leslie the impression I was rifling through important DHSS documentation. 'Ah, here we are, a Mrs Clementine Dupree.'

'I'm not familiar with that name. Are you sure she's one of ours?'

'That's what the paperwork in front of me says.'

'Bear with me one moment while I check our records.' I heard the phone being placed onto a hard

226

surface; moments later, the opening of a metal drawer and then the rustling of paper. Half a minute later Miss Leslie was back on the line.

'As I thought, we have no one by the name of Dupree residing here at Brislington House.'

I was about to thank the woman and wish her a good day when a thought struck me. I rustled the edges of the phonebook again, pretending to go through the motions of a paper search. 'My apologies, there seems to be a typing error on the document I've been given. Some confusion over the payee's correct name.'

'Oh, well if there's nothing else?'

'Ah, if I could get you to take another quick look at your records for me again, please?' I heard Miss Leslie sigh heavily down the line. I cradled the phone to my ear and turned a couple more pages of the directory. 'Same Christian name, Clementine, but with the surname of Walker.'

'One moment.'

This time the phone on the other end of the line was dropped onto the desk, followed by the sound of a filing cabinet drawer being wrenched open and paperwork rifled through. A minute or two later my friend, Miss Leslie, was back on the line and snapping at me.

'Miss Clementine Walker. Born fourth of May 1900.'

'And she's currently a resident with you?'

'Of course,' the woman snarled. 'Been with us for the past twelve months. She's staying on the south-east elevation of Brislington. Carisbrooke Court wing.' A few seconds of irritable silence passed. 'Now, can I be of any further assistance, Mr Pagett? I really do need to get back to work.'

'No, that's everything, thank you. You've been most helpful. I'll get Miss Walker's giro into the post for her today,' I lied.

I heard the connection on the other end click and die in my ear.

Outside rain was starting to fall. Within minutes the rain had turned to thick sleet. The snowy mix streamed off the windows, a solid white curtain, shutting out the world and leaving me alone with my thoughts. Hidden, unwelcome memories that I rarely ever trawled back through. I dredged up my first meeting with the voodoo mambo known as Hoo Shoo Dupree. I dwelled upon the cruel words she'd spoken to me years before. The vile curses she'd cast upon those I'd loved and lost.

When I thought of the old sorceress, hot wires again burned within me, incandescent.

Blinding.

31

The Alexander was a private members' club just off Victoria Square in the heart of upmarket Clifton. It had a large car park at its rear that was surrounded by a twelve-foot wall. The entrance had a double-door system and a camera that monitored everyone coming through the first portal. Passing through the door, you went through a flock-wallpapered hallway and encountered the second gate. This was pulled open by a giant of a man, his face as pale as a ghost, wearing a well-pressed penguin suit.

'Joseph Ellington?' the doorman asked.

I'd never met this particular bouncer b-ut I wasn't surprised that he knew my name because of my relation, Victor 'the Jah' Ellington. Vic was a criminal from sun-up to sun-down, but it didn't stop him from obtaining membership at a place like the Alex, as it was known about town. Vic was connected to organised crime in London, Birmingham, Liverpool, even over the borders into Scotland and across the Irish Sea to Belfast. In the last decade, Vic's criminal connections had gone global, his business interests stretching from as far as the United States to Italy and the Far East. Thanks to these affiliations, even a high-end establishment like the Alex, one that usually turned away black faces, was not stupid enough to shut the door on Vic.

'Yes, I am,' I said.

'Come right on in, sir.'

Sir.

229

The dining room of the Alexander was a perfect circle with a dozen round tables taking up the main floor. There were semi-secluded booths which ran along one wall. The waitresses, all white, wore heavily starched white blouses and neatly pressed, knee-length, pleated black skirts.

The Alex was neither bordello nor strip club, but rather a five-star gathering place for businessmen and sensualists of all persuasions. I'd never been further than the front door up until now, but it was rumoured that there were bedrooms and other chambers nestled on the third floor where members and their guests could enjoy all kinds of pleasure, pain and euphoria.

Word was the wine list at the Alex was as good as you'd find anywhere in France and their steaks well-aged. The waitresses were the very best, but the rule was that you couldn't press them; the management needed their servers smiling and friendly.

First impressions of the club were good. The only thing that took me back was the smell. Not a powerful odour, but just a whiff of something too sweet, like something had been sprayed to hide the scent of something decadent or, worse still, rotting.

Vic was sitting at the very end booth. He wore a black suit, with the same colour waistcoat over a black silk shirt, which was open at the neck. A waitress stood next to him, laughing loud enough for me to hear her across the nearly empty room.

I walked up to them. The tabletop was linen covered. The polished silverware and cut crystal wine goblets set out by someone with an eye for perfection.

'Just leave me yuh number on a slip o' paper when yuh come back ovah 'ere, baby,' Vic was saying.

From the charmed look on her face, the waitress

was clearly happy to oblige.

'Vic,' I said.

'JT!' Vic's grin was warm and gated by a glittering gold crown in his right upper tooth. 'Cheryl, dis 'ere is my cousin and oldest friend, Mr Joseph Ellington.'

'Hi,' Vic's new-found squeeze said. She held out her hand and I shook it, gently.

I slid into the booth and Cheryl asked Vic: 'Should I bring over the wine now, Mr Ellington?'

'All the way, baby.'

The waitress departed and I settled in, wondering about the words *oldest friend*. They were not Vic's words. I'd never heard him use them: not about me or anyone else he knew. He was an intelligent conversationalist and, some would even have said, something of a raconteur, but I knew his language to be stripped down and bare, like our hardscrabble lives had been back home.

But our meeting wasn't about Vic's vocabulary. It was about finding Trista Walker.

'You have any trouble at the door?' I asked, perhaps foolishly.

'Trouble? Bettah not be naw trouble.' Vic coughed and stuck his head out of the booth and looked across the room. 'Dat lanky honky at de door give yuh any crap?'

'No.'

'Good, 'cause if he pulled any shit wid yuh, I'll go kick de muthafucka's arse five ways in tuh Sunday.'

I laughed and Vic appreciated the respect. 'I thought that since you were living a more rural existence you may have lost touch with the folk running this kinda place.'

Vic looked insulted. 'Lost touch. Are yuh fuckin'

231

kiddin' me?' He inched forward in his seat. 'I just bought me a' eighty per cent stake in dis joint. Niggah yuh callin' cousin, now owns de lion's share o' dis ole honky house. Whadda tink 'bout dat?'

I looked behind me at the opulent dining room, turned and smiled at Vic. 'I think that's pretty amazing.'

Vic sat forward, both hands palms down on the table, more like an excited child than a cold-blooded killer. 'Amazin'. Man, it's a fuckin' miracle! Niggahs bin dragged ovah 'ere in chains on ships an' now dey got one o' 'em ownin' a snazzy place like dis. Shit, by de time am finished am gonna be ownin' de best part o' Bristol.'

Vic was not a businessman in the conventional sense. He was an enforcer, a boss man. Victor was a force of nature. Guile, violent impulse, silent strategic planning and muscle had got him where he was today, and I saw no reason to doubt or question his prediction that he would one day become one of the city's major power-players. He'd achieved great things: created an impressive business empire that was now the envy of other powerful criminal fraternities. In just over a decade, he'd gone from stealing knock-off rum down at the docks to heading up a drug- and arms-dealing ring across three continents. Nearly all of his wealth and power had been accumulated by illegal means. For me, it was not an admirable way to create so much personal wealth, but I'd be a fool not to recognise my cousin's ambition and determination to succeed, to become top dog. I watched his smile widen, his eye lighting up as he thought of the huge possibilities his lawless and corrupt future held.

Cheryl the waitress returned, a silver serving tray

in one hand, on top of it, two expensive-looking wine bottles. We watched as she uncorked both bottles with well-practised ease. 'Shall I pour, gentlemen?'

'Baby, yuh pour away.' The neck of the bottle had barely left the edge of Vic's glass before he had the goblet to his lips and was knocking the claret back. I watched him gulp back the rest of the wine, cough then stare at the empty vessel in his hand.

'Dat is some real good shit!' He held out his glass and smiled at the waitress. 'Fill it right up, baby.' I watched as she poured the fancy claret into our crystal goblets then returned the bottle to the tray and placed it in the centre of the table. Vic sniffed the contents of his glass and took another mouthful of wine. 'I ordered fo' us al'ready. I'm as 'ungry as a muthafucka.' He gulped more of his claret then rested back against the cushioned booth wall. 'Fillet steaks an' a shit load a potato.' He knocked the remainder of his drink back then refilled his glass 'Once we've filled our bellies, we'll take us a ride ovah to Queenie Blue's place.'

'How'd you know she'll even be home?'

Vic hunched his shoulders and gave me a dismissive glare. 'Dat skanky bitch 'on't be outta dat pit o' hers till af'ta de sun goes down.' Vic took another swig of wine. 'Cock rat like her don't do bid'ness in de daylight. She'll be catchin' hersel' some shut eye befo' goin' out tuh flog he' arse.'

Our steaks came out ten minutes later and Vic ate like two men. We made small talk in between stuffing ourselves with the rare-cooked steaks and knocking back glasses of expensive red plonk. Vic had finished his meal while I was still only halfway through mine. I watched him light up a cigar, take a heavy hit then begin

233

to cough his lungs up. When I gave him a concerned look, he curled his top lip at me, stuck the Monte Cristo in the corner of his mouth, lifted his right butt cheek and let out a plaintive fart. He slouched back, his stomach full, his appetite sated, then snapped his fingers to catch the attention of Cheryl on the other side of the room. The waitress quickly shimmied over, all teeth and smiles.

'Yes, Mr Ellington?'

Vic leaned forward, his voice almost a whisper. 'Can yuh go git me mistah Stolworthy, baby?'

The waitress stood back and nodded obediently. 'Certainly, Mr Ellington.'

Vic watched her walk away then turned and gestured with his head at me. 'Yuh bring dat snapshot like I tole yuh?'

I nodded. 'Yeah.'

'Good.' Vic curled a couple of fingers. 'Give it 'ere.'

I handed Vic the photograph. He looked at it for a moment, chuckled to himself then turned it over so that the image was face down on the table. A short while later a white man in his early sixties joined us. He was short and thin. He wore an elegant grey suit and thick glasses that made his eyes seem too big for his face. Vic forced a grin and shook the white man's hand.

'This 'ere's Stollie. He's de Alex's *maître d'* . . . among utha tings.' Vic winked at the well-dressed waiter.

'I got sum'ting I want yuh tuh take a look at.'

'Certainly, sir.'

Vic handed the photograph over. 'Yuh recognise anybody in dat snapshot?'

The man called Stolworthy held the photo close to his face for what seem like a lifetime, scrutinising

234

every inch of the thing without saying a word.

'Big niggah on de left is dead. It's de masked bwoy I'm interested in.'

'Very difficult to tell, sir, what with the gentleman's face being obstructed.' The head waiter cleared his throat. 'However.'

Vic's grin glittered up at the well-spoken attendant. 'However, wha'?'

Stolworthy handed Vic back the photograph. 'I can be of assistance in confirming where this photograph was taken.'

Vic's eyes drifted away from the maître d' to mine for a moment. My cousin slid the photo back across the table to me before refixing his stare back on Stolworthy. 'Stollie, dis where yuh gonna tell me dat snap was took in one a your cribs upstairs, reet?'

The *maître d'* nodded. 'That's correct, sir. The Tyndall suite if I'm not mistaken.'

Vic glanced up, his expression like stone. 'Git me de names o' any ponce who had 'im a private party upstairs, say in the last twelve months, got it?'

Stolworthy's face flushed. His head stooped, his torso bowing into the booth. The man's subdued tone was coated in reverential fear. 'Our members expect discretion, Mr Ellington. Guest lists for our evening soireés are protected.'

That got a long whistle from Vic.

Stolworthy began to sweat.

Vic snatched out his hand, grabbing the *maître d'* between the legs, dragging him down toward the floor by his nuts. Stolworthy howled in pain, gasping in air at the same time as he yelped; the resulting high-pitched sound similar to the screech of bird downed in mid-flight by larger, clawed prey. I watched my

235

cousin tighten his grip as Stolworthy struggled to both breathe and remain on his feet.

'Git me de fuckin' names.' Vic squeezed tighter. Stolworthy gasped and sank even lower, his knees almost ready to give way. 'Don't keep me waitin' and don't let me af'ta axe yuh agin. Understand?' I could see Vic's words transforming Stolworthy as he heard them.

'I . . . I . . . under . . . stand.'

Vic let go of the doubled-up *maître d'*, who let out another pain-induced squeal. He fell backwards, stumbling away from the table towards the kitchen. I watched the man limp away then hitched forward in my seat. I leaned across the table; my voice low when I spoke.

'You knew that damn photograph had been taken in here when I showed it to you last night, didn't you?'

When Vic smiled the gold in his tooth sparkled as it caught the light. 'Crib sure looked fuckin' familiar, dat's all am sayin', brother.' Vic's eyes tightened a little, making it feel as if a shadow had fallen across the booth table. He reached over and placed his hand on my forearm. The cold shudder that ran through my body felt as if it had been bestowed by the devil himself.

Vic met my eye with a sombre face.

'Don't yuh evah go tinkin' dis niggah's gone an' lost 'is touch. Yuh 'ear me?'

32

We took my car. Vic had Bitter Lemon drive him up to Bristol in his Daimler and before leaving the Alexander club had ordered his right-hand man to head over to Loretta's place to wait for him there while we went to track down Queenie Blue and brace her. On our way into St Pauls, I told Vic more about my visit from Richard Peace, the stranger calling himself a police liaison officer, and everything Floyd Council had coughed up about Trista Walker and how he claimed to have seen the minister's wife in the Gambling House, the Shady Grove, the Black and White Café and the Inkerman pub.

'Fuck de Babylon!' The word 'police' immediately triggered my cousin's already volatile temper. 'You ain't a fuckin' dog, man. You ain't 'ave to sniff 'bout fo' no pigs. Tell 'em to go piss up a rope.' He shifted angrily in his seat, stabbing at the dashboard with his finger. 'An' as fo' Dipper Council, dat drugged-up, thieving niggah always had a big mout'. Most o' what he bin spoutin' fo' years is bullshit. Jus' anutha brother went an' sold his shit to de pigs fo' thirty pieces.' Vic began to cough, finally hacking up a mouthful of phlegm. He wound down the window, spat out into the road and wiped his mouth with the back of his hand. Out of the corner of my eye, I could have sworn I caught sight of blood smeared across the tops of his fingers. Vic, sensing I was watching him, quickly hung his arm out of the window.

'You checked out all de joints he tole you 'bout?'

I shook my head. 'Nah, only the Shady. That's where I found Loudon and got my first lead. The Black and White has every face in St Pauls and Montpelier walking through its doors, all times of the day. You know as well as I do most folk going in there are minding their own business. Picking up anything about Trista in there was always gonna be slim.'

Vic nodded in agreement. 'Whaddabout the Gambling House an' de Inkerman?'

'That's the Jah's territory.' I glanced over to check Vic's reaction; he was already nodding to himself appreciatively.

'Too fuckin' reet,' he muttered under his breath.

'I wanted to check in with you first before setting foot in either of those places. Didn't want to put any of your people's noses outta joint. Me asking them questions they'd rather not answer.'

Vic drew his arm in, wiping his palm over the back of his hand, the anger in his eye fading a little. 'Looks like I best go axe fo' you den.'

There was something very ugly in the words and the way Vic used them. But ugly was the life my cousin lived.

★ ★ ★

The Gambling House was a large building occupying what had once been a mortuary. It had one big room with a bar and five smaller rooms for private poker games and illegal betting. In the old days, before I came to Britain, the undertakers had a bookmaker plying his trade behind the coffin repository. Mourners would come in grieving and leave with new hope.

Vic had bought the place for a song about three years ago. The Gamb's, as it was known locally, wasn't even a joint that the local St Pauls residents frequented. It belonged to degenerates, thieves, pickpockets and quick-tempered men who dared you to try and look them in the eye so they could beat you to a pulp. It was the kind of place that, if you had any sense, and wanted to keep your cash in your wallet, you steered well clear of.

Sam Cooke was singing about the chain gang on the juke box. Lonnie Reed, a terracotta-coloured man, stood statue-like behind his marble top bar. Vic had done the burly man a big favour years before and now Reed was living on borrowed time because of what my cousin had done.

'Jah,' Lonnie called as we walked in the door.

I looked around for trouble but all I saw were men and women hunched over small tables, drinking and talking under a haze of ganja smoke.

Vic lit a joint and let it burn between his fingers for a moment while he searched the room for folk he recognised or didn't like. He snapped his fingers at me. 'Gimme de photographs.' I did as he ordered.

Vic settled at the bar, took a pull on his spliff and laid the photos out in front of his employee. I kept my distance and let my cousin conduct business. He pointed at the picture of Trista Walker.

'Lonnie, you recognise dis bitch?'

Lonnie wagged his head, sniffed deeply, resting one hand, which owned only three fingers, on the marble top. 'I 'naw she de minister's woman. Seen her 'bout, nevah spoke to eh.' The barman sniffed again. Scratched his neck. 'If you axin' if she evah bin in 'ere, I ain't seen her fo' sure.'

239

'Little bird tole me she gone walkabout. Needs findin'.'

Lonnie shrugged. 'She nevah got herself lost in de Gamb's, Jah.' The barman gave both pictures another once-over, then concentrated his yellowy eyes back onto Vic. 'I can swear on dat.'

Vic nodded, shot a thumb over his shoulder. 'My man 'ere is lookin' fo' de Walker woman an' de niggah wearin' de mask.'

Lonnie looked at the photograph again, grinned and gave me a fleeting suspicious glare. 'Good luck wid dat, man.'

Vic perched the reefer in the corner of his mouth and rested his palm over Lonnie's three-fingered hand, curled his hand around the remaining digits and squeezed. 'You gonna loose de utha t'ree o' dem fuckin' nose pickers, you keep speakin' like that to ma kin.' Vic released his grip and sucked on the cannabis cigarette while a much-pained Lonnie Reed found some respect, by giving both Vic and myself a deferential nod.

Vic bent forward across the marble and I watched the bartender tremble. 'Lonnie, now listen up, bwoy. I want you to put de word out to de punters in 'ere dat de Jah is lookin' fo' de pastor's wife. Dat I'm lookin' to 'ear anyt'ing 'bout her. Who de bitch hangs out wid. Where she might be, whether dat hidin' out some place or if she bin buried six feet under. I wanna 'naw.' Vic stabbed at the bar with a finger, then pointed into Lonnie's face. 'Send one o' you boys ovah to de Inkerman an' let 'em 'naw de same ting. Got it?'

Vic's demand got him another reverential bow from Lonnie.

'I 'naw de drill, Jah.'

'Good.' Vic gave a slight shrug. ''Remember whatta told you all dem years back, Lonnie?' Vic headed for the door.

'We all gotta die sum'day.'

Vic dropped his joint to the floor. Stubbed out the roach with the toe of his shoe then turned and looked back at the bar. 'You jus' don't wan' it to be you any-time soon.' He winked at Lonnie. 'If you git ma drift.'

Vic's threat reverberated in my head as we walked out from a room that had once held a few dozen coffins.

The Miner's Arms was another two-storey red-brick monstrosity that sat on the corner of Seddon Road in the St Werburgh's district. The old ale house was well known for fistfights, bad beer, late night lock-ins and little else. I followed Vic across the road and peered into one of the dirty windows, then looked around the dark, empty bar. I knew that the courtyard at the rear of the Miner's led to a narrow alleyway. At the end of it were a half dozen or so small ground-floor apartments, built after the Second World War by the brewery that owned the pub and were now little more than rat-infested squats.

Dipper Council had said that Queenie lived over the pub. I suspected she was holed up in one of the dwellings behind the place. Despite what Vic had said, I was pretty sure that Queenie Blue wouldn't be home and was surprised when a black woman in her late fifties yanked open the gate door into the court-yard. She was short and skeletal but there was life burning in those eyes.

'Yeah?' It was more an accusation than a question.

'I'm looking for Queenie Blue.' Vic rested his back

against the wall.

'You don't look like de Babylon.'

'No, sister, sure as hell ain't.' After staring me out in a way that I don't believe Joe Frazier could have matched, the woman took a step towards me. I was more than half convinced she was most probably armed with something.

'If you ain't de law, whadda you wantin' wid Queenie at this time o' de day?'

Vic stood away from the wall, pushed me aside and backed the woman a few paces into the yard.

'Bitch, don't be fuckin' round wid de man. I ain't in de mood fo' no vexation. Jus' point your scabby finger at de cock rat's crib an' git de fuck outta me way.'

The woman continued to maintain her standoff for the best part of three seconds. Any test of strength she wished to impart on me was lost at the sight of Vic looming in front of her. Sweat beaded on her forehead and she was breathing hard. Eventually she pointed unsteadily towards the alleyway behind her.

'Queenie, she probably shacked up in de last den on de left.'

Vic shoved her aside and I followed after him.

The alley led down to a cobblestone street. A woman was washing clothes at a courtyard tap probably shared by half a dozen other squatters. Another woman was emptying cold ashes into a dustbin standing under her front window. Scenes like these looked like they had been lifted straight out of the Bristol of 1900, but I knew there were black people across St Pauls and Montpelier who were forced to still live in the past. Not in any figurative sense, but quite literally — in tiny one- or two-roomed houses built with scant

242

regard for either hygiene or comfort the best part of a century ago. The cave-like dwelling we were about to enter now defied the category of 'home'. Just chipped bricks and crumbling mortar, stacked one on top of the other, just waiting for a good gust of wind to come and blow it down.

The last building on the left had throwaway newspapers and beer bottles piled up at the threshold. And there was so much other junk mail jammed into the letterbox that some of the envelopes had fallen among the rubbish that littered the front step. I was sure no one was home but still knocked, out of some ridiculous deference.

Vic shot me a disgruntled look. 'Git de fuck on wid it.'

I had to take a breath before putting my hand on the knob.

'Ah, shit,' Vic said as I turned the handle and let out the ripe stink that had been trapped inside. We were both all too familiar with the unpleasant odour that was now hitting our nostrils. I'd seen a lot of death in my time; from the backstreets of Barbados to the backwoods of Louisiana. The cold hand of death had followed me from paradise, across the ocean, all the way to Bristol.

Vic reached inside his jacket and drew out a Browning 9mm pistol. He gave a curt nod and I took another breath and pushed open the door.

The hall stank of urine, faeces and blood. We found Queenie Blue in a darkened front room a few feet from the front door, the only light coming from a crack in the hessian curtains strung up over the filthy window. She was laid up against her bed, hands and feet bound and her pink blouse cut open, exposing blood-soaked breasts, with the rest of her body smeared crimson and naked. Her hands and feet were bound tightly with thin cord. A knife protruded from her chest. Her dead eyes stared up at the ceiling. Above her head, written on the damp plaster wall in blood was the word, TRAITOR.

We both stood motionless for a moment, taking in the scene.

Then I heard Queenie Blue take in a gurgling breath.

We both jumped. I am not ashamed to admit that I would have turned and ran from that damn filthy room if it wasn't for Vic standing right behind me. My cousin stepped around me, the Browning held out at arm's length in front of him. He scanned the barrel of the gun around the tiny room but there was no immediate danger — it quickly became very clear that there was just the three of us inside.

There was a straight-back wood chair set near the head of the ancient brass bed. I imagined Queenie's Johns threw their sweaty clothes and underwear down onto it before they slid between the sheets with her. I moved quickly over to Queenie's side, dropped down onto it. Death peered at me through the woman's watery, bloodshot eyes and decided that I had to be trusted.

'It . . . it . . . was . . . the Obeah's chil',' she stuttered. Blood bubbled around her dark lips and trickled from the corner of her mouth and dripped down onto her bare skin.

'What de fuck she babblin' on 'bout?' Vic growled.

I flung my arm out behind me, my palm outstretched. 'Shut up, will you?' I heard Vic mutter a string of obscenities under his breath. I leaned across the bed, drawing my face close to Blue's blood-tinged

244

lips. The foul bouquet coming off her flesh and out of her mouth took my breath. 'Queenie, was it Trista Walker . . . did she do this to you?'

Queenie turned her hot, confused eyes on me. 'Obeah,' she whispered. Her head rose a few inches then quickly sank so that her chin rested against the top of her sweating torso. I watched, unable to do anything, as she began to drift off into a feverish, final sleep.

I had about a dozen questions for Queenie. I wanted to know why Trista Walker had done this to her. Where was the minister's wife now? But Queenie didn't have either the time or strength and I knew I'd never get the answers I needed from her. I turned to Vic. He gave the dying Queenie Blue a fleeting, icy glance and sucked his teeth.

'I gotta call this into Peace.'

'You gotta be crazy, man!' Vic snapped, refusing to look me in the eyes. 'To hell wid dis Peace fella an' de rest o' de fuckin' Babylon.'

I got to my feet. 'I'm calling for an ambulance.' Vic grunted and holstered the Browning. He rubbed at his nose and shook his head at me like an angry parent would to a badly behaved child. I knew if I hung around, my cousin would try his best to prevent from doing what I knew to be the right thing. I headed back out into the hall. 'Then I'm calling Peace.'

'Tell 'im to bring a fuckin' undertaker wid 'im!' Vic hollered back.

I found a call box on the corner of Boyce Drive a few hundred yards down the road from the Miner's Arms. I took the slip of paper Richard Peace had given me and dialled the number written on it.

'Peace,' he said, answering on the third ring.

'I got another body for you, Mr Peace. This one's just about to give up on breathing.'

33

Vic and I left Queenie Blue's squat before the police and the ambulance turned up. I told Richard Peace that's what I would be doing, and he didn't argue the point. I told him the details of how and why I'd found her, and also that I would appreciate it if my name was not mentioned in dispatches for now. Peace had laughed like a drain after hearing my plea. It was the same shifty roar he'd cackled in my living room. He said, in between chuckling, that he would handle Superintendent Eve who in turn, he assured me, would keep his hounds, Locke and Mapp, from sniffing around. Before I rested the receiver in the cradle, Richard Peace piped up his well-worn mantra: 'Remember, you have anything else for me. Call me, day or night, and nobody else.'

I walked out of the phone box thinking Vic had been right. That I should have heeded his warning about contacting the police and left Peace in the dark about Queenie Blue. In Vic's eyes, reaching out to a man like Richard Peace made me about as trustworthy and reliable as Floyd 'Dipper' Council.

Aiding the police made me little more than an Uncle Tom as far as my cousin was concerned. He'd always hated the fact that I'd served in the Barbados police force. He'd chosen, long ago, to remain silent about my service on the force, and like Kipling's shrewd elephant, Hathi, he never forgot, nor did he forgive me. The way Vic saw it, a man prepared to betray his own cultural or social allegiance, to work hand in hand with the much-detested Babylon was a man obedient and servile to his white masters.

I headed back to the car. I had the feeling that my long-dead ancestors' cruel history was suddenly weighing me down as I trudged along the pavement. I felt the iron slave's collar biting around my neck. I knew that Richard Peace's clenched fist was grasping hold of the shackles and chains that would forever keep me in my place.

* * *

We didn't dwell on Queenie's fate and instead headed straight for the Printer's Devil Inn on Broad Plain. It was an unlikely acquisition to bolster Vic's already considerable array of properties: situated in a strictly white part of town, the old pub-cum-bed and break-fast sat between Bristol Temple Meads station and the offices of the local paper, the *Bristol Post*. Most of the rest of the businesses on the road were white collar: solicitors, accountants and insurance offices, alongside taxi ranks and newly built corporate high rises. It was, however, another respectable front for Vic's many business ventures and a useful staging post when travelling up to Bristol. Vic always preferred to stay out of St Pauls on his increasingly rare visits to the city, preferring the Devil's cosy accommodation and low-key location.

Driving around to the alley that ran behind the Printer's Devil, I parked up in the covered garage that always had one spare place kept available for when Vic was in town. From there we ascended the rear stairway. A few moments later we were identified by the peephole and the door came open.

George Berry was a better version of me. Taller by at least a quarter foot and an inch or two broader. He had a friendly smile, a slight limp and a right hook that Leon Spinks would have been cautious of. John had been a friend of Vic's since the sixties, when beer was cheap and black lives mattered even less than they did now.

'Vic, what you doin' comin' up the back stairs like some thief?'

Vic slapped George on the arm and grinned. 'I'm thievin', ole fella. What you tink?'

'I'm tinkin' same ole Vic then, eh?' George had already turned around and was hobbling back down the slender, dimly lit corridor towards a distant red door while laughing to himself. 'What you need?' he growled.

'What do most folk need when dey come to de Devil's?' Vic asked, following in his friend's wake.

'Most o' my customers come to drink your knock-off rum.'

'Well, dem brothers and sisters they got good taste, George. Keep 'em coming and fillin' dat cash register fo' me.'

'Till's full most nights. Cain't complain 'bout bid'ness, Vic.'

'Dat whadda like to hear, brother. Drinks only de primer, George. Your punters need to come to de Devil to feel welcome and be with utha fools . . . and talk to you miserable mug 'bout their foolishness.'

George made a huffing sound. 'Any vexations Vic Ellington's got is way beyond a poor brother like me.' He passed through the red door into a bright cream hallway that was half the length of the first.

Vic laughed and we followed the landlord until we

came to the bar. The drinking room we faced was small, brightened by wide stained-glass windows gathering the little sun from the late afternoon sky. There was a half dozen customers. All of them men, probably shift workers from the railways, all of them caked in the dirt of their hard labour, all intent on their libation. I didn't recognise anyone.

'Where's Herbie?' Vic asked.

Herbert White was the 25-stone bouncer who was usually perched on a high stool behind the rear door.

'Herbie don't come in till the sun go all the way down. Fucka's like Moses deliverin' the Eleventh Commandment from on high.'

We made our way to the other side of the bar and sat on the tall oak stools.

'What's your pleasure?' George inquired.

Vic pointed at the unopened bottle of rum sat on the back of the bar. 'Just crack dat fucka open an' set up t'ree glasses.'

George did just that. I sat there counting the scars on the barman's face accrued over many years of doing business for Vic while he poured three fingers of dark liquor into three glass tumblers. Vic raised his glass and sank the contents.

'Gonna need my usual crib fo' a couple o' nights, George.'

The barman nodded. 'Sure, no problem.' He took a sip of his rum. 'I'll git one of the girls to make up your bed with fresh linen and put in some extra towels.'

Vic took the rum bottle from the bar, refilled his glass and took a swig. He directed the neck of the bottle towards George. 'An' don't fo'git to send a couple o' bottles o' dis down wid de clean sheets.'

George gave Vic the thumbs up and wandered down

to the other end of the bar to serve a waiting customer. Vic refilled my glass and topped up his own.

'I'll git Bitter Lemon to pass de word round. Let Stollie 'naw ovah at de Alexander Club an' anyone else I got sniffin' 'bout. I'll be bunkin' here at nights fo' de time being. At least till you got dis shit sorted.' He chucked back the rum in his glass and charged it again. He suddenly conjured up a contemplative look which surprised me. 'You 'naw, whoever carved up Queenie Blue, dey one sick piece o' work.'

Vic's frank statement threw me. Hearing him offering an opinion on someone else's violent behaviour seemed highly unusual, especially coming from a man, who had, over the years, shot, stabbed, decapitated and burned his enemies.

'Sick enough to kill twice and leave the same calling card. The traitor thing, it doesn't make a lot of sense. Why do it?'

Vic shrugged and drained his glass again. 'Whoever's doin' de butcherin's making a point.'

'Which is?'

Vic's top lip rose into a half smile. 'Fuck wid me sucka, an' dis is what you git.' He took a deep breath and poured another two fingers of booze. 'So, what next?' he asked.

'We take a trip out to Brislington retirement home.' I retrieved my notebook from my inside pocket and flipped the pages to retrieve the rest home's number I'd scribbled down earlier.

'Why de hell we goin' to some ratty care home?'

''Cause that's where Hoo Shoo Dupree's lodging these days.'

'Hell, not dat creepy ole fucka agin.' Any trace of Vic's smile disappeared behind a look that was

251

suddenly aggrieved. 'Brutha, you really 'naw how to show a man a good time. Scabby squats, dead whores, an' now an' institution fo' ole folk.' My cousin syphoned the booze in his glass in a single gulp. He looked into my eyes, hesitated, then said. 'Shit.'

I called to George. 'Can I use your phone?'

'You know where it's at, man.' Over Vic's shoulder I saw the barman lift his rum in toast.

The gesture sent a feeling of warmth running through my veins.

But my blood had already chilled by the time I'd finished dialling the number to the witch's coven.

34

Snow.

Falling faintly at first, soon to become a blizzard.

When Vic and I had pulled into the car park at the rear of the Printer's Devil earlier in the afternoon I'd noticed dark clouds forming in the sky above and felt a cold wind picking up. But I never imagined that we'd be hit with such an icy squall in the short time that we'd been sat drinking and chatting. In the space of an hour the pavements and the roofs of the buildings outside had gone from granite and slate to being ice-capped with a thick layer of white.

The heavy flurries had all but ceased as the two of us set back out for me to pay Hoo Shoo Dupree a surprise visit. What was falling from the sky now was the kind of fine snow I'd always hated; the icy stuff that works inside your neckline and melts, bitter, against the skin. As I knocked snow from the car windscreen, Vic stood awkward and silent for a moment, his breath rising white towards the thin passing flakes. He coughed loudly and kicked in disgust at one of the tyres.

'Why de 'ell you still drivin' round dis ole shitbox?'

He reluctantly climbed in and I joined him behind the wheel.

'Some of us don't have the luxury of being chauffeur-driven in a Daimler.'

I turned the key in the ignition and listened to the engine struggle to turn over. Vic shook his head, snarled and beat his arms with the palms of his hands.

'Like bein' in a four-wheeled fuckin' chest freezer.'
I saw him comb the dashboard trying to locate the
blower controls. 'Git dis piece o' shit movin' so we
can fire up de damn heater,' he snapped, inhaling a
breath of air that was as sharp as a razor to my throat.

It was a little after five and the final hint of day was
still lingering in the darkening evening sky. We drove
in silence through the slush-covered streets of Bristol
out along the Bath Road and kept going for another
three miles, the interior of the car slowly heating up,
the meagre warmth thankfully calming my cousin a
little. I knew that Vic didn't want to talk about Hoo
Shoo; not because he feared her reputation as a *mambo*
priestess or the hexes she was renowned for casting
back in the day. No, Vic hated Dupree because he
associated her with my past. My bad luck. My sadness
and loss. Vic saw a woman like Hoo Shoo as being little more than vermin. A fly-blown pest best swotted
and swiftly despatched.

Away from the yellow melting snow of the city,
everything in the countryside looked white and clean,
like an Alpine landscape. We reached the outskirts of
Brislington just as the last of the light was about to
extinguish. The retirement home was a walled estate
with an ornately arched wrought-iron gate and large
bronze letters in the brickwork; the house itself a
three-storey, sandstone Georgian building that looked
more like a university than it did an old folk's home.

I pulled into the car park at the front of the main
building and turned to Vic. 'I'll be as quick as I can,
okay?'

Vic nodded and put an unlit reefer into his mouth.
I heard him mumble something as he peered through
the trees along the roofline of the care home. He

rubbed at his chin and looked back at me.

'What you thinking?' I asked.

'Like we bin 'ere before.'

'No . . . not to my knowledge, we haven't.'

Vic made a disgruntled tutting sound. 'No 'ere, you eediat. Me talkin' 'bout de time all dem years ago, I took you out to Dupree's place in St Andrew's.'

'Dupree's an old woman.' I stepped out and dropped my head back inside the car. 'She'll have lost some of her bite since I last spoke to her.'

I slammed the car door, hoping to trap what was left of the warmth inside. 'Don't you fuckin' believe it,' my cousin bawled back at me.

Brislington House had been built as a private lunatic asylum. Rumour has it, that when it opened in the early 1800s, it was one of the first purpose-built institutions of its kind in England. From the outside it resembled the kind of crestfallen haunt that Dickens's jilted spinster, Miss Havisham, had rattled around in. Inside, the old recluse would have felt right at home. The place stank of misery: every inch of the building was archaic and cold.

Brislington came complete with walls a pale, institutional green, and grey linoleum flooring, clean enough to operate on. A glass-topped admissions desk was built into a recessed alcove along one wall. Across from it hung a large oil portrait of a bulldozer-faced dowager who I guessed was either one of the first lunatics to stay in the place or had helped build it. I had no interest in reading her name on the little plaque screwed to the gilt frame, and headed for reception. Straight ahead I could see a gleaming corridor where a white-clad orderly pushing an empty wheelchair turned a corner and disappeared from view.

I'd barely set foot through the door and Brislington House was already starting to make my skin crawl. There was something depressing about the efficient sterility of the place. The hushed tread of rubber soles down bright hallways reeking of Dettol. Faceless attendants anonymous in crisp, milk-white uniforms.

I imagined that the staff in these kinds of hell holes carried out routines so monotonous that even emptying a bedpan probably took on some kind of ritual importance. As far as I was concerned, care homes were like prisons; all seemed the same from the inside. A woman behind the admissions desk was young and homely. She was dressed in starched ivory and wore a black nametag that said, C. HICKMAN. The alcove opened onto an office lined with filing cabinets and polished wooden desks.

'May I help you?' Miss Hickman had a voice as sweet as angel's breath and a face as icy as the weather outside. Fluorescent light glinted on her thick, rimless spectacles.

'I certainly hope so,' I said and smiled. 'My name is Otis Walker.' I glanced at my wristwatch. 'I apologise for the lateness of my visit this evening. I have an elderly aunt residing here at Brislington. I was hoping that it may be possible to see her?'

Miss Hickman regarded me suspiciously, her eyes wavering behind the thick lenses like tropical fish in an aquarium. I could tell she didn't like the cut of my suit, the way I spoke or the colour of my skin.

'My wife and I travelled over from Jamaica last weekend. Something of a whirlwind trip to visit family dotted across the country before we move on to the rest of Europe.' Miss Hickman's face remained stony. 'We're only here in Bristol overnight and this is very much a spur of the moment decision to swing by, if you see what I mean.'

The receptionist looked at the clock on the wall behind her then shifted back to me. 'I'm afraid our residents will be heading to the dining room for supper shortly.' She glanced down at the snow on my shoes and made a face like she'd just swallowed a handful of slugs.

'I really do only want to say the briefest of hellos and see how the old girl is.' Miss Hickman gave me the kind of look a teacher reserves for class dunces. That withering glare didn't stop me from persisting. 'Just five minutes, so I can take word back to her family in Jamaica. Let 'em all know she's doing fine here at Brislington.'

'What is the name of your aunt?' the receptionist, asked experimenting a weak smile.

'Walker . . . Clementine Walker.'

'One moment please.' Miss Hickman retreated into the inner office and pulled out a drawer of one of the filing cabinets. She returned carrying a slate grey register and slid it across the glass in front of me. 'Miss Walker can be found on the Carisbrook wing, third landing, room thirteen.' The receptionist stuck a shapely arm out of the window towards the corridor. 'Once you reach the end of the hallway, turn right and follow the signs above your head. You'll find the Carisbrook wing next to the entrance of our chapel.' She glanced back at the clock before offering me a final red flag. 'Residents are called for their evening meal at six. I'd be grateful if you would be mindful of that fact and be gone before then.'

I waved my thanks and didn't hang around. On my way down the corridor, I passed two elderly residents,

257

a man and a woman, sat on banquet-style chairs, both hunched over, their heads bowed towards the floor and mumbling to themselves in a language I had never heard before. I wished them a 'good evening'.

They did not greet me nor look up as I passed.

35

A musky, pungent odour hung in the air as I approached Hoo Shoo Dupree's room. It was the scent of stale incense, of rotting vegetation, an earthy smell like that of mud and water-life, the kind that flourished in the swamplands back home. The number 13 was pinned dead centre in the middle of the Dupree's door, the brass digits buffed to a glinting shine. I knocked once and moments later heard a familiar voice from my nightmares call back from the other side.

'Come on in, chil'.'

I slowly opened the door but stayed put in the hall-way. The room was not much bigger than a cell and was illuminated by a low-watt bulb emanating from a small lamp on the edge of a dark wood dressing table. Dupree was sat directly in front of me, bolt upright in a tubular aluminium wheelchair. She was barefoot, wearing a maroon ankle-length short-sleeved dress. Her ash grey, thinning hair pulled tight across her scalp and tied in a small bun on the top of her head. Her parchment-thin ebony skin on her face, arms and hands had shrivelled and was pinched to the bones.

'Come on in and close the door.' Her command was both fragile and feminine, but it strangely still carried weight. I did as the old woman asked and Dupree pointed at a high-back chair at the foot of her bed. 'Sit yourself down.' She smiled at me faintly. Her teeth appeared perfect. As I sat and looked up at Hoo Shoo, the room around me seemed to blur for a second or two, the walls and furniture without specific detail or special form. Dupree pointed a finger at something behind me. 'I see you still have all those poor, lost souls clinging to your hide, Mr Ellington.'

I ignored the remark, already feeling the tears welling up in my eyes. I concentrated so hard that I began to tremble. 'You remember me, Miss Dupree?'

The old woman nodded her head. 'Oh, I remember you, son.'

As crazy as it seemed, I could feel Dupree's strange power and magnetism beginning to anchor itself at my already floating thoughts. She slowly sat forward in her seat. 'An' I've long waited for you to come back an' visit me.' Dupree's eyes searched mine. A strange sensation filled my ears and began to affect my balance. I felt weightless in the chair; my arms and legs growing heavier, my breathing quickly becoming laboured as if the air was being sucked out of the room. Dupree reached her hand into the bedside drawer next to her wheelchair, took out a small brown leather pouch and a thin white candle. She dropped the bag in her lap and lit the candle with a match. I watched as she dripped a small pool of wax onto the top of the table and held the base of the candle in it until both had fused together. She kept her eyes on the flame and began silently praying.

It took all my concentration to find the right words. 'I'm looking for your daughter, Celestine.'

Dupree ignored me for a moment or two then gradually raised her head. She opened her eyes, turned and smiled. 'Bin a long time since I heard anyone speak that name to me.'

'When was the last time you saw her?'

Dupree gave a weak shrug. 'Chil' come by now an' then. Flits in on the breeze when the mood takes her.'

She cleared her throat and just for a second, I thought I saw her eyes cloud over. 'Why you asking?'

'Because she's missing and people are worried about her.'

'People worried; I don't think so. You must be talkin' 'bout the pastor?'

'I am. It was Celestine's husband, Mervyn, who asked me to try and find her.'

Hearing the pastor's name mentioned clearly amused Dupree. Her leathery face puckered, her lips creasing towards another smile, one that seemed crueller than kind. 'Oh, I bet he did.'

I felt a chill run down my back as she cast out the words.

'He's concerned for her wellbeing, Miss Dupree.'

'And his bank balance too, I suspect.'

'I beg your pardon?'

'No man can serve two masters: for either he will hate the one, and love the other; or else, he will hold to the one, and despise the other.' Dupree's eyes widened, the candlelight catching in her pupils.

'Matthew six, chapter twenty-four,' I said.

'Exactly. You know your scripture, son.'

'Thank Sunday School for that, Miss Dupree. I seem to recall an old white woman teaching me and a bunch of other kids about the sins of man and money.'

'The honky woman was right. Man can't serve God and mammon; Pastor Walker would do well to be reminded of that fact.'

'I'll remember to mention it to the reverend when we next speak.'

Anger flashed in her eyes, but then it was gone in an instant like lightning. 'You'd be wise not to mock me, Mr Ellington.'

261

'I'm not here to ridicule, just to try and get your help.'

'And why would I give you that?'

'Because I think you're the only person who can perhaps shine a light on where your daughter may be.' Dupree gave me an odd look. 'If I can find her, then I can maybe help her, perhaps go some way in easing the pastor's fears too.'

'My chil' don't need yours or anybody else's help.' Dupree muttered something under her breath, similar to the words I'd just heard the elderly couple speaking. She showed me her pearly incisors, like a hungry reef shark about to take a bite out of me. 'The minister deserves a little grief in his life, trust me.' Dupree hacked up a wad of phlegm and spat into a waste basket at her feet.

I looked at my watch. 'The receptionist told me you eat at six.' Dupree fixed me with a steely stare which I fought hard to freeze out. 'How about you stop playing games and start being straight with me?'

Dupree cackled and stroked at her hair but remained silent.

'You just said you were anticipating my return. You gotta have something worthwhile to cough up after all this time?'

'Mebbe, I have.' Dupree rubbed the bridge of her nose and searched my face with a deific gaze. 'Truth is, I've waited a long time to tell you about that child of mine. Tales about how she's been captivating men like you and Mervyn Walker since she was no higher than my waist. How she's enchanted men by candle-light, by firelight, by moonlight an', if Baron Samedi had instructed her, by starlight too. I've watched Celestine pleasure and dance for the great and good

262

of this city since she was a little girl. Aldermen and councillors, doctors, barristers, politicians and policemen. They all came to watch her whirl and sway. She danced for them, naked with a white snake named Damballa wrapped around her, taunting those rich white men who visited my home, mocking them while they stared wide-eyed at her. Over the years my voodoo child worked her magic through each and every one of those men. She got strong feeding off their money and power. By the time she was fourteen, I'd have men and women queuing to lay down with her, to touch her. Men loved to feel her young flesh, caress that soft skin. Some of them paid good money to feel those young loins and I encourage her to touch theirs. For Celestine, it was an act of healing through lust, Mr Ellington.'

Hearing what Dupree was telling me made me feel sick to the pit of my stomach. Beads of perspiration spiked across my forehead and temple. I ran my hand across my mouth and cheek, felt the five o'clock shadow of my beard catching against my fingertips. 'You let that happen to your own child?'

Dupree gave another shrug and offered a lofty grin. 'Erzulie, the love goddess, permitted it. Not I.' The crazy old woman looked me in the eye as she continued to speak. 'I was powerless to prevent her intervention. It was not my place to interfere in such sacred practices.'

'You're insane.'

Dupree's disdainful smirk quickly melted into a frown of disgust. 'Celestine has resided in the House of Whispers since she was a babe in arms. Erzulie guided her into the woman she has become. Drawn her to men she craves and feeds off.'

'Men like Mervyn Walker?' My voice cracked; there was a foul taste of bile in my throat.

'Uh-huh.' Dupree sighed softly. 'The pastor is a *bokor*.'

'Speak English.'

Dupree shook her head and gave me another shot of her dark eye. 'I better educate you fast, son, what with my supper about to be served up, right?' I felt the bruised knuckles in my right hand start to throb. I saw Dupree staring at my fingers before speaking again. 'A *bokor* is a *hungan-macoutte*.'

'A *hungan*, what?'

'A soul who is evil, whether they realise it or not. He is a priest of Obeah. Same as a *mambo* like me, only a man.'

I laughed. 'Are you telling me that Mervyn Walker is a devil worshipper?'

'I'm telling you that the pastor was drawn towards the dark long before my daughter got her hands on him. He was already bad. Over here people might have different names for that badness. Where I come from, we'd call a man like the pastor a *hungan*.'

'You're not making any sense.'

'Make sense.' She hissed the words rather than spoke them. I heard Dupree's breath come in short angry snorts. 'What I'm telling you is the truth, up to you whether you want to believe me or not.' The old woman folded her hands in her lap and sneered at me. 'Celestine had been away for a long time before she came back home to Bristol. By then, my girl was on the lookout for a certain type of soulmate. A weak man who thought he'd be holding the whip hand but who would be easy to manipulate. Celestine struck lucky the day she found Mervyn Walker.'

264

Dupree's breathing had settled into long sighs that cut into the tiny room like a hot spoon into lard. 'My girl could tell that the pastor was weak. Covetous. A fool who thought he was cleverer than the woman he was falling in love with. In truth the man is too slick for his own good.'

I heard Chloe's voice unexpectedly chime in my head, whispering the words, 'Elder Slick.'

'The pastor was easy pickings for Celestine. She saw the darkness in him. His greed, his need for power and status. She had him fooled with a phony name and a sham past life that she'd gone and fashioned for herself.' Dupree spat into the wastebasket again. 'She had that man wrapped around her little finger from the day she decided to lure him in, even after they were hitched and he thought he was going to be ruling the roost.'

'And what did she have to gain from all this subterfuge?'

'Well, that's for you to go find out, son.'

I reached into my pocket, took out the colour photograph of Dupree's daughter with Troy Loudon and the masked man. I moved forward, my fingers trembling and held the picture up close to her face.

'Can you see the people in this photo?'

'Just about.'

'Your daughter is lying next to two men on that bed. One of the men is dead. The other fella, the one with his face covered, I'm looking for a name to pin on him.'

'Then you came to the right place to ask, son.' The candlelight flickered across her face and Dupree smiled coyly at me. 'That boy's name is Mack Hurbon. He'll be in the deep waters by now.'

'The what?'

'The deep waters are where the souls of the dead must pass through to be finally reunited with their ancestors. I can see that Hurbon's already making that final journey.'

'Why are you telling me all of this so freely, Miss Dupree?'

Hoo Shoo Dupree looked at me for a long time. While she did, she seemed to get older and older; her eyes became tired, the folds in her face deepened. 'I told you how long I've been waiting for you to walk through that door. I had a story to tell and now you've heard it. And 'cause the women you came in here with are asking me to.'

My mouth went dry, my lips stuck as I spoke. 'What women?'

Dupree gestured towards the door. 'The woman stood behind you who's with chil', holding her pick-ney's hand and the pretty white woman stood next to her.'

I wanted to turn and look behind me, but I felt frozen to the spot. It was if an invisible wall had suddenly come down between Dupree and me. The old woman was talking, but I could no longer hear her words. I wanted to know everything about the women she spoke of, but I couldn't speak. Dupree seemed to be slowly moving backward, as if her chair was being drawn away by cables into the depths of a featureless realm. As she moved off into the distance the candle-light dimmed and then seconds later became bright again. Hearing the old woman's words returned me from the dead and the dreaming.

'You brought death with you too, Mr Ellington.'

I shook my head, partly insisting that Dupree was

wrong, partly to shake some sense back into myself. 'No, not that I'm aware of.'

'I can smell it on you.' She held up the little leather bag by the tips of her thin fingers, slowly swinging it from side to side.

'Take it, son.'

I reached over and took the pouch from her. Whatever was inside was lumpy, uneven, filled with tiny twigs and stones, and it stank to high heaven. 'What is it?'

'*Gris-gris*,' Dupree muttered. 'Just like the women in my family have been making for generations.'

I weighed the bag suspiciously in the palm of my hand. 'Why are you giving me this?'

'It's not for you.' The old woman turned to the wall, staring as if she could see through the plaster and brickwork. 'Give it to your friend out there in the cold. Tell them to keep it with 'em at all times.'

'And why would I do that?'

'It will keep them safe.'

'Are they in danger?'

Dupree took a deep breath, held it for a second, then let it out. 'More than you realise,' she said solemnly. 'Your friend may be sceptical now. But I feel what he's already feeling.'

'And what's that?'

'Why, the call of the deep waters, of course.'

267

36

It was snowing hard again when I got back to the car.

''Bout fuckin' time,' Vic snapped as I climbed in. 'Man, am freezin' my nuts off in 'ere. Jus' fire up de engine an' git us the fuck outta 'ere.'

I knew only too well that my cousin would not enquire how I'd got on with Hoo Shoo, nor did he have the patience to listen to me give a blow-by-blow account of what had transpired in her room. It would have taken another dead body or a bucket of blood to jolt Vic's idle curiosity. The information I'd garnered from Dupree, no matter how flighty it may have seemed, rang true in my head, but my cousin would have found her rambling hard to swallow.

I decided to keep most of what she'd told me, including Vic being in danger, to myself for now. He had never believed in the superstitions and arcane folklores which we'd grown up around back home. My cousin had, to my knowledge, no belief in any god, nor had he subscribed to any faith or religion, and had in the past used his look purely as disguise. Vic's dreads had never been worn to make a statement. They were not spiritual, nor did they symbolise the letting go of material possessions as those of the Rasta faith believed. Vic used his particular look as one big con job, and likewise, he believed that he and people like Hoo Shoo Dupree shared one thing in common — that they both knew how to bait and switch. Both were masters of sharp practice.

I turned the key in the ignition and listened to the

engine rattling and fire up. 'You ever hear of a fella name o' Mack Hurbon?'

'Naw. He a brother?'

'I'm guessing so.'

'Who is dis niggah?'

'Maybe a skeleton lurking in Trista Walker's wardrobe. He may be somebody, may be nothing. Any chance you can sniff the dirt on him?'

'Uh-huh. I'll give Bitter a call. He can git on it. The fat man can put de word out. Git you sum'ting fo' you head hit de pillow tonight.'

'That quick?'

Vic gave me a dirty look. 'Niggah can't git me whadda want faster than shit thru a goose, den I got naw use fo' 'im in my fuckin' army.'

As we left the grounds of Brislington I began to experience a strange feeling in my chest. It was both electric and respiratory. The sensation pulsed outward through my limbs and contorted my face in the rear-view mirror.

The emotion-based palsy made me shudder and flinch.

I pulled to the kerb outside the gates of the care home and took a deep breath. Sitting in the driver's seat, Vic at my side, both of us quiet, I began to understand the physical symptoms I was exhibiting.

I was, for the first time in a very long time frightened — like a child left alone in the dark. Maybe it had something to do with me being in the presence of Hoo Shoo Dupree, or worse still knowing I had the old witch's *gris-gris* bag, full of hexes and incantations sitting in my coat pocket. After speaking to Dupree, I was more certain than ever that I was set against more than just one bad man and maybe even a woman too, who intended to either do me or those I loved serious harm. As a small child, my father had told me that fear and danger force you to appreciate life; to understand its frailty, transience and its incalculable value.

The panic and dread inside of me now was not based on paternal wisdom or any concern for my own safety and welfare, but I was afraid for the wellbeing of Chloe, Loretta and Vic. They were all that mattered to me in the world. They were my world. My only remaining family. As part of me as a wolf is part of its pack.

My head was telling me that I should walk away. Let the likes of Richard Peace and his police buddies pick up the bloody mess Trista Walker was leaving in her wake. The wolf in my heart did not want to see those I cherished hurt, but my soul, whatever that is, still yearned to uncover the Walkers' secrets and, possibly, their lies.

We stopped at a Shell petrol station on our way back into Bristol to we could fill up the tank and so Vic could make some calls. While he was barking orders at Bitter down the pay phone, I had a moment to ponder. One thing about being a detective is that your actions often seem repetitive and even arbitrary: like an ant zigzagging its way across the floor, seemingly aimless, maybe even lost. My problem was that Pastor Mervyn Walker was so convincing. I'd believed him, and one thing detectives can never afford to do is believe anyone. So, with that in mind, I decided to double back on my tracks and go pay the reverend another visit later on in the evening. I'd try and shake him up a little. See if anything useful fell out.

If Vic was to tag along, I'd need to get him to promise that he'd keep his gun in his belt and his knife in his pocket. Putting Vic in the face of a possible enemy more often than not ended up in a war. Even if he crossed his heart and hoped to die, it wouldn't count for much if the pastor got on the wrong side of my cousin. Vic didn't need to be armed to draw blood. In the past he'd killed people with his bare hands, his feet and once with his teeth. No god nor prayer could protect a man if Vic decided to turn against him. Taking him along for the ride had its benefits, but the downside could be the prospect of all-out carnage.

Vic returned with a smile on his face and a joint burning between his fingers. 'Bitter's on to your man, Herpes.'

'It's Hurbon.'

My cousin shrugged, sucked on the end of his reefer and stepped inside the car, grinning through a veil of ganja-scented smoke.

'Word from de fat man, Queenie Blue nevah made it to de 'ospital alive.'

I nodded, not knowing really what to say to such miserable news. 'I want to go speak to the pastor later.'

Vic shrugged again. 'Scoop on' a dead whore an' a trip to church.' My cousin inhaled deeply on his reefer. He blew another plume of hoary smoke at me, his brows knitted. 'Shit, dis fuckin' night jus' keeps gettin' betta an' betta.'

271

37

Loretta had summoned Vic and I to join her, Bitter Lemon, Carnell Jnr and Chloe at her kitchen table for supper. Neither of us would have been dumb enough to decline such a demand. On the way back into St Pauls, Vic got me to stop at an off-licence on Ashley Road, where he picked up a crate of Dragon stout and bottles of cola and lemonade for the kids. When we walked into the Harris home, Chloe was already waiting to greet her uncle. She flung her arms around him, and the two hugged in the hallway while I stood on the step and watched like the proverbial third wheel. Loretta stood at the kitchen door, one hand on her hips, a wooden spoon in the other, her apron dusted with dumpling flour.

'You gonna shut dat fuckin' door or wha', Joseph?' Loretta shook the spoon at me. 'I look like I'm made o' money or sum'ting. May as well be heatin' de fuckin' street too fo' all you care!'

I inched inside and did as I was told.

'Both you fuckas stomp your damn shoes. Don't be trackin' snow an' shit thru ma house!'

It was the kind of warm welcome I remembered hearing as a child, and strange as it may have seemed, hearing my friend bawl at Vic and me was enough to cheer a low-spirited man's heart.

Loretta had made Bajan pepperpot thickened with okra. We ate for a while and Chloe explained to her captive audience around the table how the works of Joe Orton had a clear trajectory from Oscar Wilde's

The Importance of Being Earnest to the dead play-wright's, *What the Butler Saw*. Bitter and Vic, on their second bowls of pepperpot, listened intently. Bitter, who rarely smiled, seemed spellbound by Chloe's detailed oration. She was coming to the end of her bowl and her speech. I was about to tell her to go up and take a shower when Vic spoke.

'If your momma could see you now. What dat woman be feelin' hearin' you speak like dat.' Vic took a swig of his stout and Bitter grunted in agreement through a mouthful of food.

Chloe put her spoon down and slanted herself back. She already knew the broad strokes of her mother's life and death, but this was the first real chance she had at hearing about her from Vic.

'And my papa . . . what about him, what would he be feeling?'

Chloe's sudden enquiry set Vic off coughing. I saw the light dim a little in my cousin's eyes as he fought to cut short his cawing and wheezing.

'Proud,' Vic crackled. He took a deep breath and smiled at Chloe. 'Same as we all duh, baby.'

'How'd my papa die, Vic?' she asked delicately.

'Badly.' Vic pushed his bowl away from him. 'An' dat's all you evah need to 'naw, chil'.' Vic got up from his seat. Took a spliff from out of a silver cigarette case and lit it. He walked towards the back door. Chloe leaned across the table and placed her fingers over the back of my hand.

'You think one day, we could go see his grave, Papa?' Chloe's voice quavered, her eyes searching mine.

Vic swung open the door and answered Chloe's question before I'd even had chance to open my mouth.

'Uh-uh . . . You ain't gotta snowball's chance in hell, chil'.'

Everyone had their eyes on Vic's back.

Everyone except Loretta. Her steely glare was set on me.

★ ★ ★

While Vic and Bitter stood smoking and talking business outside in the yard, and Loretta, Carnell Jnr and Chloe washed and dried the dishes, I seized the opportunity to call Richard Peace's number from Loretta's phone in the hall. The line rang twice.

'Peace.'

'Evening, Mr Peace . . . Joseph Ellington.'

'Joseph. You have something for me?'

'I gotta name you should check out.' I heard the police liaison officer shuffle paper and click the top on a pen.

'Okay, give it to me.'

'Mack Hurbon.'

'You just giving me a name, or do you have more to tell?'

'For now, that's really all I've got. Whisper on the street is, Hurbon's connected in some way to Trista Walker.'

'In some way . . . do you want to try to be little more specific, Joseph?'

'I get the feeling Hurbon's been keeping Mrs Walker warm at night. I get the feeling he might be the sort of guy that's into Trista for more than the hugs and kisses. That a little more specific for you?'

Peace was silent for a moment. 'I'll get one of my people to run him through the system.'

'And I'll get back to you when I have more.'

'Do that, Joseph. And do it quick,' he snapped and hung up.

'Life's one long side street wid 'bout a million crossroads,' my momma used to tell me when I was a boy. 'Every hour, sometime every minute, you gotta make a choice 'bout which way to go. Some o' dem turns don't matter, don't let that fool ya. De minute you start tuh tink dat one way is jus' like t'otha, dat's when de shit come down.'

The shit was definitely coming down. I'd always believed I could survive any path set before me if I had Vic at my side. But hearing him speak so bluntly about Chloe's dead father had brought back into crystal-clear view what I'd always known; that my cousin's heart, when he chose it to, could quickly turn to stone.

Loretta, Bitter Lemon, Vic and I shared a cruel secret. Chloe's father, Conrad Monroe, was a degenerate white landowner and corrupt businessman who had, along with his equally depraved family, had in one way or another control over the Ellington family since before my mother's time.

The Monroes had taken our freedom centuries before and continued to have control over us for generations. Chloe was not born in wedlock or out of love; rather she came into the world as the end product of the years of abuse her mother had endured at the hands of Conrad Monroe. Conrad had murdered Bernice in a fit of rage, and my return to Barbados all those years ago was to bury my sister and lay old ghosts to rest.

It was Vic who had telegrammed me, informing me of Bernice's death, and in time, it would be Vic who would rid the earth of the monster that was Conrad

Monroe. Vic had prevented me from taking the life of my sister's killer. Instead, my cousin beat the man to a pulp, then hog-tied Monroe by his wrists, legs and ankles and had him thrown into a cherry wood coffin and watched while Bitter Lemon nailed it down. Vic and Bitter had then driven up into the mountains to a place where my cousin had already been, and prepared a funeral pyre. The coffin was placed on top of a huge bonfire in a shaded clearing surrounded by tall, bearded fig trees, then the coffin was doused in gallons of petrol. Vic had lit a gasoline-soaked rag with a match, then thrown the torch down into the base of the pyre and watched Monroe slowly burn to death in the coffin.

How do you tell a child of fifteen a horror story like that?

How do you make right what can never be remedied?

At around eleven that evening, I went and shook Vic from the nap he was taking in one of Loretta's kitchen chairs, his feet resting up on her dining table. Bitter Lemon had been charged with keeping an eye on the girls and Carnell Jnr, while Vic and I went out into the night under a black flag.

As we walked out of the front door, I was aware of someone standing on the stairs behind me. I turned to see Chloe on the top step staring down at me. I thought she'd been asleep for some time and was surprised to see her. I smiled up at her and she gave me a questioning glance before turning and heading back to the spare room; her crossroad chosen — and mine too.

276

38

'How you wanna hit dis prick Walker, den?' Vic asked from the backseat of my car. After he'd deposited a large brown canvas holdall in the boot he'd chosen not to get in beside me and was sitting forward, both hands on the back of the passenger seat, more like an excited child than a cold-blooded killer.

'We play it cool, that's how.'

Telling Vic to play it cool or to go easy on something when he was in an unpredictable or enthusiastic mood was as dangerous a task as moving nitro-glycerine in a truck with no shock absorbers.

Vic gave me a fierce look. 'Shit. When you say cool, you talkin' 'bout goin' easy on de niggah.'

'I'm talking about being cool. Not jumping down the fella's throat. Give him a chance to hang himself by choosing the right questions to trip him up.'

'Be quicker if I jus' hang de fucka fro' de ceiling. You git what you want outta de sucka, den. I promise you dat.'

'*Jesus* . . .' I heard myself mutter under my breath. I knew I needed back-up for what I was about to do, I knew there was only one man who could take that ride with me and he was sat behind me. And it scared me to death even to consider his help. But it was my kin's aid that I needed, again.

'What you say, JT?' Vic snapped at me.

I looked at my cousin as he stretched out on the backseat.

'I said, when the hell did I suddenly become your

277

damn chauffeur?'

The evil stare turned into a grin and a shrug.

'Day you dropped outta you' momma nuk-nuk, bwoy. Dat's when.'

We drove to Montpelier just as the snow was finally starting to let up. Being out with Vic, under the cover of darkness, about to commit an act of breaking and entering to question Mervyn Walker when I hoped he'd be at his most vulnerable, felt exhilarating and chilling. I knew that it was wrong to feel such elation, that what Vic and I were about to do was both illegal and immoral, but I could see no other way of opening up the case than to begin at the beginning. To brace the pastor for something that resembled the truth. A little bit of Christian rectitude. As I pulled up on a side street close to the vicarage, I told myself that it was my wayward cousin who had brought out the worst in me, that what we were about to do was all down to him.

But I was only lying to myself.

The worst was already in me. Always had been.

I remembered, a long time ago, Mervyn Walker telling me: 'Joseph, man is capable of greatness, love, nobility and compassion. Yet never forget that his capacity for bad is infinite.'

Ain't that the truth.

Having Richard Peace and the rest of the police on my back, believing Mervyn Walker had perhaps lied to me, had started to make me feel I was becoming rotten to the core and part of a blossoming war. A war being fought between black and white under the skin of Bristol and St Pauls. I had become a soldier, an unwilling conscript who had no idea why he was fighting or what victory or defeat might mean.

'Are you armed?' I asked my cousin.

'I ain't totin' no gun, not to a vicar's joint.'

'That's good. Mervyn's not trouble. I might just need you to intimidate him a little, that's all.'

I took a torch from the boot, handed it to Vic and we headed for the Walker residence in the shadows, keeping out of the soft orange glare of the streetlights.

Vic had come prepared with a set of picks and a slender metal slat in a comb sleeve in his pocket. That slat could crack most simple locks and latches and it didn't take my cousin long to have the pastor's kitchen door open. The downstairs was in total darkness and Vic checked each room downstairs, satisfying himself that no one was about, while I kept an ear out in the hall.

At the foot of the stairs was a photograph of Trista Walker. She was dressed in an expensive evening gown, her face beautiful as she looked back at the camera over her bare shoulder. But she didn't look healthy. There was none of the forced sensuality in the photo taken of her with Troy Loudon and Mack Hurbon, but the pain I could see in her eyes told me more than I had a right to know. It told me about the torment she'd suffered as a child, at the hands of strangers. Every one of them encouraged to defile Trista by her demented mother, Hoo Shoo Dupree.

Knowing all of the madness Trista had endured turned my stomach.

We crept on to the landing like a couple of seasoned housebreakers. Quiet as the grave. The nursery door was open, the child's cot empty. Vic swung open another bedroom door and then peered inside the bathroom to make sure both were clear. All we were left with was the pastor's bedchamber.

I eased the door open and stood against it. Vic walked inside and shone around the room, scanning for the bed. We found Mervyn Walker, lying on his side, one arm out of the bed sheets, fast asleep. I ran my hand along and up and down the wall until I found the light switch. I flicked it on and saw the pastor's eyes flicker. Vic kicked at the foot of the bed with the toe of his boot.

'Wakey, wakey, padre.'

Walker shot bolt upright, rubbing his hand across his face, his free arm reaching out in front of him, the fingers splayed out, then grasping as if he were about to catch hold of a bothersome mosquito which had pestered him from his placid slumber.

The reverend caught sight of Vic and panicked. He forced himself further up the bed, pulling the bedclothes up around his chest like a petrified child who'd just woken from a nightmare. The pastor's face span through a series of reactions as he clapped eyes on me; brief alarm, then confusion, then sadness, and pity and finally, resignation. I pointed at my fellow intruder.

'This here is my cousin, Vic.'

Vic winked at Walker.

The pastor rubbed at one eye with a knotted fist, ignoring my introduction. 'What in the name of sanity are you doing here at this time of night, Joseph?'

Vic kicked at the foot of the bed again, this time with a lighter touch. 'My bwoy 'ere, he couldn't sleep on account tings vexin' 'im.'

Walker ignored Vic, and directed his bluster at me. 'How the hell did you get in here?'

280

I rested my hands on the top rail of the bed. 'It wasn't hard, Mervyn. Believe me.'

Vic pulled up a chair next to the reverend and stuck an unlit spliff into his mouth. Walker stared at Vic, and shook his head.

'You're not going to smoke that in here, are you?' the pastor asked.

Vic didn't bother to answer. He struck a match against his thumb and lit the end of the reefer. Mervyn Walker watched in disbelief as my cousin inhaled deeply, then was rewarded with a thick canopy of hemp smoke blown towards his face.

Mervyn jabbed his finger in the air, shaking it for emphasis. 'You're a very rude man, you know that?'

Vic scratched at his chin. 'You ain't de first to be tellin' me dat shit.'

'Take no notice of Vic, he's house-trained.' Vic shifted the chair a little closer to the mattress and I saw the pastor flinch. 'I want you to tell me about Mack Hurbon.'

'Mack, who? I've never heard of anyone called Mack.' Walker shot a quick glance at Vic after I'd mentioned Hurbon's name.

'Are you sure about that, Mervyn?'

'Of course I'm sure. Do you think I'm senile? That I can't remember people's names?'

'I don't know what to think about you. That's why I'm here speaking to you now, at this ungodly hour of the night.' My mentioning God's name made the pastor wince.

'So, I'll ask you again. Mack Hurbon. What do you know about him?'

'Nothing. I told you, I've never heard of the man.'

Vic's hand suddenly flew up and cuffed Walker

across the side of the head. The pastor yelped and cracked the back of his skull on the headboard.

'Are you going to tell me what this is all about?'

'Enough with the bullshit, Mervyn. Who's Hurbon?'

'I told you . . . I don't know!'

Vic cuffed Walker again, this time harder.

'Look, Joseph, I'm happy to cooperate.' Walker stabbed another accusatory finger towards Vic. 'He doesn't need to behave like that.'

'I said he was house-trained, not well-mannered.'

'Now, for the final time, and bearing in mind, I don't want you to be suffering a headache in the morning.' Walker opened his mouth to interrupt, but I beat him to it, quickly holding my finger to my lips. The pastor rested his back against the headboard. 'What do you know about a man named Mack Hurbon?'

'Joseph . . .' The pastor's voice had taken itself down a notch or two. His voice suddenly calm and pious, like he was about to preach a sermon. 'I really don't know who you are talking about, I honestly don't.' Walker looked at the bed clothes drawn up around his chest, then back at me, his hands trembling.

I saw Vic shift in his seat. His face became devoid of expression, as though he'd floated away into a serene environment no one else could see. He seemed to gaze above the pastor's head like a man about to fall sleep. He blinked and rested his hand on top of his thigh. The crow's feet at the corners of his eyes had flattened and turned into thin threads, the skin around his temple and cheek as smooth as clay. He pursed his lips and breathed slowly through his nose and smiled at Walker.

The pastor seemed bewitched by Vic's tranquillity and appeared to have no idea what was occurring.

Vic shot up out of the chair, snatching Walker by the throat, binding his hand around his neck then driving his face into the cast-iron headboard, smashing it again and again against the metal.

I yelled at Vic to stop and darted around the bed and grabbed him by the shoulders and tried to pull him back. I could smell the heat and funk and rage and trapped booze-sweat in his clothes, saw the acne scars and the muscles flexing across his neck, the moisture glistening on his skin and knew there was no way I could restrain him, any more than I could save a drowning man who would take down his rescuer if necessary. Vic knocked me off his back as if he was swatting a fly from his face. I fell against a dressing table, sending perfume bottles, brushes and combs onto the carpet.

Vic ripped back the bedding and wrapped a sheet around Walker's throat, then dragged him squirming and twisting into the bathroom, spittle and blood running from the corners of his mouth. He drove the pastor's head into the toilet bowl and slammed down the seat repeatedly, crushing Walker's head between polished white ceramic and wood, blood stippling the bowl. Vic pulled the pastor to his knees. Walker's face and hair were soaked with water from the toilet. Blood was pouring from his nose and front lip. I saw Vic reach into his back pocket and pull out a knife. The stiletto's blade made a swishing sound as it clicked open. Vic yanked Walker to his feet and pinned him up against the wall. He tightened the sheet around the pastor's neck and slid the tip of the blade into Walker's left ear.

'Mack Hurbon . . . who de fuck is he?'

Walker stupidly hesitated, so Vic jabbed the knife

deeper into his ear. Mervyn Walker let out a scream, his entire body shaking from head to foot.

'He's . . . he's Trista's lover.'

That revelation brought a smile to Vic's face. 'And?'

'And . . . and he's the child's father.'

'Which child?' I asked.

Walker kept his eyes focused on Vic when he gave me the answer. 'Our child, Noah,'

Vic yanked Walker forward, tightened the sheet around the pastor's neck and hammered him back against the bathroom wall. 'You gotta be fuckin' kiddin' me?'

'I'm not . . . I'm not . . . we couldn't . . .' Walker, in a cold sweat, struggled to find the words. Vic shook him again to prompt his vocabulary. 'I couldn't give Trista a child. She became besotted with the idea of being a mother. If I couldn't give her what she wanted, then she said she'd find someone who could.'

'If that was the case, why the hell did she walk out and leave her baby with you?'

'Because Hurbon didn't want it under his feet, that's why. She chose him over Noah.' Walker hesitated again for a moment. 'And me.'

'Who is Hurbon?' I asked again.

'He's a pimp, a loan shark, a conman . . . take your pick.' Walker tried to shake his head, but Vic was holding on to him way too tight for such free and easy movement. 'He's a Londoner. Trista met him when he was visiting one of those damn clubs she liked to hang around in.'

'You knew about the clubs. The places I found out she been going to?'

Walker's eyes sank to the floor. The shame slowly creeping across his face. 'Of course, I did.' He began to retch. Vic smacked him against the wall. 'I knew about the blues nights, the sex parties, the hanging out at all times of the night in places she had no right to be. When I found out that she was pregnant, I begged her not to leave. Assured her that I would give her anything she wanted if she gave her word to stay away from Hurbon and maintain that the child was mine. Can you image the disgrace, the public shame, if people found out?'

I wasn't interested in shame or public outrage. It was the word 'anything' that really had me sitting up and taking notice.

'What was it you promised your wife, Mervyn? What really made her stay with you while another man's child was growing inside her belly?'

Walker's eyes darted from me to Vic. I took a deep breath and Walker measured it.

'What did you promise your wife?'

There was a long hesitation from the pastor. Vic looked at me coldly, his eyes flat. 'All dis bullshit, it ain't 'bout naw fuckin' pickney.'

My cousin plucked the blade from Walker's ear canal and flicked the tip through the fleshy top. The pastor screamed out in agony, blood spurting over Vic's face and the bathroom wall. Vic knotted the sheet tight in his fist. He wrenched Walker forward, tossing him from side to side like a rag doll, then pounding him back against the wall. Walker's head snapped forward. Vic stuck the tip of the stiletto into the fleshy curve at the top of Walker's right ear and pushed his blood-stained face closer to the pastor's, the men's noses practically touching.

'Niggah, am 'bout to start cuttin' pieces outta you. Now, you can pray. You can beg. Brutha, you can scream dis fuckin' place down fo' all I care. Vic scraped the tip of the blade around the edge of Walker's ear and down the side of his cheek and jaw. 'Now, padre, I promise you, unless you start answerin' dis man's questions, you gonna start seein' parts o' your skanky, lying body piling up on duh top o' dat shithouse behind you.' Vic angled the blade into Walker's jugular. 'Or, I could jus' slit your throat an' watch you bleed out like a stuck pig.'

The pastor looked at me. 'It was pillow talk.'

'What?'

'Trista knew I had money squirrelled away. She told Hurbon about the cash. Trista knew how to get the money, took it and ran to Hurbon.'

'She snatched it from a joint bank account?'

Walker shook his head weakly. 'No . . . it wasn't the kind of savings that could be kept in plain sight.'

'What kind of money can't be kept in a bank, Mervyn?'

'Stolen money.'

'Stolen from where?'

Walker's voice suddenly changed, like that of a man who had spent a lifetime hiding who he really was. 'It was church money . . . it . . . it belonged to the church.'

I felt a hole open up in the bottom of my stomach. 'How much money?'

The pastor dipped his chin and bit at his bottom lip.

'Would it be enough to kill people for?'

Walker didn't try and turn his head towards me to answer; he glared into my cousin's face and spoke.

'A little over twenty-five thousand.'

I heard Vic let out a long, high-pitched whistle.

'Which you stole?'

The pastor nodded. His eyes were out of alignment and there was a repressed ferocity in his stance as Vic continued to pin him against the wall. He knew he was beaten, his secret in the open, and yet there was an arrogance about the man that was hard to define. I watched as his hands shook at his side.

'How'd the hell did you think you could ever get away with stealing that kind of cash?'

Walker shrugged, continuing with this new air of arrogance. 'If the worst came to the worst, I always had a wife who'd come from the wrong side of the tracks that I could point the finger of blame towards.'

'You knew about her past. About her childhood, the kind of place she'd come from?'

The pastor gave an embittered nod. 'That she was the daughter of a procuress. A woman who worshipped false idols, who'd called her bastard child Celestine.' He continued to nod his head. 'Yes, I knew.'

I slumped against the wall. 'Just like you knew I'd come running to help you out, if you begged enough, right?'

'I needed you to find Trista so I could get the money back. That way I could make things right. With the church and with Trista.' Walker saw the disbelief on my face. He heard the madness in his voice, the insanity of his reasoning. He saw my disgust and bellowed. 'She was going to ruin me.'

I stepped out onto the landing and looked at the open door into the nursery. 'Where is Noah now?'

'Staying with Evison and Carmen Foster.' Mervyn squeezed his eyes tight. 'I was worried that Trista would come back for him, perhaps bring Hurbon with her and try and take him from me.' He swallowed hard. 'He's all I have left of her, you see.'

Mervyn Walker stared down at the bathroom floor, his emotions, whatever they were, as dead as wet ash.

'Mervyn, this may be a stupid question, but do you have any idea where Trista and this Hurbon could be hiding out?'

I saw Vic apply a little pressure to Walker's throat with the stiletto blade. The pastor looked at me blankly.

'She always said that she'd go home.'

'Where's home?'

'Where Dupree came from, I suppose . . . back to the West Indies.' Walker smiled to himself. 'She spoke on more than one occasion about leaving the country with him. I hid her passport at first, then when she went searching for it, starting to make a fuss, I burned it. She said she didn't care, that she knew a little smelly man who could get her a false one. Get her a new name, new identity . . .' The pastor's voice crackled. 'A new life. I guess that's what she's planning to do right now.'

'A little smelly man?' I asked.

Vic tickled the blade underneath Walker's ear lobe to keep him on point.

'I don't know who the man is. All I can tell you is that about six months ago I overheard her speaking to someone on the telephone. She didn't know I was eavesdropping. I heard Trista tell whoever was on the other end of the line that she was looking for someone who could help her get a new passport. I heard her say that if they helped her, then Loaves and Fishes would help them.'

A little smelly man.

Loaves and Fishes.

288

Charity, and one good deed deserving of another.

Especially if there was easy money to be made.

My old friend. Floyd Dipper Council.

I gestured with my hand for Vic to release Walker. My cousin let go of the sheet around Walker's neck. The pastor slumped to his knees. Vic folded the blade then stepped out onto the landing and headed down the stairs. As I walked away, I glanced back at Mervyn Walker before joining my cousin. He was getting to his feet, trying to steady himself against the side of the tub. He stumbled against the bath, blood streaming from his ear, tears rolling down his cheeks, frozen. He stared at me, silhouetted by the bathroom light against the darkness outside, like a cutout without features or humanity.

Out in the street it had started to snow again. Small gossamer flakes, captured in freefall by the lampposts as they dropped out of the sky.

'Man, I thought you said you were unarmed!' I said through gritted teeth when we got back in the car.

'I jus' said I didn't 'ave no gun, JT.' Vic took another reefer from his pocket and twirled it between his fingers before leaning forward to punch me on the arm. 'You 'naw a knife, shit, it don't hardly even count.'

My cousin laughed weakly and coughed hard.

39

Vic made a call to Bitter Lemon and a couple of other cronies he had on the books from a phone box just outside of Montpelier. My cousin had the sort of committed and loyal disciples who would, at the drop of a hat, undertake any order or enquiry if the Jah commanded it so. Ten minutes, and two return calls later, he clambered back into the car, a huge smile on his face. Vic rubbed his palms together gleefully, like a man who'd just won the bank at a high-stakes poker game.

'Our man's playin' de late-night bones.'

'Where?' I asked.

'Black an' White café.' He winked at me mischievously. 'Dat bwoy as predictable as evah.'

Dipper Council hung around in places most folks knew were no good for them. Dog tracks, gambling houses, off-the-books horserace meetings, side-street billiard halls and back-room card schools were Dipper's venues of choice. The fact that Vic had been able to locate him so easily shouldn't have come as any surprise to me. Someone like Council had a relatively small 'social circle' and although he was bright enough never to hang around with the same faces or in one place for too long — like all gutter-life criminals, Dipper was generally carefree, a born chancer and, for most of the time, lived for the moment. Tonight, such happy-go-lucky behaviour was to be his downfall.

As I drove back into St Pauls, I suddenly felt tired. It wasn't just fatigue from the day. No, it went deeper than that. I was tired of pursuing people like Council. Weary of being on a course that seemed to have no resolution, of hearing men lie, of walking about in what seemed to be a waking nightmare, and of feeling that I deserved all this misery. That, somehow, I'd asked for the troubles that had befallen me after foolishly agreeing to help Mervyn Walker. Witnessing Vic dishing out such a brutal beating to the pastor had once again made me realise why I had left my life of policing and detective work and the violence and cruelty that came with those jobs.

Looking back, I now realised how Dipper had been getting a free pass out of me. He'd been playing me from the day he'd approached me outside Loaves and Fishes and tapped me for a fiver. I'd stupidly overlooked how devious and slippery he could be, and I was paying a heavy price for letting the little weasel slide.

He was like one of those nasty little creatures who live in the murk at the bottom of an aquarium — the kind of slimy predator that one day you discover has eaten everything in the tank.

I had the feeling that Dipper had swallowed me up whole.

The Black and White Café was a late-night drinking joint and home-from-home for so many residents living in St Pauls. The two-storey blue brick and wood frame box-like structure stood proudly, one of only three remaining pre-war buildings in a back alley off the Grosvenor Road. I don't think the alley had a name. It had been paved at one time but most of the tarmac had worn away, leaving a rutted dirt path that ruined the alignment on any car that drove down it and spoiled the leather of any hapless pedestrian who

291

troubled themselves to walk along it.

The Caribbean food café had a reputation as a drug den and some patrons proudly boasted that it had been raided more times by the police than any other drinking premises in the country. But the Black and White was much more than a place of crime. It was also a respected institution, much loved and well frequented by the local community.

I parked on the street and Vic and I walked the hundred yards or so to the screen door. The bar smelled of cigarette smoke, ganja and stale beer. The Black and White's landlord, Bertram Oliver, stood behind the brass-topped bar, his face shiny and stretched tight on the bone. When Bertram saw Vic, he gave him a friendly nod then quietly descended the stairs behind him into the cellar. At a few minutes after midnight, the bar's only inhabitants were Trixie Hill and Floyd Council.

They sat across from each other in the gloom, under a dim light playing dominoes. Trixie had sixty years, twenty-one stone, and one of the best singing voices I had ever encountered. Dipper slapped down his last bone, and laughed.

'Pay up, Trixie. You owe me five pound, woman.'

Trixie Hill was slow and deliberate, more than twice the size of Dipper. She looked at the winning domino and looked at the bones left in her hand. She finally clicked the two together in defeat and took a blue note from her purse and threw it at Council.

'Another game?' he asked.

Trixie ignored both Council and my presence and fixed her newly troubled gaze on Vic standing behind me. 'Not . . . not right now if you don't mind, Dipper.' She clambered out of her seat, snatched her coat off the back of her chair and ambled for the door, her eyes glued to the floor as she squeezed past me and my cousin. Vic pushed me to one side and rapped the top of a table next to him to get Floyd Council's attention.

'I need your company, Dipper.'

Council swung round in his chair, his mouth hung open, a look of horror on his face.

'How you doin, man?' He made a snuffling sound in his nose and brushed at one nostril with the back of his hand.

Vic shifted a finger towards the ceiling. 'Up.'

Dipper's eyes were shining now, his lower lip trembling. 'You . . . you ain't 'ere to hurt me, are you, Jah?'

Vic shrugged. 'Me hope not,' he said. 'But you nevah 'naw.'

Dipper began to tremble in his seat. He shot his eyes on to mine and smiled nervously. 'Well, if I can beat Trixie den I must be on a winnin' streak. Nevah 'naw, I might even be lucky enuff to survive a chat wid de Jah.'

With those words he stood and walked out into the alley with Vic and me glued to his sides.

We drove out of St Pauls, east into the city. Vic was sat in the backseat with Dipper, the doors locked and Council's hands bound tight with thin nylon rope. Vic instructed me to head along the Anchor Road to the Canon's Marsh gas works down by the quayside. I headed along the unmaintained dock road doing less than fifteen miles an hour, my headlights dipped low. I kept close to the shadows created by the high-sided warehouses and turned left into the grounds of the old shipyard, down a pot-holed tarmacked lane with wire strung between concrete posts on one side and dark brick on the other, finally pulling up underneath the rotting canopy of a corrugated iron bike shelter.

I turned the key in the ignition, listened to the engine rattle and die and shifted in my seat to face Vic and Council. No one uttered a word. I eyeballed Dipper for a second or two then reached over and slapped him across the side of the face. The crack of skin meeting skin rang around the inside of the car. Vic's immediate reaction was one of utter incredulity. He stared at me, his stunned expression telling me that he was still processing what I'd just done.

And that's what I was hoping for.

I needed to take control of the situation. Needed to try and prevent the kind of savagery I'd just witnessed back at the pastor's home. Vic had got himself a taste of blood and I could tell that he was eager to spill a little more. Dipper was easy meat for a beast of prey such as Vic, and my cousin would care little how he tore at Council's flesh to get the answers we were searching for. Dipper had lowered his head, but I could still see his lips twitching.

'You lied to me, Floyd. A lie is an act of theft. It steals people's faith and makes them resent themselves.'

I could see the fear growing in Dipper's eyes as he looked into my face and heard my words, the realisation that all the rules of constraint and protocol that a recidivist like Dipper expected when being questioned by, say the local law, had just been vacuumed out of his life. I watched him think, the lies already forming in his crafty little mind, clinging onto a futile hope of saving his neck.

'No, don't open your mouth, Floyd.'

I slapped his face again, then struck him twice

more, backhanding the top of his scalp.

'Wrong time to be thinking of opening your trap. If you lie to me now, if you try and lead me down the garden path again, then I'm going to climb out of this car and take a long walk. By the time I return the Jah here will have made sure you've uttered your last tall story. Am I getting through to you?'

Dipper nodded again. He wiped at his nose with his wrist.

'Answer my question!'

'Yeah . . . yeah . . . you gittin' t'ru to me.'

'Trista Walker.'

Dipper fell silent and tried to stare me down at first. Vic sensing Council's reticence to answer, shook his head disapprovingly and slid across the seat. He glided his arm across the top of the upholstered seat behind Dipper's head.

'Whadda you wanna 'naw 'bout her?'

'Everything.'

'I al'ready tole you every'ting I 'naw.'

Vic let out a long, angry sigh, his arm falling off the back of the seat and curling around Dipper's shoulder. He drew Council close to him, his palm cupped around the top of Dipper's arm.

'Man, earlier I 'eard you talkin' 'bout bein' lucky, right?'

Dipper nodded. 'Right.' A thin vein pulsed in his temple. He lifted his eyes to Vic's. They were electric, the pupils as tiny as pinheads. A solitary drop of sweat rolled off the tip of his nose and formed a dark star on his grubby tan jacket. Vic tightened his grip around Council, his mouth inches from his ear.

'You 'naw, a black man he gotta be luckier an' any honky you evah met.'

'H . . . ow, how . . . so, Jah?' Dipper stammered. He was trying to turn and look at Vic from under his brow, his face sticky, his paunch resting on his belt, his body quickly starting to stink.

'Well, you see through history honkys dey had it easy, man. Dey had jobs, an' money, an' property. All we had was chains an' nooses an' shit like dat. Fo' a white man's father's father to survive wus nuthin'. Naw if one o' our people survived it wus only 'cause o' de best o' luck.' Vic let his hand fall towards his leg. He drew a snub-nosed Smith & Wesson revolver from a concealed holster strapped to his ankle. He raised the pistol, let the barrel stroke the side of Council's cheek then sunk it into the side of his jaw. Dipper let out a pathetic yelp and I felt my guts sink.

Vic began to cough. He held on to Dipper tight while he continued to hack. Moments later he'd cleared his throat and was back on cue with the threats.

'Dis gun am holdin'. It called a drop or throw down. When de Babylon cap an unarmed man, worse still sum poor niggah, de t'row down gits put on his body. Dis gun 'ere got its numbers burned off it. Means another clever honky in police ballistics gonna trace it to me or any fool I 'naw. It's a sweet little ting to 'ave wid you when you dealin' wid sum rasclat needin' a bullet in de mout'. You git de picture?'

Dipper made a gagging sound, saliva falling from the corner of his mouth, his eyes wide with fear. Vic rammed the gun barrel deeper into Council's gullet.

'You gonna need to be de luckiest niggah on earth to stop me blowin' your brains out if you don't start tellin' ma man what he wants to 'ear.'

'We've just paid ourselves a visit to Mervyn Walker's home,' I said, calmly. 'The Jah, here, he had a long, productive talk with the reverend. And the pastor had a lot to say to the Jah. He told him how his wife had been unfaithful. How he's not the father of the child she was carrying and gave birth to. How a fella called Mack Hurbon is the kiddie's rightful kin.'

I saw Dipper swallow when he heard Hurbon's name mentioned.

'Mack's real bad news. Crazy bastard, just like de Walker woman. You don't want to be messin' wid either of 'em, Mr Ellington.' Council bit at his lip and made a feeble attempt to look down at his lap. Vic dug the gun barrel deeper into Dipper's throat pushing his head back. When Council looked at me again there were tears on his eyelashes.

I heard Vic slowly cock back the hammer of the .38.

I eased myself further around in my seat and fixed my eyes on Dipper's.

'You know any little men who can put their hands on a forged passport?'

Dipper gasped and writhed, the tears beginning to roll down his face. 'Am gonna piss myself, man.'

Vic drove the gun deeper into Council's face. 'Piss you' pants now an' you ain't takin' anutha fuckin' breath.'

Council screamed, spittle flew from his mouth, hitting me square in the face.

'She's . . . she's holed up in some fuckin' farmhouse just outside Bath.'

I wiped the back of my hand across my cheek and mouth. 'What farmhouse?'

'Sum . . . sum place called Monkton Combe.' Council sucked in air as if they were his dying gasps. 'Walker's duh wid dat fuckin' monster, Hurbon. Dey waitin' on me to bring 'em what dey want.'

'Passports?'

Dipper, scared out of his wits, goggled-eyed and tongue-tied, bawled at me.

'YES!!' Dipper, unable to move his head with Vic's .38 still lodged deep underneath his jawline, began to sob uncontrollably. 'Yes, fo' Christ's sakes.'

The next words he uttered were barely discernible over his weeping.

'Passports, visas, immigration papers. Dey payin' me fo' de ole fuckin' nine yards.'

I looked away from Council's face and swallowed, then cast my gaze towards Vic. He stared back at me like an avenging angel weighing sin. His face as cold and unyielding as black granite.

40

There are epiphanies most of us do not share with others. Among them is the hour when you make your peace with death. You don't plan the moment; you don't acquire it by study. Most likely, as I was now finding, you stumble upon it. It's a revelatory moment, a recognition that death is simply another player in our midst, a fellow actor on Shakespeare's grand stage, perhaps even one more vulnerable than we are, one who is unloved, excoriated, condemned to the shadows, and denied either rest or joy. I realised the insignificance of my own death as my cousin had been putting the screws on Mervyn Walker and Floyd Council.

Both men feared they were going to die at Vic's hand.

Their screams and cries, their begging and denials had brought about in me the most unusual melancholy, unlike anything I had felt before. The terrible feeling that I too was soon to meet my own dark inquisitor, and that I too would feel the icy hand of death touch my soul. Fears of the grim reaper, my musings on my own mortality, had also perhaps begun to cloud my normally reliable judgement.

Vic and I had continued to brace Dipper for every ounce of information we could draw out of him. Council obliged by spilling his guts, giving us Trista Walker's exact whereabouts; a secluded farmhouse on the outskirts of the tiny North Somerset village of Monkton Combe, close to the Kennet and Avon

Canal. Walker's intentions were to hide out there with the pastor's stolen church funds and her lover, Mack Hurbon. The two of them would be holed up in the countryside until Council had secured the various travel documents and delivered them. Once the pair were in receipt of their new passports, Dipper assumed the idea was for them to quietly disappear out of the country, most likely by sea, to set up a new life in warmer climes, just as Mervyn Walker had suspected.

Dipper, aided by Hurbon, had already made a couple of trips down to the couple's rural bolthole. Like all good grasses, he'd been squealing to them to line his own pockets. He'd had his nose to the ground and was sniffing out anyone I'd spoken to, ferreting around after me, then filtering that information back to Hurbon, who, Dipper told us, was moving freely in and out of St Pauls, going unnoticed at night. I assumed that it was Hurbon who had shot his friend, Troy Loudon, and carved up Queenie Blue. Both of them traitors for speaking to me and jeopardising his and Trista's plans to make a clean break of things with more money than either of them had dreamed of owning.

Knowing all of that, having all that evidence at my disposal, I could have simply got Vic to drive me to Bridewell police station, haul Dipper out of the car and stand him in front of the night-shift desk sergeant. He could have made a call to Richard Peace, got him out of bed and with any luck, before the sun rose on a new day, all my troubles would have been over.

But that wasn't the way things were going to pan out.

I think I already knew that things would go to the

wire and that I'd continue with my search to uncover where Trista Walker had disappeared to the moment Vic and I walked into the Black and White café and picked up Floyd Council.

Perhaps it was because I'd been lied to by so many people. Made a fool of by Mervyn Walker, a man I'd previously admired.

Perhaps it was because there was still a small part of me that enjoyed playing at detective, despite knowing that a life lived among other people's miseries was no good for me.

Or maybe it was the fact that, despite all of his brutal, reprehensible ways, I was again enjoying being in the company of my wayward, violent kin.

Maybe it was the nagging sensation I had that this was perhaps the last time the two of us would walk into the night and cause havoc.

Or maybe death was finally ready to take me on that last journey with him?

One thing I did know for sure was that we couldn't let Dipper go. We were stuck with him. I knew that he was our get out of jail card, if things went pear-shaped and the police tried to muscle in on either of us. Dipper was the missing link to this mystery, to the murders and to Trista's disappearance.

It had been Trista who had approached Dipper one Sunday morning at the Old King Street chapel, where she'd singled him out and struck up a conversation with him. One brief chat about Christian matters became a series of more unusual exchanges each Sunday after her husband had made his sermon and stood down out of his pulpit. Council mentioned talk of Trista's unhappy marriage and the need to escape. About how she asked him if he knew of people who could help her with new travel papers. He'd been promised that he would be well rewarded for both his assistance and silence. Dipper's natural inclination to make easy money, his connections within the local criminal underworld and his magpie-like abilities had been quickly rumbled by Trista — all she'd had to do was set the bait, then when Council snapped at it, lure him in and get him to do her bidding.

It was Trista who had arranged for Dipper to join the Loaves and Fishes project on St Andrews Road, which was clearly a way for her to keep tabs on him and for Dipper to keep her up to date on his progress. Obtaining hooky passports and a host of new identification had proved difficult, and when the right man was secured for the job, the work would be both protracted and costly. Council had embraced the idea of becoming a volunteer.

It was a golden opportunity which offered the perfect foil; a way for a man so distrusted by his own community, a man who was constantly under the watchful eye of both the police and his probation officer, to be seen as turning over a new leaf. A repentant man, cleansed after finding God, attending church and labouring for others less fortunate by undertaking charity work.

It was all a sham.

Just as Trista Walker's marriage had been.

Both Council and Walker had their secrets, and both had found ways of using each other for their individual dark needs and wants.

I remembered a saying my wife, Amelia, used to recite on those days when I'd encountered the very worst of humanity patrolling the streets of St Philip parish back in Barbados:

'I fear not the dark itself my love, only those that

302

lurk within it.'

Looking back at Floyd Council in my rear-view mirror I could see the darkness clinging to him like a shroud on a corpse.

Vic had told me that the best time to hit Walker and Hurbon would be dawn when hopefully the two of them were still asleep or, worst case scenario, just rising. Either way, my cousin wanted the element of surprise. There'd be just the two of us. Low risk with everything to gain.

'Let's jus' sneak on in, pop de pair o' de muthafuckas. Go in high an' hard an' come out laughin',' he said and began coughing again.

'Why are you doing this?' I asked him.

Vic waited for his latest bout of hacking to subside and gave me a confused look. 'What you talkin' 'bout, why me doin' dis?'

I shrugged. 'I'm talking about the fact that you have an army of men who you could snap your fingers at, and they'd go wipe Walker and Hurbon off the face of the earth. You wouldn't even have to get your hands dirty.'

Vic, surprisingly, reflected on my words for a moment. He nodded his head in agreement at the point I'd just made. 'Ah 'naw me got good people. Most of 'em die fo' me. Sum'time, JT, a job like dis needs a personal touch. I don't want nuthin' comin' back to bite me on de arse.'

I open my mouth to thank my cousin but, sensing some kind of gratitude speech was coming, he quickly interrupted me to save any further embarrassment. He nudged my ribs with a sharp prod of his elbow.

''Sides, I wus gittin' fucked off sittin' a' home doin'

nuthin' utha than screwin' an' watchin' de money roll in.'

Vic got me to stop off at the gym he owned on Grosvenor Road. He wanted to make a couple of calls and to, as he put it, 'stock up'. He returned ten minutes later, coughing like an old man, carrying a large gym bag, which he deposited in the boot. He climbed into the front seat next to me without saying a word.

By the time I was heading out of Bristol, Vic had already dozed off, his head on his chest. He looked older, tired; the line of small moles in relief under his left eye. His body shook suddenly, and he made a sound in his throat but didn't open his eye.

Dipper barely uttered another word as we travelled along the solitary main drag from Bristol to Bath. Once we hit the icy, bucolic Somerset arteries, we were the only car on the road. Villages shrouded in the dark with names like Englishcombe, Charlcombe, Whitchurch, Newton St Loe, North Stoke came and went. Sleet fell out of the sky every few miles, topping up the heavy snow that had already fallen on the hedgerows and fields.

Three miles outside of Monkton Combe I turned into a country lane that was surrounded on either side by a dense coppice of ferns and oak trees and pulled up in a slender pass at the side of a dry-stone wall. It was a little after four-thirty. Another hour and the sun would be coming up. Vic had said he wanted to have eyes on the farmhouse and get a feel for the terrain at least a half hour before we hit the place. I checked my wristwatch and looked at Vic, who was still dead to the world.

I decided to kill the engine and let him sleep a little longer.

For the next forty-five minutes I sat in the dark, worrying about what the coming hours may hold for the three of us, and listening to the noise of my cousin's deafening snoring and Floyd Council's stomach churning over.

At just before five-fifteen I turned the key in the ignition and headed back onto the road that led to Monkton Combe. Fog had begun to drop, making the visibility on the roads more difficult. I dropped my speed as Dipper spoke in a whisper, directing me along the twisting lanes canopied with giant oaks, the long branches arcing high above us. Council mumbled for me to take a right. The mist rolled across the fields in thick clouds. I drove alongside more dry-stone walling and wooded countryside. Another mile down the road I crossed a humpback bridge over the canal then took a left down a cracked stretch of asphalt road that quickly turned to a filthy mire of wet snow and mud. A further half a mile down that track and, before long, Dipper stuttered to me to cut the headlights.

As I flicked up the switch to turn off the lamps I drove over a rise in the road and hit a pothole. Vic's head jerked up.

'We there?' he grumbled.

I swung the car under the deep awning of a row of chestnut trees and pointed to the farmhouse down in the valley below.

'This is it,' I said.

He rubbed at his face and peered out of the windscreen. 'I wus havin' anutha o' dose fuckin' dreams agin.' He yawned and scratched at the back of his head. 'Was I talkin' shit in me sleep?'

'No.'

305

Vic pinched his eyes with his finger and thumb then shook his head to knock the sleep out of it.

He got out of the car, popped the hatch on the boot and, blocking Dipper's view in case he turned to look through the rear window, took out a black shoulder holster. He worked his arms into it then snatched the Beretta from its cradle. He took a short, black silencer from the bag and screwed it on to the tip of the barrel then pulled back the receiver, eased a round into the chamber, reset the hammer and set it back in the holster.

Reaching back into the bag, he took out two Browning .9mm automatics and handed one to me, as well as another shoulder holster. While I took off my coat and put the holster on, Vic went through the same process of checking his second handgun before chambering a round into the Browning. He slipped the barrel of the .9mm into the front waistband of his trousers, then reached back into the holdall, took out four magazines of spare ammunition and a couple of large torches. He handed me a lamp and a couple of spare clips.

Vic took the holdall from the trunk and shook it to make sure it was empty and threw it back inside. He walked around the side of the car, opened up the rear door and hauled Dipper out. He marched Council round to the boot and pushed him inside. Vic thumped him in the back as Dipper got on his knees. He turned to Vic and went to speak.

'Don't say a fuckin' ting, Dipper.' Vic put his hand on the butt of the Browning tucked behind his belt. 'Jus' tink yourself lucky I ain't gagging you ugly mout'.' Dipper's head had barely touched the base of the boot when Vic slammed the lid down on him.

We began walking through the fog, moving quickly off from the path that cut through the coppice towards the farmhouse at the bottom of the valley. Vic moved closer towards me and whispered.

'JT, don't be takin' any chances. Go down towards de house slow an' quiet. Keep an eye on your back. Anyt'ing you ain't sure 'bout, check it out first, den move on. Either o' dese crazy bastards could be hidin' out any'place down there.' Vic stopped suddenly, gazed into my face and grinned. 'How'd we git into dis shit?'

'What?' I whispered back.

'Why us? It's like we didn't have a choice comin' 'ere, like we wus supposed to meet up wid dis pair an' clip 'em.'

I did not want to dwell on the implications of my cousin's word. Vic was not one given to extravagant rhetoric. The fact that he had said what he said made my breath come short in my chest. I removed my Browning from my holster, pulled back the receiver and slipped a round forward into the chamber.

We continued to trudge down the hill, now fifteen feet apart, the mist lifting every now and then to occasionally reveal the two-storey farmhouse below. I felt a chilly breeze hit me full in the face as I came to where the treeline began to thin. We slowly moved out from the cover of the trees as we neared the fields that surrounded the farmhouse. To the right of the property behind a tall hedge ran the canal, to the left of the house, a waist-high, fenced-off paddock, which looked to be free of livestock. At the rear of the building I could just make out the roof of a large barn. A white picket perimeter ran the length of the front of the farmhouse, a short gravel drive with what looked like rough lawn either side of it.

Vic gave a short whistle to get my attention. He moved in closer towards me and pointed across to the barn and the rear of the building, mouthing the order for me to move across towards the paddock and barn, and try and enter the house via the back door. My cousin then pointed to his right, letting me know he'd be covering the farm from the canal path.

We separated and I watched Vic slowly disappear into the mist as he ran down the hill towards the canal. I weaved through the last of the trees before breaking out into open ground. Aided by the cover of the thickening fog, I ran the two hundred yards over to the paddock, climbed over the fence and headed round towards the rear of the farmhouse. The ground beneath my feet was wet, the mud sticking to the soles and heels of my shoes. My heart was pounding in my chest, my stomach knotted tight. As I swung around to the rear of the house, I found a dark blue Ford Cortina parked behind the barn.

Another older vehicle was parked close by, partially covered by tarpaulin and pooled with wet slush, rotting leaves and bird shit. I wiped my face with my coat sleeve. The air round me stank of stagnant mud and raw sewage, which I suspected was perhaps coming from a backed-up septic tank. I felt a sudden wave of nausea and fear wash through my system, a pressure band like a strip of metal tightening against my head.

I pressed myself against the front of the barn, the .45 pointed upward, the pressure band on the right side of my head squeezing tighter. The barn door was ajar. From inside I heard a buzzing sound and smelled an odour like gone-off meat.

I ripped open the door and went inside, pointing the

308

.45 into the gloom with both hands and was hit with the all too familiar stink of death. I gagged as I took a couple more tentative steps inside. Thin shafts of daylight broke through the roof slats above my head. Unable to make anything out properly, I fished for the torch in my coat pocket, turned it on and strafed the beam around the inside of the barn.

The torch's glare picked out some rusting farm machinery, a half dozen or so rolls of tall bailing wire, six feet of chopped firewood stacked at one side of the door and what looked to be thousands of bottle flies buzzing everywhere. As I moved deeper into the barn the noise from the flies became louder, and the stench ranker.

I heard the scuttering of rats as they darted along the sides of the barn. The torch picked out one as it shot from one wall to another. The light from the torch beam illuminated where the putrid smell was coming from. The bloodied remains of a corpse.

A man's bloated body was sat in a wooden, high-backed carver chair. Around him, stacked a foot high, were bales of old, rotting straw. The head of a chicken rested on the top of one of the bales. Bloodied hand-prints were smeared across bundles of dried hay. The body looked like it had been positioned on a throne in some kind of arcane shrine. His legs were splayed wide, his wrists and ankles tied to the arms of the chair with strips of chicken wire, the ligature drawn so tight that it had bitten deep into flesh. The top of the man's head had been blown clean away, his face hung forward, his grey enlarged tongue hanging from his mouth. His trousers had been ripped open, his genitals pulled from inside his bloodstained underwear, the penis lacerated with multiple cuts. Candles, glued with wax to old porcelain saucers, had been arranged around the body.

I moved the torch beam back up the body. The man's bloodstained white shirt had been torn open to the waist.

The word TRAITOR carved into his chest.

41

Fear gripped at every fibre of my body. I knew I couldn't stay in the barn; there was nothing I could do for the man the corpse had once been. I had to keep moving forward. My hands trembled, my heart thundered in my chest and I was sweating heavily. I pushed the moisture out of my eyes with the heel of my hand, held the Browning against my thigh and slowly worked my way outside and along the side of the barn towards the back of the house.

I let my eyes sweep back and forth across the yard, hoping to catch sight of Vic. I came to a halt and scanned across the field and towards the canal path in the distance, but there was no sign of him. The cold wind had died and there were no shadows on the grass. The fog was drifting in from the water and the low-lying marshland on the other side of the bank. Back up towards the treeline that Vic and I had come from earlier everything seemed still. I could hear myself breathing in the silence, the steam rising from my mouth.

I moved quickly along the edge of the house, my feet sinking into the soft pad of pine needles and decayed leaves. At the back door I paused, held the Browning against my chest and looked around the corner, and still saw no sign of Vic. The small window in the centre of the door was veiled with discoloured net curtaining and I couldn't see inside or hear any movement. I gave the handle a quarter turn, felt the door was unlocked, then quietly turned the handle a little further till the latch bolt gave and slowly swung the door open.

I stepped inside; the Browning held out at arm's length; my finger curled through the trigger guard. In front of me, obscuring the inside of the kitchen, was a spaghetti string curtain. I let the Browning's barrel part the strands and took a couple of steps forward, the side of my face and shoulder brushing against the lines of thin cord. I shook my head free of the curtain, and for a moment didn't fully trust my eyes.

Dipper Council, his breath rife with fear, his hands still bound at the wrists was stood in the middle of the kitchen. Blood poured from a wound at the top of his right temple. To the left of him was a closed door that looked as if it could lead out into the hall and the rest of the house. On the other side of the kitchen, a second door, again masked by a multicoloured fly screen.

He made no sound, sweat pouring down his face, his swollen eyes silently watching me as they would a creature who had suddenly been released from a cage. I could see the pulse throbbing in his neck, his saliva red in his teeth. I took a step closer, then glanced around to check my back just as Trista Walker broke through a door behind Council brandishing a nickel Colt .25. Pointing it directly at the back of Council's skull, she said: 'Drop your gun or I drop Dipper and then you. Believe me. I can drill you both before you have time to blink.'

I watched her move slowly to her right, her body framed against the dull morning light coming through the window over the kitchen sink. It looked as if crystal splinters were breaking over her shoulders, like some demonic spirit rising from an everlasting fire.

Knowing I had no choice, I lowered the Browning and let it fall from my fingers. Walker moved around Dipper coming to a sudden halt at his side. She pointed the chrome .25 calibre automatic at my stomach. 'Kick the gun towards me.'

I did as she asked.

Walker prodded Dipper's arm with the barrel of her gun and Council flinched.

'I found this slimy bastard in the boot of your car.'

'He was stinking the motor out. It was the kindest place I could think to leave him.'

'That's no way to treat your friends.'

'He's no friend of mine.'

Trista Walker gave Council a dirty look. 'That makes two of us.' She turned her attention back to me, took a single step backward and raised the .25 so it was now pointing at my chest. 'I was watching you come down the hill with the other dude. I thought it made sense to go and take a look where you'd sprung up from. See if there was more of you out there in the woods. Luckily for me, your smelly colleague appears to be your only source of back-up.' A half smile lingered across Walker's mouth for a moment. 'I can't tell you how hard I had to push Dipper to get him inside the house before either of you had chance to properly sweep the place.'

I ignored her words and attempted a tone of civility. 'You must be Trista.'

She didn't answer. She looked me up and down, her eyes devoid of feeling or meaning. She wore a white halter-neck blouse that was covered in tiny red hearts, and her jeans were pulled low on her light brown stomach to expose a black and red pierced voodoo heart tattooed by her navel. I could smell beer and

313

the faint odour of marijuana in the room, which I suspected was coming from her.

'Or should I call you Celestine?'

Her mouth parted slightly when I called her that, evidently surprised.

'Momma loved that name. She always said to the punters, 'Lil' Celestine like de blackberry. She got de sweet juice."

She touched away a drop of sweat on her forehead with her finger and put it in her mouth. I felt my face heat as she stared at me.

'My husband clearly picked the right man to sniff me out.'

'I got lucky.'

I saw Walker's hand tighten its grip on the cocked .25. 'Well, your luck's just ran out.'

'I'm assuming that's Mack Hurbon tied up and butchered out there in the barn?'

Walker's tongue moved around the edges of her mouth as though she were eating an ice cream. 'It is.'

'That's some way to go.'

'The bastard deserved it. He was a piece of shit who wanted the money more than he wanted me.' Walker's eyes roamed my face. 'He made his decision. He chose unwisely.'

'Why brand him and the rest as traitors?'

Walker shrugged. 'Why not? That's just what they were . . . all of them, untrustworthy, manipulative, looking after their own ends. I remember it was something that Momma often used to call me when I was a pickney. When I'd been bad or I'd disappointed one of the men she'd sent me off with. 'You a little traitor,' she'd say.' Her eyes locked on mine, and for a second, I saw her self-assurance slip, as though the ridiculing

314

voice of her mother, Hoo Shoo, was echoing in her memory. Then the glint of cruelty came back into her eyes. The tip of her tongue moved over her lips. 'If I'd had the time, I would have gone back to that mad house I left her to rot in and slit her throat.'

'Your mother ran brothels and ran dope. The politest thing I can say about her was that she was a genuine sonofabitch. I don't think she'd even mind me saying that.'

She grinned and winked at me. 'I like you.'

'What about Mervyn?'

'Oh, I hate him. The pastor sends chills through me. He's like a buzzard on a tombstone. It was all about the money with Mervyn. Always had been.'

'So, he was just an easy meal ticket, then?'

'Among other things. He was fit for little else.'

'Fit enough to want to love and care for a child that wasn't his.'

Walker shrugged again. 'That was his damn choice. Mack wasn't the fatherly type. Trista's face suddenly went flat. 'Now Mervyn, he'd steal the last penny out of a beggar's bowl, but he had that paternal instinct.'

Walker's eyes fastened brightly on mine. I kept waiting for her to blink. But she didn't.

'Where's your buddy?' she finally asked.

'Vic? Oh, be around someplace; I can promise you that.'

'I can't wait.'

Hearing me mention Vic's name caused Dipper to break his statue-like silence and begin to panic.

'You need to clip dis fucka 'ere and go find his cousin or we both dead.' Dipper turned to Trista Walker and pointed at me. He screamed: 'Shoot him! Shoot him fo' Christ's sakes!' Council spun back to face me and

315

spat out the words. 'Shoot 'im befo' dat crazy fuckin' kin o' his teks us both out at de neck.'

Walker raised the gun a little higher at me then suddenly swung her arm away from me and fired the first round high up into Dipper's sternum. The top of his cream shirt coloured as though a small rose had just been painted on the cloth by an invisible brush. One hand jumped to his chest; his fingers splayed at odd angles from one another, as though all his nerve connections had been severed. I saw him swallow and turn his head towards me, his eyes filled with shock.

The sound that rose from his throat came to an abrupt halt as the second bullet entered the side of Council's skull, showering grey and pink brain matter, bone and hair against the kitchen wall. Dipper's face seemed to melt like wax held to a flame as his body slipped down between the wall and the dusty wood-burning stove, a vertical red line streaking the yellowing wallpaper.

'Another traitor.' Walker expelled a long breath from her chest, her shoulders sagged then tightened again.

I stumbled backwards as Walker resighted the .25 at my head. As my shoes knocked against the skirting, I heard the sound of a floorboard creaking outside in the hall.

Trista's trigger finger twitched and her face jerked at the sound. She shifted her weight, glanced quickly at the side door she had come through, an incisor tooth biting down on her lip, inadvertently moving the barrel away from my face and switching it towards the kitchen door.

When Vic barged through it, I doubted he'd have known exactly what to expect. Trista Walker careened backwards; her eyes wild. She let out a high-pitched scream.

By the time Vic spotted Trista, he had already swung the silenced Beretta towards her. Walker, just seconds faster, spun her chrome .25 semi-automatic away from me and pointed it directly at Vic's chest. Then, coward or lunatic as she was, she averted her face, glanced at me and laughed as she pulled the trigger, lest Vic got a shot off before he went down.

The report of the .25 was like a pop of a firecracker. The bullet punched a small hole in the strap of Vic's shoulder holster, inches above his heart. He crashed against the kitchen table, the Browning falling loose from his waistband and skating across the hard stone floor towards me. I could see him fighting not to go down, struggling to get his .38 Smith & Wesson loose from his ankle holster.

Trista fired again at Vic's head, but the shot went high, splintering the door frame. I threw myself to the floor and snatched for Vic's Browning, my fingers grasping at the butt. By the time I had the gun in my hand, Vic had thrown himself to one side, kicking a chair towards Trista's legs. As she stumbled backwards, Vic yanked the .38 free and fired at Walker. The shot careered above Trista's head, but close enough to scare her. As I raised the Browning to take a shot she already was bolting for the door she'd originally appeared through.

I got to Vic's Browning, spun onto my back and aimed, but Trista was already gone. I heard another door being swung open then slam shut with a loud slap.

'Git after de fuckin' bitch!' Vic bawled at me.

I clambered to my feet and ran after her, the

317

Browning raised at arm's length. The fog was thicker and whiter, the trees and hedgerow glistening with it. The only sound out in the yard was the dripping of the newly fallen wet snow on the ground. I swung the Browning to my right and left then moved slowly across the grass towards the canal path.

My heart was racing, my throat dry, sleet pelting against my face. The fog was like steam on my skin. My eyes were stinging and I couldn't trust my vision.

Then I heard feet running behind me.

I started to turn around, my right hand raising the Browning, but it was too late. Trista Walker had slowed to a brisk walk, slow enough to aim with one outstretched arm, her harridan face twisted.

'You thought you could hunt me down like an animal? Who the hell do you think you are?' she said.

And she shot me in the back.

Strangely, I felt little pain. The blow was like a smack from a fist between the shoulder blades, just enough to knock the breath out of me, to buckle my knees for a second or two, to make the trees and the river loose shape, to make me drop the Browning and stumble down the slope towards the canal path. I fell sideways, one arm extended like a man looking for a wall to lean against. Then I crashed to the ground. I felt my body slide across the wet grass, my fingers digging into the cold earth, my heels kicking at the slushy ground. I managed to roll over on to my side and saw Trista Walker inch out of the fog, the gun in her hand pointing at my chest. The sounds inside my head were impossible to separate. My ears filled with a bizarre mixture of Walker's screams and hysterical ranting and white noise; the air tannic with the smell of burned gunpowder.

I saw my chest rising and falling, my eyes narrowing, the warmth draining from my limbs as Walker drew closer. I was completely powerless and whatever happened next was out of my hands. I tried to raise my arm, to hold my palm in front of my face, but my strength had all but had deserted me.

'You listen —' I began.

But Trista Walker aimed the .25 directly at my face. At the same moment, through the mist and a red haze, I saw Vic appear like a ghost behind her. He was hunched over, off balance, leviathan and unstoppable in his course and purpose. He fired at Trista's back, the ejected nine-millimetre casings flying into the murk, shooting one bullet after another into her body, head and neck, then as she dropped to the ground in front of me, shooting her again at almost point-blank range as she lay dead and spread-eagled at my feet.

Vic came to a halt. I heard him hawk up a mouthful of mucus. He spat on the back of Trista Walker's corpse and slumped down on his knees. He grinned at me, the Beretta hanging from his bloody hand. My eyes filled with tears; my lungs swelled with air, dense with cold and musty canal water.

A huge wave of pain erupted in my chest as I tried to haul myself up in the leaves, my whole body shaking. I slowly pushed myself against the trunk of a tree and tried to clear my vision and stop the ringing in my ears. Vic had crawled over Trista Walker's body and was now squatting down in front of me, blood pouring from the wound at the top of his shoulder. He slipped the Beretta into the cradle of his holster and held my chin with one hand, his mouth moving, his words like the muted sound of submerged rocks bumping together in a stream bed.

Vic held me for a couple of minutes, then he pushed his body away from mine and cursed as he struggled to get to his feet. His left arm hung from its socket like a twisted soaked towel as he quietly lumbered down to the water's edge. He propped himself against a fencepost, close to the bank and unzipped his fly. I saw a golden stream arch onto the water's surface.

'Man, does dat feel fuckin' good,' he said, his face filled with release as he tilted it up at the sky. Vic looked at me, then at Trista Walker's body and laughed. 'Brutha, am goin' back in dat scabby shack an' findin' me a stack a muthafuckin' money.'

He hobbled back up the bank, still laughing and kneeled at my side. He put his arm around my waist and slowly lifted me to my feet. He waited until I had steadied myself, then together, we limped up the slope, a couple of vintage Barbadians left over from another era. Our wounds were severe, but I told myself we would survive them. We were out of step and out of sync with the world and with ourselves, and knowing this, we held on to each other like two men in a gale, both of us secretly praying for the wonder of another dawn.

Epilogue

I'd wished for a dramatic denouement to the events of the past few weeks, a clap of divine hands that would assure me of some kind of ethical order wherein evil was punished and good rewarded, not unlike a playwright's pen in an Elizabethan drama. But the reality was far less profound or righteous. In a perfect world it would have been right and fitting for Trista Walker to have been punished for her terrible crimes and incarcerated behind bars for the rest of her life. But that wasn't to be. Trista's comeuppance had been swift and brutal, at the hands of a man who had, over the years, taken the lives of many. I had learned long ago that justice finds us in its own time and of its own accord, and in ways we never anticipate.

I suspect that both my own and Vic's penance would be waiting for us, somewhere down the line.

Trista, as a child and adolescent, had been cruelly abused, not only by her mother, but by the depraved and lascivious men who had frequented Hoo Shoo Dupree's bordello. The little girl became a woman, the torment and secrets she held inside her never healing or fading.

I'm not making excuses for Trista's wicked deeds, but I could understand why she had been able to commit such barbarities. After all, the innate human qualities we take for granted, those of love, care and compassion, had been stripped from Trista Walker long ago.

Celestine Dupree and Trista Walker were both

victim and perpetrator. The name she was given at birth and that which she hid behind masked more pain and sadness than any poor soul should have to endure in a lifetime. I hoped that the woman who had shot me and Vic would find greater peace in death than she had in her short and miserable life.

★ ★ ★

I was laid up in hospital for almost three weeks. By some herculean feat, Vic had managed to carry me all the way back to my car then drive five miles to the Royal United Infirmary in Bath. I know that Vic and I underwent surgery shortly afterwards, both with gunshot wounds to the chest and back respectively. I know that my recovery was slow and painful. I barely remember being visited by Chloe and Loretta, my time spent in a fog of pain relief medication, going in and out of consciousness.

Vic's initial recovery and recuperation was a mystery to me, the medical staff and the Bristol police. Vic had been taken to theatre at roughly the same time as I was. A .25 bullet was extracted from his chest just below the clavicle. Still sedated, he was taken to a recovery room. Gunshot wounds in Somerset are rare: having two men stumble into the accident and emergency department of the BUI, bleeding out after being shot, warranted the police being called. Before hospital staff could liaise with the Bath constabulary to have Vic and I put under strict watch, Vic disappeared.

I later found out from Loretta, that my cousin, soporific, drugged up to the eyeballs and dressed only in a green hospital gown had managed to somehow tear the cannular from his arm and stagger, unchallenged, down three flights of stairs and out of the building. Once free and out in the open, Vic had headed for the hospital car park and selected himself a set of wheels.

He busted into a brand-new Ford Cortina, which the police later informed me belonged to one of the infirmary's most respected thoracic surgeons. Vic hot-wired the motor then proceeded to find a phone box. He made a call to Loretta's and fixed a rendezvous with Bitter Lemon.

The police found the doctor's car two days later. It had been left five miles from Bath, on a country lane next to a garden allotment, one window smashed, the driver's seat covered in glass and blood.

Vic's whereabouts remained a mystery to me for many months. The Avon and Somerset boys in blue never found out where he'd vanished to.

Trista Walker's death was described as a tragedy in the newspapers. The word was repeated so often that people probably believed it. I may have finished with Trista Walker, but she was not finished with me. I had learned a long time ago that the dead lay strong claim on the quick and do not easily take leave of the earth. Trista's ghost remained with me in the guise of weeks of police questioning and having Detective Superintendent Eve and Richard Peace breathing down my neck. Both men recognised that I had committed no criminal act; I couldn't even be charged with withholding evidence; I had, after all, done everything in my power to assist the police in locating Trista Walker, and they had played their part in cajoling me to aid them.

The police investigation later concluded that Trista had in fact murdered Troy Loudon, Queenie Blue and Mack Hurbon. The twenty thousand pounds that Trista Walker had snatched from her husband had been found by Vic back at the farmhouse in Monkton Combe. Along with me, Vic had carried the money into Bath Infirmary in two separate holdalls. Vic had made a gift of both bags to a woman on the reception desk, telling her to, 'Give dese fuckas to de Babylon when dey turn up.'

Twenty thousand was loose change to Vic. And he knew that by handing the cash over, he'd be making my life a lot easier in the coming days.

After the church diocese and the authorities had been alerted to Pastor Mervyn Walker's long-time criminal behaviour, the reverend was arrested by my good friends on the force, Detectives Locke and Mapp. Mervyn was charged with embezzlement and fraud. Not only did the Avon and Somerset police throw the book at him, but the church he had long served desired their pound of flesh too. The clergy demanded that the police left no stone unturned, and that the final punishment fitted the crime.

The moral to that story?

No matter how close to God you may think you are. No matter how long you may have served him. No matter how much good grace you may feel you've accrued. Never, ever on any account, consider stealing from his collection plate, and think you'll get away with it.

The greatest sadness of the whole sorry affair was that Trista's son, Noah, was now alone. Mervyn, never his real father, would be spending some time in prison and unable to care for him. He was taken into care and placed in the George Müller orphanage at Ashley Down, just outside of Bristol. I believe that

Evison and Carmen Foster visit him each week. Good and decent folk, whose personal faith and trust had been sorely tested by the terrible events triggered by Mervyn and Trista Walker. I think of the child often but have not as yet found the courage to set foot inside the children's home or to make a telephone call to ask after his wellbeing.

I know that the day will come when I will steel myself to the task, but not yet. I sometimes wondered if Mack Hurbon had ever seen his son, and if so, if he did not find his own room in hell when he had to look in the child's eyes.

Two days before my discharge from hospital, I overheard a nurse speaking to a colleague about the 'terrible trouble going on in St Pauls overnight'.

I had to wait until Loretta and Chloe visited that evening to be fully appraised of the shocking events that took place on the second of April.

When police raided the Black and White Café no one expected the violent riot that followed — yet somehow anyone living in St Pauls realised that it was inevitable. After my own recent run-in with the police, being stopped in the street for no reason, only a fool would not have realised that racial tensions were running high on the streets for months, and in truth, had been for years.

Loretta went on to tell me that about twenty police officers, suspecting drug dealing inside the Grosvenor Road Café, had stormed in heavy handed and itching for trouble. Local coppers like the pair who had stopped me, as well as six members of the drugs squad, raided the café at around three-thirty in the afternoon, telling the landlord, Bertram Oliver, that they were looking for illegal drink and drugs.

325

The exact details of what followed were to become the subject of much rumour and debate on the surrounding streets.

Some believed the police had ripped Bertram's trousers during a scuffle and refused to pay there and then for the damage; others said the uprising started when crates of booze were being taken from the café and piled into a Black Maria in the street outside.

Bricks and bottles soon started to be thrown at the coppers surrounding the outside of the café. A concrete block was hurled through the windscreen of a police car — injuring an officer.

Bertram tried to calm the situation but to no avail. The residents of St Pauls had had enough. The raid on the Black and White, the disrespect shown to Bertram, was the straw that broke the camel's back. More coppers were called in. They turned up without riot gear and began shielding themselves with dustbin lids against the missiles being launched at them. St Pauls had begun to look more like the Falls Road in Belfast than a Bristol suburb. A Panda car was turned over and set alight, and soon the violence had spread right across the area, the police now mostly cornered and outnumbered.

Lloyds Bank on Ashley Road was looted. As well as the bank, the post office, a row of shops and a warehouse in Brighton Street were also attacked and robbed. By seven-thirty that evening there were around a hundred police officers in St Pauls, but the situation was still not under control. Firefighters tackling the police cars going up in flames were also coming under fire from the crowd.

The police set up roadblocks around the perimeter of the district stopping people coming and going.

There were hours of violent clashes that ended with twenty-one people arrested and thirty-three injured.

By ten o'clock the next morning, tensions were still high, but the immediate violence was over.

* * *

There was a terrible symmetry to the fact that our 'uprising' took place in a city from which slave-traders had set sail in the seventeenth and eighteenth century. Bristol had been enriched by the slave trade and now the city saw fires set and barricades erected by young people who were the descendants of human cargo. Not far from the flickering flames of the Bristol riots, a statue of Edward Colston, a slave trader and member of the Royal African Company in the seventeenth century, looked on as the police were driven out of the St Pauls district.

I returned home two days later, my breath short, my gait shorter. As I got out of the ambulance that had brought me back to Banner Road, the afternoon air still smelled of smoke. Wood ash mainly, but there was also the acrid stench of burned plastic and paint in the streets. And even though I knew that it could not be true, I thought I caught a whiff of putrid flesh on the edge of the breeze.

* * *

The St Pauls I'd left that cold March night was not the St Pauls I returned to three weeks later. The sense of injustice and despair was written on every black face I saw, young and old. The sadness felt in the community was almost overwhelming. I stayed shut

327

in my home, unable to drink to drown my sorrows and without the strength to go out and stand next to my neighbours in solidarity at the injustice inflicted upon us all.

I spent much of those first few weeks taking things easy, my body repairing itself slowly, reading and being pampered by Chloe. As I grew stronger, I liked to sit in the yard and watch the gold light in the trees and the hard blue ceramic texture of the sky, content in the knowledge that I was still in one piece and breathing.

Over time, my shoulder, arm and upper chest didn't hurt anymore and I was alright unless I picked up a lot of weight suddenly. In an almost narcissistic fascination with my own mortality, I would sometimes reach over the top of my shoulder and touch the smaller spongy scar that had grown over the entry wound. Trista Walker's .25 bullet had gone through me as clean and as straight as an arrow shaft.

At first, I did not handle the nights well. I thought of Vic all the time. Missed him terribly and at night, when no one was around, would sit in my room speaking to him as if he were there with me. Often, I would feel a nameless apprehension that seemed to have no cause. I would try to hide my self-absorption from Chloe, but I knew she always read my moods accurately and saw through my disguises. Many times, during those early days, after Chloe had returned home from school, the two of us would walk over to Loretta's as much for the company as for the wonderful food she would prepare and serve. We'd all sit around the table, a gesture to the normal, happy times I'd once cherished and now craved. I think it is fair to say, that if it were not for the love and support of my child and good friend, I fear my recovery would have been a much darker affair and it would have taken me a great deal longer to get back on my feet.

The weeks passed, then months, and slowly our lives in St Pauls slipped back into routine. In June I returned to work, part-time at the Bristol West Indian Friends Association. A daily routine, being back with friends and helping others again brought about a sense of normality and purpose that much aided my final recovery. My life became as bland and unremarkable as the season was soft, warm and transitory.

Then, on a windblown evening in late July, as I was putting away the dishes after supper, I received a call from Loretta. She asked if I would come on over, told me that she had some important news to tell me, that it wasn't something she could speak about over the telephone and that what she had to say could not wait until morning.

I remember sitting down in Loretta's front room, the door closed while Chloe and Carnell Jnr remained in the kitchen out of ear shot.

I remember smiling when my friend said she had, earlier that morning, received a telephone call from Vic. My smile broke into a huge grin when she went on to tell me that he was now living back in Barbados, in a beachfront house in the parish of our birth, St Philip.

After that, I don't recall much else that Loretta said.

Just the words, 'Metastatic stomach cancer,' and 'There's very little time.'

★ ★ ★

329

On 28 July 1980, Loretta, Carnell Jnr, Chloe and I caught the 10.15 a.m. flight to Barbados from London, Heathrow. We flew first class, the return tickets for our extravagant journey back to the West Indies had no date printed on them to state when we would travel home. All we knew was Vic had paid for us to visit him in style. Three hundred and eighty-five quid a seat. Fine food. Free booze and a trio of movies to watch as we crossed over the Atlantic.

I'd flown before and hated the experience. This time the nearly nine-hour flight barely registered with me. We landed at 5.15 in the afternoon, Barbados time, at the Grantly Adams International Airport, located on the south coast of the island. Bitter Lemon greeted us there, taking my hand in his huge paw it took all my strength not to break down there and then.

It was, however, Chloe and Carnell Jnr, who would elevate some of my trepidation and inner sadness. The looks on their faces as they walked out of the airport, and for the first time felt the warm breeze and intense tropical heat against their skin was a joy to behold. This was Chloe's true home, the place of her birth.

She'd been two years old when I had brought her back to Britain from Bim after the death of her mother. Too young to truly remember the island's beauty or its climate.

Bitter drove us out to St Philip; the easternmost parish of the easternmost island in the Caribbean island chain. The parish was home to some of the most beautiful beaches and bays on the island. We passed familiar landmarks, places I'd grown up around as a kid; Ragged Point lighthouse and the Sunbury Plantation House, home of the Monroes, including Chloe's father, Conrad Monroe. Vic's new residence

330

was remote and gated from the rest of the outside world, and an altogether more beautiful place than the one-time overseer's property down the road.

The eighteenth-century former sugar plantation Vic now called home was a two-storey pile called Cove Spring that overlooked the pristine waters of Crane Beach and its powder-soft sand. The house was screened by thick vegetation and tall West Indian mahogany trees, which cast cooling shade over well-maintained lawns that edged both sides of the drive.

As Bitter pulled up outside the house, I saw Vic standing on the huge porch. He was resting his left shoulder against a white column, his right hand holding a thin black cane. Loretta and the kids immediately jumped out of the backseat of Bitter's car and ran up the polished wood steps to hug a much-missed friend and uncle.

For some reason, I couldn't move, as if I had turned to stone. I stayed put in the car, rooted to my seat, staring out at the beautiful garden, the colourful flowers and then the beach and the crystal-clear waters beyond.

Perhaps it was the feeling of being overwhelmed by the amazing view or the thought of finally being back home after such a long time that anchored me so firmly.

I told myself that my reluctance to move was because I was tired. A voice in my head blamed my immobility on jetlag. I could have thought of a dozen reasons not to get out of the car, but the truth was I was too frightened to move.

I heard the passenger door open and felt a surge of warm air hit my calves and ankles. Then a familiar voice, a little hoarser than since I'd last heard it, spoke.

'Well, you gonna git outta dat shitbox or you gonna stay in it all fuckin' night?'

I couldn't speak. I stayed stock still. My hands trembling, my mouth as dry as sandpaper, the tears welling up in my eyes. I felt my cousin's hand touch my shoulder, the warmth of his palm and fingers radiating through the fabric of my shirt. I kept looking through the windscreen down towards the beach and watched as the blue waters kissed the sand. I felt a shadow cross over the dashboard of the car, felt Vic's lips against my ear.

'Thank you fo' comin', man,' he whispered.

I felt my chest rise and the tears stream down my face. I slowly turned in my seat, one foot out on the gravel drive. Vic took my hand in his.

I felt him gently squeeze my fingers.

The strength he'd once possessed in them had waned, but the mighty spirit that had always forged through his once muscular and agile body was still very much present. Vic kept hold of my hand and guided me out of the car.

His face and body had become thin, his hair pulled tight across his scalp into a ponytail. He wore his favourite black leather patch over one eye, his other shined with the same sparkle of mischief and sly devilment.

The indomitable spirit inside my cousin was as fiery as it had ever been.

The days that followed were, I believed, akin to being in a place like heaven. Vic was, considering how unwell he was, a surprisingly buoyant and charming host. On Tuesday and Thursday, I quietly helped Vic into an imported US Chevy and whisked him off to appointments at the Queen Elizabeth Hospital in Bridgetown. He did not talk of why he was attending the infirmary, nor did we speak of the consultations. Vic was all too aware of the outcome of his condition, knew the cancer had spread to his lungs and kidneys and felt no need to speak of what the doctors had advised him.

He had made it clear that he intended to die at Cove Spring. 'Fuck de hospital. Me die in me awn bed, man.' No one would have been foolish enough to question that decision.

★ ★ ★

By the Friday of the same week, Loretta had taken on the unspoken role of carer to Vic in the late afternoons and before bedtime, administering medication and making sure her friend was comfortable. Bitter Lemon, the true friend and loyal bodyguard that he had always been, was never far from my cousin's side.

There were noticeable differences in Vic; the cancer had quickly spread throughout his body once he'd arrived on the island in early April. The recovery from the gunshot wound to his chest had been slow but, like myself, he was back on his feet within the month. The cough, which had been the early indicator that something was amiss, had become more persistent and deeper as time passed, and after collapsing in the bathroom one Sunday afternoon, he had been rushed to the infirmary. Three days later he was given the news that he had less than three months to live. Five days after that, Vic returned to Cove Spring armed with infection-fighting drugs and a determination to live his final days as he had always lived his life — at

333

full bore.

The reality of the situation was far more complex than my cousin had anticipated. His gung-ho attitude would only take him so far down the road and within a few weeks the cancer had become more destructive. He no longer drank his beloved rum but had refused to give up his daily Cuban cigar nor the half-dozen reefers of top-grade ganja which he insisted on smoking.

On the days Vic needed to rest more, I drove Chloe and Carnell Jnr across the island, down to some of the beaches that Bernice, Chloe's mum, and I had played on as children. The sea in early August was lime green in places and streaked with whitecaps as far as the eye could see, and dark patches of ocean, like clouds of ink, drifted across the coral reefs.

We swam in shallow reefs, watching the schools of clown fish and wahoo, Chloe blowing saltwater out of her snorkel, the small waves lapping across her back and thighs. Thirty feet below, the sand was like ground diamonds; you could see each black spike in the nests of sea urchins, and the coral fire was so bright it looked as if it would scorch your hands with the intensity of a hot stove.

One afternoon, as the heat was going out of the day, I borrowed Bitter's rusty Land Rover and took Chloe across the island to the home of an elderly friend of my family. Mama Esme was now ninety-eight years old. She had been Chloe's guardian for a brief few weeks before I had brought her back to Bristol. The old woman was sat in a wicker chair in the shade of her front garden when I pulled up outside the pretty beach house at Ginger Bay. Twin candles flickered in jars on either side of gate.

Mama Esme slowly rose from her seat as Chloe and I got out of the car. She smiled and held out her arms as the two of us walked along the garden path. Esme stared at Chloe as if she were a precious jewel.

'Chil', come ovah 'ere an' give Mama Esme a hug.' The old woman took Chloe in her arms and held her against her frail body, then she took her by the hand and led her through her simple home. Esme took a walking stick from a tall brass pot that was stood next to a pine dressing table. She opened the back door and led the two of us outside, through a short gate and down a path between the dunes to a small rectangular fence. Behind it, directly in the centre, was a gravestone, no more than three feet high. Fresh flowers lay in front of it.

We stood and looked down at the grave. I felt Chloe take my hand as she quietly read out the inscription bearing the names of my wife and daughter.

ELEANOR & AMELIA ELLINGTON.
EVER LOVED

The tears fell from my eyes. I sobbed for long time, Chloe squeezed tight against my side, the tears she spilled as full and lamenting as my own.

★ ★ ★

Later that evening, as the sun was setting, we bid farewell to Mama Esme, promising to return before we left for Britain, and I drove Chloe the half mile to the Ginger Bay cemetery. Chloe and I had already spoken about visiting her mother's grave before we made the trip.

335

My little girl had no doubt in her mind what she wanted to do.

Bernice's grave was a small, nondescript plot at the furthest corner of the cemetery. The simple headstone read.

BERNICE ELLINGTON.
BORN 24 DECEMBER 1925
DIED 11 APRIL 1967

Chloe stood silently for a long time. After a little while, she took my hand and said, 'Let's go back and see how Uncle Vic's doing, Papa.'

I had expected her to cry, but she didn't.

Perhaps, my brave little soldier thought that we had both shed enough tears for one day.

At the end of our second week, after an afternoon spent scuba-diving at Consett Bay and a joyous supper of salt fish, plantain and rice and peas. Vic, who was looking increasingly tired and had been strangely quiet throughout the evening meal, called Chloe to his room. I saw from the grave look on my cousin's face that he had chosen that moment to unburden himself of a family secret, which we had all been reluctant to speak of. I knew Vic would not let go of life before he had chance to confess that it was he who had been responsible for the death of Chloe's father.

More than three hours passed. Chloe had not left Vic's room in all that time nor had returned to her own to be alone after being given such difficult news. I could not help but note that we had heard no crying or the raising of voices in all the time the two of them had been alone together. At around ten-thirty, I wandered upstairs and knocked gently at Vic's bedroom door. When I got no answer, I quietly opened the door and peeked inside. Vic was lying on his bed, his legs crossed at the ankles, his head and shoulders resting high against a trio of white pillows. Nestled against his chest, with Vic's arm around her was Chloe.

Both of them were fast asleep. At the foot of the bed was a small brown case, the contents, mainly consisting of black and white photographs of Vic's parents, Gabe and Pearl Chloe as well as snapshots of Vic after he'd moved to St Pauls, were strewn across the eiderdown. Chloe was clutching a small framed photograph of her mother. I did not wake her. Nor did we speak of my cousin's confession to her until we had returned home to Bristol two weeks later.

I was comforted to hear that the time Chloe spent with Vic that evening was one of honesty and gentle humility. Hard truths were spoken, and it could not have been easy for Vic to speak and Chloe to have listened. But my little girl had a kind and gentle heart, a strong sense of right and wrong, and as I had always suspected, an enormous capacity for forgiveness.

The final days of Vic's life were spent mostly in his room, the blinds drawn, his door remaining closed. He had, in the intervening seventy-two hours deteriorated dramatically, becoming much weaker, the high doses of pain-relieving drugs numbing the terrible discomfort he was in, but at the same time stripping him of the resilience he'd shown when we'd first arrived.

We spent the weekend around the house; Chloe, Loretta Carnell Jnr and I taking morning walks along the beach, swimming in the sea, preparing meals together in the house's huge kitchen and taking turns to visit Vic. At times he was lucid and full of wit and vulgarity, at other times little more than a shell of his

337

former self.

On the Sunday evening, at around seven, while I was sat on the porch outside watching Caribbean martins swoop and soar in the sky above, Loretta came downstairs from Vic's room and whispered into my ear that my cousin wanted to see me.

I found him in a similar position to the one I'd seen him in previously; his head resting against a barrage of feather pillows, his leather eyepatch in place, his legs crossed, the crisp white sheets on the king-sized bed pulled to one side. He wore a loose black T-shirt and black silk pyjama bottoms. A half-smoked reefer burned in a glass ashtray on the bedside table.

An unopened bottle of Mount Gay rum sat behind it, next to the bottle, two crystal tumblers. I stood in the bedroom doorway for a moment; Vic unaware that I was there. I felt my heart beating against my chest, the palms of my hands laced with sweat. Vic suddenly lifted his head and smiled when he caught sight of me.

'Whatcha doin' standin' there like a sum fuckin' duppy?' He gestured with his hand then tapped his palm against the mattress. 'Park your arse down 'ere, cuz.'

I sat on the edge of the bed. Vic looked at the bottle of rum, smiled then said, 'Git dat bastard open an' pour us both a large one.' Unable to hold the tumbler, I put the glass to his lips and gently tipped the tiniest amount of rum into his mouth. I listened as he coughed and spluttered. When I began to take the glass away from his mouth, Vic snapped at me in a low tone.

'I ain't fuckin' finished yet.'

Ten minutes later his glass was empty.

He had me refill the tumbler and I obliged, but he did not take another sip from the glass.

For the rest of the evening, we sat uninterrupted. We spoke about our childhoods, about Vic's parents, Gabe and Pearl, about the scrapes we been through as kids, and how our lives had panned out since emigrating to Britain.

I was certain during our time together that my cousin wanted to forget the violence of his past and the faces of the men and women he had slain. He made no mention of his criminal past and I, in turn, did not wish to relive the often truly terrible times we had endured together.

At a little after eleven Loretta came in to give Vic his bedtime medication. He took it without complaint. When Loretta caught sight of the opened rum bottle and the filled glasses on the bedside table, she frowned at the two of us but said nothing. She tipped towards Vic, caressed his temple with her fingers then dipped her face towards him and kissed his forehead.

As she began to walk away, she looked at the rum bottle again and shook her head disapprovingly. She wagged her finger at Vic.

'You sum bad man, you 'naw.'

As she turned to leave, Vic called after her in a hushed tone.

'You betta fuckin' believe it, sister.'

I remained with Vic throughout the night, listening to his breathing becoming increasingly more laboured, watching him fall in and out of consciousness. At around four in the morning, Vic suddenly woke and called out my name. I took his hand and watched as he focused his eye on my face.

'I jus' bin dreamin' 'bout you an' your wife, Ellie.'

339

I listened to him take in a short, sharp gasp. He tried to lift his head from the pillow but couldn't find the strength. I hotched up the mattress and dipped my ear down towards his lips, his voice now little more than a whisper. 'I gotta let you 'naw sum'ting. Ellie, she tole me to tell you dat sum'times tings happen to you dat ain't evah bin your fault. She tole me dat you paid your dues, Joseph, an' you got your own church wid a private pew.' He took in another rattling breath. 'She wanted you to 'naw dat, brutha.'

A gentle frown creased my cousin's brow as he closed his eye, then I felt his hand softly press against my fingers. I saw his mouth move, his lips parting as if he had more to tell me, I moved my head closer to his. I felt his chest rise and fall weakly against my side.

The last word my cousin murmured to me was, 'Home.'

★ ★ ★

Vic's funeral was held two days later, the service, if it could be called such, was held on the beach below the grounds of Cove Spring. It was short, without hymn or prayer, and attended by only five mourners, Bitter Lemon, Loretta and Carnell Jnr Harris, Chloe and me. We each took turns to say a few words about our beloved friend and kin. Vic had asked for Jimmy Cliff's 'Many Rivers to Cross' to be played before the coffin was taken to Coral Ridge crematorium.

Vic's expressed wishes were that his ashes were to be brought back to England and scattered on his parents' grave at Arnos Vale Cemetery in Bristol.

Later that evening, Bitter Lemon went out into the rear garden and stacked a brazier with logs cut from a sandbox tree. As dark began to fall, he lit it and arranged a table with five glasses and a bottle of rum then came indoors and asked us all to join him. We sat around the fire, leaf bats rowing in the air above our heads, and toasted Vic. Bitter Lemon recharged our glasses, insisting that Chloe and Carnell Jnr had another tiny measure. Bitter's final duty for his friend and employer was to read his last will and testament.

From humble beginnings, my cousin had amassed over the years a considerable fortune, every penny he'd squirrelled away in covert offshore accounts obtained through illegal means. To my surprise, Vic had been prudent enough to draw up a will in the weeks before he'd contacted Loretta, requesting that we all fly out to him. His final bequest had been considered thoughtfully, and generously.

My cousin had arranged for a considerable trust fund to be set up for Chloe. Money to be made available to her if she chose to further her education at eighteen, and the remaining much larger sum to be released to her when she was twenty-one. 'Sum'ting to keep de wolf fro' de door,' was how he put it. I was left the house at Banner Road and was bequeathed the family heirlooms Vic had long treasured: mainly old sepia photographs and ornaments that had once belonged to his parents or, as my cousin put it in his will and last testament, 'Every fuckin' ting you wanna ransack outta me house.' Vic had always known I would never have accepted 'cash' which had been 'earned' by nefarious means. He was bright enough not to insult me in life with that fact, why would he be any different in death?

My cousin was equally generous to Bitter Lemon, the money he handed down setting his old friend up for life.

Finally, there was the matter of Vic's business. What do you do with a criminal empire when its crime lord ceases to exist?

Vic had no natural descendants. No one from his own bloodline to pass on the heavy mantle of responsibility that would come with the life he'd chosen to lead and the way he made his living. There was no man fit for the job.

But there was a woman.

Someone as steely, as hard-nosed, as capable in the theatre of crime and as foul-mouthed as Victor Ellington.

Loretta Ann Harris.

Vic's entire organisation, his remaining fortune and all associated assets, including his home in Brislington, he left to Loretta.

'The King is dead; Long live the Queen.'

★ ★ ★

The day before we were to fly home, Chloe and I packed a rucksack with sandwiches and drinks, and I drove the two of us out to the parish of Saint Andrew. I parked up in a wooded area close to the foot of Mount Hillaby and we set out to hike to the summit, all one thousand feet of it. Forty minutes into our trek I needed to stop because of the thin air and the steepness of the gradient. We sat on a large rock to let me catch my breath and gazed out at the marvellous views to the east, the rugged Atlantic coast and the beautiful beach of Bathsheba.

'Vic and I used to climb Hillaby as kids,' I said.

Chloe nodded and moved a little closer towards

342

me. I stared out across the ocean, thinking of Vic. 'If your uncle could see me now, gasping like some old fella.' I shook my head and grinned. 'He'd be cursing me for sure.'

As always, whether as a child or adult, Vic would have given no credence to the seriousness of a situation, of injuries incurred, of psychological wounds or increasing old age; in life he'd treated the world as a giant playground where misfortune became a problem only if you allowed it to be. I decided at the very moment, sat on that huge piece of stone, as I was fighting to fill my lungs with warm mountain air, that such a simple outlook would be the way I would live out the remainder of my years.

Living life to the full, with those I loved and not caring a jot for what may or may not be around the corner.

I looked up towards the peak of Hillaby, rested my palms on my thighs then turned and smiled at Chloe. 'You ready to go see the top of the world?'

My little girl cupped a hand on my shoulder.
'When you are, Papa.'

Thank You

A writer's life is, in my opinion, a privileged one, but the possible success she or he experiences involves so many other people, most of whom receive little or no credit for their contributions. In my case, I owe a debt to large numbers of people who have been at my side in one form or another since I became a published author in 2014.

The readers are at the top of the list. Where is any writer without the 'constant reader'? I've been exceptionally lucky to find a readership for the JT Ellington series and have received much support from those fantastic folks who have faithfully dipped into each novel. It would take a whole new book to thank everyone, so if I've missed anybody out, please accept my apologies. You're a grand bunch, and it's an honour to share my work with you.

I thank my wife, Jen, for her encouragement, her love and patience and for keeping a regular beer supply constant! Thanks to my daughters, Enya and Neve, for their loyal love and inspiration. My heartfelt gratitude goes out to my parents, Ann and Pat, and to my dear friends, Vic and Nathan Spong and to Jack Peberdy. A huge thumbs-up to my oldest friend and comrade, the wonderful noir specialist Ken Hooper, and to the crime fiction historian John Martin, BBC Radio Leicester's Ady Dayman, Church End Brewery's Karl Graves, crime writer Nick Quantrill, crime reader Brian Clarke and to the uber-talented Leicester artist Simon Farrow.

My thanks go to my superb publishers, Campbell Brown and Alison McBride, and the entire team at Black & White Publishing, who have been by my side since *Heartman* hit the shelves in 2014. What a ride it's been!

My undying appreciation to my literary agent, Philip Patterson and his colleagues, the brilliant Leah Middleton, Sandra Sawicka and the formidable Guy Herbert at the Marjacq Agency, London.

My gratitude to a trio of crime fiction gods, Ayo Onatade, Ali Karim and Mike Stotter of *Shots* magazine. And to the book bloggers and reviewers who have offered such support; thanks to Jackie at Raven Crime Reads, Abby Jane Slater, Linda Wilson, Sharon Wheeler, Richard Latham and Graham Paul Tonks. You are all stars.

Finally, I doff my cap to the crime writer and former journalist, Tony R. Cox. Your wisdom and guidance, invaluable; your friendship and encouragement, a true blessing. I owe you a great deal. Thank you.

We do hope that you have enjoyed
reading this large print book.

Did you know that all of our titles
are available for purchase?

We publish a wide range of high
quality large print books including:
Romances, Mysteries, Classics
General Fiction
Non Fiction and Westerns

Special interest titles available in
large print are:
The Little Oxford Dictionary
Music Book, Song Book
Hymn Book, Service Book

Also available from us courtesy of
Oxford University Press:
Young Readers' Dictionary
(large print edition)
Young Readers' Thesaurus
(large print edition)

For further information or a free
brochure, please contact us at:
Ulverscroft Large Print Books Ltd.,
The Green, Bradgate Road, Anstey,
Leicester, LE7 7FU, England.
Tel: (00 44) 0116 236 4325
Fax: (00 44) 0116 234 0205